If no
24/7
v

The
RULES
of
MAGIC

ALSO BY ALICE HOFFMAN

Faithful	*Local Girls*
The Marriage of Opposites	*Here on Earth*
The Museum of Extraordinary Things	*Practical Magic*
The Dovekeepers	*Second Nature*
The Red Garden	*Turtle Moon*
The Story Sisters	*Seventh Heaven*
The Third Angel	*At Risk*
Skylight Confessions	*Illumination Night*
The Ice Queen	*Fortune's Daughter*
Blackbird House	*White Horses*
The Probable Future	*Angel Landing*
Blue Diary	*The Drowning Season*
The River King	*Property Of*

YOUNG ADULT NOVELS

Nightbird
Green Heart
Green Angel
Green Witch
Incantation
The Foretelling
Indigo
Aquamarine

NONFICTION

Survival Lessons

The RULES *of* MAGIC

ALICE HOFFMAN

SCRIBNER

LONDON NEW YORK TORONTO SYDNEY NEW DELHI

First published in Great Britain by Scribner, an imprint of Simon & Schuster UK Ltd, 2017
A CBS COMPANY

1 3 5 7 9 10 8 6 4 2

Simon & Schuster UK Ltd
1st Floor
222 Gray's Inn Road
London WC1X 8HB

Simon & Schuster Australia, Sydney
Simon & Schuster India, New Delhi

www.simonandschuster.co.uk
www.simonandschuster.com.au
www.simonandschuster.co.in

A CIP catalogue record for this book is available from the British Library

Hardback ISBN: 978-1-4711-5767-7
Trade Paperback ISBN: 978-1-4711-5768-4
eBook ISBN: 978-1-4711-5769-1

Many thanks to Harvard University Press to quote from *The Poems Of Emily Dickinson: Variorum
Edition*, edited by Ralph W. Franklin, Cambridge, Mass.: The Belknap Press of Harvard
University Press, Copyright © 1998 by the President and Fellows of Harvard College. Copyright
© 1951, 1955 by the President and Fellows of Harvard College. Copyright © renewed 1979,
1983 by the President and Fellows of Harvard College. Copyright © 1914, 1918, 1919, 1924,
1929, 1930, 1932, 1935, 1937, 1942 by Martha Dickinson Bianchi. Copyright © 1952, 1957,
1958, 1963, 1965 by Mary L. Hampson.

The
RULES
of
MAGIC

There is no remedy for love but to love more.

—HENRY DAVID THOREAU

PART ONE

Intuition

*O*nce upon a time, before the whole world changed, it was possible to run away from home, disguise who you were, and fit into polite society. The children's mother had done exactly that. Susanna was one of the Boston Owenses, a family so old that the General Society of Mayflower Descendants and the Daughters of the American Revolution were unable to deny them admission to their exclusive organizations, despite the fact that they would have liked to close the door to them, locking it twice. Their original ancestor, Maria Owens, who had arrived in America in 1680, remained a mystery, even to her own family. No one knew who had fathered her child or could fathom how she came to build such a fine house when she was a woman alone with no apparent means of support. The lineage of those who followed Maria was equally dubious. Husbands disappeared without a trace. Daughters begat daughters. Children ran off and were never seen again.

In every generation there were those who fled Massachusetts, and Susanna Owens had done so. She had escaped to Paris as a young woman, then had married and settled in New York, denying her children any knowledge of their heritage for their own good, which left them with nagging suspicions about who they were. It was clear from the start that they were not like other children, therefore Susanna felt she had no choice but to set down rules. No walking in the moonlight, no Ouija boards, no candles, no red shoes, no wearing black, no going shoeless, no amulets, no night-blooming flowers, no reading novels about magic, no cats, no crows, and no venturing below Fourteenth Street. Yet no matter how Susanna tried to enforce these rules, the children continued to thwart her. They insisted upon being unusual. Eldest was Frances, with skin as pale as milk and blood-red hair, who early on had the ability to commune with birds, which flocked to her window as if called when she was still in her crib. Then came Bridget, called Jet due to her inky black tresses, a girl as shy as she was beautiful, who seemed to know what others were thinking. Last there was Vincent, the adored youngest child, a surprise in every way, the first and only boy to be born into the family, a gifted musician who whistled before he could talk, so charismatic and fearless his worried mother took to keeping him on a leash when he was a toddler, to prevent him from making an escape.

The children grew up quickly in the last years of the 1950s, their odd behavior increasing with time. They had no desire to play games and no interest in other children at the park. They sneaked out the windows of the family's shabby town house on Eighty-Ninth Street on the Upper East Side after their parents went to bed, cavorting on the roof, scurrying down fire escapes, and, as time went on, wandering into Central Park at all hours. They wrote with black ink on the living room walls, read each other's thoughts, and hid in the basement scullery, where their mother could never find them. As if it were their duty, they broke the rules one by one. Franny wore black and grew night-blooming jasmine on her windowsill, Jet read every novel written by E. Nesbit and fed stray cats in the alley, and Vincent began to venture downtown by the time he turned ten.

All three had the gray eyes the family was known for, but the sisters were opposites in every way. Frances was sulky and suspicious, while Jet was kindhearted and so sensitive that a negative remark could make her break into hives. Jet was fashionable, following in her mother's stylish footsteps, but Frances was usually rumpled, her hair left uncombed. She was happiest when her boots were muddy as she navigated the park, wandering through Sheep Meadow. Her gift with wild birds allowed her to bring them to her merely by lifting her hand. From a distance, when she ran so fast she was nearly flying, it seemed as if she spoke their language, and was meant for their world more than her own.

As for Vincent, he possessed such an unearthly charm that only hours after his birth a nurse in the maternity ward of Columbia-Presbyterian Hospital had tucked him into her coat in a failed kidnapping attempt. During her trial she'd told the court that the abduction was not her fault. She'd been spellbound, unable to resist him. As time went on, this wasn't an unusual complaint. Vincent was spoiled rotten, treated by Jet as though he were a baby doll and by Frances as if he were a science experiment. If you pinched him, Frances wondered, would he cry? If you offered him a box of cookies, would he make himself sick by eating every one? Yes, it turned out, and yes again. When Vincent misbehaved, which was often, Frances made up stories filled with punishments for little boys who would not do as they were told, not that her cautionary tales stopped him. All the same, she was his protector and remained so even when he was far taller than she.

The school they attended was despised by all three children, though Susanna Owens had worked hard at getting them accepted, throwing cocktail parties for the board of the Starling School at the family's town house. Though their home was ramshackle due to a lack of funds—their father, a psychiatrist, insisted on seeing many of his patients gratis—the place never failed to impress. Susanna staged the parlor for school gatherings with silver trays and silk throw pillows, bought for the event and then returned to Tiffany and Bendel the very next day. Starling was a snobby, clannish establishment with a guard stationed at the front door at Seventy-Eighth Street. Uniforms were required for all students, although Franny regularly hitched up her gray skirt and rolled down the scratchy kneesocks, leaving her freckled legs bare. Her red hair curled in humid weather and her skin burned if she was in the sun for more than fifteen minutes. Franny stood out in a crowd, which irritated her no end. She was tall, and continued to grow until finally in fifth grade she reached the dreaded six-foot mark. She had always had especially long, coltish arms and legs. Because of this her gawky stage lasted for ten years, from the time she was a glum kindergartener, who was taller than any of the boys, until she turned fifteen. Often she wore red boots, bought at a secondhand store. *Strange girl*, was written in her records. *Perhaps psychological testing is needed?*

The sisters were outsiders at school, with Jet an especially easy target. Her classmates could make her cry with a nasty note or a well-aimed shove. When she began hiding in the girls' bathroom for most of the day, Franny swiftly interceded. Soon enough the other students knew not to irritate the Owens sisters, not if they didn't want to trip over their own shoes or find themselves stuttering when called upon to give a report. There was something about the sisters that felt dangerous, even when all they were doing was eating tomato sandwiches in the lunchroom or searching for novels in the library. Cross them and you came down with the flu or the measles. Rile them and you'd likely be called to the principal's office, accused of cutting classes or cheating. Frankly, it was best to leave the Owens sisters alone.

Franny's only friend was Haylin Walker, who was taller than she by three inches and equally antisocial. He was a legacy doomed to be a Starling student from the moment of his birth. His grandparents had donated the athletic building, Walker Hall, dubbed Hell Hall by Franny, who despised sports. In sixth grade Hay had staged a notorious protest, chaining himself to the dessert rack in the lunchroom to demand better wages for workers in the cafeteria. Franny admired his grit even though the other students simply watched wide-eyed, refusing to join in when Haylin began chanting "Equality for all!"

After the janitor apologetically cut through the chains with a hacksaw, Haylin was given a good talking-to by the headmaster and made to write a paper about workers' rights, which he considered a privilege rather than a punishment. He was obligated to write ten pages, and handed in a tome of nearly fifty pages instead, duly footnoted, quoting from Thomas Paine and FDR. He couldn't wait for the next decade. Everything would change in the sixties, he told Franny. And, if they were lucky, they would then be free.

Haylin despised his background of wealth and privilege and wore torn, threadbare clothes and boots so old there were holes in the soles. All he wanted was a dog and permission to attend public school. His parents denied him both of these wishes. His father was the largest shareholder in a global bank that had been based in Manhattan since 1824, which was a great cause of shame for Hay. By the time they were in high school, he had considered legally changing his name to Jones or Smith so no one could connect him with his family and their infamous greed. One of the reasons he trusted Franny was because she was utterly unimpressed by externals. She didn't care if he lived in a penthouse on Fifth Avenue, or that his father had a butler who had been to Oxford and wore a morning coat and polished boots.

"What a lot of bother," Franny always said.

Most important, they had science in common. Haylin was currently studying the effects of cannabis on his calorie intake. So far he'd gained five pounds in less than a month, becoming addicted not to marijuana but to jelly doughnuts. He seemed easygoing, except when he talked about biology or injustice or his dedication to Franny. He trailed after her, not seeming to care if he made a fool of himself. When they were together, he had an intense gleam in his eye that Franny found disconcerting. It was as if there was a whole other part of him, a hidden self that was fueled by emotions neither he nor Franny was ready to confront.

"Tell me everything about you," Haylin often asked her.

"You already know me," Franny answered. He knew her better than anyone. Better, she sometimes feared, than she knew herself.

Unlike Franny and Jet, Vincent made his way through school with ease. He had taken up the guitar and in no time had surpassed his teacher, and soon enough packs of infatuated

8

girls followed him through the school hallways. His interest in magic began early on. He pulled quarters from classmates' ears and lit matches with a puff of breath. In time, his talents increased. With a single look he could make the electricity in the Owenses' house go haywire, with lights flickering, then fizzing out entirely. Locked doors unlatched when they hadn't been touched, windows opened and closed when he was near. When Franny asked how he accomplished such things, he refused to divulge his methods.

"Figure it out," he said with a grin.

Vincent had posted a sign on his bedroom door, ENTER AT YOUR OWN PERIL, but Franny walked right in to search the place. There was nothing interesting in the desk drawers or the closet, but when she reached into the cobwebby space beneath her brother's bed she discovered an occult handbook called *The Magus*. Franny knew its history, for it was on their mother's list of forbidden books. It had been so popular when it was published, in 1801, that not enough texts could be printed. People committed robbery in their desire to own it, and many devotees kept it hidden under the floorboards. Vincent's well-worn copy was still just as potent as ever. It smelled like sulfur, and as soon as Franny saw it, she had a sneezing fit. If she wasn't mistaken, she was allergic to the thing.

The Magus was so hot to the touch she burned her fingers on its binding as she plucked it from its hiding place. It was not the sort of item a person picked up on a whim. You had to know what you were looking for, and you had to have the courage to handle it.

Franny flung the text on the kitchen table as Vincent was having his lunch. There went the potato salad and the coleslaw, splattering across the tabletop. The spine of the book was black and gold, cracked with age. When it hit the table the book groaned.

"Where did this come from?" she asked.

Vincent stared at her and didn't flinch. "A used book kiosk outside the park."

"That is not true," Franny said firmly. "You've never been to a bookstall in your life!"

Vincent could flimflam other people, even Jet could be fooled by his charm, but Franny harbored an instinct for such things. Truth felt light and green, but a lie sunk to the floor, heavy as metal, a substance she always avoided for it made her feel as though she was trapped behind bars. Still, Vincent was the most appealing of liars and Franny felt a swell of love for her brother when he shrugged and told the truth.

"You're right. They couldn't sell it in a bookstall," he confided. "It's still illegal."

Any copies that had been unearthed at the turn of the century had been burned on a bonfire in Washington Square and there was a little-known law forbidding the book to be kept in libraries in New York City or sold in bookstores. Inside the book now splayed upon the table Franny spied images of witches led to a gallows hill. The date printed below the illustration was 1693. A chill of recognition ran through her. She'd recently written a report for history class on the Salem trials and therefore knew this to be the year when many of those set to be tried escaped from New England in search of a more tolerant place, which they found in Manhattan. While the antiwitchcraft mania raged in New England, spurred on by politics, greed, and religion, ignited by Cotton Mather and the infamous and cruel judge John

Hathorne, in New York only two witch trials had taken place, in 1658 and again in 1665, one in Queens, the other on Long Island, then called Yorkshire, in the town of Setauket, both involving residents who had ties to Boston. In New York, Franny had discovered, it was possible to be free.

"Why would you want this thing?" Franny's fingertips had turned sooty and she had a strange feeling in the pit of her stomach.

Of course it *would* be like Vincent to be interested in the occult, rather than something ordinary, like soccer or track and field. He was suspended from school on a regular basis for general mischief, pails of water tumbling down, cans of pepper spray going off. His ongoing behavior was a great embarrassment to their father, who had recently published a book titled *A Stranger in the House*, an analysis of troubled adolescents dedicated to the children, none of whom had any intention of reading it, though it was something of a bestseller.

Franny could guess where *The Magus* had come from. The place on their mother's list they were never to go. Downtown. It was rumored that what was outlawed in other parts of Manhattan could be found there. Hearts of beasts, blood of men, enchantments that could prove to be lethal. The chief reason their mother did not allow them to journey to Greenwich Village was that it was viewed as a society of bohemians, drug addicts, homosexuals, and practitioners of black magic. Yet Vincent had managed to find his way there.

"Trust me, it's nothing to worry about," he muttered, quickly retrieving *The Magus*. "Really, Franny, it's just a lousy book."

"Be careful," Franny admonished him.

Perhaps she was also speaking to herself, for she was often

alarmed by her own abilities. It wasn't only that birds were drawn to her or that she'd discovered she could melt icicles with the touch of her hand. There was some scientific logic behind both of those reactions. She was calm and unafraid when birds flapped about, and her body temperature was above average, therefore it was logical for ice to melt. But one night, while standing on the fire escape outside her bedroom, she'd thought so hard about flying that for a moment her feet had lifted and she'd hung in the air. That, she knew, was empirically impossible.

"We don't really know what we're dealing with," she murmured to her brother.

"But it's something, isn't it?" Vincent said. "Something inside of us. I know our mother wants us to pretend we're like everyone else, but you know that we're not."

They both considered this. The girls had their talents, as did Vincent. He could, for instance, see shadowy bits of the future. He'd known that Franny would come across *The Magus* today and that they would have this conversation. In fact, he'd written it down on his skin with blue ink. He now held up his arm to show her. *Franny finds the book.*

"Coincidence," Franny was quick to say. There was no other justifiable cause.

"Are you sure? Who's to say it's not more?" Vincent lowered his voice. "We could try to find out."

They sat together, side by side, pulling their kitchen chairs close, unsure of what bloomed inside them. As they concentrated, the table rose up, hovering an inch off the floor. Franny was so startled she hit the tabletop with the palms of her hands to stop the rising. Immediately it returned to the floor with a clatter.

"Let's wait," she said, flushed with the heat of this strange moment.

"Why wait? The sooner we know what this is, the better. We want to control it, not have it control us."

"There is no *it*," Franny insisted, logical as always, well aware that her brother was referring to magic. "There's a rational explanation for every action and reaction."

After the incident in the kitchen, the table was always tilted, with plates and glasses tending to slide off the top, as if to remind them that whoever they were, whatever their history might be, Vincent had been correct. They were not like anyone else.

None of this experimentation would have pleased Dr. and Mrs. Burke-Owens, had they known of such games. They were elegant, serious people who spent evenings out nursing a Tom Collins or whiskey sour at the Yale Club, for after receiving his B.A. at Harvard, the doctor had attended medical school in New Haven, a town their mother admitted she hoped never to visit again. They were both constantly on the lookout for signs of hereditary malfunctions in their offspring, and so far they were not especially hopeful. In his writings, Dr. Burke-Owens proposed a theory of personality that placed nature over nurture, stating there was no way to change a child's core personality. Not only was the brain hardwired, he proposed, but the soul was as well. There was no way to escape one's personal genetics, despite a healthy environment, and this did not bode well for Frances and Bridget and Vincent.

Luckily for them, their father was preoccupied with his patients, who furtively made their way inside through a separate entrance before descending to a basement office in the Owenses' town house. While therapy was in progress, Vincent often sneaked down to the coat closet to search a patient's pockets for cash, mints, and Valium. Then all three children would lie on the kitchen floor, relaxed by the little yellow pills Vincent had found, sucking on Brach's Ice Blue mints as they listened in to the sobbing confessions that filtered up through the heating vent. Due to these eavesdropping sessions they knew about obsessions, depressions, manias, sexual appetites, and transference long before most people their age knew what a psychiatrist was.

Every year a box of lavender-scented black soap wrapped in crinkly cellophane would arrive from Massachusetts. Susanna refused to say who the sender was, yet she faithfully washed with it. Perhaps that was why she had such a creamy, radiant complexion. Franny discovered the potential of the soap after she nicked a bar one Christmas. When she and Jet sampled it, the soap caused their skin to shine, but it also made them so silly they couldn't stop laughing. They filled the sink with bubbles and splashed water at each other and were soon soaked to the skin. When their mother found them throwing the slippery bar of soap back and forth like a hot potato, she snatched it from their grasp.

"This is not for children," she said, though Franny was nearly seventeen and Jet would turn sixteen next summer.

Surely their mother was hiding something from them under the clouds of mascara she wore. She never spoke of her family, and the children had never met a single relation. As they grew older their suspicions grew as well. Susanna Owens spoke in riddles and never gave a straight answer. *Uncross your knives,* she'd insist if there was a quarrel at the table. Butter melting in a dish meant someone nearby was in love, and a bird in the house could take your bad luck out the window. She insisted that her children wear blue for protection and carry packets of lavender in their pockets, though Franny always threw the packets away the minute she was out of her mother's sight.

They began to wonder if their mother wasn't a spy. Russia was the enemy, and at Starling students were often made to crouch beneath their desks, hands over their heads, for bomb-safety drills. Spies had no family connections and dubious histories, just as their mother had, and they spoke in double-talk, as she did. They fudged their histories to protect their true backgrounds and intentions, and Susanna never mentioned attending college nor did she discuss where she grew up or reveal anything about her parents, other than claiming they had died young while on a cruise. The Owens children knew only the slimmest facts: Susanna had grown up in Boston and been a model in Paris before settling down with the children's father, who was an orphan with no family of his own. Their mother was terribly chic at all times, wearing black and gold sunglasses even on cloudy days, and lavish designer clothes from Paris, and she always wore Chanel No. 5 perfume, so that every room she was in was deliciously scented.

"And then you all came along," Susanna would say cheerfully, when anyone could tell having children had been a trial for her. It was obvious she wasn't meant for domestic life. She was a terrible cook and seemed puzzled by all household duties. The washing machine caused her endless grief and often overflowed. The stove was on the fritz more often than not, and every culinary dish she attempted came out half-baked. Even macaroni and cheese was an ordeal. A hired woman came in once a week to mop and vacuum, but she was fired after Susanna found her teaching the children to use a Ouija board, which was confiscated and burned in the fireplace.

"You know the rules!" she cried. "Do not call up darkness when you are unprepared for the consequences." Susanna looked quite mad, stuffing the Ouija board into the flames with a poker.

Her penchant for the rules only made her children more curious. Why did their mother draw the curtains on May Day, leaving them in the dark? Why did she wear sunglasses on moonlit nights? Why did she panic when they ran out of salt and quickly rush down to buy some at the market? They looked for clues about their heritage, but there were few keepsakes, although one day Franny discovered an old photograph album wrapped in muslin on the top shelf of the hallway closet. There were faded pictures of women in a lush, overgrown garden, a troupe of girls in long skirts grinning at the camera, a black cat on a porch, their mother when she was young, standing in front of Notre-Dame. When Susanna found Franny curled up on the settee in the parlor studying the album, she immediately took it away. "It's for your own good," she said tenderly. "All I want for you is a normal life."

"Mother," Franny sighed. "What makes you think that's what *I* want?"

What is meant to be is bound to happen, whether or not you approve. One June morning, their lives were forever changed. It was 1960, and all at once there was a sense that anything might occur, suddenly and without warning. It had been a great relief when the end of the school year arrived, but life at home was stifling. New York City was a cauldron of pollution and humidity. Just as the temperature climbed into the nineties and the siblings were already bored out of their minds, a letter arrived in the mail. The envelope seemed to pulse, as if it had a beating heart. There was no stamp, yet the U.S. Post Office had seen fit to slip it through the mail slot in their front door.

Susanna took one look and said, "It's from my aunt Isabelle."

"We have an aunt?" Franny asked.

"Good God, not her," Dr. Burke-Owens remarked. "Don't open that letter."

But Susanna had already slid her nail under the flap of the envelope. She had a strange expression, as if she were opening a door long closed. "It's an invitation for Franny. Everyone gets one when they've turned seventeen. It's a tradition."

"Then I should go," Franny was quick to say. Anything to get away from her mother's rules.

"If you do, nothing will ever be the same," her mother warned.

"Unlikely," Franny said, retrieving the envelope. Above all she was brave, and when no one dared to step in, she always would. And the letter *was* addressed to her, not their mother.

"Massachusetts must be avoided at all costs," their father interjected. "Contact with any of the family will inflame characteristics which are currently dormant."

Franny ignored her father, intent on the old-fashioned handwriting that resembled the tracks of a bird.

You may leave home this afternoon and arrive by dinnertime.

"Did you go when you were seventeen?" Franny now asked her mother.

Susanna blinked her wide gray eyes. Caught in Franny's gaze, she couldn't tell a lie. "I did," she admitted. "Then I left for Paris and that was the end of that. But you." She shook her head. "I don't know about letting you go alone. You're so rebellious as it is."

"I am not!" Franny said with her customary defiance.

Vincent stepped on Franny's foot to silence her. He was desperate to have an adventure. "We'll go with her," he said.

"We can watch over her," Jet added.

Their minds were made up. They would escape for the summer. While their parents argued, Franny and Vincent and Jet went off to pack, shouting to each other not to forget swimsuits and sandals, excited to at last discover where they'd come from.

When they brought suitcases and backpacks and Vincent's guitar into the kitchen, their mother was sitting alone at the table, her eyes rimmed red. They gazed at her, confused. Was she ally or enemy?

"It *is* a formal invitation," Susanna said. "I've explained to your father that it wouldn't do to be rude to my aunt, but I'm not certain he understands." She turned to Vincent and Jet. "You will watch over Franny?"

They assured her they would.

"Isabelle will surprise you," Susanna told them. "There will be tests when you least expect them. You'll think no one is watching over you, but she'll be aware of everything you do.

And you must promise that you'll come back to me," she said tearfully. She was rarely so emotional, and her children took note of her despair. It made going to Massachusetts seem all the more worthwhile.

"Of course we'll come back," Franny said. "We're New Yorkers."

"It's only for the summer," Jet reassured their mother.

Everyone had to leave home eventually, didn't they? They had to set out on their own and find out who they were and what their futures might bring. But for now all Vincent wanted was a bus ticket, and when he looked at his sisters he could tell they agreed. No going back, no retreat, no settling for the ordinary lives they had been made to live every day.

They arrived on Midsummer's Eve, the summer solstice, when the day is so long it seems for once there is all the time in the world. The roses were in bloom and a green blur of pollen drifted through the darkening air. As they walked through the small town, neighbors came to stand at their windows and gawk. It was common knowledge that any strangers dressed in black would likely be heading to Magnolia Street. Most people avoided the Owens family, believing that any entanglement with them could taint not only your present, but your future as well. It was said that some members of the family could place a single horse hair into a pan of water and turn it into a snake. If they threw dust in a circle, you had best not cross over, not even when the dust disappeared, for you might fall into a hole of desire or regret and never arise again.

"Not very welcoming," Jet said in a worried tone as the neighbors glared at them.

"To hell with them," Fanny remarked. Had her sister learned nothing at the Starling School? Other people's judgments were meaningless unless you allowed them to mean something.

At fourteen, Vincent was already too handsome for his own good. He was six four and imposing despite how skinny he was. Now he shook his fist in the air and jeered at the local spectators. In an instant, there was the clicking of locks up and down the street.

"Excellent," Vincent said. "We won't have any trouble with them."

He stood out wherever he went, but especially here, in a small town where boys his age were playing baseball in a dusty field, wearing baggy jeans, stopping their game to observe the outsiders walking through town. Vincent wore his black hair slicked back and had his guitar slung over one shoulder despite his father's declaration that a guitar, like a sports car, was an extension of a damaged male ego. "So I'm damaged." Vincent had shrugged. "Who isn't?"

When they reached the end of Magnolia Street they stopped, daunted for the moment. The house was huge, with tilted chimneys and scores of windows fashioned out of green glass. The entire property was encircled by the wrought-iron fence, but there wasn't a gate in sight.

"Do you feel something here?" Vincent asked his sisters.

"Mosquitoes?" Franny guessed. She surveyed the muck-laden puddles in the huge vegetable garden. "Probably a good chance of dysentery."

Vincent made a face and said, "No pain, no gain," then went

to investigate. The garden was so lush and green it made one dizzy. There was a henhouse, where some brown and white clucking chickens pecked at seed tossed on the ground; a potting shed surrounded by plumy weeds that were taller than Vincent; and a padlocked greenhouse, which looked extremely promising as a potential hideaway.

"Over here," Vincent called after clearing away some of the thorny shrubbery. He had managed to discover a rusted gate that led to a bluestone pathway. His sisters followed to the porch, charging up the steps. Franny was about to knock on the door when it opened of its own accord. All three took a step back.

"It's just an old door," Franny said in a measured voice. "That's all. It's a hot day and the wood frame expanded."

"You think so?" Vincent drew himself up to his full height and peered through the shadows. He could feel the current in the air. "There's a lot more here. Hundreds of years of it."

Isabelle Owens was in the kitchen, her back to them as she puttered about. She was a formidable woman; her frame might be small, but her attitude was commanding. Her white hair was pinned up haphazardly, and yet despite her age, her complexion was perfect. She had worn black every day of her life and she did so today. Franny stared until their aunt suddenly turned in her direction, then Franny impulsively ducked down behind a potted plant, her heart pounding against her chest. Vincent and Jet followed suit, sinking down beside their sister, holding their hands over their mouths so as not to explode with laughter. They'd never seen Franny so flustered.

"Hush," she hissed at them.

"I thought you'd all show up, so what's stopping you from

coming inside? Are you rabbits or brave souls?" their aunt called. "A rabbit darts away, thinking it will be safe, and then is picked up by a hawk. A brave soul comes to have dinner with me."

They did as they were told, even though they had the sense that once they did they would be entering into a different life.

Franny went first, which was only right, as she was the first-born and the protector. Plus she *was* curious. The kitchen was enormous, with an ancient pine table long enough to seat a dozen and a huge black stove, the sort that hadn't been sold for decades. Isabelle had made a vegetable stew and a plum pudding, along with freshly baked rosemary bread. Willowware platters and bowls had been set on the table along with old pewter silverware in need of a shine. The house had no clocks, and there seemed the promise that time would go at a different pace entirely once they stepped over the threshold.

"Thank you for inviting us," Franny said politely.

One had to say something when one didn't really know the person with whom one was about to spend an entire summer vacation, especially when she appeared to possess some sort of power it was clearly best to respect.

Isabelle gazed at her. "If you really want to thank me, do something about what's in the dining room."

The siblings exchanged a look. Surely, this was one of those tests their mother had warned about.

"All right." Franny rose to the challenge without even asking what it was. "I will."

Her brother and sister trailed after her, curious. The house was enormous, with three floors. All the rooms had heavy draperies to keep out the sun, and, despite the dust motes in the air, all contained gleaming woodwork. Fifteen varieties of wood had been used to craft the mantels and the paneling on the walls, including golden oak, silver ash, cherrywood, and some varieties of trees that were now extinct. There were two staircases, one a chilly back stairs that twisted around like a puzzle, the other an elegant stairway, fashioned of mahogany. They stopped to gaze up the carved staircase to where there was a window seat on the landing. Above it was a portrait of a beautiful dark-haired woman wearing blue.

"That's your ancestor Maria Owens," their aunt told them as she led them to the dining room.

"She's staring at us," Jet whispered to her brother.

Vincent snorted. "Bullshit. Pull yourself together, Jet."

The dining room was dim, the damask curtains drawn. As it turned out, there was no spirit to dispel, only a small brown bird that had managed to slip in through a half-opened window. Every year on Midsummer's Eve a sparrow found its way in and had to be chased out with a broom, for any bad luck would follow it when it flew away. Isabelle was about to hand over a broom that would help with the job, but there was no need to do so. The bird came to Franny of its own accord, as the birds in Central Park always did, flitting over to perch on her shoulder, feathers fluffed out.

"That's a first," Isabelle said, doing her best not to seem impressed. "No bird has ever done that before."

Franny took the sparrow into her cupped hands. "Hello," she said softly. The bird peered at her with its bright eyes, consoled by the sound of her voice. Franny went to the window and let it into the open air. Jet and Vincent came to watch as it disappeared into the branches of a very old tree, one of the few elms in the commonwealth that had survived the blight. Franny turned to their aunt. Something passed between them, an un-spoken wave of approval.

"Welcome home," Isabelle said.

Once they'd settled in they couldn't imagine why they hadn't spent every summer on Magnolia Street. Aunt Isabelle was surprisingly agreeable. Much to their delight it turned out she couldn't care less about bad behavior. Diet and sleeping habits meant nothing to her. Candy for breakfast, if that's what they desired. Soda pop all through the day. They could stay up until dawn if they wished and sleep until noon. They weren't forced to tidy their rooms or pick up after themselves.

"Do as you please," she told the siblings. "As long as you harm no one."

If Vincent wanted to smoke cigarettes there was no need for him to hide behind the potting shed, although Isabelle let him know she disapproved. Smoking fell under the category of harm, even if the person Vincent was harming was himself.

"Bad for the lungs," Isabelle scolded. "But then you like to tempt fate, don't you? Don't worry, it will all work out."

Their aunt seemed aware of parts of Vincent's psyche even his sisters weren't privy to. Vincent had never let on that he often experienced a rush of alarm when he passed a mirror. Who, in fact, was he? A missing person? A body without a soul? He was hiding something from himself, and perhaps it was best if he listened to some advice. He stubbed out his cigarette in a potted geranium, but remained unconvinced that he should care about his health or his habits.

"We're all killed by something," he said.

"But we don't have to rush it, do we?" Isabelle removed the cigarette butt to ensure that the nicotine wouldn't poison the plant. "You're a good boy, Vincent, no matter what people might say."

The only light in town turned on after midnight was on the back porch of the Owens house. It had been lit for hundreds of years, first by oil, then by gas, now by electricity. Moths fluttered through the ivy. This was the hour when women came to visit, looking for cures for hives or heartbreak or fever. Local people might not like the Owens family, they might cross to the other side of the street when they saw Isabelle on her way to the market with a black umbrella held overhead to ward off the sun, but as soon as they were in need, they battled the thornbushes and vines to reach the porch and ring the bell, knowing they were welcome when the porch light was turned on. They were invited into the kitchen, where they sat at the old pine table. Then they told their stories, some in too great detail.

"Be brief," Isabelle always said, and because of her stern expression they always were. The price for a cure might be as low as half a dozen eggs or as high as a diamond ring, depending on the circumstances. A token payment was fine in exchange for horseradish and cayenne for coughs, dill seeds to disperse hiccoughs, Fever Tea to nip flu in the bud, or Frustration Tea to soothe sleepless nights for the mother of a wayward son. But there were often demands for remedies that were far pricier, cures that might cost whatever a person held most precious. To snatch a man who belonged to another, to weave a web that disguised wrongdoings, to set a criminal on the right path, to reach someone who was standing on the precipice of despair and pull them back to life, such cures were expensive. Franny had stumbled upon some of the more disquieting ingredients in the pantry: the bloody heart of a dove, small frogs, a glass vial containing teeth, strands of hair to boil or burn depending on whether you wanted to call someone to you or send them away.

Franny had taken to sitting on the back staircase to eavesdrop. She'd bought a blue notebook in the pharmacy to write down her aunt's remedies. Star tulip to understand dreams, bee balm for a restful sleep, black mustard seed to repel nightmares, remedies that used essential oils of almond or apricot or myrrh from thorn trees in the desert. Two eggs, which must never be eaten, set under a bed to clean a tainted atmosphere. Vinegar as a cleansing bath. Garlic, salt, and rosemary, the ancient spell to cast away evil.

For women who wanted a child, mistletoe was to be strung over their beds. If that had no effect, they must tie nine knots in a strong rope, then burn the rope and eat the ashes and soon enough they would conceive. Blue must be worn for protection. Moonstones were useful in connecting with the living, topaz to contact the dead. Copper, sacred to Venus, will call a man to you, and black tourmaline will eliminate jealousy. When it came to love, you must always be careful. If you dropped something belonging to the man you loved into a candle flame, then added pine needles and marigold flowers, he would arrive on your doorstep by morning, so you would do well to be certain you wanted him there. The most basic and reliable love potion was made from anise, rosemary, honey, and cloves boiled for nine hours on the back burner of the old stove. It had always cost $9.99 and was therefore called Love Potion Number Nine, which worked best on the ninth hour of the ninth day of the ninth month.

After listening in, Franny had decided that magic was not so very far from science. Both endeavors searched for meaning where there was none, light in the darkness, answers to questions too difficult for mortals to comprehend. Aunt Isabelle knew her niece was there on the stairs taking notes, but said nothing. She had a special fondness for Franny. They were alike in more ways than Franny would care to know.

Fortunately, Isabelle was up late with her customers, and could be depended upon to nap in the afternoons. Francis and Jet and Vincent therefore had the gift of long languid days when they were left to their own devices. They trooped into town, past an old cemetery where the only name on the headstones was Owens. They stopped at the rusty fence and stood in silence, a bit overwhelmed by all those mossy stones. When Jet wanted to explore, the others refused.

"It's summer and we're free. Let's live a little," Franny said, grabbing hold of Jet's arm to pull her past the cemetery gates.

"Let's live a *lot*," Vincent suggested. "Or at least as much as we can in this hick town."

They ordered ice cream sodas at the linoleum counter of the old pharmacy, lingered on leafy lanes, and sprawled on the grass in the park to watch the territorial swans chase badly behaved children through the grass, which left them in gales of laughter. Their favorite activity on especially hot days was a hike to Leech Lake, a spot most people avoided, for if a swimmer waded into the murky depths past the reeds, scores of leeches awaited. Franny kept a packet of salt in her backpack to disperse any of the leeches that attached themselves, but for some reason none even came close.

"Be gone," she cried, and they were.

The Owens siblings spent hours sunbathing, then they dared each other to dive off the high rock ledges and take the plunge into the ice-cold, green water. No matter how deeply they dove, they immediately popped back up to the surface, shivering and sputtering, unable to sink or even keep their heads underwater.

"We're oddly buoyant," Jet said cheerfully, floating on her back, splashing water into the air. Even in her old black bathing suit she was gorgeous, the sort of young woman in bloom who often incites jealousy or lust.

"You know who can't be drowned," Vincent remarked from his perch on a flat rock. He had learned all about this in *The Magus,* with illustrations of women being tied to stools and sunk into ponds. He shoved his long hair back with one hand, knowing his father would pitch a fit when he arrived back in the city with this thick mop. When his sisters didn't respond and merely looked at him with confused expressions, he provided the answer. "Witches."

"Everything can be explained with scientific evidence," Franny said in her blunt, forthright manner. "I don't believe in fairy tales."

"Franny," Vincent said in a firm tone. "You know who we are."

She didn't like her brother's implication. Were they subhuman beings, among those creatures to be feared and chased by mobs through the streets? Was that why the neighbors avoided them, and why, on that odd day in the kitchen when they had tested themselves, the table had risen?

"I love fairy tales," Jet said dreamily. She felt like a water nymph when she floated in the lake, a pure elemental spirit. She toweled off before placing a lace cloth over a table-shaped rock, where she set out a lunch of egg-salad sandwiches and celery sticks. She'd filled the thermos with Frustration Tea from a recipe she'd found in Aunt Isabelle's kitchen. Anyone partaking of this drink would be granted good humor and cheerfulness, attributes of which Jet believed Franny was sorely in need.

A grin spread across Vincent's face as they discussed their inability to sink. "I think what we are is pretty clear." He raised his arms and the finches in the thickets took flight in a single swirling cloud. "See what I mean? We're not normal."

"*Normal* is not a scientific term," Franny said dismissively. "And anyone can frighten a finch. A cat could do that. Try calling them to you." She held out one hand and several finches alit, chattering in her palm until she blew on them to shoo them away. She was quite proud of this particular ability.

"You're proving my point!" Vincent laughed. He jumped into the lake, and then all but bounced, as if repelled. "Check it out!" he cried cheerfully as he floated just above the water.

That night at supper, Vincent gave his sisters a look, then turned to their aunt and asked if the stories he'd heard about the Owens family were true.

"You know who you are," Isabelle responded. "And I suggest you never deny it."

She told them of an Owens cousin named Maggie, who had come to stay one summer, and tried her best to befriend the locals, telling tales about her own family. How they danced naked in the garden, and took revenge on innocent people, and called to the heavens for hail and storms. She went so far as to write an opinion piece for the local newspaper, defaming the Owens name, suggesting they all be incarcerated.

The family locked the door and told Maggie to go back to Boston. The outside world being against them was one thing, but one of their own? That was another matter entirely.

Maggie Owens was so enraged when she was cast onto the sidewalk with her suitcase that she took up cursing, and with every curse she grew smaller and smaller. Some spells work against you, or perhaps the Owens cousins inside the house threw up a black reversing mirror. Each wicked word Maggie spoke was turned back upon her. She couldn't even unlatch the lock on the door. Whatever magic ran through her blood had evaporated. She'd denied who she was, and when that happens it's easy enough to become something else entirely, most likely the first creature you see, which in her case was a rabbit darting through the garden. Maggie went to sleep in the grass a woman, and awoke as a rabbit. Now she ate weeds and drank milk that was left to her in a saucer.

"Keep your eyes open," Isabelle told the siblings. "You may see her in the yard. This is what happens when you repudiate who you are. Once you do that, life works against you, and your fate is no longer your own."

Jet's favorite place to be was the garden. She adored the shady pools of greenery where azaleas and lily of the valley grew wild, but ever since they'd been told their cousin's story, she was anxious when rabbits came to eat parsley and mint and the curly Boston lettuce that was planted in neat rows.

"We'll never be turned into rabbits, if that's what you're thinking," Franny said. "We're not so foolish."

"I'd rather be a fox," Vincent announced. He was teaching himself a Ramblin' Jack Elliott song on the guitar. "Stealthy, sly, under the radar."

"I'd prefer to be a cat," Jet said. Their aunt had six black cats. One, a kitten named Wren, had grown particularly attached to Jet and often followed her as she pulled weeds. Jet had a nagging suspicion that Isabelle had told the story of their wayward cousin directly to her, as a warning for all those times she'd wanted to be an ordinary girl.

A large, fearless rabbit was glaring at them. It had black whiskers and gray eyes. Jet felt her skin grow cold. "Maggie?" she said in a soft voice. There was no answer. "Shall we give her milk?" she asked Franny.

"Milk?" Franny was contemptuous. "She's only a rabbit, nothing more." Franny tossed some tufts of grass in the rabbit's direction. "Shoo!" she commanded.

To their dismay the rabbit stayed exactly where it was, solemnly chewing dandelion greens.

"It's her," Jet whispered, nudging her sister.

"Maggie?" Franny called. She didn't believe their aunt's story for a minute, yet there was definitely something odd about this creature. "Get out!" she told the thing.

Jet thought it might be better to ask than to command. "O rabbit, please leave us be," she said respectfully and sweetly. "We're sorry you're no longer a woman, but that was your doing, not ours."

The rabbit obeyed, hopping into the woody area where the beehive stood. While Jet piled up ragweed and brambles she decided she would faithfully set out a saucer of milk every morning. Franny watched the retreat of the rabbit and wondered if beneath her sister's gentle nature there wasn't more than she and Vincent had imagined. Perhaps they didn't know her as well as they believed.

By now Franny had her own suspicions about their heritage. She had taken to going off by herself on rainy afternoons. While the others were lazing about she'd spent time at the public library, paging through old, inky issues of the *Salem Mercury* and the *Essex Gazette*. She'd discovered a legacy of witchcraft associated with the Owens family. In the town ledger, kept in the rather shabby rare book room, there was a list of crimes members of their family had been charged with in an era when any woman accused of unnatural acts might be drowned in Leech Lake. Witches, however, couldn't be drowned unless they were properly weighed down with stones in their pockets or their boots or stuffed into their mouths, which were then sewn shut with black thread. The Owenses' wrongdoings included bewitchment, enchantment, theft of a cow, using herbs to relieve illness, children born out of wedlock, and enemies who had suffered bad fortune. The first accuser had been John Hathorne, the judge at the trials that had been responsible for the deaths of so many innocent people.

Franny had come upon a notation that suggested Maria Owens's journal was stored in the rare book room. The journal was stowed in a drawer that the librarian had to unlock with an iron key. The lock stuck, coming free only after much prodding. Inside the drawer was the thin book with a stained blue-gray cover, meticulously secured in plastic wrapping.

"Be careful with that," the librarian warned. She was clearly afraid of the slim volume, which she herself refused to touch. She offered a pair of white gloves to Franny to slip on to ensure that she wouldn't damage the delicate paper. There was so much dust in the room Franny had a wicked sneezing fit.

"You have exactly twenty minutes," the librarian said. "Otherwise trouble could ensue."

"Trouble?" Franny was curious.

"You know what I mean. This is a book of spells Maria Owens wrote while in prison. It should have been set on fire, but the board of the library refused to do so. They thought destroying it would bring bad luck to us, so we've kept it all this time, like it or not."

Beware of love, Maria Owens had written on the first page of her journal. *Know that for our family, love is a curse.*

Franny worried over the mention of a curse. For all the time they'd been away she had been writing letters to Haylin. On Friday afternoons she brought them to the post office and picked up the ones he sent her via general delivery. In New York, Haylin was studying the ecosystem of the Loch, the meandering stream in a wooded area of Central Park called the Ravine. Fireflies that gathered there blinked on and off in sync. It was as if they had a single heartbeat, sending out the same message through the dark. Such incidents had been reported in the Great Smoky Mountains and in Allegheny National Forest, but Haylin seemed the first to have discovered the phenomenon in Manhattan.

That summer, Franny went to the rare book room every day to read the journal. The librarians grew to know her, becoming accustomed to the tall red-haired girl who came to examine spidery script so tiny she had to use a magnifying glass to make out the words of the remedies and cures. Franny brightened up the place with her quest for information and history, and a few of the librarians allowed her a full hour with the text, though it was strictly against the rules. They believed all books should be read, for as long as the reader liked.

When Franny came to the last page of Maria's journal, she understood that a single broken heart had affected them all. Maria had been cast out by the father of her child, a man she never named. *Suffice it to say he should have been my enemy, instead I fell in love with him and I made the mistake of declaring my love.* She wanted to protect her daughter, and her granddaughter, and all of the Owens daughters to follow, ensuring that none among them would experience the sorrow she'd known or ruin the lives of those they might love. The curse was simple: *Ruination for any man who fell in love with them.*

Reading this, Franny paled.

It's not the same here without you, Haylin had written in one of his letters.

Then, clearly embarrassed that he'd overstepped certain boundaries, he'd crossed out that line and wrote *Boring here* instead. But Franny had seen through the smear of black ink and knew the truth. It wasn't the same without him either.

Do not ask what the spell is, or how it was accomplished. I have been betrayed and abandoned. I do not wish this for any member of my family.

"Don't you think I look like her?" Jet asked one day when she found Franny sitting pensively on the window seat studying the portrait. One of Maria's remedies called for the beating heart of a dove to be taken from the bird while it was alive. Another included collecting the hair and fingernail clippings of a disloyal man and burning them with cedar and sage.

"You don't want to look like her," Franny was quick to respond. "She ended unhappily. Trust me, she was miserable. She was accused of witchery."

Jet sat beside her sister. "I wonder if that would have happened to me if I was alive at that time. I can hear what people are thinking."

"You cannot," Franny said. And then, after a look at her sister, "Can you?"

"It's not that I want to," Jet said. "It just happens."

"Fine. What am I thinking right now?"

"Franny," Jet demurred. "Thoughts should be private things. I do my best not to listen in."

"Seriously. Tell me. What am I thinking right now?"

Jet paused. She gathered her long, black hair in one hand and pursed her lips. Since coming to Massachusetts she had grown more beautiful each day. "You're thinking we're not like other people."

"Well, I've always thought *that*." Franny laughed, relieved that was all her sister had picked up. "That's nothing new."

Later, when Jet went out into the garden, she stood beneath the lilacs with their dusky heart-shaped leaves. Everything smelled like mint and regret.

I wish we were like other people.

That was what Franny had been thinking.

Oh, how I wish we could fall in love.

One bright Sunday the sisters awoke to find a third girl in their room. Their cousin April Owens had come to visit. April had been raised in the rarefied world of Beacon Hill. With her platinum blond hair pulled into waist-length braids, and the palest of pale gray eyes, she looked like a painting from an earlier era, yet she was oddly modern in her demeanor. For one thing, she carried a pack of cigarettes and a silver lighter, and she wore black eyeliner. She was bitter and fierce and she didn't give a hoot about anyone's opinions other than her own. Strangest of all, she kept a pet ferret on a leash; it ambled beside her, instantly making her far more interesting than any other girl they'd met.

"Cat got your tongue?" she said as the sisters stared at her mutely.

"Most certainly not," Franny said, snapping out of her reverie. "If anything I'd have the cat's tongue."

"Well, meow," April purred.

April had visited this house last summer when she'd turned seventeen, and now she'd run off from Beacon Hill and come back to the one place she'd been accepted. Her presence was an unexpected surprise and, in Franny's opinion, completely unnecessary. April dressed as if ready for Paris or London rather than a small New England town. She wore a short black skirt, a filmy blouse, and white leather boots. She had on pearly pink lipstick, and her long pale hair had a thick fringe that nearly covered her eyes. She'd begun to unpack: chic clothes, makeup, several candles, and a battered copy of *Lady Chatterley's Lover*, which had been banned and had only recently been published in America.

"I'd love to read that," Jet said when she saw the racy novel everyone was talking about.

April tossed her cousin the book. "Don't get corrupted," she said with a grin.

Their cousin was clearly far more sophisticated than they. She was a wild child, doing as she pleased, refusing to be constrained by the social mores of Beacon Hill. There was a blue star tattooed on her wrist that had caused her to be grounded for several months. She had another on her hip, but that one hadn't yet been detected by her prying, fretful parents. Ever since childhood she'd rarely been out of eyeshot of a nanny, a tutor, or Mary, the long-suffering housemaid, whose hair had turned gray as she dutifully did her best to keep up with her charge's shenanigans. According to Dr. Burke-Owens's theories, such ingrained behavior couldn't be stopped; it was like a tide, rising to flood-like proportions despite anything placed in its way.

April had been to several private schools and each time had been asked to leave. She didn't believe in authority and was a born radical. She told the girls that she could turn lights on and off at will and recite curses in four languages. She had been sent on trips to Europe and South America and had learned things from the men she met that would have made her parents woozy with anxiety had they known about her exploits. She seemed to have no fear of consequences, or perhaps it was only that Aunt Isabelle had allowed her to see her fate and she knew there was no way to avoid her future. She would fall in love once, and with the wrong man, and she wouldn't change it for the world.

"I hope you've had some fun while you've been here," April said to the sisters. "Isabelle doesn't care what we do. You're entitled to enjoy yourself, you know, and you might as well do so now, because it will most likely end badly for all of us."

April was such a know-it-all Franny couldn't stand her. "Speak for yourself," she said with a scowl.

"We've had a grand time here," Jet offered in an effort to change the subject. "We've been swimming at the lake almost every day."

"Swimming!" April rolled her eyes. "No curses? No spells? Have you even *looked* in the greenhouse?" When they stared at her, she was exasperated. "This is pathetic. You're wasting your time. There's so much you could learn from Isabelle and you're blowing it by being children."

"We are not children." Franny stood up. The lamp beside her bed rattled and came perilously close to the edge of the table. At six feet, with her blood-red hair curling with anger, she was enough of a presence so that even April took heed.

"No offense," April backtracked. "I'm just telling it like it is." She lit a fragrant sage candle and began tossing her belongings onto a chair in a jumble of socks and bras and teeny Mary Quant outfits she'd bought on a trip to London. Jet picked up one of the lovely shirts and examined it as if it were a treasure.

"I imagine you've heard about the Owens family curse," April said. She sat on the bed and made herself comfortable, with the ferret immediately falling asleep in her lap.

"Curse? That sounds dreadful," Jet said.

"Oh, Jet, you can't believe anything she says," Franny warned. She'd kept Maria's writings to herself so as not to upset her sensitive sister.

"Well you should," April responded. "We have to be careful or we can ruin ourselves and the other person. The other person will fare far worse. It's always been this way, so take my advice and don't bother falling in love."

April continued to pat her ferret, which she referred to as her *familiar*, implying he was more of a soul mate than a pet. Such things occurred when creatures of different species were drawn to one another and were so intimate in their relationship they could read each other's minds.

"He knows what you're thinking," she assured her wide-eyed cousins.

"Unlikely," Franny responded. There was no scientific proof to suggest such a thing was possible.

"Well, he just let me know you pretend to have no feelings but you really care much more than you let on. I agree with him."

"You're both wrong." Franny sulked, though she worried that she had somehow revealed her innermost self to a member of the weasel family.

"Well, wrong or right, my parents plan to kill Henry," April said matter-of-factly. The ferret was surprisingly docile with bright, unblinking eyes, reminiscent of April's. "They think we have an unhealthy relationship. If they ever dare to do so, I plan to get back at them any way I can. I suggest you do the same when the need arises. Our parents want to keep us locked up. Remember, it's us against them. In fact, don't trust anyone."

"Not anyone?" Jet said, distraught.

April studied her cousins, shaking her head. They clearly knew nothing.

"There are people in this world who wish us harm. Especially in this town. It's been that way since the 1600s." April sprawled back and made herself comfortable. "I'll need to have one of the beds. Bad back. Ballet accident. Who gets to sleep on the floor?" she said with the authority of one who had been a guest the summer before. "And I get all of the down pillows."

The sisters exchanged a fleeting look. If they didn't watch out their cousin would take over. They excused themselves and went directly to Aunt Isabelle to ask if April could sleep downstairs in the extra guest room. It was so much larger, they explained, plus April had informed them that she snored, so it would be far better for the sisters to have the attic to themselves. Also, it was possible that they were allergic to the ferret.

When they told April that she wouldn't be sleeping in the attic, she had the nerve to thank them. "Reverse psychology," she said with a grin. "I wanted the downstairs bedroom. More privacy."

Franny narrowed her eyes. "We're not susceptible to reverse psychology. We know all about it. Our father is a psychiatrist."

"I've been to more headshrinkers than you'll ever meet," April informed them. "Tell them you can't sleep and your parents don't understand you and you can pretty much get any drug that you want."

Vincent heard voices and came to the topmost stair.

"Well, well," April said when he appeared on the attic landing. "Aren't you gorgeous."

It was not a question, and so there was no need to answer. Vincent shrugged, but he didn't disagree.

"An Owens man is bound to have more power than the seventh son of a seventh son. I suspect you're a wizard."

"Well, thank you," Vincent responded, pleased by her attentions.

"He's hardly a man," Franny said dismissively. "He's fourteen. And learning magic out of a book does not make him a wizard."

April gave Franny the once-over. Perhaps she had met her match, but she doubted it. Franny had a hard exterior, but she was also quite innocent.

40

By now, Jet and Vincent were drawn in by their cousin's brash glamour as April held forth, enlightening her younger cousins. She told them how to slip out the window and climb down the drainpipe if they wished to sneak out, and warned that there were mice hiding in the bureau drawers and beneath the beds.

"Watch out for the beehive," she recommended. "The honey is so sweet anyone who eats it immediately wants to have sex."

Jet and Franny exchanged mortified glances, while Vincent grinned and asked, "How do you know?"

April threw him a world-weary look. "I've tried it," she said.

"Sex or the honey?" Vincent teased.

"What do you think?" April stared at him with such intensity that he shrugged and gave up. She'd won that round. "You do understand that we're different from other people." When met with silence April knew she had them in thrall. "I can't believe how naïve you all are. Where do you think your power comes from? We're bloodline witches. Which means we have no choice in the matter. It's a genetic factor. Like blue eyes or red hair. It's who you *are*."

"Don't tell *me* who *I* am," Franny shot back.

"You can argue all you want," Vincent said. "I don't care where it comes from, as long as I have it. While you debate, I'm actually going out to live my life, wizard or not."

He took the narrow stairs two at a time all the way to the first floor. He then went out through the kitchen, letting the screen door slam behind him. They could hear his boots clattering on the porch steps. The girls went to the window to watch him stride down Magnolia Street.

"Headed for trouble," April said cheerfully.

"How do you know that?" Jet wondered.

April grinned. There was definitely a family resemblance. "Because I'm headed for the very same place."

During the time April stayed with them, she and Vincent left the house together each morning. They said they had taken up running, which they vowed would become a huge trend some-day. But whenever they returned they were wearing their black clothes and boots and they clearly hadn't broken a sweat. Jet and Franny both resented being cut out of their mysterious do-ings. Franny was jealous of the time Vincent spent away from them, but it was April whom Jet wanted to know better, if only to borrow some of her cousin's fabulous clothes.

Still, each day April and Vincent continued to disappear without a trace, clearly looking for the trouble they would one day find. At last Franny spied them in the rare book room at the library, intent on *The Magus*. The two of them had gleefully set the glass-drop chandeliers to shaking, which had the librarians frantically calling town hall to see if there had been an earth-quake. The cousins were so engrossed they didn't notice that Franny had entered the room until she threw herself into a chair directly across from them. Then they looked up, blinking, caught in the act. They were glad they had earlier set a spell on Franny so she would never know what they were up to.

"Brilliant," Franny scolded. Her eyesight was fuzzy, as if she couldn't quite see the trouble they were brewing. "Prac-ticing the dark arts in a public place. That will make the locals love us."

"Screw the locals," April responded. "Did you know this

was the spot where the old jail stood? Maria Owens sat here in chains. It has enormous power."

"It's a library. Somehow I didn't think of you two as library hounds."

"I am not a hound," Vincent said.

"I can't believe this is where you spend your time," Franny said.

"We also smoke pot at the lake," April cheerfully revealed.

"*Our* lake?" Franny said to Vincent, truly hurt now.

"We don't own it. April has a right to go there." Vincent seemed even more reckless than usual. "And we only go there occasionally."

"So what *are* you up to?" Franny asked her brother.

"What trouble could happen in a library?" When Vincent's languid smile spread across his face Franny nearly forgave him for sharing secrets with April. But not quite.

"If you're with her," Franny said, nodding to their cousin, "plenty. Just be aware that April is a narcissist." She'd heard her father use this term for many of his patients, devil-may-care people who never thought about anyone but themselves. "I think you'll regret this alliance," she told her brother.

"He won't," April said. "And you're not the first one to tag me with that diagnosis. I'm disappointed in you, Franny. I thought you were more original. If you're doing so much research here, did you find out anything about the secret?"

"What secret?" Franny said.

"If I knew, it wouldn't be a secret," April said smugly. "I've heard my parents whispering about it. It's probably something horrible and unexpected. I suppose it will hijack us when we least expect it. It has something to do with the curse. Some dark past that everyone wants to forget. So it looks like you don't know as much as you think you do."

After that Franny had nothing to do with April. Jet, on the other hand, continued to find their cousin fascinating. She loved to try on April's miniskirts and skintight jeans and lacy dresses. When Jet dressed up in them she looked like someone completely different, and she liked what she saw.

One night, when thunder was rolling across the sky, Jet looked out the window to spy April and Vincent playing strip poker in the garden, laughing and tossing off shirts and shoes. Not even the rain stopped them. April certainly didn't seem Vincent's type, yet they were thick as thieves. Those two instinctively knew how to have fun, something at which Jet and Franny were both painfully inept.

There came a hot morning when Vincent was sleeping late and Franny was at the library when April knocked on the attic door. Jet was in bed reading an annotated copy of Emily Dickinson's poems that she'd found on a bookshelf in the parlor.

April grabbed the embossed edition from Jet's hands. "Let's get out of here." When Jet hesitated, April made a face. "You can't read and pull weeds for the rest of your life. Try doing as you please and see how it feels."

If this was an offer of friendship, who was Jet to decline? So off they went to Leech Lake on a whim, with a cooler of beers bought at the corner store thanks to a fake ID April had obtained in Harvard Square for twenty dollars and the promise of a kiss that was never granted.

When they reached the lake, Jet undressed behind some shrubbery. She was wearing her old black bathing suit under her dress, but was still modest. April, however, hadn't bothered with a suit. She merely slipped off her clothes, dropping them onto the grass. She was even more beautiful naked, a pale exotic creature so daring she climbed to the highest rock, then dove in without a moment of hesitation. Like the siblings, she floated right back up to the surface. She shook her fist in the air. "Just try to drown me!" she called out to some invisible enemy. "Oh, come on," she crooned, when Jet looked scandalized. "Don't be such a baby."

Later, while they dried off in the sun, April unbraided her hair, which looked like snow as it fell down her back. There was a smear of mud on her face, and she had a lost expression, appearing more thoughtful than usual. "I can see the future, and I thought that would help me know my path, but I keep walking right into every mistake."

"Everyone makes mistakes," Jet said. "It's part of being human."

April gave her a contrary look. "That's not exactly what we are. Or don't you get that?"

"We're human enough."

"You must have a special talent."

"I can tell what people are thinking," Jet admitted. April was the first person other than Franny to whom Jet had confided this skill. She was always embarrassed to be anything other than normal, as if she were proving those dreadful girls at the Starling School right.

"Really?" April's interest in her cousin was piqued. Perhaps Jet wasn't as mousy as she seemed.

"I don't *want* to know. It's so intrusive, it seems morally wrong, but I can't seem to stop it unless the person blocks me by putting up a force field around her mind. Franny's good at that. She just shuts down emotionally. She never lets anyone in. I guess that's her strength."

"Try with me," April insisted. "I won't block you. What am I thinking right now?"

Jet knew this was dangerous business. She kept her eyes downcast. "You wish you could stay here," she said in a consoling voice.

"Anyone could guess that. Tell me something no one else would know. Show me your talent."

They were sitting across from each other. The rest of the world dropped away when they took each other's hands and looked into each other's eyes. They both cleared their minds. They could hear bees in the tall grass and the flickering of birds that skimmed over the lake, and then, all at once, they couldn't. Everything around them fell silent. It was just the two of them, and as April's mind opened to her cousin, Jet gasped, startled by April's deepest thoughts. By now she had realized that people were surprising creatures. Still, she would have never guessed Vincent was the problem.

Jet thought it best not to reveal too much. Beneath all the bluster and sophistication, April was terribly vulnerable. Jet realized that when April left, she would miss her cousin. To avoid any embarrassments, she simply said, "You wish you could come back to New York with us. You asked Vincent, but he said it was impossible."

Tears rimmed April's eyes. "You know. I can tell that you do."

"I wish I could help you." Jet had never wanted the sight less than she did right now.

April shrugged. "It doesn't matter. My parents would never let me go. They want me to be like everyone else. My mother says I don't apply myself and that's why I don't fit in. She doesn't believe it, but I've tried to be like other people. It doesn't work." April's skin was hot and flushed, her usually perfect complexion blotchy. "It's very difficult to live with parents who disapprove of your every thought and deed."

"You'll get away from them," Jet assured her. "Just not yet."

"I'm fated to lose everyone I ever love," April said. "I already know that."

"Of course you are," Jet responded in her calm, measured tone. "That's what it means to be alive."

The next morning a long, black car pulled up in front of the house. April's parents had hired a driver, sent to retrieve her and bring her back home. The horn honked several times and an annoyed Isabelle went out to make sure the driver hushed, which of course he did as soon as he set eyes on her. April could have made the departure difficult; she might have hidden in the cellar or run out the back door and found her way into the woods. But in the end her fate had come to meet her and it always would.

"Here I go. Back to Beantown, where I'll never hear the end of my failures." She took Henry and went to pack, running into Franny in the hall. The ferret looked especially sad, as if he knew his fate as well. "We'll always be involved with each other," April told Franny. "You know that, don't you?"

Franny had the sense that her cousin was right, still she said, "I doubt it. We live in different worlds."

"Actually, Franny, we don't."

Because of the sad tone of her cousin's voice, Franny offered to carry her suitcase to the door.

"The next time I see you everything will be different," April mused.

"Isn't it always?" Franny said, sounding harsher than she felt.

"I suppose your brother can't be bothered with saying good-bye," April said.

"Vincent does as he pleases," Franny remarked. "Anyone who truly knows him knows that."

When Jet came to say her good-byes, she and April lingered near the green-tinged windows. From this vantage point, they could see through the glass into the garden. Vincent was out there, dozing in the hammock. He picked up his head when the horn beeped again, gazing at the limo with disinterest before resuming his nap.

April turned away from the window. "What's done is done."

Jet went to embrace her cousin, for she knew what April was thinking. *He couldn't even say good-bye.* April certainly wasn't the first person to have fallen for Vincent, or the first to be wounded by his indifference. She'd been new and daring and exciting, but that had faded as time went on. Now she was just a girl who could easily be hurt.

"Good luck," Jet said.

"Thank you." April's eyes were filling with tears. Not everyone was who she pretended to be, including their out-of-control cousin. "Good luck to you, too."

Franny and Jet continued to work in the garden early in the mornings, before the heat of the day was upon them. They wore heavy gloves so they could tear out the poisonous plants that grew wild: jimsonweed, holly, foxglove, nightshade, mandrake, rue. While they sweated, Vincent lay in the hammock strumming his guitar. He had been composing a song about April. Called "The Girl from Boston," the ballad was about a young woman who will do anything to win her freedom. In the end she drowns in Leech Lake, sinking into the green water.

"Can't it end differently?" Jet asked her brother. "Can't love conquer all?"

"I think it's a perfect ending," Franny piped up. "She should get her comeuppance."

"A song is what it is." Vincent shrugged. "This one's tragic."

Despite the warning girls in town had been given by their mothers, many of them came to peer over the iron fence, enthralled by the handsome young stranger, won over by his long, dark hair and his pure, expressive voice and his tender rendition of "The Girl from Boston." Vincent would occasionally wave, which sent his fans into hails of giggles. The girls applauded and shrieked as if they were in the presence of a star.

"Don't they have anything better to do?" Vincent muttered.

"You know this town," Franny answered. "Apparently not."

Vincent was beginning to wish he could be released from his own rakish charms. His reputation had reached fever pitch, with increasing crowds of high school girls circling the house. Finally he gave in and let them have him. He tried one girl after another, but none held his interest. In the end he couldn't tolerate their foolish notions. The locals seemed silly and unsophisticated. When it came down to it, he simply didn't feel anything for them; they barely registered.

Then came an evening he was seduced by someone far more experienced, a neighbor who'd come to buy Aunt Isabelle's black soap, the very stuff their mother used every night. When Mrs. Rustler spied Vincent in the kitchen she was instantly in thrall. How lazy and gorgeous he was, so tall and darkly charismatic. As soon as Isabelle left the room to fetch the soap, the neighbor went right over to Vincent to whisper in his ear, saying she would make his dreams come true. She slipped one hand down his jeans to entice him. No one could call her subtle, but Vincent was drawn to rule breakers. Who was he to deny her the opportunity to defile him? She told him it was only an inappropriate flirtation; no one could fault them for that. After all, she had a son his age who was away at summer camp.

Vincent began climbing into their neighbor's window at night. He learned far more about sex on this summer vacation than most fourteen-year-old boys learn in a lifetime, for Mrs. Rustler seemed insatiable. Vincent tolerated her because when he closed his eyes, she might have been someone entirely different, and sometimes he was surprised by his own imaginings. All the same, he considered his escapades to be an education, nothing more.

When Mrs. Rustler's husband went on a business trip, Vincent was convinced to spend the night and then it went too far. She'd suddenly said something about being in love. Fear coursed through him at the very idea. Mrs. Rustler was in her late thirties, the age of his mother. He realized how old she was when he stayed all night and saw her in the glare of the bright morning sun. It was something of a shock. She was haggard and dull, with sagging breasts. Her nose appeared to be crooked, and there were hairs in her chin he hadn't noticed before. If anything, she reminded him of a very large rabbit.

Vincent came to his senses all at once. This was not what he wanted. He climbed out the window in a panic, not bothering to dress, while Mrs. Rustler slept on unawares, snoring softly. Vincent fled in shame, clothes in hand, desperate to get away. To his chagrin, he bumped into Aunt Isabelle on the porch. He was stark naked and mortified, thankful the vines cast shadows in which he could hide himself, at least a bit, from the spotlight of his aunt's fierce glance.

"Your fling not what you thought it would be?" she asked in a knowing tone.

Though Aunt Isabelle had a sober expression, Vincent could tell his exploits were a source of amusement for her. She turned her back while he dressed, then brought him out to the greenhouse, where there were dusty pots of Spanish garlic and rosemary. In a corner there grew lemon thyme and lemon balm and lemon verbena. Vincent had already broken in and explored and it was here that he and April had often come to smoke marijuana.

There were varieties of plants that needed special care on the shelves, including night-blooming cereus, jasmine, foxglove, miracle leaf, angel trumpet, and comfrey. From beneath the rows of plants, Isabelle looked through a heavy black book Vincent hadn't previously noticed.

Isabelle opened the book. "It's easy to bring love to you," she told him, "but getting rid of it is another matter entirely. If you can call whatever just went on love."

"I wouldn't call it that," Vincent admitted.

"I'd agree with you there." She leafed through the book. "There are rules to all this, you know. First, do no harm. You need to remember that."

"I'll try," Vincent said.

"Trying is not quite good enough." Isabelle turned to a page marked *Protection*.

Black cloth, red thread, clove, blackthorn.

When Mrs. Rustler woke to find Vincent gone, she had rushed after him, not caring if she caused a scandal. She was enchanted; much like the nurse who had tried to kidnap him hours after his birth, when her attraction to him was impossible to fight. They could hear her on the porch, banging on the door so hard the sound echoed across the garden. She really had no shame. Isabelle muttered a few words, which forced their neighbor to retreat to her own home. Then Vincent's aunt turned to him. "You seem to be addictive, so you'd better learn to deal with the problem now. I assume you already know your fate. Or do you fear knowing?"

"I don't fear it," Vincent said, bravely, but in fact he did.

Isabelle reached for the black cloth that covered an object stored on the floor beside the potting soil and the bulbs which would be planted in autumn. There stood a three-sided mirror, the glass painted black. There were no mirrors in the old house, and when he now spied his image he understood why. Members of their family saw not only their current reflections but also the images of what was to come. There in the greenhouse, on this cool morning, Vincent saw his future before him. It was a twist of fate he had guessed at before. But seeing it so clearly, he turned chalk white.

Aunt Isabelle offered him a glass of water, but he shook his head and continued to stare. There were blurred images of a little girl on the grass and of a man on a hillside and of a park he didn't recognize where the paths were made of stone. And larger than any of these images there was the shadowy twin he had caught sight of throughout his life, whenever he peered into mirrors or passed by store windows. A self inside him, one he'd done all he could to avoid. Now, however, he had no choice but to look. In doing so, he understood who he was. In that moment, in his aunt's greenhouse, he felt more alone than ever.

Isabelle made the charm for him, sewing so quickly her fingers seemed to fly. Vincent had to wait through the day, for he was told to leave the amulet on Mrs. Rustler's porch when the moon was waning, then he must draw a circle around himself in the dust and stand in place until he knew it was time to go.

"How will I know?" he asked.

Isabelle laughed. "You'll know."

Vincent kissed his aunt, thanking her.

He lay low for the day, holed up in the greenhouse, ignoring his sisters when they called to him. At last it was time. As he walked back to the neighbor's he realized that the magic tricks he'd taught himself were childish foolishness. What mattered was the blood that ran through him, the same blood that had flowed through Maria Owens. Once, when he'd cut himself in a tangle of brambles on the way to the lake, drops of his blood had burned through the fabric of his shirt. This was what bloodline magic was. It was inside him.

On this night he followed his aunt's instructions. He left the charm on a wicker chair on Mrs. Rustler's porch and stood within a circle of dust until he felt her attraction to him evaporate. The electricity around him fizzed, and the air turned calm. There was the sound of crickets calling and a wind arose that would end later the next day. Upstairs, in her bed, Mrs. Rustler fell into a dreamless sleep and when she woke she had no aspirations other than to have a decent cup of coffee and a toasted English muffin. Her son came home from summer camp. Her husband returned from one of his many business trips.

When Vincent next ran into Mrs. Rustler, in his aunt's kitchen, come for a bottle of vinegar from an old Owens recipe that used molasses and rainwater, he felt a chill. The vinegar was useful for impotent men, of which her husband was one. When Mrs. Rustler raised her eyes to meet his, Vincent could tell she didn't recognize him. It was as if she had never seen him before, let alone taught him the intricacies of what a woman such as herself wanted in bed.

In the days that followed, Vincent tried his best to uncover his natural abilities. As he sat with his sisters on a wooden bench in the park, he decided to teach the two vicious swans in the pond a lesson. He studied them with absolute concentration, and soon enough they rose into the air, hanging above the water for a terrified instant before splashing back down. They were stunned for a moment, then took off on wing across the pond, squawking like chickens.

"That should teach them," he said.

"All swans fly," Franny insisted. "That's not magic."

But between April's assertions and the swans' reactions, Franny was intrigued. She embarked on a quest to methodically test her siblings' abilities.

When she began her experiment, Vincent shook his head. "It's a waste of time. We have the sight, Franny. Just admit it."

Still, Franny wanted evidence. She had her brother remain in the parlor and stationed Jet in the attic, with no possibility of communication as they scanned duplicate index cards. Each could guess the word that the other had seen one hundred percent of the time. Franny tried it with numbers as well.

"We may simply have ESP," Franny said. "I'll need further documentation."

Vincent laughed at that assessment. "Franny, we have more than that."

Secretly, Franny had also been testing herself. Interested in the idea of levitation, she placed small items on the cherry-wood desk in the parlor, then closed her eyes and willed them to move. When that didn't work she asked nicely and soon had the ability to cause a tape measure to jump off the desk. She practiced daily, but it was clearly Vincent who had the strongest power. He didn't even have to try. When he sauntered into the room books leapt from the library shelves. It was so effortless, like a bird lifting into a tree, the papers fluttering, the volumes crashing to the floor. *You have the gift,* Franny thought as he sprawled onto a velvet love seat. She hadn't before realized how much he resembled Maria Owens. She thought it likely that he had as much power, perhaps more.

Vincent laughed, as if she'd spoken aloud. "Yes, but I'll probably waste it," he said. "And don't kid yourself, Franny," he told his sister. "You have it, too."

As it so happened, Franny soon found herself pulled into consciousness in the middle of the night, awaking with a gasp. It was as if someone had reached into her soul and grabbed her to pull her out of her sleep. Her name had been spoken, although how, and by whom, she had no idea. It was the green heart of the summer, and cicadas were calling as heat waves moved through the air. It was a perfect night for dreaming, but Franny felt she had no choice but to answer the call. She left the attic and slipped down the back stairs in her nightgown. She pushed through the screen door and went past the porch, where the wisteria was so twisted children in town swore the vine had been fashioned out of an old man's arms and legs.

It was pitch dark, and Franny crept forward carefully, doing her best not to trip over the holes the rabbits had dug. When she narrowed her eyes she noted that she wasn't the only one out in the yard. Aunt Isabelle was making lye by pouring water through wooden ashes while talking to herself in a low tone. Now that Franny's eyes had adjusted to the dark, she spied a mound of dried lavender on the ground, along with a basket of spices, and a pail of what looked like liquid midnight, but was in fact licorice-infused oil.

"The best soap is made in March in the dark of the moon. But since you're here now, we'll do it tonight. Soap must be made by someone in the family. That's why I called you. If you weren't the right person you would have gone on sleeping. But you woke, so the job is yours."

Isabelle had interrupted a curious dream Franny had been having about a black bird eating from the palm of her hand as she sat on a bench in Central Park. The crow had told her his name, but now that she was awake she'd forgotten what it was.

She'd read that Maria Owens was thought to have the ability to turn herself into a crow in order to accomplish her witchery. This conclusion was based on the account of a farmer who had shot at such a bird in his cornfield. The very next day Maria was seen with her arm bandaged.

"I don't see why it has to be me." Franny was barefoot and the earth felt damp. "Jet can do it."

Isabelle gave her a hard look. Her expression sent a deep chill through Franny. It was to be her, that much was clear.

Franny noticed the book that was kept in the greenhouse had been brought outside. The fat, overstuffed tome reminded her of a black toad, for it was bound in a covering that resembled frog skin, cool to the touch. It was filled with deeply personal information, some too dangerous ever to repeat. If there were no family member to inherit it, it would be burned when the owner died, out of respect and according to tradition. Some called such a collection a Book of Shadows, others referred to it as a *Grimoire*. By any name it was a treasured text of magic, and was imbued with magical power. Writing itself was a magical act in which imagination altered reality and gave form to power. To this end, the book was the most powerful element of all. If it wasn't yours and you dared to touch it, your hand would likely burn for weeks; small raised lumps would appear, causing a rash that was often impossible to cure.

The journal in the library had been written during the last year of Maria's life, but this, her secret book of spells, had been hidden beneath the floorboards of the house. The *Grimoire* contained instructions on how to craft talismans, amulets, and healing charms. Some formulas were written in ink that was specially made from hazelnuts or madder; others were written in the writer's blood. There were lists of herbs and useful plants; remedies for sorrow, illness, childbirth troubles, jealousy, headache, and rashes. Here was a repository of a woman's knowledge, collected and passed on.

"This is where the recipe for our soap came from. They may have the journal Maria wrote in her last year at the library, but we've kept the important book hidden. It may be the oldest *Grimoire* in this country. Most are burned when the owners pass on, to ensure that they don't get into the wrong hands. But this one never gets into the wrong hands. We make sure of it. From Maria onward, it has gone to the strongest among us." The *Grimoire* was so crammed with papers that scattered pages fluttered to the ground as Isabelle handed it over. "When the time comes, you'll be next."

The book opened in Franny's hands. On the first page were the rules of magic.

> *Do as you will, but harm no one.*
> *What you give will be returned to you threefold.*
> *Fall in love whenever you can.*

The last rule stopped Franny cold. "How is this possible?" she asked. "We're cursed."

"Anything whole can be broken," Isabelle told her. "And anything broken can be put back together again. That is the meaning of Abracadabra. *I create what I speak.*"

"Are you saying the curse can be broken?" For a moment, Franny felt her heart lift.

"It hasn't been in several hundred years, but that doesn't mean it can't be."

"I see," Franny said moodily. Clearly, the odds weren't on their side.

Together, they lifted the old black cauldron to hang on a metal pole over the wood fire. Ashes floated up in a fiery mist. To the mix they added roses from the garden, lavender that had grown by the gate, herbs that would bring luck and protect against illness. Sparks flew and changed color as they rose, from yellow to blood red. Making this soap was hard work, and soon enough Franny was overheated. Sweat fell into her eyes and her skin turned slick with a sheen of salt. It seemed like a wonderful science experiment, for the ingredients must be carefully measured and added slowly so they didn't burn. She and her aunt took turns stirring the mixture, for it required a surprising amount of strength, then poured ladles of liquid soap into wooden molds that were kept on the shelves in the potting shed. The liquid soap in the molds hardened into bars. Inside each was a dash of shimmering color, as if each contained the essence of the roses they'd added. They wrapped the bars in crinkly cellophane. As they did, Isabelle appeared younger, almost as if she were still the girl she'd been before she'd come to Magnolia Street. Franny's own complexion was so rosy from the hours of handling the soap that drowsy bees were drawn to her, as if she were a flower they couldn't resist. She batted them away, unafraid of their sting.

By the time they were done the sky was filling with light. Franny felt invigorated, so fevered she slipped off her nightgown and stood there in her underwear. She could have kept at it for another twelve hours, for in truth the job had seemed more pleasure than work. She collapsed in the grass, observing the sky. A few pale clouds shone above them. Aunt Isabelle handed her a thermos of rosemary lemonade, which Franny drank in thirsty gulps. "That was fun," Franny said.

Isabelle was clearly pleased. She had packed up the *Grimoire* until it was next needed. "For us it was. It would be drudgery for most people."

Franny pursed her lips. She had always been a practical girl, and was one still. "I know there's no such thing as what you say we are. It's a fairy tale, a compilation of people's groundless fears."

"I thought that, too, when I first came here." Isabelle sat in an old lawn chair.

"You didn't grow up here?" Franny asked, surprised to learn that her aunt had a history that predated Magnolia Street.

"Did you think I had no other life? That I was born in between the rows of lettuce and was an old woman from the day I could walk? Once upon a time I was young and beautiful. But that is the fairy tale, because it all passes in the blink of an eye. I lived in Boston, under lock and key, not unlike April. I didn't know who I was until I came here to visit my aunts and learned the rules."

Franny felt herself flush. "What if I don't wish to be what I am?"

"Then you will face a life of unhappiness."

"Did you accept it?" Franny asked.

She could see the regret in Isabelle's expression. There had definitely been a *before* in her life.

"Not fully. But I grew to enjoy it."

Jet's initial mistake was to go to the pharmacy that day, or maybe the error was made when she sat at the counter and ordered a vanilla Coke, but disaster was definitely set in motion as soon as she began chatting to the two handsome brothers who were entranced by her as soon as they spied her. She was, without a doubt, the most beautiful girl they had ever seen. They were so utterly enchanted they followed her to the house on Magnolia Street, which they should have known well enough to avoid. Franny was sprawled in the grass, eating raspberries and reading one of Aunt Isabelle's books on how to raise poisonous plants when she heard the rumble of voices. The cats were sunning themselves, but as soon as the strangers approached, they leapt into the shadows.

Jet came bursting into the yard, waving at her sister, but the boys hesitated at the gate. Seventeen-year-old twins, one with brown hair, the other fair, both daring and brave. When she saw the strangers Franny grew quite pale; the freckles sprinkled across her face stood out as if they were spots of blood.

Jet cheerfully gestured to the boys. "They've heard it's dangerous to come here."

"It *is*," Franny said to her sister. "What *were* you thinking?"

The blond boy, called Jack, geared up his courage and came traipsing through some blustery raspberry bushes that pricked the hand of anyone who tried to pick their fruit. The lovestruck boys begged Jet and Franny to meet up with them that night, and frankly both girls were flattered. Jet turned to Franny and pleaded. "Why can't we have some fun? April would."

"April!" Franny said. "She's in trouble more than she's out of it."

"She's right about some things," Jet said.

They climbed out the attic window after midnight, then shimmied down a rain pipe. All the while, Franny thought about how Hay would laugh if he could see her sneaking out of their aunt's house. *Don't you even check the weather report?* he would have asked. *Is it really worth climbing onto the roof?*

The night was indeed cloudy, with a storm brewing. It was Massachusetts weather, unpredictable and nasty with sparks of electricity skittering through the air. As they made their way down Magnolia Street, a pale drizzle had already begun to drip from the overcast sky. By the time they reached the park, buckets were falling. The girls were so drenched that when Franny wrung out her long hair, the water streamed out red. That's when she knew they had made a mistake.

The boys were making a mad dash through the park. Even the swans were huddled beneath the shrubbery. A clap of thunder sounded.

"Oh, no," Jet said, overwhelmed by the turn fate was taking.

The sisters signaled for the boys to run back to safety, but it was now impossible to see through the sheets of rain and the boys raced onward. The sisters were at the edge of the pond when lightning struck, but even before the incandescent bolts illuminated the sky, Franny could smell sulfur. The boys were hit in an instant. They stumbled as if shot, then fell shuddering to the ground. Blue smoke rose from their fallen bodies.

Franny pulled Jet along with her, for an alarm had been sounded and patrol cars already raced toward the green. If the sisters were present, they would surely be suspected of wrongdoing. They were Owens girls, after all, the first to be blamed for any disaster.

They fled to Magnolia Street, then flew through the door and up the back stairs. Breathless, they sat in the attic listening to sirens. People in town said it was an accident, they said that lightning was unpredictable, and the boys had been foolish to run through the stinging rain in their Sunday clothes. But Franny knew better. It was the curse.

They dressed in scratchy black dresses scented with mothballs they'd found in the attic but made certain to stay away from the crowd of mourners, remaining poised under some old elm trees. Jet cried, but Franny was tight-lipped; she blamed herself for what had happened. April's point was well taken. This was what love did, even in its mildest forms, at least in their hands.

When the girls came home sweating through their woolen dresses, Isabelle offered them advice along with glasses of lemonade flavored with verbena. "Avoid local people," she said simply. "They've never understood us and they never will."

"That's *their* problem," Vincent commented when he overheard.

Perhaps he was right, but from then on, the sisters rarely ventured beyond the garden. They wanted to make sure there were no more tragedies, but it was too late. People ignored Franny, with her glum expression and blood-red hair, but Jet had become a legend. The beautiful girl worth dying for. Boys came looking for her. When they saw her on the far side of the old picket fence, with her long black hair and heart-shaped mouth, they were even more ardent, despite the fate of their predecessors, or perhaps because of it. Vincent came out and threw tomatoes at them and sent them running with a snap of his fingers, but it didn't matter. On one day alone, two unhinged fellows went ahead and did crazy, senseless things for the love of a girl they'd never even spoken to. One stood in front of a train barreling toward Boston to prove his mettle. Another tied iron bars to his legs and jumped into Leech Lake. Both sealed their fates.

The sisters went directly to the attic in a state of shock once they'd heard the news. They would not eat dinner or speak to their aunt. When night fell they stole out of the attic window and climbed onto the roof. There were thousands of stars in the night sky. So this was the Owens curse. Perhaps because no one had yet figured out how to break it, it was stronger than ever. The whole world was out there, but for other people, not for them.

"We have to be careful," Franny told her sister.

Jet nodded, stunned by the events of the summer.

Then and there they made a vow never to be in love.

Franny told Jet not to go to the funerals of the boys whose names she didn't even know. She wasn't responsible for other people's illogical actions, but Jet sneaked out the window and went anyway. She stood in the tall grass, her hair tied up, her eyes rimmed with tears. She wore the black dress, though the weather was brutally hot. Her face was pale as snow. The same reverend had presided over the grave site services for all four funerals. Now Jet could hear his voice when the wind carried as he recited a quote from Cotton Mather.

Families are the Nurseries of all Societies: and the First combinations of mankind.

A boy in a black coat had come through the woods. He had a somber expression, and kept his hands in his pockets. Like Jet, he was overdressed for the hot summer weather.

Wilderness is a temporary condition through which we are passing to the Promised Land.

At first Jet thought she should run, the stranger might be another suitor, ready to do something crazy to win her love, but the tall, handsome boy was staring at the gathering, his eyes focused on the speaker. He paid her no mind.

"That's my father," he said. "Reverend Willard."

"They killed themselves over me," Jet blurted. "They thought they were in love with me."

The boy gazed at her, a serious expression in his gray-green eyes. "You had nothing to do with it. That's not what love is."

"No," Jet said thoughtfully. "It shouldn't be."

"It isn't," the boy assured her.

"No," Jet said, feeling something strange come over her. She felt comforted by his calm, serious manner. "You're right."

"Unable are the Loved to die, for Love is Immortality," the boy said. When he saw the way Jet was looking at him he laughed. "I didn't come up with that, Emily Dickinson did."

"I love that," Jet said. "I love Emily Dickinson."

"My father doesn't. He thinks she was depraved."

"That's just wrong." This summer Jet had become a huge admirer of the poet. "She was a truly great writer."

"I don't understand many of the things my father believes. He makes no sense. For instance, he'd have my hide if he caught me talking to you."

"Me?"

"You're an Owens, aren't you? That most certainly would not

fly with him. He wishes the Owens family had disappeared long ago. Again, depraved."

Perhaps it was this thought that made the two edge farther into the woods for some privacy. All of a sudden their discussion felt secret and important. The light fell through the leaves in green bands. They could hear the mourners singing "Will the Circle Be Unbroken?"

"We're related to Hawthorne," the boy went on, "but I've never been allowed to read his books. I'm grounded for life if I do. Or at least while I'm in this town, which believe me will not be long. My father has all sorts of rules."

"So does my mother!" Jet confided. "She says it's for our protection."

The boy smiled. "I've heard that one."

He was called Levi Willard and he had big plans. He would attend divinity school, hopefully at Yale, then head to the West Coast, far from this town and his family and all their small-minded notions. By the time he'd walked Jet to Magnolia Street in the fading dusk, she knew more about him than she did most people. It was nearing the end of the summer and the crickets were calling. She suddenly realized she didn't want the summer to end.

"This is where you live?" Levi said when they reached the house. "I've never been down this street before. Funny. I thought I knew every street in town."

"We don't really live here. We're visiting for the summer. We have to go back to New York."

"New York?" he said. "I've always wanted to go."

"Then you should come! We can meet at the Metropolitan Museum. Right on the steps. It's just around the corner from us." She had already forgotten the pact she had made with her sister. Perhaps the world was open to them after all. Perhaps curses were only for those who believed in them.

"To friendship," he said, shaking her hand with a solemn expression.

"To friendship," she agreed, although for the longest time they didn't let go of each other and she knew exactly what he was thinking—*This must be fate*—for that was what she was thinking as well.

The siblings packed up their suitcases. The summer was over. It had vanished and all at once the light falling through the trees was tinged with gold and the vines by the back fence were turning scarlet, always the first in town to do so. Vincent, bored and edgy, fed up with small-town life, was eager to throw his belongings into his backpack and sling his guitar over his shoulder. He'd been itching to return to Manhattan and get his life back on track. On the morning of their departure they had an early breakfast together. Rain was pouring down, rattling the green glass windows. Now that it was time to leave, they felt surprisingly nostalgic, as if their childhoods had ended along with their summer vacation.

Aunt Isabelle handed them their bus tickets. "You'll have a good trip. Rain before seven, sun by eleven." And sure enough the rain ceased while their aunt was speaking.

When Franny finished packing and went downstairs, Isabelle was waiting for her with two fresh pots of tea. Franny grinned. She knew this was a test. It was likely Vincent and Jet had already been assessed in the same manner, but Franny had always excelled at such things. She wasn't afraid to make a choice.

"Let's see what you'll have," their aunt said. "Courage or caution?"

"Courage, thank you."

Isabelle poured a cup of an earthy fragrant mixture. "It contains all the herbs you've tended this summer."

Franny finished one cup and asked for another. As it turned out, she was desperately thirsty. Her aunt poured from the second pot.

"Isn't that caution?" Franny asked.

"Oh, they're both the same. You were never going to choose caution. But take my advice. Don't try to hide who you are, Franny. Always keep that in mind."

"Or I'll be turned into a rabbit?" Franny quipped.

Isabelle went to embrace her favorite niece. "Or you'll be very unhappy."

As they headed toward the bus station, doors and windows along the street snapped shut.

Good riddance was whispered. *Go back to where you belong.*

Jet straggled behind. She had felt at home in the garden on Magnolia Street, and even more at home whenever she met up with Levi Willard, whose very existence she kept to herself, a secret she hadn't revealed to her brother and sister. They had the sight, but they hadn't even bothered to look into what Jet was doing when she went out in the evenings. She said she was going to pick herbs, and they let it go at that. Their dear Jet, why would they even suspect her? Why would they guess she had learned something from Franny, and had thrown up a barrier inside her mind?

Franny walked on ahead with Vincent, taking his arm, discussing the test with brews of tea. "What did you choose? Courage or caution?"

"Is that even a question?" Vincent had his guitar slung over his shoulder. He'd had more girlfriends than he could count this summer, yet didn't feel the need to say good-bye to a single one. "Caution is for other people, Franny. Not for us."

They sat in the back of the bus. People avoided them, and for good reason. The Owens siblings looked grumpy and sullen in their black clothes, with their overstuffed luggage taking up a good deal of the aisle. As they sped along the Mass Pike, Franny felt homesick for Manhattan. She had tired of the attitude of the neighbors, and the unnecessary tragedies they'd witnessed. She'd missed Haylin and had all of his letters bundled at the bottom of her suitcase. Not that she was sentimental; it was purely for archival purposes, in case she should want to refer to a comment he'd made.

In Massachusetts everything had a faint green aroma, a combination of cucumber, wisteria, dogwood, and peppermint. But the scent of the city changed every day. You never could predict what it might be. Sometimes it was a perfume of rain falling on cement, sometimes it was the crispy scent of bacon, or a sweet and sour loneliness, or curry, or coffee, and of course there were days in November that smelled of chestnuts, which meant a cold snap was sure to come.

When the bus neared Manhattan, Franny opened the window so she could breathe in the hot, dirty air. She was still having that same dream about a black bird that spoke to her. If she hadn't thought psychotherapy was utterly ridiculous she might have asked her father what on earth her dream might mean. Was it flight she wanted, or freedom, or simply someone who spoke her language and could therefore understand her confusing emotions?

"Careful," Vincent told her with a grin when he saw her moody expression. "I foresee complications of the heart."

"Don't be ridiculous." Franny sniffed. "I don't even have one."

"O goddess of the rational mind," Jet intoned. "Are you made of straw?"

Vincent took up the joke. "No. She's made of brambles and sticks. Touch her and be scratched."

"I'm the Maid of Thorns," Franny said gamely, even though she had already picked up the scent of Manhattan through the open bus window.

Tonight it smelled of love.

PART TWO

Alchemy

The most glorious hour in Manhattan was when twilight fell in sheets across the Great Lawn. Bands of blue turned darker by the moment as the last of the pale light filtered through the boughs of cherry trees and black locusts. In October, the meadows turned gold; the vines were twists of yellow and red. But the park was more and more crime-ridden. The Owens siblings had ridden their bikes on the paths without adult supervision when they were five and six and seven; now children were forbidden to go past the gates after nightfall. There were muggings and assaults; desperate men who had nowhere else to go slept on the green benches and under the yews.

Yet to Franny, Central Park continued to be a great and wondrous universe, a science lab that was right down the street from their house. There were secret places near Azalea Pond where so many caterpillars wound cocoons in the spring that entire locust groves came alive in a single night with clouds of newly hatched Mourning Cloak butterflies. In autumn, huge flocks of migrating birds passed over, alighting in the trees to rest overnight as they traveled to Mexico or South America. Most of all, Franny loved the muddy Ramble, the wildest, most remote section of the park.

In this overgrown jumble of woods and bogs there were white-tailed mice and owls. Birds stirred in the thickets, all of them drawn to her as she walked by. On a single day waves of thirty different sorts of warblers might drift above the park. Loons, cormorants, herons, blue jays, kestrels, vultures, swans, mallards, ducks, six varieties of woodpeckers, nighthawks, chimney swifts, ruby-throated hummingbirds, and hundreds more were either migrating flyovers or year-round residents. Once Franny had come upon a blue heron, nearly as tall as she. It walked right over to her, unafraid, while her own heart was pounding. She stayed still, trying her best to barely breathe as it came to rest its head against her cheek. She cried when it had flown away, like a beautiful blue kite. She, who prided herself on her tough exterior, could always be undone by the beauty of flight.

Near the Ramble was the Alchemy Tree, an ancient oak hidden in a glen few park goers ever glimpsed, a gigantic twisted specimen whose roots grew up from the ground in knotty bumps. The tree was said to be five hundred years old, there long before teams of workers turned what had been an empty marshland into the groomed playground imagined by Frederick Law Olmsted in 1858, giving the city a form of nature more natural than the very thing it imitated. It was here, one chilly night, that the sisters dared to unearth the abilities they had inherited. It was Samhain, the last night in October, All Hallows' Eve, the night when one season ended and another began.

Their parents were out at a costume party, having dressed as Sigmund Freud and Marilyn Monroe. It was a night of festivity, and troops of children were scattered along the city streets. Two out of three little girls were witches with tilted black hats and rustling capes. Halloween in New York City always smelled like candy corn and bonfires. Jet and Franny cut across the park to meet Vincent after his guitar lesson. As they were early, there was time to sit on the damp grass. The summer had started them thinking: If they were not like everyone else, who, then, were they? Lately they'd been itching to know what they were capable of. They had never tried to combine whatever talents they might have.

"Just this once," Jet said. "Let's see what happens. We can try something simple. A wish. One each. Let's see if we can make it be."

Franny gave her sister a discouraging look. The last time she had said *Just this once*, two boys had been struck by lightning. Franny was definitely picking up something; Jet had an ulterior motive. There was something she desperately wanted. If there was ever a time to make a wish, it was now.

"We can find out what Mother has been hiding from us," Jet suggested. "See what we're really able to do."

If there was a way to get Franny involved, it was suggesting an attempt to prove their mother wrong. They joined hands and right away the air around them grew heavy and dense. Franny repeated a phrase she had overheard Aunt Isabelle recite when one of her clients had asked for a wish to be fulfilled.

We ask for this and nothing more. We ask once and will ask no more.

A soft fog rose from the ground and the birds in the thickets stopped singing. This was it. Something was beginning. They looked at each other and decided they would try.

"One wish apiece," Franny whispered. "And nothing major. No world peace or the end of poverty. We wouldn't want to push it over the limit and have some sort of rebound that does the opposite of the wish."

Jet nodded. She made her wish right away, eyes closed, breathing slowed. She was in a trance of desire and magic. Her face was flushed and hot. As for Franny, she wanted what she most often experienced in her dreams. To be among the birds. She preferred them to most human beings, their grace, their distance from the earth, their great beauty. Perhaps that was why they always came to her. In some way, she spoke their language.

After a few minutes, when it seemed nothing would happen and the air was still so heavy Franny's eyes had begun to close, Jet tugged on her sister's arm.

"Look up."

There on a low branch of the tree sat a huge crow.

"Was that your wish?" Jet whispered, surprised.

"More or less," Franny whispered back.

"Of all the things in the world, a bird?"

"I suppose so."

"It is definitely studying you."

Franny stood up, took a deep breath, then lifted her arms in the air. As she did a cold wind gusted. The crow swooped off its branch and came to her just as the sparrow had in their aunt Isabelle's house, as the heron had walked to her, as birds in the park were drawn to her from their nests in the thickets. This time, however, Franny was caught off guard by the sheer weight of the bird and by the way it looked at her, as if they knew each other. She could swear she could hear a voice echo from within its beating breast. *I will never leave unless you send me away.*

She fainted right then and there in the grass.

Vincent had begun to go downtown on a regular basis, most often headed for a bar on Christopher Street that he knew served minors, a rough, ratty tavern called the Jester frequented by depressed NYU students who drank themselves into oblivion before staggering back to their dormitory rooms. Ever since coming home, he'd been running away from himself, and drink was one way to do that. There were pockets of magic in some of the tavern's booths, where plans had been hatched long ago. It was a good place to have a mug of ale and disappear.

Occasionally he saw a glimmer of himself in the mirror above the bar, and then he would slink down in the booth. He wasn't ready to see who he was. In *The Magus* there was a forgetting spell, which he cast upon himself. Still, he must have recited it incorrectly because he felt a spark of his true self when he was walking through the park at night. He heard his own heartbeat then and felt a quickening in his blood. He wondered what it might be like to open the door to a different life, one in which he did not hide in taverns or walk in the dark.

Now, as he crossed the Ramble, he was shocked to see Franny lying on the ground, her face a ghostly white. She had been revived, but was still prone, her head spinning.

"I'm fine," she insisted when Vincent raced over. "I'm perfectly okay."

She had been overwhelmed by the intensity of the crow's intentions. In an instant he made it clear, he was hers. She who had no heart, the Maid of Thorns, was now beloved by a common crow, and if the truth be told, she was thrilled to be in contact with such an amazing creature. Was this what a familiar was? A being that knew you better than any human ever would?

There was a cawing from above. Vincent took note of the way

the bird appeared to be guarding his sister. "Looks like you've got yourself a pet."

"I would never have a pet," Franny said. "I don't believe in them."

"What were you two doing?" Vincent asked, for he had the sense he'd been left out of something rather important. The air still felt sticky and damp and it smelled sweet.

"Nothing," Franny and Jet said at the same time.

"Right." Vincent grinned. Their dual denial was a dead give-away.

"We wanted to see what we could do if we combined our efforts," Franny said.

"And this was the result?" Vincent said. "A bird? Really you should have waited for me. I would have come up with something far better. A million dollars. A private plane."

"We wanted simple," Franny said.

The three began walking up Cedar Hill behind the Metropolitan Museum. Milkweed was growing wild even though Fifth Avenue was on the other side of the museum. It was possible to see hummingbirds here in the summer if you lay on your back in the grass and remained perfectly still.

"Whatever we did it didn't quite work out," Franny admitted. "I asked for flight."

"You have to know how to ask for things," Vincent told her. "*The Magus* says always be specific."

When they reached Fifth Avenue, Jet stopped in her tracks. Even though the night was dark she could see what was before her. Her wish was entirely whole and absolutely perfect. She knew how to ask and had been very specific: *Send me my true love.* It was simple and there was no way for it to be misunderstood, and now there was Levi Willard, sitting on the steps of the museum. He was so handsome, it made no difference that he was wearing a threadbare black suit, a skinny black tie, and a scuffed pair of black shoes.

"Jet," Franny said. "Are you all right?"

Jet had stopped breathing, but only for a moment "That's him," she said. "My wish."

Franny spied the boy on the steps. When he stood to wave she narrowed her eyes. "Seriously? Him? What about the curse?"

"I don't care."

"Maybe you should," Franny said, thinking of all the funerals Jet had attended.

Jet took hold of her sister. "You have to cover for me."

Franny looked at the boy on the steps and pursed her lips. "This might be too much for you," she told her sister. "Sneaking into the house? Dealing with Mother if she does find out? And isn't this what we said we'd stay away from? We made a vow."

"Franny, please. I know I can do it. Isabelle tested me with the tea, too," Jet said. "Did you think it was just you?"

Surprised, Franny asked, "Caution or courage?"

Jet smiled her beautiful smile. "Do you even have to ask? Who wouldn't choose courage?"

"Go," Franny said. "Before I change my mind."

Vincent stood with his hands in his pockets, puzzled, as Jet ran down Fifth Avenue.

"What did I miss?" he asked.

"Jet's been keeping secrets."

"Has she? Our Jet? Didn't she choose caution?"

"Apparently not," Franny said.

"Is this our Jet who never breaks a rule?"

They both thought it over. Jet was something of a mystery.

"And who's he?" Vincent asked.

"I believe he's her date."

"Him? He looks like a funeral director."

"It's him, all right," Franny said. "He's the one."

In the morning, they knew they were in trouble. Vincent and Franny were awakened early, summoned to the kitchen, where their parents awaited. Their mother and father were at the table, two cups of black coffee set out before them, bleary-eyed and grim, having been up all night. It was difficult to take them seriously, for they were still in their costumes. Sigmund and Marilyn. Their mother was smoking a cigarette even though she had quit several months earlier.

"Whatever it was," Vincent was quick to say, "we didn't do it."

"Do you or do you not know where your sister is?" their father fumed.

Vincent and Franny exchanged a glance. Jet was missing?

"And what is this?" their mother asked.

There was a pool of melting butter in the butter dish, a sign that someone in the house was in love.

"Don't look at me," Vincent said.

"It's nonsense anyway," Franny added.

"Is it?" Susanna said.

"We've let you run riot for too long," their father went on. "That trip to Massachusetts never should have happened. What a mistake!" He turned to their mother. "I told you it was a matter of genetics, and once again I was proven correct."

"Shouldn't we call the police?" Franny was thinking of the boy in the black suit. She didn't even know his name or where on earth he and Jet had disappeared to.

"The police?" Susanna said. "The last thing we want is to bring in the authorities. No. Your father is the one who deals with abnormalities."

Disgusted by his parents' reaction, Vincent began pulling on his boots in order to go look for his sister. "Jet is missing and that's all you have to say? That we're not normal?"

"That's not what I said!" their mother insisted.

"It's exactly what you said," Franny remarked with a dark look. She went to collect her jacket so she might join Vincent in the search. Of course she blamed herself. She should never have agreed to cover for Jet. She'd gone so far as to stuff pillows under her sister's quilt so it would appear she was home sleeping should their mother check in.

"Do not leave this house!" Dr. Burke-Owens demanded. "We're already down one."

Vincent and Franny ignored his command and went to the door. When it was thrown open, however, there was Jet on the threshold, hair in tangles, clearly out of breath, holding her shoes in her hand.

"You're alive," Vincent said. "That's good."

"You do realize that 'Cover for me' does not mean 'I'll stay out all night,'" Franny hissed. Now that Jet was safe and sound Franny could allow herself to be furious.

"We lost track of time," Jet explained. "We were everywhere. Places I've never been to before even though I've lived here all my life. The Empire State Building. The ferry around Manhattan. Afterward we walked along the Hudson until we wound up at a diner on Forty-Third Street. He'd never had a bagel before! He'd never heard of lox! Next time he wants to have Chinese food."

"You didn't notice when the sun came up?" Franny said, no longer as angry.

"I swear I didn't. Everything just happened."

Vincent and Franny exchanged a look. This was the way people spoke when they fell in love.

"We don't even know who he is," Franny said. "He could have been a murderer."

"He is not a murderer! His father is a reverend and he's applying to Yale. I met him over the summer, when we were visiting Aunt Isabelle. Yesterday he happened to be at a national youth club meeting at Queens College. He said that he suddenly found himself thinking about me right there in Queens, in the middle of everything, and he couldn't stop. So he got on a subway. And then he just appeared."

"He sounds fascinating," Vincent said drily.

"Well, he is!" Jet said, her facing flushing with emotion. "He wants to do good in the world and make a difference and I find that fascinating!"

Their mother had come into the hallway, the color drained from her face. She'd overheard just enough to cause her to panic. "Who were you with?"

"I'm so sorry! I didn't mean to be this late."

"You were with some boy! What is his name?"

Jet had the sense that she should lie, but it wasn't in her nature. She turned quite pale as she said, "Levi Willard."

To everyone's great shock Susanna slapped Jet, hard so that her head hit against the wall. Their mother had never before raised a hand to any of them. She didn't even believe in it.

82

"Mother!" Franny cried.

"Your father is in the kitchen and I don't want him to hear a word of this. Don't you ever see that individual again, Jet. Do you understand me?"

Jet nodded. There were bright tears in her eyes.

"I will send you away to boarding school if I ever find out you've disobeyed me. It will happen so fast you won't have time to pack a suitcase."

"What's the big deal?" Vincent said. "She lost track of time."

"Just do as I say. And for now, you're all grounded. And understand this, just because you *can* love someone, doesn't mean they won't be destroyed."

"But you're married," Jet said, confused.

"I gave up love for a normal life," Susanna said. "That's all I ever wanted for you."

"You never loved our father?" Franny asked.

"Can't you tell?" Vincent threw in.

"Of course I love your father. Don't misunderstand me. I'm just not *in* love, which has saved us both in ways you can't imagine. I recommend you do the same. We are not like other people, that much is true. It has to do with our history, and if you're lucky you'll never know any more than that."

"I already do," Franny dared to say. "I spent a great deal of time in the library when we were at Aunt Isabelle's."

"Some things should be left alone," Susanna told Franny. "You won't be going back to Isabelle's or to that library." She turned to Jet. "And you stay away from that boy. Do you hear me?"

"Yes. I hear you." Jet's eyes were raised to meet her mother's. She appeared to acquiesce, but her expression was cool. "Loud and clear," she said.

Their father called to them. "May I ask what is going on here?"

They exchanged a look, agreeing it was best to keep him in the dark, but they all trooped into the kitchen.

"Well, hallelujah," he said when he saw Jet. "One problem solved and another begun." He gestured to a crow tapping on the window, clearly wishing to be let in.

Franny went to unlatch the lock and push up on the window frame. "There you are." She was actually delighted to see him.

"Oh, for goodness' sake, Franny, must you have creatures around?" their mother said.

"Yes, I must." The crow flapped inside and made himself comfortable on a curtain rod.

When they went to their room, the crow flapping after them, Jet was despondent. "She's never loved our father."

"She loves him," Franny said as she made a nest out of a sweater atop her bureau. "Just in her way."

Jet got into bed and pulled up the covers.

"Oh, no you don't," Franny said, getting into bed beside her. "Tell all."

"Mother hates Levi and she doesn't even know him. I think she hates me, too."

"We don't have to listen to her," Franny said. "Or be like her. She definitely would have chosen caution."

Jet closed her eyes. "I *won't* listen to her."

They lay there side by side, defiant, convinced that, if there were curses, then there must also be cures for every mortal plight.

In November, April Owens came to New York, having told her exasperated parents that she'd been invited to visit her cousins, which was far from true. She had already spent what should have been her first freshman semester of college working in a coffee shop in the North End. She had been accepted to MIT, delighting her stupefied parents, who had no idea she was so intelligent, but had deferred because she felt she had other things to attend to. It was too exciting a time to be tied down to school. On the eighth of the month, Senator Kennedy from Massachusetts had won in the closest presidential election since 1916. Hatless and handsome, he had given people faith in the future when he gave his acceptance speech. *I can assure you that every degree of mind and spirit that I possess will be devoted to the long-range interests of the United States and of the cause of freedom around the world.*

April came directly to the Owenses' town house. She had a packet of lavender in her pocket, for luck.

"Look who's here!" Susanna Owens tried to sound cheerful when she opened the door, but her pose was a flop. In fact, she looked panic-stricken at the mere sight of her niece. She most certainly didn't want the responsibility of overseeing this difficult girl, whose influence might lead her children to the brink.

As for April, she was unreadable as she slipped inside the house, a Cheshire cat who had arrived with a single suitcase. She looked younger than she had in the summer, her white-blond hair pulled into one long braid, her face free from makeup. She was dressed in black, with knee high lace-up boots.

"Surprise, surprise," April said. She turned to Jet, whom she considered a pal. "Although I'll bet you knew I'd be here."

The family turned to Jet. "What is *that* supposed to mean?"

Dr. Burke-Owens said, always looking for a neurosis to pin down. "Are you and April in cahoots?"

"It doesn't mean a thing," Jet said, doing her best to skirt the issue. When she and April exchanged glances, she was glad she'd said nothing and was stunned to read her cousin's thoughts. April did have something of a cluttered mind. Certainly, it couldn't be this.

"You can read me like a book," April assured her cousin. "You know why I'm here."

"Jet?" Susanna said with alarm. Since the incident with that boy, she had taken to checking her daughters' room every night, and she made sure to pick up the extension should Jet receive a phone call—which only caused Jet to be very adept at quickly hanging up.

Now Jet gazed at the floor and refused to respond. She never divulged privileged information, hers or anyone else's, though she knew why April had come. If their cousin wished to make a scene, so be it.

"It's silence, is it?" Susanna said. "Well, then April can stay the night but she'll leave in the morning."

"You're kicking me out? Just like that?" April shook her head in disbelief.

"Your parents will want you to come home," Susanna said. "I'll phone them."

"If anyone understands wanting to escape Boston it should be you. From what I've heard, we're two peas in a pod. Difficult to control. I heard you were sent to two different boarding schools, and that when you went to Paris you turned your back on who you were."

Susanna's fierce distaste for this annoying girl was evident.

86

"My dear, you are young," she said coolly. "Therefore I'll excuse your rude manner. You may stay through breakfast."

The sisters made up the spare room for their cousin. It was a cramped, chilly space with a single bed. Years ago, another family's cook had resided here, and had cried herself to sleep every night. It was still possible to see tearstains on the floor.

"Where's Henry?" Jet asked.

"My parents killed him, of course. They said he got into the rat poison, but I'll never believe that."

April lay down on the bed, weary, one arm flung over her eyes. As it turned out, she was not immune from rejection.

"Your mother hates me," she said.

"Our mother is too well bred to hate," Franny said. "She disapproves."

The crow found his way to the room and let out a shrill caw.

April opened her eyes. "You have a familiar," she said to Franny. "And your parents haven't killed him yet?"

"He's not a familiar," Franny said. "He's a foundling."

"Fine," April said. "Tell yourself that." She gazed down the hallway, then turned to Jet. "Where's your brother? Out raising hell?"

"Guitar lessons," Jet said. "He's quite serious about it."

"I suppose he has time for hell later on." In an attempt to rally, April sat up and gazed in the mirror. She unbraided her pale hair and dabbed on some lipstick. The sisters exchanged a look, for unless they were mistaken, their cousin's eyes were brimming with tears.

"April, I'm sorry," Jet said.

"Why on earth should you be sorry?" Franny asked her sister. "She's the one who arrived here without an invitation."

Instead of the smart talk they were used to from April, their cousin cried for a moment, then pulled herself together.

"Do you need some water?" Franny said, touched by the sight of her adversary in tears.

April shook her head. "Did your mother warn you not to fall in love?" she asked the sisters. "Did she say it would ruin you? Because it's common knowledge that she ran off to Paris with some Frenchman she was mad for, but he had some sort of accident, and that was that was that. She can be cautious now if that's what she wants, but as far as I can tell, love is like a train that will keep going at full speed whether you like it or not, so you may as well enjoy the ride. If you try to avoid it, you'll just make everything worse. What's meant to happen will." She looked at Jet more closely. "Congratulations. I can see it's already happened. I hope he's worthy. Who is he?"

"Levi Willard," Jet said.

April looked stricken. "That's a bad idea."

Franny was quick to defend her sister. "I don't see how this is your business."

"Well it is and it's your business, too. The Willards despise our family. There's some sort of feud. It's been going on for hundreds of years. It has something to do with the curse."

The sisters looked at her blankly.

"Don't you get it?" April said. "He's part of the secret."

"I doubt that," Franny said.

"You can doubt all you want." She turned to Jet. "Have you met the Reverend?"

"Not yet," Jet admitted.

"You probably never will. He'll refuse to be in the same room. *He's* not too well bred to hate us. I wandered into his garden during my first visit to Aunt Isabelle's and he came out and poured salt on the ground, as if I had contaminated the place. Our aunt went over there, and I received a letter of apology in the mail, but his garden died right after that; maybe it was a lack of rain or maybe it was our aunt, I don't know. I just know none of this bodes well for a happy future for you and Levi Willard."

"Things change," Jet said bravely.

"Do they?" April had begun to unpack. Along with her clothes, she'd brought several candles. "Aunt Isabelle always says that every guest should bring a gift when visiting. Even if that guest is unwanted." She handed a red candle to Franny and a white one to Jet. "If you wish to see who your true love is, prick two silver pins into the wax. When the candle burns down to the second pin your beloved will arrive. Works every time."

"No thank you. I already know my true love," Jet said stubbornly.

"I have zero interest in games like this," Franny informed their cousin.

"She believes in logic and empirical evidence," Jet informed April.

"So do I," April said. "I'm the scientist here. I've been studying arachnids in my spare time. Especially those that murder their mates after reproducing. I feel it will give me insight into the odds we Owens women have."

"If you plan on calling yourself a scientist you should be aware that odds don't matter. The natural world defies statistics."

"Does it?" April made a face that showed she disagreed. "I think the genetic realities of our family are quite obvious. It's in our blood." She took out a last candle for Vincent.

"He won't be interested," Franny said with assurance.

"You never know," April said.

"Yes I do," Franny insisted.

As usual, Vincent came home late. He peered into the sisters' room to find Jet asleep and Franny in bed reading a book concerning the migration of owls. Even from a distance, Vincent stank of cigarettes and whiskey.

"Let me guess," Franny said. "You were at a bar."

Vincent sat on the edge of the bed. "Dad said April is here."

"You spoke to Dad?" They both laughed. Conversations with their father were rare. "She's leaving after breakfast," Franny reported. "Thankfully."

"She's not so bad," Vincent said.

"Oh, please."

"She's actually sort of vulnerable."

"Hard to believe. She seems perfectly capable and extremely full of herself. By the way, she brought you a gift."

Vincent frowned. "Did she?"

Franny gestured to a black candle on her desk. "She says it will show you your true love."

Vincent pitched the candle into a trash can. "Not interested."

"Exactly as I thought." Franny nodded. "I know you too well."

"Mind if I sleep on the floor?" Vincent was far from sober, and before Franny could answer he sprawled out on the white carpet, where he snored gently through the rest of the night.

In the morning, when Franny went to the spare room, April was gone. She hadn't bothered to wait for breakfast. She hadn't said good-bye. All that remained of their cousin were a few pale hairs on her pillow and a note. *Thanks for nothing.*

Franny sat on the bed, which was still faintly warm. She felt guilty and ashamed. After all, they shared the same bloodline. Franny asked the dresser drawer to open, which it quickly did. There was the red candle. Franny placed it on the night table. She closed her eyes and willed it away. It fell onto the floor and rolled toward the door.

Vincent had come to the threshold of the room. He picked up the candle. "You've been practicing," he said admiringly.

"I don't have to practice," Franny responded. "None of us do. April was right. It's in our blood."

"Where is April?" Vincent asked, puzzled by the empty room.

"Do you care?" Franny asked.

"Somewhat," he admitted.

"Well, somewhat isn't enough. We weren't nice to her so she left."

"I was always nice to her. Wasn't I?"

"No," Franny said bluntly. "You were dismissive."

"Is that another word for cruel?" Vincent seemed remorseful.

"Of course not," Franny assured her brother. It was difficult to speak to someone who was avoiding the truth. "You're just interested in other things."

"Am I?" Vincent said.

Franny had decided to go forward with the love-divining spell to prove that love was out of the question for her. *Stick two silver pins into a candle. When the candle burns down to the second pin your beloved will appear.* Surely no one would arrive. She went and fetched two straight pins from their mother's sewing basket.

"This is dangerous," Vincent told her. "Love is easy to find, but not so easy to get rid of." As he well knew from his summer fling, which had soured so quickly.

Jet wandered into the room as Franny was lighting the candle. They could still find each other, no matter where they were, just as they had when they were children whose skills made it impossible to play hide-and-seek.

"If you're so good at reading people, what was up with April?" Franny asked her sister.

Jet flushed slightly. "Don't know."

"Look at her!" Vincent pointed to Jet. "She can't tell a lie for the life of her."

"No," Franny said warmly. "The best liar award goes to Mr. Vincent Owens, Esquire."

"Gratefully acknowledged and accepted." Vincent bowed deeply.

There was a knock at the front door. Without them noticing, the candle had burned down to the second pin.

"All I know is that I threw my candle away," Vincent reminded them. "It's for one of you."

Franny and Jet stared at each other. "It's probably for you," Franny said.

"I didn't light my candle. I can't have Levi appearing at our door. You go," she told her sister.

Franny went, her unwilling heart slamming against her chest. She was convinced that she was the last one love would ever come to. She wasn't made for such things. She wanted flight and freedom and would prefer to live among the birds, pitching a tent in Central Park and having nothing to do with humankind. Surely the caller was the mailman or one of her father's misdirected patients who had come to the wrong door.

The crow came to light on the molding of the door. "Make whoever it is go away," Franny told the crow. The bird was supposed to be her soul mate, wasn't he? But rather than help, he lifted off and winged to his favorite perch above the drapes, eyeing her with a knowing look.

The knock came again.

Vincent approached, carrying his guitar case. He'd begun to attend concerts at the Riverside Church on Sunday afternoons and had been caught up in folk music. He wore cowboy boots now, old dusty ones found at a secondhand store. He'd bought a fringed suede vest at some godforsaken thrift store on the Bowery.

"Don't open the door," Franny told him.

"I have a lesson and I'm late. This is something you'll have to handle, kiddo."

Vincent flashed his glorious grin, an expression that always meant trouble, either for him or for someone else. This time that someone was Franny. Vincent swung the door open before she could stop him. There was Haylin, leaning on the wall.

"You're home," he said. "I was about to give up. No one was answering the phone. You seem to be avoiding me."

Indeed it was true. She had hardly seen him since their return from the summer. Now she knew why she had been keeping her distance.

She took a step away from him. She'd turned pale as paper.

"Are you okay?" Hay was carrying an armful of college catalogs. They had already decided to apply to all of the same schools. They had a bet going; the winner would be the one who got into one of their top five choices: Harvard, Stanford, Berkeley, Brown, and the hometown favorite, Columbia.

"You didn't know it was going to be him?" Vincent smirked as he headed out. He didn't need the Clairvoyant Tea Aunt Isabelle concocted out of mugwort, thyme, yarrow, and rosemary. He didn't need Jet's empathy or Franny's curiosity. This one was obvious.

"Your brother's a funny guy," Haylin said.

The crow flew across the living room to perch on a velvet armchair. He studied Haylin, and Haylin studied him back, duly impressed.

"You've got a pet?"

"You know that I don't believe in pets." Franny collected the crow, then opened the window and set him on the railing.

"You're dumping him outside?" Haylin asked, bemused.

"He's a bird," Franny said. "It won't hurt him." Her heart was still pounding. This had to be wrong. Love?

Hay went to peer through the window. "Does he have a name?"

"Lewis." Franny named him on the spot. She hadn't thought to call him anything before, other than hers.

Haylin laughed. "Why is a raven like a writing desk?" he said, quoting Lewis Carroll's unanswerable riddle in *Wonderland*.

"Because a writing desk is a rest for pens and a raven is a pest for wrens? But he's not a raven. *Corvus brachyrhynchos*. The common crow."

"He doesn't look common."

Lewis was tapping on the glass.

Franny couldn't stop staring at Haylin. It had been there all along, whether she'd been aware of it or not. If she just held out it would likely pass. It had to pass. For his sake as much as for hers.

Franny had read in one of Aunt Isabelle's books that if you lit a match to a handful of snow and it melted quickly, the snow on the ground would soon disappear. By counting the knots on a lilac bush the number of cold spells could be predicted. Though the weather was chilly, the sisters escaped the house whenever they could. They liked to walk along the bridle path in the park, wearing high boots and heavy black coats. It was the season of migration and Franny stared longingly at the huge flocks passing overhead. She wished for freedom and here she was earthbound, worried about the petty concerns of human beings.

On these days Jet was often on her way to meet Levi, and Franny was her accomplice. Sisters were sisters, after all, and if they didn't stick up for each other, who would? Their mother had continued to make matters difficult ever since Jet had gone missing. She had posted a sign-out sheet on the refrigerator, and every time the girls left the house they were to jot down their destination, time of arrival, and time of return. Foolishly, their mother trusted Vincent, who disappeared to Greenwich Village whenever he had the chance.

"Good luck fighting the power," he'd say to the girls as he took off.

"Mother is *not* the power," Franny would say.

"Well, she has power over you," Vincent remarked, which they all knew was true enough.

On this particular day, Jet had until four o'clock. They said they were heading to the Museum of Modern Art to do research for term papers, but only Franny would be going. She had brought a camera along and planned to take photographs in the sculpture garden that she could have developed in case their mother demanded proof.

Levi was waiting at the Bethesda Fountain, beneath the Angel of the Waters statue, their favorite meeting place. The statue referred to the Gospel of St. John, and the angel carried a lily in her left hand, to bless and purify New York's water. Each time Levi came to the city, he had to sneak away, traveling back and forth by bus in a single day, paying for his ticket with earnings saved from odd jobs. Today he had told his father he had an interview at Columbia University, allowed even though the Reverend disliked New York City and saw it as a place of crime and greed. It was Levi's first lie and he stuttered when he told it, which made his father question him for nearly half an hour. Reverend Willard was firm in his beliefs and firmer still in his dislikes.

Jet had brought along *The Scarlet Letter* as a gift. She had signed it *To Levi with great affection*. It had taken her half an hour to decide what the dedication should be. *Love* was too much. *In friendship*, too little. *Affection* seemed perfect. At least for now.

"That's our copy! Doesn't he have his own books?" Franny groused.

"Not really," Jet said.

"And doesn't he have any other clothes?" Franny asked when they spied him.

"He was raised to be simple and kind."

Franny laughed. "Are you sure you're looking for simple?"

"Simple means he's not self-indulgent. Just so you know, Levi happens to be brilliant."

He was wearing his black suit and a scarf Jet had knitted for him. It was her first attempt, and quite uneven, but Levi had pronounced it a wonder. He had dark hair and his beautiful gray-green eyes lit up whenever he saw her. "Hey," he cried. "There's my girl."

"Don't forget to be at the museum at a quarter to four," Franny called when Jet took off. "Keep track of time!"

Franny watched her sister disappear into the park with Levi. It was such a beautiful crisp day she didn't know why she had a sinking feeling. Lewis had been following along, and now he called out with his harsh cry. He soared above the fountain, the first grand public artwork to be commissioned from a woman artist in the city of New York. Franny shielded her eyes from the thin sunlight to watch the crow perch on the angel's hand. Below him, sitting on the rim of the fountain, was a man in a black suit paging through *The Scarlet Letter,* which had been forgotten and left behind. He wore a white shirt and a black tie and shoes so old it was evident that he favored simple things. When he came to the title page and saw the dedication, he didn't need to read any further. He closed the book.

After his father's discovery, Levi was no longer allowed to leave the house unless he was going directly to work or to school. The telephone was cut off, so it was impossible to reach him. Their copy of *The Scarlet Letter* was mailed back to Jet without a note, and the handwriting on the envelope clearly wasn't Levi's. Packed with the book were half a dozen nails.

"What on earth is this supposed to mean?" Jet said anxiously.

"It means his father is deranged," Franny said.

She quickly gathered the nails and threw them into the trash. She knew from her readings at the library that witch-hunters believed a witch could be caught by nailing her steps to the ground to ensure that she couldn't run. A witch's powers were decreased when she was near metal; surround her with it and she would be helpless.

Luckily, Franny had also grabbed *The Scarlet Letter.* When it fell open in her hands she saw that someone had scrawled over Jet's lovely inscription with thick black ink and written their own message.

Thou shalt not suffer a witch to live.

Franny recognized the quote from Exodus, for it had been scrawled in the judge's notes at Maria's trial. It was the same quote that had been on the title page of *The Discovery of Witches,* written by Matthew Hopkins, the Witch-Finder General of England, in 1647, the man who was believed to be responsible for the deaths of three hundred women.

"I think April's right," Franny told her sister that night when they were both in bed.

Jet had been crying for hours, but Franny's comment stunned her. Franny had never thought April to be right about anything. She sat up in bed. "You do?"

"You should stay away from Levi."

Jet fell back into her pillow. "Oh, Franny."

"Did you hear me?" Franny asked.

"Yes," Jet said, no longer in tears and more determined than Franny might have imagined. "I heard you. And I wish I hadn't."

She went to Vincent for help. A rebel could only depend on another rebel. She trailed him to the Jester, getting on the Fifth

Avenue bus, then walking half a block behind him. She was amused that he didn't have a clue that he was being followed until she slid into the booth beside him. She had thrown up an invisibility shield that had clearly worked.

"Good God, Jet," he said, "what do you think you're doing? This is not your kind of place." All the same, he called for two beers. If his sister *was* going to be here, she might as well drink.

Jet placed a letter on the table.

"Let me guess. For Levi?"

"Just this once," Jet said.

"Yeah, I think that's what you always say. How do you propose I get it to him?"

Jet took a bus ticket from her purse.

"Massachusetts." Vincent nodded. "You seem to have it all covered." He was actually impressed. "And what do I tell the parents?"

Jet had a copy of the school newspaper. The Starling Band had been invited to play at a prep school north of Boston.

"I've joined the band?" Vincent said.

"Yesterday," Jet told him.

"I'm very clever," Vincent said. "Aren't I?"

"The music teacher said he'd been trying to get you to join for ages. He's delighted."

"Do I actually have to play?"

"There's a concert in the morning. Then you take a taxi and wait for Levi outside of his school at three."

"And if his father is there waiting, too? Have you factored in that possibility?"

Jet took a sip of the beer Vincent had ordered. "Then you use *The Magus*."

He recognized Levi right away. The white shirt, the dark hair, his serious demeanor as he made his way down the steps of the high school. He went right past Vincent, in a hurry. Vincent rose to his feet and took off running to catch up with him.

"Hey, Levi. Slow down."

Levi threw him a puzzled look. "I don't know you."

"Yeah, well I know you. Slow the fuck down."

"I have to get to work." Levi had slowed his pace. "Over at the pharmacy." He looked at Vincent more closely. "Did you want something?"

"No. But you do." Vincent took out the letter. "From my sister."

Levi grabbed the letter and tore it open, reading it hungrily.

Vincent gazed around. "Your father's not here, is he?"

"What? No." Levi went on reading. "You're supposed to give me twenty dollars."

"I am?"

"Sorry. I wouldn't ordinarily agree to this, but my father puts all of my earnings into a bank account I can't access. I need money for the bus to New York."

Vincent gave him the twenty. "You don't think you might be looking for trouble?"

Levi thanked Vincent for the loan, but laughed at the question. "Life is trouble, brother. You've got to fight for what you want."

They shook hands. Vincent didn't know what to think. He saw in Levi something he'd never felt himself. This was what love looked like. This was what it could do to you. Vincent found him-self walking to Magnolia Street. It had begun to rain, and so he ran. He wondered if he would ever feel that someone was worth fighting for, if there would ever be a person who would make him stand up and take a chance and have the courage to be reckless.

Isabelle wasn't surprised to see him. When she gave him tea and a piece of pie, he realized he was starving. He explained that he had been in the school band, but had quit once their performance was over.

"I take it you're not staying." Isabelle had noticed he had nothing with him but a jacket.

"The school reserved hotel rooms. I only came to deliver a letter for Jet." It was impossible to tell a lie to their aunt.

"Levi Willard," Isabelle said, "I used to see them walking together last summer."

"Apparently, his father hates us."

"Did he see you?"

"I don't think so."

Isabelle gestured for Vincent to lift up his left foot. She took his heavy black boot in her hand and examined the sole. There was a nail through it.

"Think again," Isabelle said. "He knew you were here. He left out nails."

Vincent fiddled with the nail, his face furrowed. "I can't get it out."

"Of course not. This is the sort witch-hunters use."

Isabelle took a small vial from a shelf. Rosemary oil infused with holly and hyssop. She dabbed some on the nail and uttered an oath. *This cannot harm you on this day. When you walk, you walk away. When you return, all of your enemies will burn.*

"What happened between our families?" Vincent asked.

"Family," Isabelle corrected.

Now he was thoroughly confused. "What do you mean?"

"I mean what I say."

"We're related?"

"Charlie is here," Isabelle said.

A battered station wagon had pulled up at the gate. None of the local taxi services would come to Magnolia Street, therefore Isabelle had called Charlie Merrill, the handyman, to give Vincent a ride back to the hotel where the band was staying.

"Is there more to the story?" Vincent asked.

"There's more to every story," his aunt told him.

On the drive, Charlie was pleasant enough, though he barely spoke. He was even older than Aunt Isabelle and had lived in town all his life.

"Do you know the Willards?" Vincent asked him.

"The Willards?"

"Yeah. The Reverend and his son."

"Did your aunt say I knew them?"

"She didn't say anything."

"Well, then, I don't know anything."

Clearly, the handyman's loyalty was to Isabelle. He didn't utter another word, other than *Good night* when they got to the hotel. Vincent was glad to have a room to himself. Something didn't feel right. He felt a chill. He wondered if what people said was true, that no one could hate you more than members of your own family.

He felt an ache, so he propped his foot up on his right knee. The nail was gone. But when he took off his boots and socks, he noticed there was a hole in his left foot. It was a good thing he had gone to his aunt for help. The nail had already drawn blood.

It began to snow toward the end of December, big flakes that stuck to the pavement. Soon the drifts were knee high, and the streets were difficult to navigate. It was the week before Christmas, and the stores were busy with shoppers. Franny was looking for a microscope at a lab warehouse. It would be an ideal gift for Haylin. She had dragged her brother and sister along.

"I thought you didn't believe in presents," Vincent said.

"This is different," Franny said. "It's practical."

Vincent and Jet exchanged a look. Their sister without a heart had spent two hours looking for the perfect microscope. On the way to the warehouse they'd stopped at a coffee shop, and when Franny ordered toast, the pats of butter melted as soon as she reached for them.

When at last she was done shopping, and the gift had been chosen and boxed, all three wheeled into the street, where the snow was still swirling down, faster now, like a snow globe, with drifts so high many parked cars were buried. It was already twilight and the world had turned an inky blue. They walked arm in arm, mesmerized by the beauty of the blue-white flakes all around them. Anything seemed possible, even to Vincent, who turned out the streetlights as they walked on.

"Let's always remember how beautiful tonight is," Jet said.

"Of course we will," Franny agreed.

But Vincent would be the one to remember this evening when his sisters had long forgotten how they'd tried and failed to get a cab, then took the subway, singing "This Land Is Your Land," and how the microscope was so heavy they'd had to take turns carrying it. When they got home, Vincent went to his room and closed the door. He sat on his messy, unmade bed. His clairvoyance was becoming more intense. He experienced the future not as a panoramic vista but as bits and pieces, like a living crazy quilt. It was becoming more difficult for him to deny what he saw. *A man standing on a hillside in California in a field of yellow grass. A street in Paris. A girl with gray eyes. A cemetery filled with angels. A door he'd have to open in order to walk through.*

One spring day, they knew something out of the ordinary had transpired because their mother had ordered a huge cake, which was set out on the dining room table. She had lit a hundred candles, which shivered with yellow light even though it was no one's birthday. Fifty candles would have been more than enough. Even more revealing that something was up: their father was putting in an appearance at the dinner table. And what's more he had actually cooked, fixing Ritz crackers with Brie and red peppers warmed up in a Pyrex dish.

Before a family meeting could commence, Vincent was called out of his room. He came into the dining room brooding, annoyed to be called away from the world of his bedroom, which reeked of smoke and magic. He had found a hanging wicker chair, with a lattice seat, which he had attached to the ceiling with bolts. He often perched there, bat-like, practicing guitar riffs for hours, in no mood to be disturbed.

Once they had all gathered, their parents let loose and roared with pride.

"Congratulations!" James Burke-Owens waved an envelope. "This just arrived from a little college on the banks of the river Charles." Anyone crossing paths with the doctor would know he went to Harvard, and then Yale, within five minutes of meeting him. He now clasped Franny to him in a bear hug. "You're a good girl, Frances Owens."

Franny, always embarrassed by displays of emotion, slipped out of her father's embrace. She took the envelope from him, barely able to contain her excitement. Inside was her acceptance to Radcliffe, Harvard's all-female equivalent, created when higher education for women was scandalous.

"You've joined the club," her father boasted.

"We all knew you were the smart one," Vincent said. "Now don't screw it up."

"Very funny," Franny responded. She knew Vincent to be the most intelligent among them all, albeit the laziest.

The admission to Radcliffe was not in the least bit funny to Jet. College catalogs had been arriving in the mail for some time, and Jet had worried that when Franny went off to Cambridge or New Haven she would be forced to deal with her parents on her own. How would she ever be able to see Levi without Franny to cover for her? She simply could not live without him. That very afternoon they had sat on a park bench kissing until they were dizzy. When it came time to part, they were upset, and they continued to embrace in the Port Authority Bus Terminal while Levi missed one bus after another.

Now, as the family was celebrating Franny's acceptance to Radcliffe, Jet did something terrible. She wished that Franny wouldn't be able to leave New York. She knew she was being selfish and she chastised herself for it afterward, but it was too late, the wish had been made. It was bitter and carried the acrid scent of smoke, and when it lodged somewhere inside Jet it made her cough, a hacking rattle that lasted for months.

"Cheer up," Vincent said as Jet despondently watched their parents open a bottle of champagne. "It won't be as bad as you think."

"What won't be?"

Vincent tousled her black hair. "Your future."

It was then she realized that Franny could provide the perfect excuse to see Levi. Every time she said she was going to visit Franny in Cambridge, she could get off the train at New Haven. Levi had gotten into Yale, and he would be there waiting for her. She thought she would bring him a new coat on her very first visit, then he wouldn't have to keep the old one his father had him wear. She had changed her mind about Franny going off to school. She even drank some champagne. She took back her wish right then and there, but unfortunately such things simply can't be done.

Haylin's letter from Harvard arrived in the mail the following day. He came around to collect Franny so they could celebrate their impending independence from their small-minded parents and their dreadful school and awful childhoods, for which they were already feeling nostalgic. They nestled close together to avoid a pale rain as they walked toward Madison Avenue, pretending to fight over a single umbrella.

"The only thing I'm taking with me when I leave is the microscope," Haylin announced. "I'm donating everything else."

At the coffee shop on the corner, they ordered waffles and eggs, and because all of Manhattan smelled like bacon that day, a side of Canadian bacon as well. Hay topped it off by wolfing down two jelly doughnuts, which he'd craved ever since his marijuana experiments. They were both starving for food and for freedom. The brilliance of the day made them dizzy and hopeful in ways they had never imagined. In Cambridge anything could happen. The rain was stopping; the air was green. Spring was thick with lilacs and possibility. Everything was delicious, their food and New York City and their futures. Hay was to live in Dunster House, Franny a stone's throw away, if you had a strong arm, which Haylin did, at South House on the Radcliffe Quad. They toasted to liberty, clinking together their glasses of orange juice. *O joy,* they crooned to one another. *O learning and books and baked beans and the Red Sox and the filthy Charles River.*

They had all spring and summer to enjoy Manhattan. The magnolias and ornamental cherry trees were blooming in the park. They met at twilight, free spirits, no longer tethered to their parents' wishes. They explored every acre of the park they so loved and would sorely miss, watching constellations from Sheep Meadow, wading in the chilly Loch, studying the white-footed mice that collected acorns along Cedar Hill, tracking the red bats nesting in the English oaks and black locusts. Lewis the crow followed them, and Haylin fed Franny's familiar bits of crusts when they brought along sandwiches.

"You'll spoil him," Franny said. "He's supposed to be wild."

"Maybe he'd rather be tame," Haylin responded thoughtfully.

Hay had already confided that if he were ever to inherit his family's money he would dispose of it, for every time he walked into their limestone mansion on Fifth Avenue, he felt he had made a wrong turn and had mistakenly come to live with a family who would have been much happier with a different son. "You're the only person who really knows me," he told Franny.

She kissed him then. She didn't plan it. She simply felt a wave of emotion she couldn't name. It was impossible for anything to happen between them. Still she kissed him again, and then once more for luck.

Vincent was at the Jester, where he had become a regular, and he was drunk. He hadn't told his sisters how much of the future he could see, because he didn't like it one bit. Luckily Franny rather than one of their parents picked up the phone when the bartender called to say the Wizard might need help getting home.

"Who on earth is that?" Franny said.

"The kid who does magic tricks. He gave me your number. He said he was your brother."

When she said that he was indeed, Franny was informed that Vincent could usually be talked into performing tricks after he'd had a few: the lights would flicker, matches would flame with a puff of breath, silverware would rattle as though there was an earthquake. Now, however, he was plastered, and likely a danger to himself. Franny took a cab, then made her way into the dimly lit bar.

The bartender waved her over. "He's been drinking since noon," he said.

Franny asked for a glass of tomato juice, extra large, then proceeded to a booth where Vincent was resting his head on the red plastic padding behind him.

"Hey there, sister," he said when Franny flung herself into the seat across from him.

She'd brought a cure for drunkenness: a powder composed of cayenne, caffeine, and St. John's wort, which she now dispensed into the tomato juice. "Drink," she said.

Vincent sipped, then shuddered in disgust.

"You're better than this," Franny said.

"Am I? I see things I can't change, Franny. When I drink I stop the visions. It was in pieces but it's coming together in one picture. And lately, what I've been seeing is an accident. A bad one. And soon."

"If you keep drinking like this, I'm sure there will be one sooner or later."

Franny sounded flip, but all the same she felt a chill. Vincent's eyes were nearly black, never a good sign.

"I'm serious," he said. "Our family. This month. When there's a full moon."

"Well, then, you don't have to worry." There had been a full moon at the beginning of the month. "It's come and gone."

Franny remembered the moon because she and Hay had sneaked out to meet at Seventy-Fourth Street in front of the statue of Alice in Wonderland. Midnight had been bright as day and they could easily read the lines chiseled in granite around the sculpture: *'Twas brillig, and the slithy toves did gyre and gimble in the wabe.* Franny had started something between them with a kiss and now what was done could not be undone, nor would she want it to be. *Brillig* was said to mean four o'clock in the afternoon, but surely it must mean more: broiling, brilliant, luminous, shimmering, unstoppable.

"Stop worrying about the moon," she told Vincent, "and start worrying about your drinking."

She gestured to the glass before him, and Vincent gulped down the rest of the drunkenness cure. He already seemed more clearheaded, but when he set the glass down it shattered into thin shards and turned blue.

"You're paying for that, Wizard," the bartender called.

Vincent looked into Franny's disapproving eyes. He seemed shocked and concerned. "I swear I did not do that."

A glass breaking on its own portended death.

"I'm telling you the truth," Vincent said. "Death is close by. I've never felt anything like this. I can almost touch it. It's like a black circle coming closer and closer."

He reached his hand into the air, and when he opened his closed fist soot appeared in his palm.

"Ashes," he said. "Franny, you have to listen to me."

Franny felt a scrim of fear. Still, she approached his prediction logically. "Certainly, somewhere *someone* will die. It doesn't necessarily have anything to do with us." She grabbed her brother's arm and shook it so that the ashes lifted into the air, where they turned white and scattered into the corners of the room. Then she used a napkin to gather the slivers of glass and brought the mess up to the bar. "He's underage," she told the bartender. "Don't serve him again."

They walked home together deep in thought. They didn't hear the bees until they reached the corner. As they neared their house they could see swarms at every window.

They stopped where they were. Bees tried to get into a house when a death was imminent.

"I'll have Mother call an exterminator," Franny said.

Vincent was suddenly stone-cold sober. "It won't make a difference. We can't stop it."

"Of course we can. You can change your fate."

"Can you?"

They stepped closer to each other.

"Do you know who's in danger?" Franny asked.

"I can't tell. I don't think it's us, because we're seeing the omen."

They stood there, shoulders touching. Bees don't swarm at night. Glass doesn't break without a cause. Ashes do not fall from above. All the same, Franny still didn't quite believe Vincent until they entered the front hallway. There on the threshold was a beetle.

"Fuck," Vincent said. He went to stomp on the creature.

He knew what it was from his readings in *The Magus,* and he now advised Franny that deathwatch beetles are wood borers that can be heard in the rafters calling for mates. They signified a death. *You cannot destroy destruction, The Magus* warned. *Though you may try.* Vincent had gotten rid of the beetle, but not its message. *You cannot unwrite a death that has been written.* There was no spell strong enough to do so.

Franny went for a broom and a dustpan to dispose of the remnants of the beetle. Jet was in the kitchen. "What's that?" she said when the creature was tossed in the trash.

"Something to avoid. From now on, no taking chances, no talking to strangers, no walking through the park at night."

"I thought we were supposed to have courage?"

"Just for now. Don't do anything out of the ordinary."

It was decided that Franny would be the one to wait up and tell the parents. They had debated and, when it came down to it, they felt that the parents had to be told for their own protection. They'd been to a party at the new Guggenheim Museum and were tipsy upon their return.

"Amazing evening," her father remarked. "That building is the future."

"Speaking of the future," Franny said, "I have information about our family I'd like to discuss with you."

"You handle this," Dr. Burke-Owens said to his wife. "It's your family."

Once he'd left the room, Franny turned to her mother. "There was an omen, and we need to pay heed."

"Franny." Their mother was exasperated. "Let's not have any nonsense tonight. I don't think I can take this any more than your father can."

"I know you don't want to believe in any of this, but there were bees swarming the house."

"Fine. I'll call an exterminator in the morning."

"And a beetle in the hall."

That stopped Susanna. "What sort of beetle?"

"The bad sort," Franny said. "A deathwatch beetle."

Susanna reconsidered. There was no reason to be impulsive

when all signs pointed to caution. "I don't see the harm in doing as you say. No chances will be taken. Now convince your sister of that since she's been so foolish lately."

"She's already agreed," Franny said.

"Fine. We will all be cautious."

Yet Franny continued to have a nest of nerves in the pit of her stomach. She went to the bedroom and perched on the edge of Jet's bed. She felt a rush of love for her sleeping sister, the most kindhearted person she had ever known. Rather than going to sleep herself, Franny crept out the open window. Lewis was there, waiting for her. She'd swiped a dinner roll, which she now broke into three pieces, signaling to each crust. She called each crust by name: *Mother, Father, Sister.*

"Which one?" she asked, but Lewis flew off, disappearing into the pitch-black sky. "You're supposed to do as I say," Franny called after him, distraught, wounded by his refusal to predict the future. Her familiar had made it clear that a crow may be a confidant and a companion, even a spy, but never a servant. In this regard, he mirrored his mistress's flinty independence. If he cried, as she now did, surely no one would ever know.

On Jet's birthday the parents surprised her with tickets to a Broadway musical and a special dinner at the Russian Tea Room. She was turning seventeen and was as near to perfect as she'd ever be. Ever since the winter Jet had collected canned food for the local soup kitchen, and she often worked there on holidays, peeling potatoes and slicing carrots. People said she resembled a young Elizabeth Taylor, whose photograph had graced the cover of *Life* magazine earlier in the year, when Miss Taylor won the Oscar for best actress in *BUtterfield 8*. Jet was an A student at Starling and had never caused her parents a single bit of worry until this Levi Willard business, but the parents were relieved that folly seemed to be old news now. Jet seemed to have turned a corner on that score. Not that they would allow her to go to Magnolia Street this summer, even though her time to visit Aunt Isabelle had come. That would be tempting fate.

"You're still the favorite," Franny remarked with zero jealousy. She was sprawled across her bed watching Jet choose her dress for the evening.

"I am not," Jet insisted. "Has our mother ever slapped you?"

All the same Jet was pleased with the fuss being made over her. Her birthday was indeed a special occasion, although no one in the family knew quite how special it would be. Franny had bought her a silver bangle bracelet in the jewelry department at Macy's. Vincent presented her with a record album by a folk singer named Pete Seeger, whose songs were so filled with humanity they brought Jet to tears. But best of all, Levi would be waiting for her at the Bethesda Fountain later tonight. He'd sold a watch that had belonged to his great-great-grandfather so he could rent them a room at the Plaza Hotel. Jet was nervous, but ecstatic. All she had to do was sneak away after the theater and she'd be free. It would be worth the trouble she'd be in when she returned in the morning.

She had tried on nearly all of her dresses when Franny suggested she wear the black minidress April had sent as a present from a shop on Newbury Street in Boston. Even Franny had to admit, April had style. "It's your birthday," Franny told her sister. "Live a little."

Vincent straggled in and threw himself onto Jet's bed, which by now was piled with discarded clothing. "Live a *lot*," he advised.

Jet was persuaded to add a floppy hat, then Franny dabbed on some lip gloss and mascara, and there Jet was, utterly gorgeous. Franny was a little in awe of her younger sister's shimmering beauty. "If those bitches at Starling could see you now they'd hate you even more. Just be careful tonight."

Once the parents had left with Jet, Vincent grabbed his leather jacket and nodded to Franny. "Let's get out of this mausoleum."

"The sooner, the better," Franny agreed.

Haylin was probably already at their usual meeting place. Franny latched the front door and they set out into the lovely summer evening. A limo sped by with a whoosh of air and Franny felt a chill, which she ignored. Surely, there was nothing to worry about on this perfect night.

When they reached the corner of Eighty-Ninth and Fifth, brother and sister went their separate ways.

"Use caution," Franny called to her brother, who waved to her before he headed downtown.

Franny then went directly to the Ninetieth Street entrance, eager to step into the cool, silent park. Lately she was disturbed by her strong feelings toward Haylin. She just couldn't seem to control them, though she tried her best. Every time they were together, she held back. They would be all over each other, and then she would pull away to stalk off by herself, not wanting him to see how she was burning for him.

"Not again," Haylin would say, twisted with desire. "Jeez, Franny, I'm dying here."

Franny had vowed she would not go anywhere near love, but here she was standing on the very edge of it, about to fall. She wasn't certain how long this denial could go on or if she even wanted it to.

Tonight she wore her usual outfit of a black shirt, black slacks, and a pair of sneakers. It didn't matter what she wore or how she might try to downplay her looks, Franny possessed a rare beauty. With her long red hair and pale flawless skin, she resembled a woodland creature as she ducked under thickets.

Caution above all else, she told herself. But there he was waiting for her on the path, and Franny had never been an admirer of caution.

They headed for the Ramble. It was a glorious evening. They stopped once to kiss and could go no farther, until Franny broke away, fevered, far too attracted to him. As they came to the model-boat pond, formally called Conservatory Water, Hay reached for some change so he could buy lemonade from the kiosk. "Hey, look at this," he said. All of the quarters in his hand were tarnished. He had no idea that the silver in a man's pockets always turns black if he kisses a witch.

There were inky clouds in the even darker sky, and the horizon was painted with a blue-black tint. What was pale glowed brilliantly through the dark: Franny's freckled skin, some renegade white nightshade growing nearby, the moon, bright and full. It was a blue moon, the name for the second full moon in a single month, the thirteenth full moon of the year. If Franny had remembered Vincent's remark about the danger of the moon, she might have heard the clamor of a warning bell; instead she and Hay went to Belvedere Lake, which they called Turtle Pond due to the dozens of pet turtles released there. It was set just below the imposing Belvedere Castle. The castle was made of gray granite, a bronze winged dragon in the transom.

Haylin grinned and said, "We could live there and no one would know."

It was the grin that always tugged at something inside Franny. He seemed so pure. *Wrong* and *Right* were fixed points in Haylin's mind. When he spoke about the many inequities facing those people who had no say in their own futures, Franny felt the sting of tender admiration stirring inside her. Still, she did not wish to have a heart, for such a thing could be broken. She thought of the women who knocked on the back door at Magnolia Street, desperate for love, crying at the kitchen table, each willing to pay any price to win the attention of some man who didn't know she was alive. Franny had been convinced it was only a rumor that Aunt Isabelle was given all manner of jewelry as payment until she saw a neighbor take off her cameo necklace and leave it on the kitchen table. And then one day, as she was searching a cabinet for the saltshaker, she found a plastic container that rattled. Inside were a dozen diamond rings.

She thought Jet was a fool to look for love, but here she was with Haylin trying to make sense of her frantic heart. Sooner or later she would figure out the curse. Mysteries could be solved, if one applied logic and patience.

As they sat on a flat rock, with the evening floating down around them, Franny and Hay traded tales they'd heard about the pond, urban legends about snapping turtles so huge they would leap into the air to catch pigeons that were then drowned and devoured, and of pet fish released from their small bowls that had grown enormous, with sharp teeth and wicked dispositions. There was a lady rumored to live in the shrubbery who was said to catch turtles for her supper. She could be spied begging for spare change on the corner near the Starling School.

Don't think this won't happen to you, she hissed at all the pretty young girls passing by. *Youth is fleeting. It's nothing but a dream. I'm where you're going. I'm what you'll be.*

They called her the Pond Lady and ran from her, shrieking, but they couldn't get her warning out of their minds. Caution, these girls thought. As for Franny, she always gave the Pond Lady a dollar when she saw her, for she had no fear of who she would turn out to be.

When the theater let out, Jet was walking on air. She quickly worked a Believe Me spell before telling her parents that the girls from Starling were having a slumber party in honor of her birthday. Wasn't that what they had wanted? For her to be popular and accepted?

"Address please," her father said.

"Ninety-Second and Third," Jet responded, having already practiced the answers to most of the possible questions she might be asked.

"Let us drop you," Susanna said, hailing a cab.

"Oh, Mother, they'll think I'm a baby."

Jet kissed her parents good-bye, then she slipped into the taxi and leaned forward to ask the driver to take her to Fifty-Ninth Street. Off they went, for there was a plan, one that had nothing to do with the girls at school, who couldn't have cared less that it was Jet Owens's birthday. But someone cared desperately, and had already been waiting for her for over an hour at the entrance to the park on Central Park South. They would spend the night together at the Plaza Hotel, the grandest, most romantic hotel in New York, built in 1907, designed as if it were a French château. In the park across the street from the hotel there was the elegant golden equestrian statue of General Sherman and his horse by the sculptor Augustus Saint-Gaudens.

In addition to selling his great-great-grandfather's watch, Levi had been saving for this special night, working overtime at the pharmacy, delivering newspapers in the early mornings. Spying Levi from the cab was the best moment of Jet's life. She was ready to fall in love without looking back. Frankly, she had already fallen. She paid, then ran out to embrace Levi. They kissed and barely noticed the world around them. Horns honked, and they were nearly run over by a bicyclist. Levi laughed and pulled Jet out of harm's way. He was carrying her birthday present. An old edition of Emily Dickinson's poems.

If I can stop one heart from breaking,
I shall not live in vain

As Jet was about to open the book, as her heart was lifting and her life just beginning, her parents' taxi roared up. They'd heard her tell the cabbie the address of the Plaza, and, suspicious, they had followed, up Sixth Avenue, turning onto Fifty-Ninth Street. Susanna opened the window now and called shrilly, using Jet's rarely used given name. *Bridget Owens, you stop right there!*

Jet looked up at her mother and panicked. The cab was racing toward them. Before her parents could leap out and drag her away, before they could ruin her life, she took hold of Levi's arm and cried out, *Let's run.* He didn't even know what they were running from, but he knew he was dedicated to protecting Jet. They headed for the park, and as they did, the parents' cabdriver was told to step on it and not let them escape. There was an oil slick on the road, beneath the pools of spilled water used for the horses pulling the carriages that took tourists and lovers through the park. It was dark and the city smelled like freshly spaded earth.

Just across from the Plaza Hotel the taxi skidded out of control. Birds in the trees took flight and filled the ember sky. Levi leapt in front of Jet as the taxi came barreling onto the sidewalk. Time slowed so that she could see his eyes dilate when he realized what was happening. It was so very slow they might have been caught in a glass jar. She could hear his thoughts. *Not yet. Not this.* And then time sped up, it rolled up right under their feet and caught them off balance. The air was alive and pushed against Jet like a wave, but it was Levi who was pushing her out of the way. She lay on the cold ground as glass shattered and fell over her, like a hard rain. There was no other sound, no birds, no traffic, nothing but the sound of her heart thudding against her chest. There was nothing else beyond this moment when she heard the taxi hit Levi, the sound of the world cracking in two. And then she heard his voice, and he said only one word, and that last word was her name.

At Turtle Pond, Franny had slipped off her sneakers and was letting her pale feet dangle over the edge of the rocks. The night was perfect and she worried about perfect things, for there were often flaws seen only under a microscope, with a very clear eye. She felt a chill go through her, as if the wind had blown directly through her chest. All at once, there were tears in her eyes.

"I'll swim here if you will," Haylin announced, already stripping off his shirt. He always wanted to prove himself to Franny, yet he never exuded the same confidence. Hay had recognized that she had a strange sort of courage. She didn't even seem to notice when she was in danger. Perhaps that was why he was driven by the need to be brave and why he stood on the very edge of the rock, his heart thudding, his emotions at a fever pitch. If courage was what she wanted, that was what he'd give her. "Seriously," he said. "Let's swim."

Franny shook her head no. She felt nerves again, right in the pit of her stomach, as if the world was about to spin out of control. Another time she might have been thrilled by Haylin's proposed leap into the muddy abyss. But she knew the warning. She must use caution. Plus, swimming with him was out of the question; she would only float and he would wonder why and there was no way for her to explain the reason.

The water was murky, filled with mysterious, mossy items. Still, Haylin didn't back down. He pulled off his boots and unzipped his jeans, then took everything off. She'd never seen him naked. He was like a statue, perfect.

Haylin inhaled, then leapt into the pond. The turtles splashed away as he disappeared into the blackness of the surface. Water rose up and slapped against the rocks, then spilled onto the path. Though the pond was filled from a tap, trash left to sink to its depths made the water appear ominous and unclean, likely chock-full of strange debris and unknown pathogens. Franny's heart was hitting against her chest. Haylin would probably need a tetanus shot.

He didn't rise. Franny thought of bees, and ashes, and broken glass. But Haylin hadn't been inside their house when the deathwatch beetle appeared, so surely he'd be safe. And yet there was a circle forming around the spot where he had disappeared. No air bubbles, no Haylin. Franny wanted to leap in after him, but she knew from the time spent in Leech Lake it was impossible. She would only float to the surface. Because she couldn't be drowned, she couldn't follow him into the depths to save him. She was frantic, her pulse pounding, fearing that the curse was happening right now.

When Hay suddenly reappeared, he broke the surface like some sort of enormous fish. He was sputtering for air, turning blue. He struggled for breath, then met her eyes. Franny sat frozen on the rock; a kind of terror had immobilized her. Caution.

Hay shook his head. "Jesus, Franny," he said.

She'd never seen anyone look as sad or disappointed. He swam to the rocks with two strokes of his long arms and hoisted himself out. His hair was slicked back. His penis looked blue from the cold. Franny had a small shiver of what she thought was fear, but it was really something else entirely, what she didn't want to feel for him and already did.

Hay reached for his clothes and pulled them on even though he was soaking wet. "There's a shopping cart down there. My leg got stuck. I almost couldn't surface. In case you care."

"Haylin." Franny spoke with emotion. "Of course I do."

"There's something wrong between us, Franny." Hay cast

his large, wet feet into his boots without bothering with socks. Then he came to her and put his hands on her shoulders; he was shaking from the frigid water and from raw emotion. "Were you going to let me drown? Seriously. Tell me the truth. You're keeping something from me. What *are* we to each other, Franny?"

Before she could answer *Everything* and explain the curse of who she really was, Franny spied a figure weaving through the trees. He was headed straight toward them with a strange, shuddering gait. It was Vincent and he was barefoot. He'd run all the way down Eighty-Ninth Street and through the park and was now sprinting forward, crying out her name. Franny pulled away from Haylin. She could hear bees, the ones that had been there on the day when she and Vincent knew someone in their house was doomed. She looked up and spied the moon and instantly knew what this night had brought. She now thought one word. Her sister's name. Jet.

"What is it?" Hay said, concerned.

When Vincent reached them, he was pale with shock. "They had an accident." He looked so young standing there, barefoot, his bravado gone. Because Franny appeared to be frozen, he grabbed her hand. "I know what you're thinking, but she's alive."

Which meant the others were not.

Franny and Vincent took off across the park together. Haylin called out, but Franny couldn't answer; she was running too hard. She didn't realize that she was also barefoot until they'd reached the pavement. She stood shivering on Fifth Avenue while Vincent hailed a cab.

They sat side by side in the ER at Bellevue, not speaking. The cold linoleum floor nearly froze their feet. When the doctor came to speak to them it was long past midnight.

"Your sister has a concussion and several broken ribs," the doctor told them. "She's quite shaken and we had to stitch up her face, but she'll be fine."

"And our parents?" Franny asked.

The doctor shook his head. "I'm sorry. It was instantaneous. And the boy also just passed on."

Franny and Vincent exchanged a look. They had completely forgotten that Jet had intended to meet Levi.

"You mean he's dead?" Vincent asked.

"He was struck by the cab your parents were in."

Franny had never felt so cold. "They followed her. They chased after them."

Vincent draped his jacket over her shoulders. "Let's go see Jet."

She was in a small private room, her black hair streaming onto the white pillow. Her face and arms were bruised and bandaged, and there was a gash on her face that had been closed with thirty neat stitches. Her eyes were rimmed red. It was her birthday, her night, her parents, her beloved. Guilt was curling around her heart with tendrils of self-hatred. In one instant she had lost everything.

Franny came to sit on the edge of the bed. "There was nothing any of us could do to stop it. You can't blame yourself, Jetty. It was an accident."

Jet leaned into the soft pillow. She was doomed to lose everything, even her gift of sight. When they'd first brought her into the hospital she could hear the patients' jumbled thoughts.

Hearts that beat stopped with a shudder, men who were racked with pain. Then all at once she couldn't hear a thing. The only sound that reverberated was the voice of the Reverend, who'd come to a room down the hall and set to wailing when he found his son, here in New York City, a place he had always believed caused ruination. He had been right about the curse, for this was what love had done to his boy, who never would have been struck if not for Jet. Although she'd never met the Reverend and he likely despised her, there was no one Jet felt she had more in common with than he, for the person they both loved best in the world was gone.

The furniture was draped with white sheets as Aunt Isabelle instructed they must do when they entered the mourning period. She had arrived late that night without a suitcase, though she carried a large, black purse. She had a black silk band around her right arm, and she wore a felted hat with one ember feather attached to the brim. She told them they needed to turn the mirrors to the wall. Then she had them sprinkle salt on the windowsills and leave sprigs of rosemary outside the doors.

"It was bad luck," she told them. "Nothing more."

She sat beside Jet, offering a cup of tea, which Jet refused to drink.

"It was bound to happen," Jet said in a small, broken voice. "It was my fate."

"It wasn't fate. It was the interruption of fate. No one can control such things."

Jet was thin and pale. She turned away from her aunt, tied

up with guilt and grief. Isabelle knew right away that her niece had lost the sight, for her eyes were a dull dove gray without light or life.

Isabelle slept in the room where the previous family's cook had cried herself to sleep every night. Franny had made up the bed with clean white sheets and had left lavender in the dresser drawers. Isabelle unpacked her purse, in which she had a nightgown and slippers and a bar of black soap.

"She never thought to choose courage," Isabelle said.

"But she did choose courage. Didn't she?"

"In life we don't always get what we choose. I gave her what she needed."

On the day of the funeral, Franny found two black dresses in their mother's closet. She was surprised to see several pairs of red shoes in the back of the closet, something her mother had forbidden them from wearing. Franny helped Jet to dress, pulling her nightgown over her head, then slipping the prettier of the dresses on her, treating her as if she were a child. Jet still hadn't slept or had a bite to eat. She thought of her parents, how she had often heard them talking late at night. If it wasn't true love that they'd had, then it was a true partnership. She couldn't imagine one without the other. Now she realized that she hadn't spent enough time with them, or told them she loved them; perhaps she hadn't even known. All she knew was that she didn't feel safe with them gone. Anything could happen now. Whatever their world had been, it would never be again. She sat in a chair in the living room, wearing her black dress, hands folded in her lap as she watched the door, as if she expected their parents to walk through, maybe then time would have rolled backward, maybe then Levi would still be alive.

Vincent, bleary-eyed and ravaged, had on a black suit he hadn't bothered to press. When he came out of his room barefoot, Isabelle insisted he go back for his boots. That was the way in which their family members were buried and it was disconcerting to see Vincent without shoes. At the funeral home on Madison Avenue the coffins were closed. The mortician had been instructed that both their mother and father must wear black and be barefoot. Franny had chosen a Chanel dress for their mother and handed over her favorite red lipstick and Maybelline mascara, for she never went without her makeup and Franny was not about to have that change. For their father, Vincent had taken a Brooks Brothers suit from the closet, along with one of the white shirts he had had tailored in London. Franny had straightened her own unruly hair with an iron and dabbed on pale lipstick so that she might look presentable. There was no way to hide the wound on Jet's face, though Franny tried with some powder from one of their mother's gold compacts. It looked as though blue flowers had been stamped on Jet's skin. Even when it healed, a jagged line would run down one side of her face.

Not that Jet cared. Nothing would be punishment enough for having lived through the accident. She kept seeing Levi put his arm out and step in front of her, and then she saw stars, and he called her name, or maybe it was only a sigh, the last of his life and breath rising up.

"You know he was related to us," Vincent told Franny.

"No." She looked at her brother. "How so?"

He shrugged. "Isabelle wouldn't tell me."

"Jet has lost the gift," Franny said sadly. "I didn't know that could happen."

Their sister was still sitting in the chair, though the car had come for them. She barely seemed to breathe.

"She'll get it back," Vincent said. "It's in her blood."

At the chapel in Manhattan vases of orange and red gladiolus were set onto the polished tables. Aunt Isabelle sat with them in the front row. No one in the family cried. Although they were crushed, crying in public was unacceptable. Several of Dr. Burke-Owens's patients who were in attendance were inconsolable. After the service, Franny and Vincent shook the hands of those who had come to pay their respects, while Isabelle sat in the parlor with Jet. Hay was there, along with his parents, who were polite and distant and quick to suggest that Haylin hurry along. But he wasn't about to desert Franny, even though a limo was waiting to take the Owens siblings to the cemetery in Massachusetts for the interment.

"She has to leave," Mr. Walker muttered. "Their car is here."

"Fuck the car. I want to go with you," Hay told Franny. "I should be there."

Aunt Isabelle had come up behind them. "I like him. He should come with us."

"Impossible," Franny said. She wanted to keep Haylin away from her family's troubles. It was bad enough that she must now introduce her aunt to the Walkers.

"You're quite rich," Isabelle said to Mr. Walker. "And yet you seem to have so little." Haylin grinned when he overheard her remark.

"You're quite rude," Mr. Walker said.

"My niece and her husband are about to be buried. Who's the rude one?"

"I think we know the answer to that one, Dad," Haylin said.

Franny took her aunt by the hand to lead her away. "Not here," she urged. "Not now."

"What do you think I would do to that horrid man?" Isabelle said. "Believe me, he'll bring on his own bad luck. His son, well, he's another story. He's the real thing." She waved at Haylin and he waved back. Unlike most people, he was completely undaunted by Isabelle Owens.

Franny went to explain that there would be only family in Massachusetts, and all of the Owenses gathered in one place was far too much for any outsider to deal with.

"I don't mind," Haylin said. "Especially if they're all like your aunt."

"I'll phone as soon as I'm back," Franny promised.

The burial was to be held in the small graveyard in Massachusetts, the one they'd once peered at through the mossy iron fence, not especially interested, not even when they realized the old headstones were all engraved with the name Owens. Now their parents would be there, even though their mother had spent her entire life trying her best to get away from her family. And yet this place had continued to have a hold over her. In the end she knew she belonged with her relations. Her will had stated that both she and her husband were to be buried there, side by side.

Driving along the Massachusetts Turnpike, Jet had to be

sedated. She took Valium on top of the painkillers she'd been given for her cracked ribs. Even then, she continued to shake. Vincent had discovered the limo had a bar. He gulped down scotch with the intention of getting good and drunk. Isabelle had insisted on sitting with the driver so she could give him directions. When she heard the clanking of bottles, she turned and gave Vincent a hard look.

"Let's not have a scene today," she suggested. "There'll be trouble enough."

"People are dead. To hell with good behavior," Vincent muttered, low enough so that their aunt wouldn't hear, but of course she did anyway and she gestured to Franny.

Franny returned the bottle of scotch to its proper place. "We need to get through this without incident," she said darkly.

"Franny, we're not getting through *anything* without incident," Vincent said. "Isn't that obvious?"

"Try," Franny urged. She nodded to Jet, who was not paying attention to anyone and seemed caught up in her own sad world. Jet stared out the window, tears flowing down her face. "Let's just get her through this," Franny whispered to her brother.

Ever since the accident she had felt the burden of being the oldest. Overnight, and without warning, Franny no longer felt young. She was not going to get what she wanted or do as she pleased. She had come to understand that as she and Vincent sat together in the hospital. Today she had pinned up her straightened hair and had taken a black Dior cape from her mother's closet, which carried the scent of Chanel No. 5, Susanna's perfume. Franny knew that from now on she would be held hostage by her responsibilities.

When they reached the cemetery, the Boston Owenses,

most of whom they'd never met before, had already gathered. They were introduced to April Owens's disapproving parents, although April was nowhere in sight. Some cousins from Maine who had a farm known for its miraculous rhubarb, which could cure almost anything, from influenza to insomnia, were in attendance, and of course Aunt Isabelle sat in the front row, beside Franny. A heat wave had begun, but Isabelle wore her long black dress and a shawl she had knitted to keep evil at bay. All of the women had bunches of hyacinths, which Jet and Franny were given as well. The flowers were to remind them that life was precious and brief, like the hyacinth's bloom.

The minister was married to an Owens and led a congregation in Cambridge.

"I look forward to seeing you in the fall," he told Franny. They all knew she'd been accepted to Radcliffe.

"Perhaps," Franny demurred, not wanting to commit herself.

Franny assisted their aunt over the tufted grass when they left the burial site. They went into a small bleak hall where cakes and coffee were displayed on a lace-covered table. There were pots of hyacinths everywhere.

Isabelle's voice held real tenderness. "We never know the end of the story until we get there. Let me suggest a possibility for the immediate future. You three could move in with me."

Franny shook her head. "It's not possible."

"At least stay for the rest of the summer," Isabelle urged. "Give yourself some time to decide what comes next."

"Thank you, no," Franny told her aunt. "We'll go back to New York."

"Suit yourself. That tall boy will be happy, but will you?"

They could hear a siren. On the street a police car led a long line of cars, including a hearse. Levi Willard's funeral procession was passing by.

"It's a shame," Isabelle said sadly.

"Because he's a member of our family?" Franny asked. She very much wanted to know the secret April had spoken of.

"Because this could have been avoided if his father had learned not to hate. I think we should refrain from telling Jet that his funeral is taking place today. It's too much for her to bear."

"So you're not going to tell me anything," Franny said.

"Yes, if you must know, we're related to the Willards."

"Why is that a secret?"

"Why is anything a secret? People want to protect themselves from the past. Not that it works."

Franny left her aunt to search for Vincent and Jet, whom she found in a corner.

"Let's get out of here," Vincent said. He was half-drunk, never a good state to be in.

"There's April." Jet pointed to the opposite corner, where April was sitting on an overstuffed chair, a baby girl on her lap. They approached with caution.

"Seriously?" Franny said, in quite a state of shock. "A baby?"

"I'm sorry about your parents." April turned to Jet. "And I'm sorry about Levi. I heard he's being buried today."

Franny gave April a look that was so harsh and foreboding April felt smacked. She understood what she was being told and quickly backtracked, surprised by how much more powerful Franny now seemed.

"Or maybe it's tomorrow," April hedged. "Don't ask me. I don't have a moment to think straight."

"Hello, baby." Vincent sat on the edge of a coffee table and offered his hand, which the baby grabbed and held on to. No female wanted to let him go. This one's name was Regina. Her eyes, of course, were gray.

"I suppose you can fight fate, but I'm glad I didn't fight this," April said of her daughter.

"You wouldn't have wanted to," Jet remarked with real emotion. "She's a gorgeous baby," she added when Franny looked puzzled.

Now Franny's curiosity was piqued. "What happened to Regina's father?"

"Drowned," April said. "Wouldn't that be my luck? Flash flood. What are the scientific odds of that?"

"Not a very high probability," Franny remarked. April's lie had fallen to the floor, heavy as lead, but Franny didn't dare kick it, for fear of what other disturbing information might spring out at them.

"Well, congratulations are in order," Vincent said, itching to have a drink. He stood and saluted, then found his way to the bar, where whiskey sours, their parents' favorite cocktails, were being served.

Jet bent to tickle the baby. For a moment she seemed to have forgotten the tragic circumstances of the day. "Adorable," she said. "Look at those big eyes."

April seemed a bit softer than she used to be. "I really am sorry for your loss," she told Jet. By now her daughter was whimpering.

"Hold her for a minute," April said to Franny, as she went to retrieve a bottle of formula from her bag. Franny begged off, saying she'd never had much to do with children and hoped to keep it that way. But a baby cannot be denied, and April grimaced and deposited the infant in Franny's arms anyway. "Nonsense," she said.

Regina instantly stopped fussing as she stared up at Franny.

"See!" April said, when she returned. "You're not who you think you are."

Franny was stung. "I'm exactly who I think I am!" She quickly gave the baby back and gazed at their new relation, her heart softening, as the baby sucked on her bottle.

They went back to Aunt Isabelle's for supper, mostly homey casseroles that the Owenses from Maine had left. Creamed spinach and macaroni with pearl onions and for dessert their famous rhubarb pie. None of the siblings could eat. Jet went out to the garden. Vincent and Franny sat in the parlor and played gin rummy, which was difficult since each could guess the other's cards a hundred percent of the time. Franny eased off her insistence on good behavior and didn't say a word when Vincent poured himself a tall glass of their aunt's scotch, hidden in a bureau, which they'd found in the first days of the summer when they'd come to visit.

After the guests departed, Isabelle went to lie down for a while, fully dressed, with her boots on. Her drapes were not drawn, and she spied Jet sneaking out the gate, clearly in a hurry. It was a two-mile walk, so once Jet got to town, she looked for the cab that was usually parked at the bus station. Luckily one was there, idling at the curb. She got in and asked to be taken to the big cemetery at the edge of town, where the four boys had been buried the previous summer. They were about to pull out when the taxi's door opened and Isabelle got in. The driver watched her in his rearview mirror, in a panic. Isabelle Owens on her way to a cemetery was a passenger no one wanted.

"Do you have business at the cemetery, Miss Owens?" the driver asked in a nervous tone.

"We all will have business there sooner or later," she answered brightly.

"I'm going alone," Jet said.

"I think it's a bad idea for you to go, but if you insist, I'm going with you." Isabelle tapped the back of the driver's seat. "Hurry up. And I'll need you to wait for us."

Levi's funeral was over, but as they walked the path they spied the newly turned earth. The Reverend was still there. He did not have any intention of leaving his son. Jet turned pale when she spied him in his black jacket, sitting on a folding chair that had been left from the service.

Isabelle linked her arm through Jet's and they walked forward over the grass. Birds were calling in the treetops and everything was emerald green. The grass had recently been mowed and the scent was midsummer sweet. The Reverend was looking down, and therefore saw their shadows before he saw them.

"Do not come any closer," he said.

"We're here to pay our respects," Isabelle said. "I'm sure you would do the same if the situation were reversed."

The Reverend raised his eyes. Gray-green, just like Levi's. "But I don't have to, because my son is dead and she's alive," he said, nodding to Jet. "This is the reason you've been cursed."

"Your relative set that in motion, ours had no choice in the matter. And really, the truth is, because of them our fates and our histories are joined."

Jet looked at her aunt, confused.

"And yet here I am," the Reverend said. "At the grave of my son."

Jet sank to the ground, dizzy. Isabelle did her best to get her back on her feet. The Reverend stood and watched, alarmed.

"Help us," Isabelle commanded.

The Reverend took one of Jet's arms and Isabelle the other and they guided her to the chair.

"Breathe slowly and deeply," Isabelle said. She went to stand beside the Reverend, her cousin, since his side of the family were direct descendants of the man who was the father of Maria Owens's daughter. "She's just a young girl who happened to have fallen in love," she said to the cousin who denied their shared family lineage. "In what world is that a curse?"

The Reverend couldn't answer. He was broken and carried three hundred years of history and hatred.

"When we can forgive one another, we can begin to break the curse. You know that as well as I."

The Reverend looked at Jet and Jet could see how he'd been devastated by what had happened. She managed to get to her feet. She stood before the grave, wishing she could be buried there as well, that her hands could be intertwined with Levi's, and she could live in this place beside him.

"We should go before they close the gates," Isabelle said.

The Reverend followed them at a distance.

"He should hate me," Jet said to her aunt. "He has every reason."

"Hatred is what got us here in the first place," Isabelle said.

When they reached the taxi, Isabelle told the driver to wait. As soon as the Reverend arrived at the gates, Isabelle asked the driver to get out and assist him and have him sit in the front seat so he could be driven home. The Reverend looked surprised, but he was exhausted, so he did as he was told. He got into the taxi and stared straight ahead and there was no talk of any kind until they reached his house on the far side of town. The taxi stopped and the Reverend got out without a word or a look back.

When they returned to Magnolia Street, Isabelle asked Franny and Vincent to join them in the garden. They would be leaving for Manhattan in the morning, so it was time. On some nights it was best to remember the past, and not shut it in a drawer. Three hundred years ago people believed in the devil. They believed if an incident could not be explained, then the cause was something wicked, and that cause was often a woman who was said to be a witch. Women who did as they pleased, women with property, women who had enemies, women who took lovers, women who knew about the mysteries of childbirth, all were suspect, especially to the fiercest and cruelest judge in the area, John Hathorne, a man so terrible that his great-great-grandson, the author of *The Scarlet Letter*, tried to deny his own heritage by changing the spelling of his name.

The affair happened when Maria was young, and it was unexpected for both of them. Hathorne showed her one side of him, for he was a brilliant man, a magistrate, a justice of the peace in Essex County, and he had a soul, before it had been shattered by unhappiness and pride when he sent nineteen innocent people to their deaths and ruined the lives of many others. But when Maria met him none of this had happened, and she was enamored of him and perhaps he truly loved her. He was the one who gave her the sapphire and sent her away with a small bag of diamonds when the affair ended, hoping to ensure she would never be back, for he had a wife and a family and she was a young girl with whom he should never have tampered. Perhaps he felt he'd been enchanted, for from then on he looked for witchery in the world, and was the only magistrate associated with the trials who had never repented his actions.

They were therefore all descendants of a witch-finder and a witch, and therein lay the very heart of the curse's beginnings, for they were fated to try their best to deny who they were and to refute their true selves. The Willard side of the family was related through one of Hathorne's granddaughters, who had married a relation of John Proctor, hung as a witch when he tried to defend the innocent women being brought to trial.

"We were not there when these dreadful things happened, when women were accused of being crows and messengers from hell. We were neither the judge nor the accused, but we carry these things with us, and we have to fight them. The best way to do this is to be who you are, every part of you, the good and the bad, the sorrowful and the joyous. You can never run away. There is nowhere to run *to*. I think your mother knew that in the end, and that is why she came back here to be buried. We are who we are from the start."

It was very late by now and the moon was red. Jet sat in the grass, her mouth set in a thin line. When you are young you are looking forward and when you are old you are looking back. Jet was young but she was already looking back. On this evening, when the crickets were calling, when the birds were all sleeping in the thickets and even the rabbits were hushed, Jet didn't know how it was possible to forgive those who had wronged you or how it was possible to forgive yourself for those you had wronged.

They sat in the garden where Maria Owens had planted seeds so long ago. Life was short, it was over in an instant, but some things lasted. Hate and love, kindness and cruelty, all lingered and, in their case, all had been passed on. When they finally straggled inside, rain had begun to fall. It was a green, fresh rain, the sort most needed in summer, when everything is burning hot and thirsty. Usually the sisters shared the attic, but on this night Jet said she was too hot to go upstairs. Instead she sat in the parlor, waiting for the sun to rise, her suitcase packed. In the morning she told everyone she was perfectly fine, even though she wasn't, even though she wished she was still on that green hill where Levi had been buried, where the grass smelled so sweet, where there was no beginning and no end.

The limo drove them back to Manhattan through a gray drizzle. The streets were empty and hot. They piled out onto Eighty-Ninth Street and stood on the sidewalk. They'd lived here all their lives, yet it didn't feel like home. Franny found she couldn't bring herself to go inside. Vincent helped Jet out of the car, then looked at Franny, wanting to know what was to happen next.

"Go on," she told him. It was now thundering but Franny wouldn't budge. "Go," she insisted, and so they did while she remained where she was, though soon enough the clouds opened, leaving her soaking.

She had lost not only her parents but her future as well. Cambridge was no longer a possibility. How could she leave Jet and Vincent and go off to school? Though she was eighteen, little more than a girl, she, too, had begun to look backward.

When it came to the future she was certain she would never get what she wanted.

When Haylin didn't hear from her as promised, he sprinted to Eighty-Ninth Street. He spied her standing in the driving rain and ran faster. When he reached her, he pulled her close and bent to kiss her. There was no need to say anything. The weather was still hot and pavements steamed as raindrops hit the cement. All of Manhattan smelled of hyacinths. "I'm always going to love you," Hay said.

He came upstairs with her. They slipped through the parlor and went to the cook's bedroom. They could hear the wet gusts of rain as the windows rattled. Hay took off Franny's sopping clothes. She was shivering and couldn't stop. The sky outside was murky and black with yellow heat waves rising from the pavement. Haylin kissed her, and when he grabbed off his own clothes they fell onto the bed together and neither thought about anything but each other. It was a single bed covered with the white coverlet that Susanna Owens had bought in Paris when she was a young woman mourning her lost love. The more

Haylin loved her, the more Franny broke apart. Was this what had happened to her mother in Paris?

She told Hay that she wanted his hands all over her, and he was happy to oblige. She yearned to forget everything that had ever occurred in the past and only be in this moment.

"Oh, Franny," Haylin said. This was his first time, too, which was what he had always wanted. To only be with Franny. When they were done, Haylin was lying on the floor on his back, naked and exhausted, terrified that he had already lost her as she drifted away. He watched Franny where she was poised on a chair by the window. The rain had stopped and Lewis was outside, his plumage gleaming wet as he pecked at the glass. Franny let him in and toweled off his slick feathers.

"Come back," Haylin called to her.

Franny shook her head. She was naked except for Haylin's T-shirt. She had exquisite long legs.

"Franny!"

She ignored him, for she had already decided what was between them must end. After what had happened to Levi, she no longer had the courage to take the chance of ruining Hay.

"We'll be all right," Hay said as if he knew her thoughts. "We'll be happy in Cambridge."

But it wouldn't be all right. Franny went to lie down beside him. She stroked his shoulders and torso. He was so beautiful and young. "Where did we meet?" she asked. She wanted to remember everything when it was over.

"Third grade. The lunchroom. You had a tomato sandwich, which I thought was very strange. Who eats a plain tomato sandwich?"

Tomatoes were in the nightshade family and Franny had

always adored them. "How do you recall these things?" She kissed his cheek, which was rough with stubble.

"I remember everything about you. I was waiting all that time for you to love me."

They could hear music from the living room. The night had passed for them without sleep, in a dream of heat and longing. It was already noon. Vincent was playing guitar. They could hear him singing "Stand by Me" in a haunting voice.

Franny had no choice but to tell him. "I can't leave Jet and Vincent." She'd known it ever since the hospital.

Hay had no intention of letting go. "They'll be fine. You have to go forward with your life."

Franny kissed him and didn't stop. Let him remember only this. The softness of her mouth, how her thighs opened to him when he wanted to be inside her. Maybe then he would forgive her more easily on the day her gray eyes turned to ice, when she appeared not to care, because she knew that was her fate, to avoid love at all costs and then to pretend it didn't break her apart when she finally told him they were through.

Now that they had their freedom, they didn't know what to do with it. No one put out the garbage. There were piles of trash in the kitchen that had begun to stink. Before long two rats had taken up residence in the broom closet, creatures Franny dealt with by flinging blocks of Swiss cheese inside for them. All at once she noticed how dilapidated everything was: the paint was chipped, the lights flickered, only one burner on the stove worked, and then not until Franny blew on it to light the flame.

The town house had been deteriorating for some time, with no funds for repairs. As it turned out, the family was in debt and had borrowed heavily from the bank. So many of their father's patients had been seen gratis, and their mother had spent whatever small inheritance she'd had years ago. The house would have to be put on the market. Jet hated the idea, and barely left her room. It therefore fell to Vincent and Franny to attend a meeting at their parents' attorney's office and listen to the lawyer address their dismal financial situation until Vincent said roughly, "Who the fuck cares?" storming out when he realized how broke they were.

"I believe the meeting is over," Franny said. Before she departed, she signed all the necessary paperwork. As the eldest she was assigned to be her brother and sister's legal guardian. It was up to her to make decisions. And, without a word to the others, she'd already made several of them.

Occasionally, their father's patients would leave bouquets of flowers at the back door, which Franny immediately threw in the trash barrel. Several members of the psychoanalytic society had sent sympathy cards, which were burned in the fireplace. What was done was done and could not be undone. How much Franny missed her parents was unexpected. She wished she could sit down and talk to her mother, whom she discovered had convinced the local shopkeepers into giving them credit. She wished she could ask her father how to get rid of the flying ants in his office and how he had found time to write his book early in the morning before anyone else in the family was yet awake. She now understood why they had chased after Jet that night. It was fear of the Willards and their shared history of judges and victims. *If only*, Franny thought, but the list of what she wished she could have changed was too long and there was no way to rewrite their history.

Vincent spent most days sleeping, then he crept out in the evenings, not saying where he was headed, although they all knew the only place that currently interested him was the Jester. He didn't come home till the wee morning hours, clearly having been up to no good, smelling of whiskey. He'd stopped going to school, and perhaps that was just as well; they could no longer afford Starling's high tuition. When Vincent was at home, he wasn't alone. He brought home countless girls, including Kathy Stern, the nymphomaniac, kleptomaniac patient of their father's. Once she was ensconced in Vincent's bedroom, she refused to leave. From listening in through the heat vents during Kathy's therapy sessions, Franny knew Kathy had a wicked fear of birds. She let Lewis into the room, and before long Kathy ran screaming out the door in her underwear as the crow pulled on her hair, fistfuls of which were left on the floor. Later they realized Kathy had stolen their mother's gold and pearl Chanel necklace.

"She was hilarious," Vincent said. "She has a notebook listing all the men she's ever slept with. She took photographs of their dicks and taped the photos in her book. She said she was going to make a collage out of them. So how could I deny her?"

There wasn't anyone to tell Vincent *no*, except for Franny. Since their parents' deaths, he refused to take anything seriously.

"Don't you get it, Franny?" he said. "We have to live now,

while we can. It will all be over soon enough." He was almost sixteen, tall and dark and brooding, usually carrying a guitar, which made him all the more attractive, and all the more dangerous both to whoever might fall for him and to himself.

As for Jet, she remained in bed long after the doctors insisted she was fine. Her cracked ribs had healed, her bruises were fading, and what had been gashes in her hands and knees were thin red striations no one would recognize as wounds. The only thing that remained was the scar on her face, a jagged line shaped like petals on a stem that could be seen only in certain sorts of light.

"What's the point?" she would say when Franny suggested they go for a walk.

Jet's hair was so tangled a brush would no longer go through it. She didn't bathe and ate only crackers and ginger ale. She slept with the edition of Emily Dickinson that Levi had given her. Inside he had written *Forever—is composed of—Nows.* Because they could hear Jet crying at all hours, Franny nailed the second-floor windows shut just to make sure her sister couldn't make the rash decision to leap.

More and more Franny turned to Haylin, though she knew it was a mistake to do so. She had vowed to be with him only once, yet they were together every day. The closer they became, the harder the inevitable break would be. She should have told him about the future that loomed, but she couldn't speak it aloud. *Not now and not ever,* she should have told him. *Not if it will bring you to ruin.* Every day she planned to end it, but instead of breaking up with him, she had sex with him in the spare room until they were both depleted and euphoric. Then they would lie there entwined and watch the crow fly through the room like a shadow.

"My mother would be mortified," Franny confided. "She had an aversion to animals."

"Lewis is not an animal," Haylin said. "He seems to know what you're thinking."

"Are you saying he's my familiar? That would make me a witch." Franny rested her face against Haylin's chest. She could hear his heartbeat, which gave her great comfort. She thought of the entries in Maria's journal, and kept quiet even though she longed to tell him everything.

"I don't care what you are, as long as you're mine," Haylin told her.

On the day Jet finally came out of the bedroom her stunning black hair was shorn as short as a boy's. She'd used a pair of nail scissors and the ends were choppy. She was paying her penance. She had ruined all of their lives. She knew why Franny's eyes were often brimming with unshed tears, and why her sister was still wearing the dress she had worn to their parents' funeral. Franny had locked herself in her father's office, the desk strewn with scattered papers, dust motes spinning through the air, and there she had telephoned the admissions office at Radcliffe to withdraw her acceptance. She did so in secrecy, but her voice had risen through the vents, the way their father's patients' tearful confessions had during their therapy sessions, and Jet had overheard.

"Oh, Jet, you've cut your hair," Franny said when she witnessed what her sister had done.

Jet was still in her nightgown, barefoot. She resembled a

cat, with a cat's suspicion and mistrust, a gorgeous creature despite her attempt to ruin herself. Jet had already decided she would not be finishing high school. She felt far too old for that, and from that day forward, she wore only black. She rid herself of the girlish clothing she'd favored in the past—frilly, floaty dresses in shades of pink and violet—giving it all to Goodwill. Her clothes no longer suited her, for she wasn't the same person she'd been before her birthday. That girl was gone forever. Sometimes she went back to the scene of the accident. She could no longer hear other people's thoughts and was so alone she felt like a moth in a jar. She sat on the curb, like a beggar woman, but no one passing by could grant her forgiveness and that was something she certainly couldn't allow herself.

Her one salvation was the novels she read. On nights when she thought it might be better not to be alive without Levi in the world, she opened a book and was therefore saved, discovering that a novel was as great an escape as any spell. She favored Jane Austen and the Brontës and Virginia Woolf, reading one book after another. On most days, she was happy not to leave home. She, who was once the most beautiful girl in two states, who had inherited their mother's gorgeous features, now seemed mousy and unremarkable, a bookworm who could hardly be convinced to look away from the page. Boys no longer noticed her, and if they did, she made it clear she wasn't interested. She walked late at night, when the avenues were deserted, as if tempting fate. She felt a kinship with the lonely, forsaken people drifting through the streets at that blue hour.

Seeing her sister's distress, Franny wrote to their aunt. Surely there was a remedy to help Jet through this terrible time. Two days later a crate arrived with Jet's cure. Franny laughed when she looked inside, then immediately went to wake Jet.

"Isabelle sent you something."

Jet sat up in bed and wiped the sleep from her eyes.

"It's not a rabbit, is it?" Jet asked.

"Goodness, no."

Jet rose from bed and knelt to peer inside. There was a small black cat. Wren, who had followed her in their aunt's garden. She scooped it up and dissolved into laughter, a lovely thing to hear after such a long period of mourning. The cat sat completely still, surprised by the attention.

"Oh, she's perfect! You have your crow," Jet said to Franny. "Now here's my Wren."

Jet let the cat onto the bed to play with a ball of blue string. She stroked her and told her what a lovely little cat she was, but her eyes never lit up, and Franny remembered what Isabelle had written on the card that had accompanied the cat.

A remedy such as this can only last so long.

A real estate agent soon began showing the neglected house to prospective buyers. Every now and then the siblings would discover strangers being led through as they were told how a little remodeling could easily restore the true beauty of the house. Vincent kept his room locked and he drew a skull on the door in black ink.

"Stay the fuck out," he told the shocked Realtor, who wore a pillbox hat, of the sort Jacqueline Kennedy wore.

The agent had known Susanna Owens from the Yale Club

and was showing the house as a favor. Anyone else would have quit in light of Vincent's shenanigans. The nearly tame rats in the broom closet, the flickering lights, the smell of spoilt milk in the kitchen sink. The Realtor didn't dare to open Vincent's door, and made what she hoped were reasonable excuses. Just a small child's room, potential buyers were told. You'll need to paint and plaster. This was the way to avoid the drained bottles of whiskey, the hashish and marijuana, a fancy glass hookah pipe, piles of unwashed clothes, stinky boots, books of magic, and an amazing collection of record albums stored in orange crates. Even Franny was told she must knock before entering his room. Now that they were leaving, Vincent, who'd never seemed to give a damn about their home, was in despair. "I don't see why we have to sell the place," he complained.

"Because we're broke," Franny said with a forthrightness her brother didn't appreciate.

"You can't make me leave if I don't want to," he groused.

He kept his locked room dark. So much the better. Less costly electricity bills. They were counting pennies now. Dodging the shops where their parents had run up tabs: the butcher, the baker, the liquor store. They sold the living room furniture at a bad price, and did the same with a rug from Persia that had always been in the dining room. The entire town house was shadowed by the siblings' spiritual agony, therefore Franny tried her best to get her brother and sister out when prospective buyers came by, not that it did a bit of good. They hung around the home they couldn't wait to escape from in the past. In the end, Franny paid Vincent ten dollars each time he vacated before a showing. He then stomped out of the house and went to the Ramble, where he could concentrate on the only thing other than music that held his interest. Magic. He was focusing on his powers of intense concentration. He could make larger and larger objects move, at first with a shudder, then with a leap. Rocks fell from the cliffs above the paths. People stayed clear of any area Vincent claimed for himself when he set a circle that couldn't be crossed. He carried *The Magus* under his coat, studying it so closely he had much of it memorized before long.

At last the house was sold to a lovely family who hoped to enter their girls into the Starling School. They wanted to move in as quickly as possible. Their lawyer suggested that Franny put whatever money they made from the sale into real estate. It was a good investment and they wouldn't have to worry about making the rent. They could forget the East Side, however, it was much too expensive. It was suggested that Franny look downtown.

She took the M1 bus to the end of its route, then walked to Washington Square Park, where she stood beneath the historic white arch. Long ago, Minetta Creek flowed here and Washington Square was a swamp. In 1794, Aaron Burr changed the course of the stream, so his own nearby property would have a pond, and later, when the city began encroaching upon the creek, muskrats still abounded. It was an extraordinary place, but it also held great sorrow, for Minetta Creek, known by the Indian people as Devil's Water, was a boundary for a cemetery that was in use from 1797 to 1826, a potter's field where twenty thousand bodies were buried and where they rested, uneasily or not, to this day.

The Hangman's Elm, said to be over three hundred years

old, stood in the northwest corner of Washington Square Park. That was where witches were said to gather. The last execution in Manhattan took place here in 1820, when a nineteen-year-old slave named Rose Butler was hanged for burning down her master's house. After that most people avoided the tree after dark, or at least they made certain to keep lavender in their pockets to bring them luck when they passed by. Folk magic could always be found in Manhattan, from the time English colonists valued the almanac in order to read astrology and magic parchments were sold as maps for treasure digging, along with divining rods and secret incantations. Divination and palmistry were studied. After the Revolution magic was so rampant, with peddlers selling forbidden books hidden in black covers, that ministers preached against it from their pulpits. The craft was dangerous and unpredictable, and witches were difficult to control, for they had minds of their own and didn't hold to keeping to the law.

As Franny walked on, the neighborhood smelled like patchouli and curry. It was the end of summer and everyone who could afford to be out of the city was. The Village felt like a sleepy town. It was a different city here; the buildings were smaller and it was possible to see the sky. No one cared what you looked like or what you wore. Franny stopped at a café for a strong cup of coffee. Listening to the waiters argue in Italian, she felt transported. She went to a flower shop and bought a rose that was so dark it appeared black. At last she turned onto Greenwich Avenue and there she stopped. She had come upon a tilted little house that had a For Sale sign in the street-level window where there had once been a shop. There was a school next door and the children were out at recess. When Franny looked through the window she could see a pie-shaped yard filled with weeds. Shifting her gaze she spied a twisted wisteria and a few spindly lilacs. It was then she felt her heart lift.

She wrote the phone number of the Realtor on a scrap of paper and went on, across Sixth Avenue, past the Women's House of Detention at 10 Greenwich Avenue. It was a huge prison plunked down in the center of the city, built in 1932 in the Deco style on the spot where the old Jefferson Market Prison once stood. Women shouted rude comments through the bars that guarded the open windows. It was hot on the street and far hotter inside the prison.

Help a sister, someone called.

Franny did the best she could. A cool wind rose to flit through the windows, down the hallways of the prison. For a moment, there was some relief from the heat. In response there were hoots of laughter and applause. Franny looked around. No one on the street was watching so she blew a kiss to those women who were locked away, and she left the wind gusting all the rest of the day.

Franny found Vincent in the Jester on Christopher Street. He was drinking absinthe and lemon juice, a sugar cube tucked into his cheek.

"Hey, Franny," he said when he caught sight of her. "Fancy meeting you here."

Two attractive girls from NYU sat in the booth with him, the prettier one slouched in the hollow of his arm. The girls seemed annoyed to see Franny and sent looks of frustration Vincent's way. As if he cared about them. Franny didn't know why he bothered. Was it to prove something to her or to himself?

"Let's go," Franny said with a nod. Vincent could tell from her tone that she was deadly serious. "We're moving."

"What?"

Franny had received a notice from the attorney. They had enough to buy the ramshackle place on Greenwich and still have a nest egg of cash to survive on a shoestring for a while. After that they were on their own.

"The movers come this week. Our house has been sold and we're going to a place we can afford. Or at least I hope we can." She paid Vincent's bill and waited for him on the sidewalk while he told his girlfriends good-bye. Then they walked side by side, boot heels clattering, two tall moody individuals with scowls on their faces. People crossed the street to avoid them.

"So we just leave home?" Vincent asked. "And what about Radcliffe?"

Franny gave her brother a sidelong glance. "You knew I was never going."

"I wish you could have."

They splurged on a taxi uptown. Then they stood in front of the house where they'd grown up and gazed at it sadly. They would likely not come back to Eighty-Ninth Street once they were gone. They would avoid it after they were settled downtown. You don't go back to a place where you've lost so much.

"What about Haylin?" Vincent asked.

Today New York smelled like wet grass and jasmine tea.

Franny shrugged. "He'll give up."

"You're selling him short. He'll never let you go."

When Haylin phoned, Franny told him he must go to Cambridge alone. He wouldn't listen. He continued to call, so she stopped answering the phone. He came to their door at all hours, but she didn't respond. Sooner or later he'd have to leave New York. It was now September. Everything in the park was fading to yellow, and huge clouds of migrating birds lit in the trees.

"You're staying for me," Jet said.

Franny shrugged. "You're my sister."

"But Hay?"

"Hay will be fine."

"Will he?" Jet wondered.

"Yes, he will, but he won't listen to me. You tell him the truth," Franny said in a surprisingly small voice. "Cover for me."

"What if you lose him for good?"

"Then it was meant to be."

Jet was convinced she must talk to him. Haylin had posted himself at the Owenses' town house, a determined expression on his face. He looked the way he had when he chained himself in the school cafeteria. Jet told him Franny had withdrawn from school and would not be leaving for Cambridge. In fact, they were moving downtown. There was no way to change Franny's mind. Jet had already tried.

"If I just saw her," Hay said. "If I could talk to her I think she would leave with me."

"You know Franny, she's stubborn."

Haylin was already two days late for the semester and had missed registration; if he waited any longer they might retract his acceptance.

"Go," Jet told him. "And don't feel guilty."

She went inside and locked the door, leaving Hay to stand

there, dazed and despairing. He had no idea why Franny had done her best to stop love's hold on him. He looked upward, shielding his eyes. The movers were packing up the town house. Vincent had suggested they leave everything behind—all he was taking was a backpack of clothes and his guitar—but Jet had taken great care in wrapping up the china her mother had brought home from Paris and had filled a trunk with Susanna's chic clothing. She had boxes and boxes of books stacked in the hall. As for Franny, she took only the letters Haylin had written to her the summer she was away, and some of the clothing she'd worn when she was with him. She was packing it all into a single cardboard box when she happened to gaze out and see Haylin on the sidewalk. Her heart broke then; she could feel it tearing in two. He looked so alone out there.

The crow was peering out the open window. "Take care of him," Franny said.

When Haylin turned to leave, the crow plummeted down to perch on his shoulder. Hay didn't seem the least surprised. He had a cracker in his pocket, which he offered to his new companion. The two disappeared down the street, into the yellow haze of the park. They were both gone, her heart and her soul. The scent of chestnuts was in the air. It would be autumn soon. Hay would be in Dunster House, the crow would be perched on a rooftop in Cambridge, and Franny would be living at 44 Greenwich Avenue, following her fate, even though what she wanted most of all was headed in the opposite direction.

PART THREE

Conjure

*T*hings *without all remedy* should be without regard. But what you can cure, do so willingly. What ails the human body and soul may be difficult to diagnose, but just as often there is a simple resolution. Black pepper for aching muscles, linden root and yarrow for high blood pressure, feverfew for migraines, ginger for motion sickness, watercress to ease labored breathing, vervain to quiet the pangs of unrequited love.

Before the sisters opened a shop on the first floor of the house, they made soap, prepared in an iron pot on nights when the moon was waning, a pale sliver in the sky above St. Vincent's Hospital on the northeast corner of Seventh and Greenwich Avenues. This was the institution that had given the poet Edna St. Vincent Millay her second name, for her uncle's life was saved there in 1892. Their own Vincent liked their downtown location so well he didn't mind helping to improve the little house. He investigated construction sites, salvaging discarded windows and lumber. Once lugged home, what had formerly been trash was used to create a makeshift greenhouse, where herbs could be grown from seed. When it rained the place flooded, but that only seemed to help even the most delicate plants grow; they burst through the glass roof, and before long the entire green-house was covered with vines.

As for the shop, it was a disaster when they moved in, with peeling plaster and water-stained ceilings, but soon enough everything was painted a pale dove gray. For weeks they all had streaks of gray paint in their hair, as if they had prematurely aged. Franny bartered with a local plumber. If he would stop the pipes from leaking, they would dispose of his wife's boyfriend; it was easy enough to do with a bit of Be True to Me Tea. For the carpenter who built shelves, the sisters concocted a hex breaker composed of salt, coconut oil, lavender, lemon juice, and lemon verbena. If he gave the mixture to the ex-client who was badmouthing him, the slanderer would fall silent.

Soon enough there were copper sinks and countertops made of white marble, salvaged from the boys' and girls' rooms of a school in the Bronx that was being torn down. The floor-to-ceiling shelves were filled with bottles of every shape and size collected from junk shops, all containing herbs that would be necessary. The pine floors, which had been stained a blotchy maroon, were refinished until they gleamed. A stuffed blue heron that was too wonderful to leave behind had been found in an antiques store on the Lower East Side. He reminded Franny of the heron who had come to her in Central Park, and she paid an exorbitant price for him. He was too tall to be taken home in a cab, and so the sisters rented a flatbed U-Haul truck. Vincent applauded when they set the heron up in the window of the shop and named the bird Edgar, for Edgar Allan Poe's ghost was said to roam their neighborhood, and for a time from 1844 to 1845 he had lived at 85 West Third Street, writing *"The Raven."*

Franny often frequented a discount store that sold chemistry equipment, buying beakers and a Bunsen burner, along with tongs and funnels and goggles.

"Science teacher," the checker guessed.

"In a manner of speaking," Franny answered.

Despite everything, she still considered science to be her main interest. She set up a lab in the back room of the shop, and there the sisters readied their inventory, concentrating on love potions, for that was what Aunt Isabelle's customers had always been most eager to buy. They consulted with Isabelle, who sent pages of notes in thick manila envelopes.

Remind customers they must be careful what they wish for, Isabelle instructed. *What's done cannot be undone. What's set into motion takes on a life of its own.*

They mixed henna with limes, roses, tea, and eucalyptus and let it simmer overnight, for henna's hue reflects the strength of love of a woman for a man, the thicker and deeper the color, the more genuine the love. Amulets that carried apple seeds were made in the evenings as they sat out in the yard, meant to bring the wearer love, for apples signify the heart. For those who wished to gain willpower, and say no to a lover who would bring only heartbreak, there was a cure of rosemary and lavender oil. Bathe in it, and when you next saw the one you had once cherished, you would send him packing. They now had the recipe for Fever Tea, composed of cinnamon, bayberry, ginger, thyme, and marjoram, and for Frustration Tea, a combination of chamomile, hyssop, raspberry leaf, and rosemary, which Jet brewed for her sister in the mornings so that the day would go smoothly. Aunt Isabelle refused to hand over the formula for Courage Tea. That, she said, was one recipe you had to discover for yourself.

Though Jet had lost the sight, she was more than competent when it came to concocting remedies. A good thing, for they needed the income. Often the sisters were in the shop from early in the morning till long past suppertime. There was no complaining, no slacking off. Jet seemed perfectly fine unless you yourself had the sight, and then you knew she was not. She went to bed early, and too often Franny could hear her crying. Jet refused to speak about Levi and the loss of their parents. She hadn't admitted she had lost the sight, but Franny and Vincent both knew. Usually they could trade thoughts, but when they approached Jet's mind they were greeted by a wave of darkness. Franny mentally tried to send her a list of what she needed for the store and there was no reply, only a blank stare.

"Did you want something?" Jet asked.

"No, I'm fine," Franny said. "You?"

"Perfect," Jet replied.

She had lost so much that she had lost herself as well. She had a secret that she carried with her, and it hurt, as if she stored a stone beside her heart. It was her hatred of herself that was her burden, and it grew each day. At first it was tiny, a mere pebble, then it was as big as her heart, and then it was the largest thing inside her. She had decided it wasn't the curse that was at fault. It was her.

During the day, she worked at the shop and never once complained. But at night she had begun to roam. She went to bars and after midnight found her way to Washington Square, where she smoked marijuana with strangers. She wanted to lose herself, get rid of her past, and forget the pain she carried when she thought of Levi. On the weekends she went uptown to Central Park. It was here, on Easter Sunday, that she walked farther than she had planned. Once there she heard bells and music and followed as if enchanted.

The park was crowded, the meadow was filled with a wash of love and acceptance. It had been a long time since Jet had felt part of anything. There were balloons drifting into the bright sky and garlands of flowers wreathed around necks and arms, and people in love, some in stages of lovemaking, some of them giving out LSD, not yet illegal. Fluff, Ghost, Sacrament, Sugar, named for the design on the blotter paper the liquid was dotted upon. Whether it caused happiness or confusion, the drug certainly created ripples in the texture of the world.

"Here you go," a man ambling by said to Jet. He took her hand and was gone before she could see his face. "This will cure you," he called over his shoulder.

"Nothing can cure me," Jet said. She saw that she had a tab of acid in her hand. People said it was magic. One taste could transport you. And perhaps, if she were very lucky, she would no longer be herself or carry her burden.

She placed the tab of LSD on her tongue and let it melt. She had a shiver of expectation, and wasn't that the sign of magic to come? She waited, but nothing happened, so she went on, drifting through the crowds. When she got a bit lost she stood still and tried to get her bearings. She had somehow blundered into a maze that everyone else seemed able to navigate. What path led uptown? Where was north? Where was her soul? Was it up above her in a tree, perched there like a goblin?

She must have looked as if she were setting off on a voyage because a young woman passing by said, "Happy travels."

"I'm not going anywhere," Jet replied. And then she realized that she was. She saw it happen in fast motion, in a whoosh. The grass was thrumming with life, a shimmering hallucination coiling and uncoiling in long stalks, populated by thousands of ants and beetles. There was music and someone grabbed her arm to dance with her, but she slipped away.

Forty minutes of real time had passed, but it seemed as if only moments had gone by. Surrounded by so many people, she felt even more alone. She experienced sickening waves of paranoia and lowered her eyes so no one could see into her mind. She had lost the gift of sight, but now she could see the air was crumpling into hard, little waves; the earth itself was folding, like a piece of paper. Perhaps there had been a small earthquake.

Jet darted down a path, dodging into the Ramble, where she could catch her breath. She was hyperventilating, so she counted to ten with each breath and raced on. Sunlight fell through the overhanging branches, and the shadows on the ground formed lacy patterns. Before she knew it she was at the Alchemy Tree, which was pulsating with green blood within its bark, so alive it might as well have been human.

She stood with her arms out and ran her hands over the tree. Everything glowed and shimmered, undulating before her eyes. She could actually taste the air. It was vanilla and moss. There were black weeds beneath her feet and when she wished them to bloom they did so, in shades of lilac and persimmon. She lay down in the brambles, sinking into them, yet she didn't feel the stickers. They drew blood but the thorns didn't hurt and each bruise of blood resembled a rose. If she were dead, would she be reunited with Levi? Was he waiting for her right now?

There were yellow warblers flickering by as they migrated, as if specks of light had broken off from the sun. The brightness of the little birds in the fading shadows was blinding. Jet closed her eyes. Still she couldn't escape the light. Inside her eyelids there were fireflies. How had they gotten there? Everything was too bright, dazzling.

She thought she saw Levi, and she ran after him, but when she blinked he was gone. Now she was in the dense woods. Her breath was composed of filmy black sparks that rose up whenever she exhaled. She definitely heard his voice. She tracked the stream called the Gill and traipsed through the mud, not stopping until she came to the lake. The black water had turned into a mirror. Jet crouched on hands and knees and looked at herself. What she saw loomed. The girl who had ruined everything she touched.

She crawled closer to get a better look and as she did she tumbled into the lake. In no time she was in up to her waist. She deserved this. This was what was done to witches. Though she was freezing she plunged farther into this watery looking glass. She wanted to sink down, to be punished and done away with, but she felt the buoyancy inside her, and she floated when she meant to drown.

It was no good. She would not sink. She swam to the edge and sloshed through the mud. The grass was still pulsing with life. Jet struggled to breathe. It had been six hours since she had taken the tab of acid. It was no longer daytime. Stars filled the sky. There were still a few fireflies behind her eyelids.

She walked all the way home, following Fifth Avenue to the very end. When she came inside Franny saw that her clothes were wet, and that her dark hair was damp around her face.

"What did you do?" Franny asked. There was a circle of sorrow around her sister, a pale gray-blue, as though she were still walking through water.

"Nothing," Jet said. "I wasn't paying attention."

"You tried to drown yourself." Franny could see it. The edge of the lake, the water weeds, the moment when her sister gave in to the call to go deeper.

"It was an accident."

Franny went to embrace her sister. "The world will do enough to us, we don't have to do it to ourselves," she said. "Stay away from water. Promise me."

Jet promised, she crossed her heart, but in fact she now knew that if a witch wanted to drown herself, she could do so. All she needed was some assistance. A stone, a rock, a spell, a cup of poison, a steely heart, a world of sorrow. Then, and only then, could it be done.

Once a week Jet walked uptown to the Plaza Hotel at Fifth and Fifty-Ninth Street. No one knew where she was. To the crowds rushing by she was nothing, just a young woman in black standing on the sidewalk crying. She always went directly to the place where it happened, and when she did she could feel the last moments she had spent with Levi before his accident. Even though she'd lost the sight, those instants were so powerful they hung in the air and were threaded through the trees. Everything glowed with a peculiar bright light. He'd held her near. He'd told her to close her eyes. She'd said, *Don't be silly,* but he had insisted. At last he'd placed something in her hands. *Now look,* he'd said.

What is this? She'd laughed, feeling the small circular surprise in her hands. *A bottle cap?*

But when she opened her eyes she saw he had given her a ring, a thin silver band with a moonstone. She hadn't taken it off since, though the silver had tarnished.

In the park in front of the hotel she watched the trees for a sign, but there was none. No dove, no raven, no spark of light. Then one day as she was working in the shop, she stumbled upon what she needed. The potion. That week she walked into the Plaza Hotel and rented the room Levi had reserved. He had showed her the reservation so she knew the room number: 708. Sometimes that number came up in the oddest places. On the cash register in the shop when someone bought a bar of black soap. In the grocery store when she went to pay for bread and milk. If it was over the door of a restaurant she then must stop, whether or not she was hungry.

Jet told the bellman she didn't need help, then she tipped him five dollars and went up alone. There was no one in the elevator, or in the hall. It was very quiet. She was glad she couldn't hear the thoughts of those inside the rooms she was passing. She appreciated silence now. Even the door to her room made no noise when she slipped inside. She drew the curtains and flung open the windows. Then she peered into the bathroom to see the huge tub and all the lovely bath salts and soaps, and finally she lay down on the bed fully clothed. She could spy the tops of the trees in the small park in front of the hotel and a wedge of blue sky. She thought about what might have been if the accident hadn't happened. How they would have walked into the hotel together, come up to their room, this very room. They would have sat on the bed, shyly at first, before daring to embrace. He would have been gentle, and kind, although mad for her, and they might have cried together afterward, overwhelmed by sex and emotion. She supposed she was weeping as she thought about this, and the sound carried, and there was a knock on the door.

She didn't answer. Perhaps guests nearby had complained. She forced herself to be quiet. But as it turned out, she had left the door unlocked and someone came into the room.

"Are you all right, miss?"

It was the bellman. Jet didn't answer, so the bellman pulled up a chair and sat down. He was young and had a worried expression.

"When people check in without luggage you never know what they're going to do," he said. "And then I heard you crying. I put two and two together."

"I'm fine," Jet managed to say. "Please go."

"You're not going to kill yourself or anything like that?"

Jet shook her head. It was safer not to speak.

"Because I would feel responsible. I would be the last person to have seen you. That would mean that I forever would carry this moment around, and think of what I could have done to stop you. My life would probably be ruined. I'd get off track and start to drink and I'd drop out of school and after a while this place would fire me, because everyone would blame me, and worst of all, I'd blame myself."

Jet began sobbing anew. She turned away from him. There had been a plan and he was ruining it. She felt the bed sink as he lay down beside her.

"Don't cry," he said. He stroked her hair. "I can get you room service."

In spite of herself, Jet laughed. "Room service? Why would that help?"

"The room service is great," he protested. "You shouldn't pass it up."

Jet turned to face him. They lay side by side looking into each other's eyes. His were very dark, flecked with gold. He told her his name was Rafael and he was taking night classes at Hunter College. She told him she had lost the man she loved and that she no longer believed in love and wanted nothing to do with it. He told her he planned never to marry and thought love was probably a foolish endeavor. He had seen what had happened to his mother, who had raised three children without any help, and who worked two jobs, all due to love, while his father went on and married twice more and had other families and never looked back. Jet had found her perfect bitter companion. She felt at ease in his presence.

"What do they have here for room service?" Jet asked.

"Everything. You name it, they've got it."

She wanted roast chicken, string beans, and a hot fudge sundae.

"Give me fifteen minutes," Rafael said. "Maybe twenty."

She fell asleep while he was gone and she dreamed of the Angel of the Waters at the Bethesda Fountain. The angel arose and was free from the shackles of metal and stone. She put out her hand and stopped time, and everything in Manhattan was motionless, except for the swirling stars above the city. It was then Jet knew what she wanted. To go back to that day and relive it.

When Jet woke, Rafael had returned with a tray that he'd arranged for them. He brought enough for two. They ate together, except for the sundae, which Jet alone devoured. He'd been right, the room service was fabulous.

"Are you going to get fired?" she asked.

"No, my uncle is the head bellman."

"I don't want your life to be ruined. I would feel bad if you did get in trouble."

"Trouble's actually my middle name," he told her. "Rafael Trouble Correa."

They both laughed. Then Jet looked serious. She got up her nerve.

"What if I wanted you to be him?" she asked.

"The dead man?"

"And we would never see each other again and it would have nothing to do with love. You would just be him once."

Rafael thought this over. He had had many strange requests working in the hotel. People wanted privacy or they wanted women or they wanted drugs or drink. He always said he couldn't help them, because that was what his uncle, who'd hired him in the first place so he could put himself through school, had said to do. This, however, was different.

"I think I'd have to be myself. I can't be a dead man."

They had begun to drink the whiskey in the minibar. There were several varieties, all excellent. They'd had quite a few.

"You'll be him to me," Jet said. "That's what's important. I don't want to mislead you."

Rafael nodded. "I understand. Can you at least tell me his name?"

"Levi."

"From the Bible." That seemed to make him feel better about the situation. "Was he a good man?"

"He planned to go to Yale," Jet said. "Divinity School."

Rafael got up and went to lock the door. When he came back he said he could wait in the hall vestibule while she undressed and got into bed. He felt as though he had wandered into a dream, and sometimes in a dream you just follow the path you're given without asking too many questions. For once you do, the dream is over.

"That's not the way it would happen," Jet told him.

So he sat on the bed beside her and kissed her and they kissed for a very long time. This was the way it would have begun. At first she thought she would cry again, but then Jet kept her eyes closed and the bellman was Levi to her. She said Levi's name. Rafael might have been offended, but inside he pitied the dead man for all he had missed out on. He unbuttoned Jet's blouse and undressed her gently, just as Levi would have. He had a condom in his wallet, though he hadn't expected to use it today. Jet kept her eyes closed. When Rafael touched her he expected her to be cold, but she wasn't. She was hot under his touch.

"I want you to look at me," he told her. When she did he said, "I don't want to be the dead man." Jet turned away and began to cry, but he insisted. "We can't pretend. We're both alive. We have to do this like living people. Otherwise I wouldn't feel right."

She really looked at him. He was a handsome young man who was worried about her even though he didn't know her. She kept her eyes open as he made love to her. She was supposed to have had her first time with Levi, but instead she was here in a bed with a stranger. They could hear traffic on Fifth Avenue. They could hear the wind in the trees. When she embraced him he was himself, and that was fine.

"Is this one of these things where I have to be responsible for you for my whole life now?" Rafael asked. "Like when you save someone from death, and then you're their angel, and you can't have any peace until you know they're all right."

"I *am* all right," Jet said.

"Then why am I still worried?"

It was dusk now and the room was dark. Jet was pretty certain Rafael would get fired despite his uncle. "If you lose your job, it would be the reverse. Then I have to be responsible for you."

"If I lose my job, it's fate," he said.

"We make our own fate," Jet said, and then all at once she realized that they did. They could not control it, but they could choose how to respond to what happened. She insisted he get dressed and go back to work. He did so, although he seemed reluctant to go.

"So this isn't a relationship," Rafael said.

"Absolutely not." She told him about the curse, and the trouble people in her family had in matters of love. There was no reason not to tell him everything since they would remain as strangers. The truth was, he looked different to her now. He was even more good-looking than she'd thought at first, and he had a concerned expression. He wasn't Levi and he wasn't going to be no matter how hard she tried to pretend that he was.

"We should meet here in six months. Check in with each other," he said. "Then I would know you didn't kill yourself."

Jet shook her head. "I won't. But we're never going to see each other again. Let's just get that straight."

"You miss him," Rafael said. "Even right now."

She did, but the day of the accident now felt as though it belonged to the past. She was glad she had kept her eyes open.

"I'm glad you were you," Jet said.

He kissed her good-bye as himself and then they both laughed. "So am I," he told her.

When Rafael left, Jet took a long bath, then she put on a white robe and finished what was left of the chicken. She got into bed and phoned Franny to tell her where she was.

"You are not at the Plaza Hotel," Franny said. "That costs a fortune."

"I had to stay here. I needed to complete what should have happened that night."

She could see the lights come on along Fifth Avenue now. Rafael would be checking out of work and heading for night class. He had told her he wanted to be a teacher. She went to the window and gazed out. She thought she saw him, but she wasn't sure. She barely knew him after all.

"It's beautiful here," she told her sister. She'd forgotten how lovely the sky was at this hour of the day.

"Will you come home in the morning?" Franny wanted to know. "We can't afford another night at the Plaza."

"Yes," Jet assured her. "I promise I will. After I have break-fast from room service."

The Plaza Hotel was the least of their financial problems; there were heating bills and electricity and taxes, things their parents had seen to in the past. Even before the shop opened their savings had all but disappeared. Jet set a paper spell, hoping to bring money their way, burning a dollar bill coated with honey and milk in the fireplace. The only result was an order from a small pharmacy on Bleecker Street for a box of black soap. Franny had altered the recipe, adding city ingredients that were available. There were no blooming roses outside the door, no lush herbs and flowers as there were in Isabelle's garden. So she made good with what she had. A branch from an ash tree in Washington Square Park, two dappled feathers of a nesting dove on West Fourth Street, leaves from the wavering lilacs in their yard. The result was grittier than Aunt Isabelle's recipe, with more intensity. Wash with it, and not only were you beautiful, you were ready to do battle. It was especially good for anyone riding the subway or walking down a dark street after midnight.

The pharmacy ordered several more boxes in the ensuing months, but the sale wasn't enough to sustain them. When their money ran out they had no choice but to divest themselves of family belongings. They sold their mother's good Limoges china at a bad price. They sold the French cooking pots, and then the costume jewelry their mother favored, jeweled bugs and starfish and butterflies. One gray day, when they hadn't enough to pay the electricity bill, they brought nearly all of Susanna Owens's Chanel suits and Dior dresses to the secondhand store on Twenty-Third Street near the Chelsea Hotel. Franny bargained as best she could, but in the end they collected only a few hundred dollars for the timeless clothes their mother had bought in Paris when she was young and in love. They sat in the lobby of the Chelsea Hotel and counted their money.

"You could have stayed here instead of the Plaza," Franny said. "Then maybe we wouldn't be so broke."

"My fate wasn't here." Jet had a small smile on her face that gave her away.

"Oh really." Franny now understood. "What was your fate's name?"

"It doesn't matter," Jet assured her.

Franny narrowed her eyes. "Love?"

"Absolutely not. We never intend to see each other again," Jet said cheerfully.

"Perfect," Franny said. "Then you're the new Maid of Thorns."

"Oh, no," Jet said. "You'll always hold that title."

"Will I?" Franny said thoughtfully.

Jet went to her sister and sat beside her. "Franny, that was a joke. You have the softest heart of any of us."

"Untrue," Franny shot back, though she was near tears. She had hated seeing her mother's clothes hung on wire hangers in the thrift shop.

"Very true. This just means I know you better than you know yourself," Jet said. "But what else is a sister for?"

Posters were affixed to every lamppost in the neighborhood and Franny took a small ad in *The Village Voice*, the alternative newspaper whose offices were right around the corner in Sheridan Square. On the day of the grand opening, the shelves were stocked with cures and Edgar the heron was set in the window and festooned with ribbons and bows. By noon, only a smattering of people had showed up, a huge disappointment. Two teenage girls with long straight hair in search of true love sneaked in, giggling, afraid of the stuffed heron, nervous about magic, eyeing the bones and teeth set out in jars.

Franny threw up her hands, preferring the drudgery of cleaning the storeroom, but Jet found she enjoyed dispensing cures, and was happy to offer the girls the most basic potion: rosemary leaves, anise seeds, honey, and red wine. Since the Plaza Hotel, she had retained a deep empathy for those in love. She told the girls about a home remedy they could use when their money ran out, not wise for a shopkeeper to give away free advice, but true to Jet's nature. To grow a lover, she told them, they must plant an onion in a flowerpot and add plenty of sunlight and water. The girls were amused to hear that such a plain, smelly thing as an onion could bring love to them.

"That's all we have to do?" they cried, delighted.

Jet told them yes, an onion and a pure heart were the best ingredients. She'd had a pure love too once upon a time. These girls were too young and innocent for doves' hearts or spells written in blood. They hadn't the faintest idea of what love could do. Jet, on the other hand, knew only too well, and should she ever forget, should she wake up in the middle of the night and not know where or who she was, there was always the scar on her face to remind her. You had to squint to see its delicate outline, but it was there. Jet could run her hand over her face and feel it and then she thought about the glass breaking and the sound of the thud as the taxi had hit Levi. That was when she would phone Rafael, who at this point knew her better than anyone. It wasn't love, not at all, but he'd been right. He'd saved her from what she had intended to do at the Plaza Hotel that night and now he felt responsible for her. In some way she was his. He'd known what she'd planned to do. She'd brought along a tincture of belladonna that night, a mixture that quickly induces dizziness and nausea, then weakness and breathing complications. She had planned to ingest it, then get into the bath, and when she passed out she would drown, which seemed only fitting. No one could float after partaking of this tincture, not even her. Rafael had derailed her plans when he came into the room and lay down beside her. He'd reminded her that she was alive.

The last time they'd met she'd showed him the Alchemy Tree. They'd brought along a six-pack of beer, and after the second bottle, Rafael admitted that he had guessed her plan when she'd said she didn't need help getting to her room, yet tipped him five dollars anyway. In return he had saved her life. He was her secret, one she kept close. It wasn't love, but for her it was something more. He was someone she trusted.

Vincent had stopped bringing random women home, which was a relief to both sisters. They'd never known whom they might find in the kitchen when they went to fix their morning coffees. A teenager from Long Island in her T-shirt and nothing else, a waitress from the Kettle of Fish, a college girl from NYU, all wandering through the house with spellbound, confused expressions.

"Why do you bother?" Franny had asked once. She was at the table eating toast. Some woman had just made herself scrambled eggs before leaving, without even bothering to introduce herself.

"What is that supposed to mean?" Vincent snarled, defensive, brooding over why he could never feel anything for the girls he brought home.

"Fine. Never mind."

"Why do *you* bother?" Vincent tossed back at his sister.

"I don't!"

They were not the sort to discuss their emotions, or even admit they had them, so Franny kept her insights to herself.

"I think we have a disorder. Maybe we should have read Dad's book," Vincent wondered. "We might have been more normal."

Actually, Fanny had been reading it. She'd expected to find it preposterous, filled with crackpot theories about genetics. But as it turned out, *A Stranger in the House* was a love letter to Dr. Burke-Owens's children, something none of them would have ever guessed. Certainly, Franny was shocked by her father's warm, loving attitude.

They may be nothing like you, he had written, *they may surprise you, they may even repel you when their behavior is out of control, when they climb out their windows and drink underage and break every rule, but you will love them in a way you had not thought possible before, no matter who they turn out to be.*

All that year Vincent had earned cash by busking on corners and in subway stations. His exceptional voice made people cluster around, especially when he sang of the troubled times. He felt connected when he performed; he found that if he put away his guitar, there was nothing inside him. It was as if when he had been stolen as an infant, he had come back as a changeling, as if someone had reached inside him and grabbed his heart to keep under lock and key.

He had always been a night owl, but now he had found a coterie of late-night rovers. He frequented the clubs on Eighth Street—Cafe Au Go Go, The Bitter End, the Village Gate—and often dropped by the San Remo, the hangout of poets, both unknown and great, including Burroughs, Ginsberg, Corso, and

Dylan Thomas. Vincent listened to the poets who had no hope of ever making it, and those who were on the cusp of changing the meaning of what poetry was and could be. Whenever possible he caught Bob Dylan at Gerde's. Dylan was making his mark as a poet and musician with a voice that was unmistakably his own. That was true beauty. That was the map of one's soul. To do so meant to reveal some inner part of yourself, and that Vincent was unable to do.

By now he was known in the clubs. Some people knew him from the Jester, and when they called him the Wizard the nickname stuck. When he spoke his voice was so soft that whomever he was addressing had to lean in to hear, and then some sort of enchantment happened. He was more handsome than ever, but that was only part of the spell he cast. Rumors began. People said he could pick your pocket without ever touching you. He could swipe a song lyric right out of your head; he seemed to know what you were thinking or maybe you'd blabbed a chorus to him and when he added a few words he made it so much better than anything you could ever dream up, that in the end you wouldn't even recognize your own music. He carried a book of spells with him, and for the right payment he could make things happen for you. The unexpected became real before your eyes. A girl who never looked at you before would follow you home. A job for which you weren't qualified would be yours. A letter would arrive informing you of an inheritance from a relative you hadn't known existed.

Vincent worked briefly as a waiter at the Gaslight, where he gratefully ate for free from their quirky menu: date-nut bread and cream cheese, grilled cheese, beefburger, pink lemonade, and a series of sundaes he sneaked home for Jet. Mint, brandy, rum, chocolate, and vanilla. He'd have to run all the way home to Greenwich Avenue so the ice cream wouldn't melt and leave sugary puddles on the sidewalk. Eventually, the management fired him when a ticked-off waitress he had rejected ratted him out as being underage.

On the weekends he usually made a quick stop in Nedick's, a hot dog place on Eighth Street and Sixth Ave, before heading down to Washington Square Park, where folk musicians gathered on Sunday afternoons. He still had his same old Martin guitar he'd bought when he was fourteen, an instrument that seemed to feel and emote in a way that eluded him. He was inspired when he performed, his voice blessed with a soaring grace. And then he would stop and feel empty all over again, a hollow reed the wind blew through, another young man in a black jacket hanging out on the corner of MacDougal and Bleecker.

"Are you sure you're seventeen?" the best guitar teacher in New York, Dave Van Ronk, asked after Vincent sat in to play with a group of older men at the park. Van Ronk was known as the mayor of MacDougal Street, a pal of Dylan's, and a legend himself.

"I'm not really sure about anything," Vincent said, shaking the big man's hand, making sure not to run his mouth for once in his life.

"Well, keep playing," Van Ronk said. "That's one thing you should be sure of."

These were the times when children dreamed about nuclear testing and falling stars. There was an undercurrent of unrest, like a wave, racial division in the cities, the war halfway around the world blooming with blood. When Vincent walked through Washington Square Park he could hear the thoughts of the people he passed by, such a ragged outcry of emotion he sometimes thought he would go mad. He understood why Jet seemed not to care that she had lost her gift. It was awful to hear the voices of dead paupers buried in unmarked graves beneath the cement paths. All but forgotten, they cried out to anyone who might hear them. For them the world had been a veil of tears. The murdered, the abandoned, the ill, the ruined, victims and criminals alike all cried out to him. He wished he'd never had the sight. What had been a game when he was a boy had become an affliction. He had no desire to tap into other people's pain, to know them better than they knew themselves.

He took to wearing a black cap woven out of metal thread in an attempt to shut out his clairvoyance. He'd found the cap on the Lower East Side, where he'd bought his first book of magical instructions. He'd never admitted the truth to Franny, but he'd first read about *The Magus* in a book he'd found on a shelf in their father's office, for Dr. Burke-Owens had studied folklore and ancient magic and Jungian archetypes. Vincent had been a kid, but one who knew what he wanted. He wanted to be the best at what he did, no matter the price. He searched for *The Magus*, but in every bookstore the clerks laughed at him and told him all of the copies had been burned long ago. Then he had come upon a shabby vendor strung out on drugs who peddled magic from a makeshift room in an abandoned building. There, hidden in a wheelbarrow, beneath a threadbare blanket, Vincent found the book. In exchange for the text, Vincent had handed over a fifty-dollar bill filched from the coat pocket of one of his father's patients and a strand of his mother's pearls, stolen from her jewelry box. He'd assumed the vendor had no idea of the true worth of this treasure, but then the old man had said to Vincent, "I've been wanting to get rid of that. It will lead you down the wrong path if you're not careful. It's a burden."

When Vincent returned to search for the iron hat, he'd looked up the old vendor, but the magic man had long ago disappeared. Squatters had claimed the building he'd once occupied. They'd tried to turn Vincent away when he examined his predecessor's space, discovering the hat left on a shelf, as if meant for him. Harassed, Vincent began a fire without flame or wood, and the squatters backed off. Standing in the ruin of a place, he'd felt oddly at home. He knew the creed he'd been taught by their aunt, the first rule of magic is, *Do no harm*, but that was not the world he was drawn to. Hexes, curses, conjuring for causing spiritual sickness, such practices could be addictive, especially when customers were willing to pay high prices for them.

He set up shop in his predecessor's room. It was sympathetic magic he dealt in, some so exhausting he had to sleep for days to regain his strength. In no time, he had a list of wealthy clients who didn't care about the rule of three. They took it upon themselves to turn evil back on the one who had created it, which meant that a candle must be burned backward or a container spell with mirrors must be put into use. Wicked magic was used to bind an enemy, often in business, wherein a photograph or doll or other image was used to represent the one who would be cursed. Some of the spells were painful and risky. All were unethical. And yet, Vincent began to collect and sell the paraphernalia of jealousy and hate: coins, mirrors, combs, pyramids, figurines, amulets to protect and those meant to harm. Franny had been right about his magical leanings. They led to trouble, and always had.

His sisters loved him, but he couldn't be the person they wanted him to be. There was no reason for them to know how he earned his money. When he brought home bags of groceries and footed all the bills, they asked how he could afford to do so. He simply remarked, "What can I say? I'm a great waiter." He didn't bother to mention he'd been fired from the Gaslight. Did they truly believe the expenses were paid off in tips? Or from the profits of their shop, empty of customers most days?

There was a fellow in Washington Square Park who dispensed certain illegal items needed for such spell work—vials of blood, the hearts and livers of animals—who warned Vincent to be careful in the occult world. *What you send out will come back to you,* this fellow had whispered in a thick voice. *Not once but threefold. What do you think happened to your predecessor? Are you ready for that, brother?*

Vincent ignored the advice. He knew he was squandering his talents, but he didn't give a damn. There was always a price to be paid. What you get, you must also give. But he had cash now, and he didn't seem in the least bit jinxed. At least, not yet. In fact, he was gaining an audience in the Village. He'd helped this along with invocations from *The Magus,* but so what? Fame was addictive, even the tiny bit he'd garnered. People crowded round him in the park, and often a group was gathered there waiting for him before he arrived. But he wondered if it was magic that drew them to him, and, when they dispersed, he felt more alone than ever. He could make it happen if he wanted to, the crowds, the fame, the records, the stardom. But what would the price be? He thought of a story Franny had told him when he was a boy. A minstrel used sorcery to climb to the heights of fame. *Don't worry about the price,* the wizard the musician had gone to had advised. And then the time came for reparations, when it was too late to change his mind. Only then did he discover that the price was his voice.

On the night of his birthday Vincent wandered home in the September dusk, a tall, stark figure, rattled by the magic in which he'd recently been complicit. Every time he had sold a spell for some perverse intention—to ensure that a rival would fail or a wife would disappear—he felt he'd sold a portion of his soul. It paid the bills, but he slept fitfully and then not at all. In the middle of the night he dressed and walked the streets in a daze, with a hollow feeling, as though he were famished and couldn't get enough to satisfy his hunger. He wanted to stop, but magic took hold and wouldn't let go.

He was turning eighteen, but he felt so much older. Master of denial, master of dark magic, master of lies and loneliness. What good was it to be a conjurer if he couldn't conjure his own happiness?

Now he was late for his own birthday dinner. Jet was making his favorite meal to celebrate: coq au vin, with potatoes and fresh peas. Franny had baked Aunt Isabelle's tipsy chocolate cake, the mere scent so intoxicating a person could get drunk on it. Still, he wasn't ready to face a celebration and pretend to be happy. He found an empty bench in Sheridan Square and gazed at the old streetlights, there for over two hundred years. He made them dim, then go black. He could go in a bad direction and he knew it. What would happen then? Would he lose his voice? Be unable to make amends?

He smoked a joint and tilted his head up. There were no stars in the sooty sky. Eighteen years of being a liar, he thought. When he looked down he saw that a creature was staring at him.

"If you've come for me, you've made a mistake," he warned it. "I'll turn you into a rabbit."

The animal came close enough for Vincent to feel its hot breath. It was no rabbit, but a black German shepherd, without a collar or leash. The dog faced him with a serious expression, his eyes flecked with golden light. Vincent smiled despite his glum frame of mind. "Friend or foe?" he asked. The dog offered his paw as an answer, and they shook. "You're very well trained," Vincent said admiringly. "If you have no name, I'll call you Harry after the greatest magician, Mr. Houdini. I would discuss your situation further, but it's my birthday and I have to go home."

The dog trailed him across Sixth Avenue, following to Greenwich Avenue. Vincent looked over his shoulder before coming to an abrupt halt. "If that's what you have in mind we might as well walk together. We're late for dinner."

Vincent had no friends, yet after he'd come home, Franny overheard him conversing with someone in the entrance hall. Curious, she went to peek. There was an enormous German shepherd who waited patiently as Vincent hung up his coat. Male witches were often known to have black dogs, or so the texts in the library had stated. Immediately, Franny knew this beast was Vincent's familiar, his double and alter ego, a creature of a different genus that had the same shared spirit.

The dog shadowed Vincent into the kitchen, then lay beneath the table, waiting for his master's next move. Jet's little cat let out a howl when it spied the huge dog, then leapt from Jet's arms and raced from the room, skittering up the stairs to the safety of the second floor. The dog merely watched impassively. He clearly wasn't about to humiliate himself by giving chase.

"Poor Wren!" Jet sighed. "Her home life has been ruined by a sibling."

"Like ours?" Franny teased.

"You know you were both thrilled when I was born. Or did you hire that nurse to get rid of me? I could forgive you if you tell me there's a tipsy chocolate cake," Vincent said, far more upbeat than usual, delighted to find he could be surprised by fate.

"If you tell us who your friend is," Franny countered. As his birthday gift, she'd wished he wouldn't be so alone, and had burned a paper coated with honey to complete the spell, and now here he was with a companion.

"He's Harry." At the mention of his name the dog picked up his huge head. "He'll be staying with us from now on." When the sisters exchanged a look, Vincent added, "You have to admit, we won't have any robberies with him around."

"We wouldn't anyway," Franny said, "we've got a fixed spell on the door." But she'd already filled a plate with chopped chicken and rice for the dog. She was pleased; everyone knew a dog was an antidote to alienation. "Happy birthday, dear Vincent."

It was a cheerful dinner, and when it was over, Vincent took out the trash without being asked, around to the alley where there were a dozen garbage cans. He was actually whistling. After all, he'd never liked his youth, maybe he'd prefer being older. He inhaled the night air and listened to the city sounds he loved: sirens in the distance, laughter and catcalls on the street.

It was then he noticed a card atop the trash can. The ink was faded, nearly invisible to the naked eye, but he managed to read the message. *Abracadabra.* It was Aramaic in origin, meaning *I create what I speak*, the most mystical and powerful blessing and curse. *Begin by walking down Bleecker Street.*

Vincent glanced around. No one was in sight, only the dark silky night. But he felt his pulse quicken. Clearly, he had somewhere to go.

He went out after his sisters had gone to bed. He did this nearly every night, but this time was different. He was not headed for the Jester and a night of drinking that would leave him blotto. He felt unusually elated as he headed down Greenwich to Bleecker. At the corner, he noticed the street sign was unfamiliar. It read Herring Street, the original street name of the address where Thomas Paine had lived, a name that hadn't been used for over two hundred years. Something odd was happening. There had been a fusion between the present and the past; things that were logical and those that were impossible were now threaded together. Well, if this was the way his eighteenth birthday was to be celebrated, so be it. He was a man tonight. Legal in the eyes of New York State.

There was a mist rising from the asphalt as he followed along Grove Street, where Thomas Paine had died in 1809. In honor of Paine's *The Age of Reason,* the surrounding lanes had virtue names: Art Street, now part of Eighth Street; Science Street, which became Waverly Place; and Reason Street, renamed Barrow. Only Commerce Street, running between Seventh Avenue and Barrow, was left with its initial name, a remnant of the past. Vincent realized he was headed onto an even tinier lane, one he'd never before noticed. Conjure

Street. There he found a wood-and-brick town house with a knocker in the shape of a lion's head. Once he went inside, he realized it was a private club, yet no one stopped him from approaching the bar.

He ordered a whiskey, not taking note of a man who came to sit beside him until he spoke. "I'm glad you could make it," the stranger said. "I'm a fan."

"Of folk music?"

"Of you."

Vincent turned to him. The man beside him wore a gray suit and a shirt made of fine linen. For some reason, Vincent felt flustered. For once in his life he fell silent.

"I hope you don't have a rule about not talking to strangers," the man said.

He let his hand fall upon Vincent's arm. Vincent felt stung, yet he didn't pull away. He just let the sting he felt go on, as if he wanted it, as if he couldn't understand how he'd ever lived without it.

"I've heard you play in the park. I go most Sundays."

Vincent's gaze settled on the man's dark, liquid eyes. When he tried to answer, there was a catch in his voice. He, who had talked himself in and out of trouble his entire life, who had charmed the nurse who had stolen him on the day he was born and every woman since without ever caring about a single one, had fallen silent, as if bewitched.

"I'm thinking I should be an exception to the rule. Talk to me," the man urged. "You'll be glad you did." Vincent's new companion introduced himself as William Grant, who taught history at the progressive university the New School, although he seemed far too young to be a professor. "I've been waiting for you to notice me, but since you haven't, I thought I'd invite you here. The card was from me. You know as well as I do, Vincent, we don't have all the time in the world."

William lifted his hand away to signal to the bartender for another round. In that instant something happened to Vincent. He realized he had a heart. It came as a great surprise to him. He sat back on the barstool, stunned. So this was it, and had been all along, the way a person felt when he was enraptured, when he didn't care about anyone else in the room, or in the city for that matter. It had finally transpired, what he had seen in the mirror, the man he would fall in love with.

They went to William's apartment on Charles Street. If there was anything Vincent might have done to stop it he wouldn't have done so, for this occurred only once in a person's life, and then only if he was lucky. It happened the way things happen in a dream. A door opens, a person calls your name, your heart beats faster, and everything is familiar, yet you don't know where you are. You are falling, you're in a house you don't recognize and yet you want to be here, you have actually wanted to be here all of your life.

Vincent was shocked by the depth of his feelings. All of the women he'd had and he'd felt nothing. Now he was burning, he was at someone's mercy, embarrassed by his own need. He, who prided himself on being a loner and not caring what anyone thought, cared desperately. When William ran his hands over Vincent's body, his blood was hot, he wanted to be here and nowhere else. In the past the sex was only about what others might do for him. He had been selfish and thoughtless, but now he was a different man entirely. What they did together was a form of magic, maddening and ecstatic.

Vincent didn't go home that night. He didn't care if he ate or slept or if his sisters worried over what had become of him. William set up a Polaroid camera and took photographs of them together. They appeared as if by magic, lifting off the page. In each image, they embraced each other. It seemed they were one person, and that was when Vincent began to worry. If you were one, what befell you hurt the other as well. In a sudden cold sweat, he remembered the curse.

He cared nothing about the ruination of himself; trouble didn't have to look for him, he went right toward it. But William's fate was another matter. Not love, he and Franny always said to each other, for look at what had happened to Jet. Anything but that. And yet Vincent stayed, unable to give up this dream he'd stumbled into, the one he'd always had but had made himself forget.

On their seventh day together Vincent fell silent, exhausted by sex and by his own fears, which now had grabbed hold of him and wouldn't let go.

"What's wrong?" William asked.

Vincent couldn't bring himself to speak of the curse or let the idea of it into the room with them, even though William would have understood in a way another man would not. He was a bloodline whose relative Matthew Grant had been tried for witchcraft and then acquitted in Windsor, Connecticut, before disappearing. There was no official record of William's ancestor after his trial, but there didn't need to be. He'd come to New York, where the family had settled on Long Island, and William had spent every summer at his family's house on the shore. He had an easy manner, but was direct and comfortable with himself. He'd been to Harvard, so he understood Massachusetts as well, and he'd written his thesis on John Hathorne, the witch-finder and judge who had sentenced so many of their kind to death, and several of the classes he taught at the New School centered on outsider societies.

"Do you know your fate?" Vincent asked as they lay together, entwined.

"I know yours." William laughed. "I told you when I met you."

"To sing in Washington Square Park?"

William grinned. "To be mine."

When Vincent went missing Franny was worried sick the first two days, furious over the next two days, and hurt every day that followed.

"He'll be back," Jet insisted. "You know Vincent."

Franny walked the dog, who continually pulled on his leash to the corner of Bleecker Street, then would stop, puzzled, refusing to walk on until Franny dragged him home. She wondered if her birthday wish had gone wrong, and had driven Vincent further away.

"You would know if something was wrong," Jet assured her sister. "You still have the sight."

At last Vincent phoned to say he was sorry to have been out of touch.

"Out of touch?" Franny had barely slept a wink since her brother had disappeared. "I was afraid you were murdered."

"Worse," Vincent told her. "I'm in love."

"Very funny," Franny said.

He'd had so many admirers and he'd never cared about a single one. He laughed, understanding his sister's response. "This is different, kiddo."

"You don't sound like yourself." Franny was already looking for a canister of salt and some fresh rosemary to dispel whatever afflicted him.

"I am myself," Vincent told her.

He gave her an address and told her to come see for herself. Franny packed up the ingredients she thought she might need, then leashed the dog and took off. Vincent's instructions were odd, however, and the streets unfamiliar. Finally she came to Conjure Street. It was dusk when she thought she saw Vincent on the stoop of an old town house, but Harry didn't bark to greet him and it was another man who waved to her. Franny approached, suspicious. The dog, on the other hand, went right to the stranger, who introduced himself as William Grant. Although he wasn't especially handsome he had charisma and even Franny was engaged by his manner.

"I'm meeting my brother here." Franny was studying William more closely. His dark sensitive eyes, his intensity.

"I am as well."

"Really?"

There had been so many people who'd been mad for Vincent; Franny assumed she'd simply come across one more admirer. She had persisted with her childhood task of watching over her brother. Every week she dropped a protection amulet into his jacket pocket, made of black cloth and bound by red thread, containing clove and blackthorn. Often, however, she found the amulets discarded in the street.

"And I'm here to meet you, too," the fellow said. "Your brother was too shy to be here when we first spoke."

"My brother? Shy? We're not talking about the same person."

William laughed. "This is all very new to him."

"But not to you?"

"Well it is if you mean falling in love." When Franny didn't answer, it was William's turn to study her. "You can't be surprised. He thinks you knew before he did."

She'd certainly known that Vincent had never been in love with a woman. That neighbor of their aunt's who had seduced him, the college girls, the waitresses, the fans of his music, all were meaningless. He rarely saw them more than once, and often couldn't remember their names. But William Grant was different. Franny knew it as soon as her brother came outside to join them. She could tell when he looked at William.

"So now you know," Vincent said.

"I think I always knew," Franny said.

"Well, then, now it's out in the open."

"I'm sure you don't mind if we speak privately," Franny said to William, taking her brother by the arm.

"Not at all." They left William with the dog, who seemed perfectly content to be entrusted to this stranger.

"He has the sight," Vincent protested as Franny directed him toward an alley. "There's no privately. It's *all* out in the open. You might as well speak in front of him."

Her brother could be so irritating when he pretended to be dense. "You know you're not supposed to do this," Franny said.

"Be with a man?"

"Fall in love!" They both laughed, then Franny's expression darkened. "Seriously, Vincent. The curse."

"Oh, fuck it, Franny. Aren't you sick of being ruled by the

actions of people who are long dead? Maybe everyone is cursed. Maybe it's the human condition. Maybe it's what we want."

Franny was truly worried. There was no one of whom she felt more protective. She thought of sitting beside his crib with a canister of salt, refusing to leave him after he'd been returned to them. She had seen a halo around him, the sign of a beautiful, but short, life. Franny had the salt with her now, but here he was with a grin on his face. And there was William Grant, watching them, concerned, clearly mad for her brother.

"Franny," Vincent said. "Do not argue with me. Let me be who I am."

As she threw her arms around him, she forgot about the salt and the rosemary and the curse and the ways fate could surprise you.

"Then I wish you happiness," she said, for that was really all she'd ever wanted for him.

There was a crow on the lamppost on New Year's Day. They'd had a small dinner, stuffing a goose with Aunt Isabelle's recipe, which included chestnuts and oysters sure to inflame the erotic center of anyone who partook of the meal. Vincent and William took off after helping to wash up, laughing as they packed some of Vincent's belongings. He was so often at William's apartment it seemed he lived there. After he'd gone, Franny saw that he'd left *The Magus* at home, which she took to be a good sign. She went after it, thinking she would hide it under a loose floorboard in the kitchen, and perhaps Vincent would forget about it entirely. But when she went to grab the text, it burned her fingers. "Fine," she said to the book. "As long as you leave him be."

194

As Franny and Jet stored away the dishes, Jet noticed the crow in the yard. "Isn't that Lewis?"

Franny went to greet him, having not seen him in more than two years. When she held up her arms he came to light on her shoulder. No matter what anyone said about crows, there were indeed tears in his eyes.

"Is it Haylin?" Franny asked.

The crow rested his beak against her cheek and she knew that it was. She went inside and found the phone number of Dunster House.

The crow paced on the coffee table and kept an eye on her. Jet paced as well, as Franny did her best to get through to the school. It was a holiday, and Harvard was all but deserted. At last a custodian answered. As Franny wasn't a relative, he couldn't give out any information.

"Don't take no for an answer," Jet urged. "Stand up for yourself."

Franny pleaded with the custodian, who at last gave in, telling her that the student in question had been taken to Mass General Hospital.

"Of course you'll go," Jet said. "There's no question about it."

"But what if I ruin him?" Franny asked her sister. "Maybe I should stay."

Franny had never before asked for her sister's advice and Jet was somewhat startled, especially because she had not been forthcoming about her own life. She had intended not to see Rafael again, but that's not how things turned out. They often met outside the hotel, then walked through the park. Jet read the papers he wrote for class, and later when he wrote a book about teaching kids who had been labeled unteachable he thanked her in his dedication, although no one in his family had ever met her. She had not regretted a moment.

"Go," Jet told Franny. "What's meant to happen will."

Franny stored her toothbrush and an extra T-shirt in her backpack, then had Lewis climb into the cat's carrying case, for it was too miserable a night to fly such a long distance. She took a cab to Penn Station and bought a ticket on the first train to Boston.

The car was overcrowded, and Franny had to stand until they reached New Haven, when she could finally slide into an available seat. By then she had a deep sense of foreboding. The other passengers must have felt it as well; as crowded as the train was, no one would sit next to her.

When she got to Boston she let Lewis out of his case and he lit into the sky. She stopped at a shop outside South Station and bought a bag of jelly doughnuts, then took a taxi to Mass General. This time she knew she would be questioned about her relationship to the patient. When she said she was his sister, she was told that Hay had suffered from appendicitis. His room-mate had found him curled up in a fetal position, teeth chattering, unable to respond, and had frantically called an ambulance. It was touch and go, the nurse divulged as she led Franny along the hall; they had feared septic shock and Haylin was still weak.

He was in a shared room, which meant Franny had to edge past the man in the bed closest the door. He was exceedingly old and she could tell he was dying. There was a dark circle tightening around him like a shroud, instant by instant. Franny paused to take his hand, and the old man clutched at her, grateful. "Are you here to see me?" he asked. "Will you say good-bye to me?"

"Of course," Franny assured him.

Haylin had been dozing, but he rose up through his half sleep, brought fully awake by the sound of Franny's voice. He was pale and much thinner. There was the dark stubble of a beard on his face. The old man now soothed, Franny went on to Haylin's bed. She dumped her backpack on the floor and lay down beside him, careful not to disturb the IV tubing inserted into his vein. She circled her arms around him.

"Franny," he said. "You came."

"Of course," she said.

"It's always been us," Haylin said.

Franny told him how Lewis had come to the city to fetch her. "He's never really liked me," she said. "He's always preferred you."

"You're wrong," Haylin told her. "He's crazy about you. I have a photograph of you on my desk and he sits there and stares at it, lovesick." Hay chuckled, then clutched at his abdomen, in pain. Franny had brought along a protection spell. She tied a blue string that had been coated with lavender oil around Haylin's wrist, then kissed his open hand.

"Is this to bring me back to you?" he asked.

"It's to make you well."

She delivered the bag of jelly doughnuts, which brought a grin to Haylin's face. "You remembered."

"Of course I did."

Hay then launched into praising Cambridge, how much Franny would appreciate the narrow streets and the riverside. She could take a class or two at Radcliffe. They could get an apartment in Central Square. He had been taking extra courses, and planned to graduate a year early so they would have more time to spend together. She submitted to this dream of happiness, but only briefly, until she gazed out the window. The crow was on the windowsill, watching, his head tilted. He knew what she was thinking. She was too afraid of the curse to ever place Haylin in danger. Franny slipped off the bed. It was too difficult to be near him. She poured Haylin a cup of water.

"Franny," he said. "We were meant to be together. Your coming here proves it."

She had no idea what she would do next, if she would stay or go.

"You can't leave me now," Hay urged, and she might have said she would never leave him again, but just then a tall blond girl stepped into the room, breaking their intimacy. The girl was perhaps twenty, pretty, with a huge smile, her cheeks flushed from walking along the Charles River, which she complained about as soon as she arrived. Her sleek cap of hair was in place despite the windy day. She wore a plaid skirt and a blue cashmere sweater and a scarf knotted at her throat. She, too, carried a bag of jelly doughnuts.

"I'm freezing!" the girl declared. "And oh, my God, Hay, I was out of my mind with worry last night." She went to Haylin's side. "I didn't even get to call your parents until this morning. They'll be up tonight." She pulled off her scarf. "I didn't leave here until the doctor assured me a hundred percent that you were fine."

"I am," he said roughly, his eyes still on Franny.

The girl had been so intent on Hay she hadn't even noticed Franny lurking by the window, wearing her ill-fitting black coat. "Oh, hello!" the girl said brightly. "I didn't see you there."

Lewis tapped on the window glass, but Franny was distracted. Her heart was pounding. She'd gone white as a sheet, her freckles splotchy across her pale face. "Hello," she said. Her voice cracked with the fever of resentment.

The girl came forward and stuck out her hand. "I'm Emily Flood."

Being in such close proximity to this interloper caused a series of images to flicker behind Franny's eyes. "You're from Connecticut and you went to an all-girls private school and you're Haylin's roommate."

"Why yes! How did you know all that! I'm not officially a roommate, but since I'm there every night, I guess so! It's a good thing I am. Otherwise who would have called the ambulance? Hay is so stoic. He would have shivered there uncomplaining until his appendix burst."

"Oh," Franny said. "It was you who saved him."

"Franny." Haylin seemed truly in pain now.

Emily looked at Hay, then at Franny. "You're Franny? I've heard so much about you. How brilliant you are."

"Well, I'm not. I'm actually stupid." Franny went to retrieve the backpack she'd dropped on the floor when she climbed into bed with Haylin. "And I've overstayed my welcome."

Hay got out of bed, gripping his side, lurching forward so that the IV stand nearly toppled. Emily caught the IV and righted it, but no one was paying much attention to her.

"Franny, do not leave," Hay said. "Things changed. You were gone for two years."

He had the nerve to reproach her with Emily Flood standing right there. If that pretty roommate of Hay's spoke to her again, she couldn't be held accountable for her actions.

"That's right," Franny said. "I didn't get to go to school. I couldn't be your roommate."

199

She went to the door, past the dying man. The shroud was almost completely encircling him now, but he murmured his gratitude when Franny stopped to touch his forehead. She stayed until he had passed over; it was so brief, like a sigh. Then she went on, despite Hay calling out to her. She ran all the way to South Station, her heart thudding against her chest. Emily. His roommate. Well, what had she expected? She had sent him off. She had told him to go and not to look back.

On the train, Franny smoldered with fury and hurt. At Penn Station she cut a path through the crowd and walked home in the dark. That night she cried tears so black they stained the sheets. She didn't change out of the clothes she'd worn when she was beside Haylin in bed. They still carried his scent. In the morning, she went into the garden.

Jet spied her sister from the kitchen window. She went outside and they sat together on the back steps. Snow had begun to fall but the sisters remained where they were.

"He found someone else," Franny said.

"There will never be anyone else."

"Well there is. Her name is Emily. She's his roommate."

"Only because you told him to go."

"Either way, she's the one who has him." Oh, it was horrible. Franny was crying. She was mortified. She quickly buried her face in her hands. "I let him go and now he belongs to someone else. And it's better for him that way."

"You can love him if you want to," Jet told Franny. The scar on her face bloomed in cold weather, turning the color of violets. "To hell with the curse. You don't have to make the same mistakes all the other women in our family have made."

"Why would I be any different?"

"You'll be the one to outsmart it."

"Unlikely," Franny said sadly.

"You will," Jet insisted. She didn't have to have the sight to know this. "Wait and see."

April Owens arrived on a Greyhound bus on a bright spring day in 1966 and walked to the Village from Forty-Second Street. It had been nearly six years since she had first met Franny and Jet and Vincent, but somehow it had felt as though she'd known them forever, so it made perfect sense to show up in New York without bothering to write or call. It was a long walk, but she didn't mind. All she wanted was to be free. Every mortal being was entitled to that right, no matter what her history might be. April was still fierce, but now she was most fierce in her devotion to her daughter. She didn't mind when Regina, only five and usually very good-humored, grew tired and cranky by the time they passed Pennsylvania Station, and had to be carried the rest of the way.

Regina was dressed in a T-shirt and a gauzy little skirt that she referred to as her princess outfit, but now she was an exhausted princess. She fell asleep in her mother's arms, heavier in sleep than she had been while awake. No matter. April kept going. She was wearing jeans and a fringed vest and her long pale hair was in braids, bound with beaded leather ties. She stood out in midtown among a sea of suits and proper dresses, but as she headed downtown she looked like anybody else on the street. She found number 44 Greenwich and rang the bell. She liked what she saw. The tilted house, the trees in the garden, the shop that sold enchantments, the school yard next door where scores of children were out at play.

When Jet threw open the door, she embraced April and her daughter, who resembled Franny, though her hair was as black as Jet's and Vincent's. For the first time since Levi's death Jet felt a bit of happiness when she looked into the face of the little girl. She wasn't even grumpy to have been woken and introduced to a stranger. She was very serious and she shook Jet's hand and said, "Very nice to meet you."

"I can't believe how big Regina is! And how polite! Are you sure she's an Owens?"

"She most assuredly is."

"You should have told us you were coming for a visit. I would have prepared something special. Now the house is a mess."

"That's immaterial. And this is not a visit, dear Jet. It's a jailbreak." April had an overstuffed backpack and a duffel bag, both of which she deposited on the couch in the parlor. There were dark circles under her eyes and she appeared drained. "My parents want to take Reggie from me. They want her to grow up on Beacon Hill and go to a private school in a chauffeured car. It's everything I don't want for her. Everything I wanted to escape from. They said they'd fight me in court if they had to. I think they've already retained a lawyer. So I'm headed to California. Let them try to find me there. This is just a pit stop. I hope you don't mind."

"You know you can stay as long as you'd like."

Franny came in from the garden with a basket of herbs she had just picked, comfrey, mint, and, though it was not as often needed these days due to the birth control pill, pennyroyal. City soot had veined the herbs' leaves black, so Franny always had to soak them in cold water and vinegar in the big kitchen sink. She stopped in her tracks when she saw the little girl.

Regina looked up at her and smiled. "You're the good witch," she said.

Franny laughed. She'd certainly never thought of herself that way, still she was charmed. "Have you ever heard of a tipsy cake?" she asked.

Regina shook her head no.

"Why, it's absolutely delicious. It's the most chocolaty chocolate you'll ever taste. I think I'll make you one."

Franny nodded a greeting when April came into the kitchen in search of Regina. She thought their cousin looked the worse for the wear, with her pale hair lifeless and her already slender frame now excessively thin. "We're just about to make a tipsy cake, but I'll leave out the rum," Franny said. "For Regina's sake. I must say, this is a surprise. But then that's your style, isn't it? Just show up out of nowhere."

"I won't impose, Franny. I just need a night. We're leaving for California tomorrow. I've got a ride on something called the Sorcerer's Apprentice, a van that goes cross-country."

The little girl shivered when California was mentioned. She was so sensitive she seemed a walking prediction, as if she had the sight times two.

"You don't think you'll like California?" Franny asked the child.

"Maybe. But I know what happens there."

"Which is?" Franny pressed.

"Well, people die," the little girl said.

"For goodness' sake," April said. "People die everywhere."

"You should avoid California," Franny told her cousin. "She

has a premonition. There are better places to raise your daughter."

"You sound like my mother. Say whatever you want. I've made up my mind. I've got my degree from MIT, despite my mother's protests. Biology. That's what I've been doing for the past four years. I have a friend at a geo lab in Palm Desert. I can work there and Regina can be safe for a while."

Jet came in to make tea. "Safe from what?"

April glanced over at Franny, who was studying the child. "You see it, don't you?"

Franny did. There was a halo around Regina that usually indicated a shortened life span. Such people seemed more alive when they were young, filled with light. She had never told a soul that Vincent had had the same halo around him when he was a baby, and perhaps this was why she'd always been so protective of him.

Regina sat cross-legged on the floor to play with Wren. "She's got gray eyes, Momma. Like us."

"Of course," Franny told the little girl. "That's because she's an Owens cat."

When it came down to it, Franny was sorry she and April always had quarreled. She wished she could console her cousin, but there was no way to skirt around some things. Not when they both had the sight.

"I want her to have a happy life, a free life," April said, resigned. "I'm going to do everything I can to see that she gets it. She'll find that in California. People are more open there. Not so quick to judge."

Jet had collected a pile of books for the child. "I really don't know what you two are talking about."

April turned to observe Jet. "You've lost the sight. Maybe that's for the best."

"I had no choice in the matter," Jet said. "My fate wasn't what I thought it would be."

"I know what that feels like," April said in a soft voice, just as the front door was falling open.

Vincent had arrived. Jet had telephoned and insisted he come to dinner. Hearing his cousins' voices he now knew why. He wandered in with his dog at his heels and bowed to April. "To what do we owe this visit?"

"Bad luck and the need to run away."

"It's always the same story," Vincent said with a grin. "Parent trouble."

"You know so much and yet so little," April remarked.

No one mentioned Vincent's involvement with William. Franny because she didn't think to do so, and Jet because she knew it would be painful news for April. She wanted this evening to be a happy time, and it was exactly that. Thankfully, April had never had the ability to get inside Vincent's head. Regina took to him, just as she had when she was a baby. After dinner, she begged him to read aloud from *Half Magic* by Edward Eager, her favorite book, and he obliged. Vincent thought the novel was advanced for her age, but Regina was not a typical child. She had taught herself to read, and always carried a book with her. Vincent was especially funny when he acted out the dialogue of a cat that was half real and could only half talk. Regina was soon enough in fits of bright laughter.

Vincent's dog was at his feet, his shadow, silent and dignified and more than a little mortified when Regina laid her cuddly stuffed bunny rabbit beside him.

"I call her Maggie," Regina said.

"Do you?" Vincent said, giving April a grin.

"What did you expect her to call it? Mrs. Rustler?" April teased.

"How did you know about that?" Vincent asked. Then he saw a look exchanged between April and Jet. "Does everyone know all the details of my life?"

"Not all," Jet said.

"Hardly anything," April assured him.

When the chocolate cake was ready they had it hot from the oven, served with mounds of vanilla ice cream.

"Am I allowed to have that?" Regina asked.

"Of course," Vincent told her. "Always remember," he whispered, "live a lot."

Regina ate most of her cake. "You can have the rest," she told Vincent, as she set to work on a drawing of Harry and Wren. In her rendering the two were best friends who held each other's paws.

Vincent was charmed by the child, but when he glanced at his watch he stood up. "I'm late," he said.

"For a very important date?" April said, blinking.

"Indeed," Vincent said. "I'm involved with someone."

"Don't tell me you actually care about someone?"

"We're not supposed to, are we?" Vincent joked.

"No," April said. "We're not."

Vincent grinned and kissed the little girl good-bye on the forehead, then went out with his dog, two shadows spilling into the night. "See you when I see you," he called over his shoulder.

"See you when I see you," Regina called back.

"He's still the same," April said.

"Not completely," Jet said. There was no need to go into details and hurt April any more than she already was.

"Vincent is Vincent, thank goodness," Franny said as she started in on the dishes.

April shook her head. She pulled her daughter onto her lap. "Will he ever grow up?"

"Yes," Jet said. "And we'll be sad when he does."

In the morning, the cousins were gone. Regina's drawing of a black dog and a black cat had been left on the kitchen table. Franny had it framed later that afternoon, and from then on she kept it in the parlor, and even years later, when she moved and left almost everything behind, she took it with her, bundled in brown paper and string.

PART FOUR

Elemental

*S*he saw Haylin walking down the path. At first she thought she had conjured him, and perhaps he was a ghostly image of himself, but no, it was Hay. He was so tall she spotted him right away, wearing the same denim jacket he'd had since he was fifteen. Franny sat on the rock, knees to chest. She was a mess and damned herself for being so. The last time she'd seen him, she'd caused a scene in the hospital. Now she vowed to be calm and collected. She had lost him, so her heart shouldn't be thudding against her chest. It was over, and she should be happy that he had been saved from throwing in his lot with an Owens woman.

She wore old sneakers and jeans and a black and white striped T-shirt she'd found in the ninety-nine-cent bin at the thrift store where they'd sold their mother's beautiful clothes. She hadn't even brushed her hair that morning.

Haylin spied her and waved, as if they'd seen each other only hours before. He came to sit beside her. "Don't tell me you've been waiting here all these years?" Franny laughed out loud. Hay smiled, pleased he could make her laugh. But his hurt made him say more. "I know you haven't been waiting for me. I've come here every time I'm home and you're never here. So I gave up on us."

Franny threw a hand over her mouth as if holding back a sob. Her eyes were rimmed with tears.

"Franny." He hadn't really wanted to hurt her.

"I'm not crying, if that's what you think," Franny responded, wiping her nose on her sleeve.

"I know that. Do you think I'm an idiot?" They both laughed then. "Don't answer that," Hay said with a grin.

He was attending Yale Medical School, Franny's father's alma mater. It made perfect sense that he would become a doctor. He had always wanted to do good in the world. And it made sense, too, when he revealed he'd placed distance between himself and his family.

"I don't go home anymore," he said, morose as he always was when thinking about his heritage. "It's like a fucking mausoleum with my father getting richer on the war, and my mother drinking so she won't go berserk because she's married to him."

"Where do you stay when you come to New York?" When Hay glanced away, Franny knew. "Oh." She could barely bring herself to say it. "With Emily."

"You remember her name," he said, surprised.

"Of course I do. Emily Flood, your roommate."

"You don't usually take note of people." He flushed when Franny threw him a deadly look. "Well, you don't!"

"Of course I took note of her, Haylin. How could I not?"

"Yeah," Hay said, feeling more like an idiot than ever.

"So where is she? I'm shocked that she lets you out of her sight. Maybe you'd better run on back to her."

"I don't understand why *you're* mad," Hay said, frustrated and unwilling to bear her anger. "*You're* the one who didn't want *me*."

"I had no choice! I had my brother and sister to see to. There was the accident to deal with. Or do you blame me for that?"

Franny stood up with the intention of leaving. When Hay took her arm, she glared at him. But he was looking at her the way he used to, when he was the only person in the world who really knew her.

"Don't go yet," he said.

"Why? You're with Emily."

"I am," Haylin said.

"And do you blame me for that, too?"

She was heartless. The Maid of Thorns.

Haylin shook his head. If only he would stop looking at her like that. So she took it further.

"Well I'm glad you're with her," Franny said. "You'll be happier than you would have ever been with me. She's normal!"

Lewis was perched above them, ever vigilant, upset they were arguing. Hay called the bird to him and the crow skimmed the air and came to perch on the rock. He gazed at Franny for too long, and just when it seemed he might say something that would change their path, he snapped out of it. "I should probably leave Lewis with you. I don't really have time for a pet."

"I've told you! He's not a pet! He comes and goes as he pleases. Isn't it clear? He's chosen you, Haylin. I don't blame him."

"Well, he can't stay with me anymore. Emily has a fear of birds."

"What if she does?"

"We live together in New Haven."

"Then what are you doing here?"

He looked at her, but she simply stared. She wanted him to say it.

"I'm here for you."

"But you live with her!"

"What should I have done? You never answered any of my letters. I thought you hated me because we were together when the accident happened."

"What's done is done. I don't think either one of us should come here anymore." He had made his choice, Franny thought. Emily. And there was the curse to protect him from. She refused to be responsible for any of his sorrow. "We were young and now we're not."

Haylin laughed a short unhappy laugh. His shoulders were hunched, the way they were when he sulked. "We're twenty-four, Franny, for Christ's sake. We have our whole lives to live. You're going to let me marry her? Is that what you want?"

"Apparently that's what you want."

When she walked away she felt as though she were falling. It seemed as if the world was a snow globe that had been shaken, and where she'd ended up had nothing to do with where she had begun.

When she reached the zoo, Franny stopped and sat on a bench, with Lewis perched beside her.

"I suppose you're mine," she told him. In response he did the oddest thing; he sat on her lap and let her pet him, something he'd never done before. He made a funny clacking noise, then took to the sky. Was he letting her know that if she ran she could catch up with Haylin? She knew the paths he took to cut across the park. But his life was set out before him, and he would be better off without her, and because she still had no idea how to break the curse, Franny walked home, four miles as the crow flies. When she reached 44 Greenwich Avenue she went inside alone, and only the crow knew that it was possible for a woman to claim to have no heart at all and still cry as though her heart would break.

Vincent and William flew to San Francisco, a city cast out of a dream. It was the Summer of Love. Free love and a free society had called a hundred thousand people to the city. There were indeed flowers everywhere, and along the bay the scent of patchouli and chocolate infused the air. Strangers embraced them as they walked down Haight Street. In Manhattan, theirs was a secret society, but here the doors were open to everyone. They camped out in Golden Gate Park surrounded by eucalyptus trees, and when a pale mossy rain began, they raced for the shelter of the public library. There in the stacks they met a couple who invited them to their apartment in the Mission, where they spent the night on a quilt on the floor, entwined and madly in love. It was true, Vincent was in love, despite the warnings, despite the world, despite himself. This was what he had seen in the mirror in his aunt's greenhouse, the image that had terrified him because from that moment he knew what he wanted, a life he thought he'd never have, and now, at last, he did.

In the morning they were given a breakfast of toast and honey-butter and orange tea.

"Are you always so kind to strangers?" William asked their hosts.

"You're not strangers," they were told, and it seemed in this city, at this time, they were embraced by those who saw them for who they were.

They rode around in a convertible Mustang, borrowed from

a cousin of William's who lived in Mill Valley. The cousin had informed them California was not like New York; they did not need to keep themselves hidden. They had the nerve to kiss on a dock with a view of Alcatraz and the bright blue water of the bay. They went to clubs in the Castro District where they felt completely at home dancing until they were exhausted. They drove along in the pale light of dawn in an ecstasy of freedom. Magic was everywhere. They spied people wearing feathers and bells on Mount Tamalpais, and in cafés in the North End, and all along Divisadero Street, where young girls handed out magical, ceramic talismans in the shape of a triangle or an eye. *Blessed be*, they called, and indeed Vincent and William felt blessed to be in California.

In Monterey they slept in a cabin overlooking the ocean and made love in the blaze of the pure yellow sunlight and felt something dark lift away from them. They had been hidden, casting a clouding spell wherever they went in New York, but they would do that no longer. It was the end of secrets, the end of lies, the beginning of everything they did not yet know. Something was about to happen; they could both feel it. Vincent thought about the black mirror in his aunt's greenhouse. There had been so many images, but now as his future became his present he recognized the visions he had seen.

William was acquainted with a publicist working for the record producer Lou Adler, who had come up with the idea for the Monterey Pop Festival, held on the weekend of June 16, 1967, inviting the Grateful Dead and Janis Joplin and the Who and Jimi Hendrix and Otis Redding and many others for three days of music, and love, and peace. Somehow William had talked his friend into letting Vincent perform. When Vincent heard the news he hesitated; he was a street singer, not meant for large venues, but in the end he was talked into it and William slipped a roadie ten bucks so Vincent could use a guitar. He wore black and took off his boots and socks. William placed a wreath of leaves on his head just before he went onto the stage.

It was an odd hour, dusk, a dim, murky time no one wanted to claim on the stage. So there he was. A nobody. Vincent and a borrowed guitar. No one knew him; no one cared. He seemed calm if you didn't look too closely at his beautiful, worried face. When he began people had their backs to him, but the microphone was turned up suddenly, by William's hand no doubt, and Vincent's soaring voice drifted over the crowd, as though it were an enchantment. A quiet fell as darkness sifted down from the trees.

When I was yours, who was I then?
I heard your voice, but that was when
I had a heart, I had a harp, I had your love, the knife was sharp.
I walked at night, I longed to fight.
Isn't that what betrayed is? Isn't that when fear exists?
When you hide who you are and you take it too far, when you're
*   a man.*

I called on angels when I faced a wall,
but just like Joshua's, it began to fall.
I cried blood-red tears, despite my fears.
Isn't that what betrayal is? Isn't that when fear exists?
I walked at night, I had the sight and still I lost despite the call.
I walk at night, without a fight.
I've tried before, I've locked the door, I've done it wrong, I've
*   done it right.*

Afterward, there was a moment of silence, then a huge wave of applause. William took Vincent's arm as they ducked behind the stage.

"Man, you cast a spell," one of the promoters said to him, but Vincent paid no attention. He was looking beyond those crowding around him. A little girl with gray eyes was standing in the yellow grass. Hadn't he seen her before?

He left the business of saying good-bye to William, and went over to the child. "I know you," he said.

"I know you back," she piped up.

She was Regina Owens, now six years old. Her mother, April, was behind her, her pale hair so long she could sit on it if she pleased, her skin tanned from her time in the desert. She looked like a creature that couldn't possibly be part of the mortal world.

"My dear cousin," she said, embracing Vincent. William, never shy, came to introduce himself. April looked at him, then at Vincent. She smiled slyly. "I see who you are now that you're a man. Let me guess. This was the date for which you couldn't be late. You certainly had me fooled."

"I thought no one could do that," Vincent remarked.

"You always blocked me," April said with a measure of sadness.

"You're related," William said, wanting to break the tension between these two. "I can tell by the eyes."

"Distantly," Vincent said as he accepted some daisies Regina had picked. "Several times removed. Probably by hacksaw." He grinned and April grinned back at him.

"No, by carving knife," she said prettily. "That's the way an Owens removes you from his life."

April and Regina were currently living in Santa Cruz in a

small wood-shingled cottage that was provided when April found employment as the gardener and housekeeper on the estate of the owners, wealthy San Franciscans who wanted to be closer to nature, but hardly ever got out of the city. She planned to return to the desert to attend to her research with spiders, but for now Regina needed school and the companionship of other children. "Stay with us tonight," April insisted. "We so rarely have interesting guests. You're here, we're here. Clearly it was meant to be."

Regina had taken hold of Vincent's hand. Because of the weight and heat of her small hand in his, he didn't say no. April had hitchhiked to Monterey with her daughter, so they drove back in the borrowed Mustang, top down. While they sped along the curving highway William slipped a recording he'd made into the tape player.

"You made a tape?" Vincent asked William.

"I wanted to save the moment. And maybe send it to a radio station."

"No," Vincent said. He knew where fame would lead him, to the darkest side of himself. It was something he didn't need.

April leaned forward, her arms on the edges of their seats. She held her hair back from her face with one hand, intent on the song.

Saul went down to the oldest road to meet the Witch of Endor.
She spoke, but he couldn't hear. She saw his fate, but he had no fear.
No predictions could make him stay. He was told the truth, but still
he strayed.
Isn't that what love makes you do? Go on trying even when you're
through.

Go on even when you're made of ash, when there's nothing left inside
      you but the past?

When I was yours, who was I then?
I heard your voice, but that was when
I had a heart, I had a harp, I had your love, the knife was sharp.
I walked at night, I cared with all my might.
Isn't that what betrayal is? Isn't that when fear exists?
Isn't that what happens when you hide who you are, even love can't
      take you that far, when you were a man.

"Who was the Witch of Endor?" Regina asked her mother.

"A wise old woman who could foretell the future."

"Could she really see a person's fate?"

"Fate is what you make of it, my aunt always says. You can make the best of it or you can let it make the best of you. My cousin knows that. He loved to get the best of other people."

William was driving and therefore didn't see the worried expression cross Vincent's face. There was something in April's knowing tone that made him uncomfortable.

In Santa Cruz they had dinner outside, at a weathered wooden table set beneath a trellis teaming with flowering vines. The pale blooms gave off the bittersweet scent of almonds, reminding Vincent of their aunt's greenhouse.

"It's so familiar," he said.

"Oleander," April responded. "It's poisonous."

She had been inspired by the greenhouse in Isabelle's garden and grew herbs that weren't native to California.

As a girl, April couldn't wait to leave home, yet now she favored wildflowers that could be found when traipsing through the woods in Massachusetts. Sunflower, wild bean, wintergreen. Blue flag, used for skin conditions. Blue vervain, for headache and fever, cardinal plant, appreciated by the native people as a love charm. Skullcap, for nervous conditions. She asked Regina to give William a tour of the greenhouse so he could see for himself. Vincent stood, about to join in, but April caught his eye and gestured for him to stay. "Don't leave, Cousin, it's been too long since we've spoken." He felt he had no choice but to sink back into his chair, though he had a feeling of dread. April was a wild card. You never knew what she'd do or say. Now, for instance, as soon as William and Regina were out of earshot she turned to Vincent. "You know, don't you?"

"April, don't play games." Vincent stretched out his long legs. He was all in black and he'd kicked off his shoes. He realized that he felt more at home singing in a subway station or in the park on a summer evening than he had in Monterey. All that time of playing around with *The Magus*, thinking he sought fame, and now it was the last thing he wanted. He was rattled by the festival, and had little patience for April's mockery. "Your charm was always telling it like it is."

"Well, you always knew what your charm was, especially that summer when you were fourteen and fucking everything in sight. Of course, this was before you knew who you preferred." April gazed searchingly after William, who was bending down to fit his tall frame through the pitched doorway of the greenhouse. He was so courteous, listening to Regina's ongoing lecture concerning the uses of poisonous plants. Vincent, too, watched William, intent on his form. He had a masculine grace that was enchanting.

"I don't care what you think about me and William, so if you want to make nasty remarks, go right ahead. It will feel like old times."

April reached over and took Vincent's hand. "Tell me you don't remember."

He looked at her blankly. Family was always such a bother.

April raised an eyebrow, disappointed in his lack of recollection. "I came to your room. Into your bed."

It had happened on a night when there was a rainstorm, when the sparrows took shelter in the branches of lilacs below the window. They'd told no one, and had never even spoken of it afterward.

"Oh, that," Vincent said. He remembered now. Of course. A quick crazy fuck with their hands over each other's mouths so no one would hear the heat of their sudden passion. Their aunt had given him a disquieting look in the morning, but his sisters, prescient as they were, seemed to have no idea of what had gone on.

"We *are* extremely distant from each other in the family tree," April went on. "Third cousins twice removed. It's fine genetically." She studied his puzzled face and laughed. He had no idea what she was getting at. "You really don't know! And you're supposed to be the one with the sight. It just goes to show, people see what they want to see."

"April," Vincent said. "Don't fuck around with me."

"I think it was quite the opposite. You were the one fucking with me, darling."

Annoyed, Vincent stood, making haste to follow William, but before he could April reached for him. Her tentative touch made him stay. She was emotionally raw, something he hadn't thought was in her nature. Although she had been so vulnerable when she'd come to visit them after the summer, running off before they'd spoken.

"All right, then," April said. "Perhaps you are clueless. Well here it is, my dear. She's yours."

Bewildered, Vincent watched the little girl in the greenhouse. She was gathering purple echinacea flowers for William. They had grown almost wild in Aunt Isabelle's garden and had been used throughout time as a cure for scarlet fever, malaria, diphtheria, blood poisoning, and the common cold. Regina laughed as William accepted her gift, then bowed.

"Can't you see yourself in her?" April asked.

"You said her father drowned."

"What was I to say? That I fucked a distant cousin who was fourteen and too stupid to use a condom? And now here she is. An amazing child we share. A double bloodline. The problem is, I think she may live twice as fast. I saw it when she was an infant, and I think Franny did as well when I came to visit."

"Franny?" He had a flicker of panic.

"Don't worry. She doesn't know you're the father. That spell we placed on her in the library so she wouldn't know what we were doing lasted. But she knows the fate. Something our girl has inherited. From both of us, really. A life line that is regrettably short."

Vincent was stricken. "You know that for a fact?"

April dissolved into tears. "I'm giving her the best life I can. She'll grow up, I know that much, and really, who knows how much time anyone has?"

"What will you tell her?" Vincent leaned forward into the last rays of yellow light. "About me?"

"I'll tell her you're a very special cousin."

Vincent nodded. His grief was in his expression.

"It's too late to have regrets," April said. "Maybe I should have told you, but you were hardly interested in such things. You were a boy. Life is a mess, that's what Isabelle told me when I decided to have the child, but all we can do is live it. She was right. I'm glad at last you fell in love."

"You know that's impossible for us," Vincent reminded her.

"Bullshit," April said, for she had been in love with him that summer. Her first and only true love as a matter of fact, and nothing horrible had happened. Instead, something wonderful had occurred. Their daughter. "We just have to fight harder for what we want."

William and Regina approached the patio, holding hands and singing their own version of "I Walk at Night." William carried the bunch of cut flowers with their purple-red blooms.

I had a garden, I had a dove, I had a tree, I had your love.

"Let's bring out dessert," April said. "If I'd known you were coming, I would have made Auntie Isabelle's tipsy chocolate cake. Instead we have a raspberry mousse."

"I thought you were making macarons," Regina said, for those were her favorites. "Vincent and William would love them."

"Not enough time," April informed the sad little girl.

"Someday we'll have macarons from Paris," Vincent said to cheer her. "But tonight we're having a moose for dessert and I want the antlers."

Regina laughed as she climbed onto his lap, a child who was completely comfortable with who she was. "Sing to me," she said. "I want to remember you when you're gone."

Vincent smoothed down her hair. It was black, like his, straight as sticks, and her smile could undo a person, at least it had done so to him.

"I'll send you a tape," William assured the little girl. "Or even better, I'll have it made into a record."

Regina clapped her hands happily and said, "Then I'll play it every night when we get a record player."

"We'll send you one of those as well," Vincent told her.

"Do me a favor," April said. She had reappeared with their dessert and some coffees and had overheard his promises. She knew Vincent as well as anyone, and she knew how easy it was for him to forget something that was terribly important to someone else. The smell of the dessert's berries and sugar was so intoxicating bees gathered round and April had to bat them away with her hand. "Don't make promises you can't keep."

Jet took the bus without telling anyone. It was the first of March, Levi's birthday, and the forsythia was blooming. She wore her black dress and tied a scarf over her head. She had her purse and nothing else. She had discussed coming here with Rafael when he'd surprised her by reserving a room at the Plaza Hotel for a night. When the elevator opened at the seventh floor Jet realized he had asked for room 708, and she said she would prefer if they could have a different room, one that was their own.

"What we are is separate from Levi," she'd said. "Even if I go to visit his grave, it has nothing to do with us."

When she got off the bus she walked to the west, stopping in a field to collect some daffodils that were the color of new butter. She tied a bunch together with blue string. The sun was pale and the air was cool and fresh. It was two miles out to the cemetery and she walked quickly, ducking behind greenery each time a car passed by.

At the cemetery gates a waiting hearse idled, which gave her pause, but the funeral that had taken place had ended, and there was no one in sight when the hearse pulled away. There were many surnames she recognized in the older section of the cemetery: Porter and Coker and Putnam and Shepard. People had been called Wrestling and Valor and Worth and Redeemed, for it was those virtues their families hoped they would possess. When Jet neared the graves of the Willard family she came upon an angel marking the resting place of a baby named Resign Willard, who had lived for one day.

Levi's grave was in a newer section beyond a huge field of grass. She set the daffodils in front of the simple stone that had been placed in the ground. He had been eighteen. Barely a life. Suddenly exhausted, Jet lay down on the grass beside him. She still wore the ring Levi had given her, even though the moment when he told her to close her eyes so he could give her this birthday gift felt so far away. They had likely been together twenty times, an entire world created in just days. She imagined Levi next to her, in his black jacket. Many of the Hathorne family had been buried nearby. They were her family as well as his, a fact that was terribly uncomfortable. No wonder the Owens family had kept this secret. No wonder so many had fled Massachusetts. Even the witch-hunter's own relation Nathaniel Hawthorne had placed the *w* in his name to distance himself from his cruel ancestor, his writing driven by his desire to make amends for all the evil his great-great-grandfather had done in the world.

Not far from here was a tree where the witches were hung, sentenced by the man who had been the father of Maria Owens's child. In 1692, he had been appointed chief examiner of the witch trials. He had sentenced and overseen the hanging of nineteen innocent people, convincing the court to accept spectral evidence, which meant what was said was gospel without any proof. Women could turn into crows. A man could be the devil's apprentice. His cruelty was legendary. He refused to hear recanted testimonies, concluding those accused were guilty before they were tried, badgering the accused, causing them to be murdered, thereby setting upon himself, and all that followed him, the curse they now shared. After a conviction, property could be taken and distributed as the judges saw fit. Hathorne had married a Quaker girl of fourteen years of age, built a mansion, and fathered six children. He did as he wished to Maria Owens, who was without parents or guardians, using her as he saw fit, and in her youth and inexperience she believed she loved him, but it was as a crow loved his cage.

Jet shaded her eyes and looked into the sky. She saw that a man was watching her and quickly scrambled to her feet. Her heart was pounding. She was so close to the hanging tree she felt dizzy. She had the blood of both accuser and accused running through her. The man stayed where he was. He was carrying a bunch of daffodils. They stared at each other, the only people in the cemetery. Before the Reverend could come any closer and chastise her and call out that she was a witch and a demon and had caused his son to die, Jet took off running. She ran so fast all she could hear was the blood pounding in her ears. She wanted to be dead and be beside Levi, but she was alive and so she ran. She didn't stop in town, she didn't wait for a bus. Instead, she found her way to Magnolia Street.

She knocked on Aunt Isabelle's door. The light was on, but no one answered, so she went round to the garden. Isabelle was in the greenhouse beginning her seedlings. She didn't seem the least surprised to see her niece on the threshold.

"You could have come here if you wanted daffodils," she said when Jet walked in.

True enough, the yard was thick with them at this time of year, a sea of yellow. Jet saw that the garden was far ahead of the rest of town. The wisteria was already blooming; the climbing roses were budding.

"Looks as though you saw a ghost," Isabelle said.

"I saw Levi's father."

"That Reverend doesn't own the cemetery and he doesn't own this town. You have your right to Levi's memory."

"I want to get rid of it," Jet said.

"Do you?"

"I want to have no memory of him. Please," she said to her aunt. "Please do this for me. I know you can do things like that. And I can pay you." Jet was in tears.

"Jet, if I did that, then you wouldn't be you."

"Good! I don't want to be me." Jet had come to sit on a wooden bench, her hands folded on her lap. "I let Franny think I drank courage."

"But you did," her aunt said.

Isabelle signaled for Jet to follow her back to the house. There was a woman pacing on the porch. She stopped when she saw Isabelle. "Oh, Miss Owens," she said. "If you could spare me a moment."

"You'll have to wait," Isabelle told her. "Just sit down and be quiet."

Jet followed her aunt into the kitchen, where Isabelle put up the kettle.

"I don't want to keep that woman waiting," Jet said.

"She's waited twenty years for her husband to love her, she can wait another twenty minutes."

When the tea was brewed they both sat down and had a cup.

"Taste familiar?" Isabelle asked.

"It's what I had before."

"You asked for caution but I gave you this. It was what you needed. And it's what you have."

Jet laughed and drank the rest of the tea. Was this what courage felt like?

"Once you forget a piece of your past, you forget it all. That's not what you want, dear."

Jet went to embrace her aunt, who was surprised by the unexpected show of emotion.

"I have a client," Isabelle said. "Time for you to go."

"Will her husband love her?"

"Would you want love you had to buy?" Isabelle asked.

Isabelle then called Charlie Merrill, who came in his old station wagon to give Jet a ride to the bus station. As they drove, Jet asked if he would take a detour. The cemetery gates were closed, but Charlie knew the trick to picking the lock with a screwdriver. He pushed the gates open for her and waited in his car, happy to listen to a basketball game on the radio.

It was nearly dark and Jet was glad she knew the way. She cut across the grass, luminous in the fading light. She was entitled to her memory and to this place.

Here lies the life I might have had once upon a time, the man I might have loved for all my life, the days we might have had.

Jet went to his headstone and knelt down. There were two bunches of daffodils. The Reverend hadn't thrown hers away.

She lay down beside him once more, and this time she told him she would never forgive the world for taking him, but she had no choice but to go on. She was alive. She walked back in the pitch dark, glad she could see Charlie's headlights cutting through the night.

"Everything all right?" Charlie Merrill said when she climbed back into the car. It smelled like cough drops and flannel.

Jet nodded. "I think I'll go to the bus station now."

He drove her there in time for the last bus. When he pulled over, Charlie handed her a paper bag. Inside was a small thermos and something wrapped in wax paper. "Your aunt sent along some tea. I think there's some cake in there, too."

Jet threw her arms around the old man, utterly surprising him.

"She's a good lady," he said, as if explaining her aunt to her. "Anyone who knows her knows that."

He waited, his car idling, until the bus pulled away. It was likely Isabelle told him to do so, and he always did as she asked. His two boys had been heroin addicts; one was in prison by the time he was twenty, the other went half-mad with drugs. She'd fixed them both with one of those mixtures of hers. Afterward there'd been a knock at their door even though everyone knew Isabelle Owens didn't call on people. She came to see the boys every night for two weeks, watching over his grown sons as if they were babies until they were well again. She charged him nothing for doing so. Now when his sons saw her on the street, or when they were working on her house and she looked in on them, the boys would elbow each other and stand up straight. They were still afraid of her even though she'd sat by their beds and fed them soup with a teaspoon.

So Charlie stayed and waved as Jet got on the bus, and Jet

waved back, and when she realized she was starving and hadn't eaten all day, she was glad to have the chocolate cake her aunt had sent along, and grateful to have been convinced that forgetting her loss would be worse than the loss itself. So she sat there remembering everything, from the beginning of her life to today. By the time she recalled the pale yellow of the daffodils she'd picked that morning, she had reached New York.

The announcement was in *The New York Times* on March 21, Franny's birthday, a day that had always proved inauspicious. It was the unluckiest day of the year, but it was also the day to celebrate Ostara, the spring equinox, when eggshells must be scattered in a garden, for new growth and transformation is possible, even for those who consider themselves to be unfortunate.

Perhaps publishing on this date was an oversight; but whether intended or not, it had the effect of injuring Franny more fully than she already was. Vincent tried to hide it, he threw the *Times* in the trash, but Franny found it when she took the garbage out to the bin. It was opened to the engagement announcements, and there it was in her hands, an arrow to wound her.

> *Haylin Walker, son of Ethan and Lila Walker of New York and Palm Beach, is engaged to Emily Flood, daughter of Melville and Margot Flood of Hartford, Connecticut. The groom is a graduate of Harvard College and Yale Medical School. The bride, a graduate of Miss Porter's School and Radcliffe College, is currently working at Talbots in Farmington, Connecticut.*

Franny couldn't read on. Not about how the groom's father was the president of a bank and how his wife was on the board of the opera, not about how the bride-to-be's parents were both doctors who raised boxer dogs that showed at the Westminster Kennel Club. Dating someone else was one thing, but this was marriage, this was the end of hope that it might ever be different between them.

Franny burned the newspaper in the fireplace. The smoke was gray and gave off the bitter scent of sulfur. Afterward, she propped open the windows, and yet her eyes continued to tear.

When Vincent came into the room there was still a gritty mist hanging in the air.

"Hay's engaged," Franny told her brother. "You shouldn't have tried to hide it from me."

"You should ignore it, Franny. How many years did you think he would wait for you? Ten? Twenty?"

"Shouldn't he have waited?"

"Not when you told him to go away. People believe you when you say things like that. You never told him you loved him, did you?" Vincent held up his hands. "Do as you please."

After he went upstairs, she did exactly that.

She phoned Haylin's parents' number, which she had memorized when she was ten years old. When a housekeeper she didn't recognize picked up, Franny said she was calling about the engagement party. The housekeeper assumed she was a guest invited to the celebration that evening. Yes, yes, Franny said. What was the time? She had forgotten.

She wore her funeral dress, for her other clothes were all too casual. She slipped on a pair of her mother's old stiletto heels bought in Paris. They were red, which made Franny feel her kinship with her mother anew.

The sky was a mottled pink and gray when she took a cab to Park and Seventy-Fourth Street. Her chest hurt when the cab pulled up at the Walkers' address. Their apartment took up an entire floor. Tonight it glowed like a firefly. Franny went inside the building, following an older couple and taking the elevator with them so she might be considered a member of their party. "Such an exciting occasion," the woman said to Franny.

"Yes," Franny murmured in response. She had worn her brilliant hair twisted up so as not to call attention to herself, but she noticed the man staring at her shoes. Her mother's red high heels. She kept her eyes downcast.

"And to think Ethan always feared his son would be a failure," the woman went on. She was older but wore a Mary Quant miniskirt, along with a silk blouse and a long rope of pearls. The elevator opened directly into the apartment, and when it did Franny felt as though she were dropping back through time.

The party was crowded with guests, but otherwise it seemed exactly as it had when they were in grade school and Haylin had first brought her home, only after she had made a solemn promise not to tell anyone how he lived. It was after they had met in the lunchroom, when she had given him half of her tomato sandwich and he had eaten it without complaint, though it lacked salt and mayonnaise. The decor hadn't changed since that time; the same pale pearly wool carpets, silk wall coverings, persimmon-colored sofas. Someone offered to take her coat.

"Oh, no thank you," Franny said. "I'm cold."

Indeed, she was shivering. She was out of place with or without her coat; nothing she had on seemed appropriate for this gathering. The women were in jewel-toned cocktail dresses, the men in well-tailored suits. Franny stayed on the edge of the huge formal parlor, where glasses of champagne were offered and hors d'oeuvres were served on polished trays. She thought she spied Emily through the crush, but there were so many tall, pretty young blond women she couldn't be sure. There was a table littered with silver gifts. Platters, serving trays, candle-sticks. Due to Franny's presence, many of the smaller silver pieces tarnished and turned black. She walked away from the table, embarrassed by what witchery could do. She avoided the other guests, but she couldn't hide from Haylin, who came up behind her and put a hand on the small of her back. She felt the heat of his touch through her coat. She tried to catch her breath.

"I couldn't send you an invitation," he said. "You never told me where you lived."

He was in an expensive suit, his hair cut short. She didn't think she'd ever seen him in a suit before. But it was still him, her dearest friend, no matter what he wore, no matter whom he had promised to marry.

There were spots of color on Franny's cheeks and her hair had begun to unwind. She wanted to say, *Run away with me. Now I know nothing else matters. I don't care if we come to ruin.*

In her black coat with her shining red hair, she was impossi-ble to miss. From across the room, Haylin's father spied her. He glared and gestured for his son to get rid of her.

"Let's step outside." Haylin led her to the elevator. He pushed the button for Lobby, but halfway down he stopped the elevator's descent and drew Franny to him. In an unexpected show of intimacy he put his mouth against hers. It was so fast and intense nothing could stop what happened next. It didn't matter where they were; it didn't even take courage to do this. It was fate and they didn't try to fight against it. Franny threw herself at him and Haylin didn't stop her or himself, although by now Emily Flood was wondering where he'd gone, worrying because she'd seen a tall pale woman with red hair. She still had nightmares about Franny, for after Franny's visit to the hospital, it had taken Emily months to win back Haylin's affections. *Don't you see?* she had told him. *She's never coming back to you. She doesn't care or she would have come to Cambridge with you.*

What Emily Flood had feared had come to pass. It all happened too fast and then they realized where they were and what they had done. Haylin backed away, pulling up his pants like a fool, pained by his own actions. He was not a disloyal man, yet he had just betrayed his fiancée. "I'm getting married," he said, shaking his head as if puzzled by his own statement.

"I know. I read about it in *The New York Times*." Franny tilted her chin up, ready to be hurt by whatever he would next say. She felt this was her last chance, and she was taking it.

"I have to marry her," Hay told her.

"Do you hear yourself? *Have to?*"

Haylin groaned and said, "You always do this to me. You make me think I have a chance."

The elevator alarm went off. Haylin did his best to stop it, but in the end he had to punch the up button for the sirens to subside. The elevator resumed, climbing back to the seventeenth floor. When the doors opened, Ethan Walker was there. Both Haylin and Franny blinked and looked guilty.

"I thought I made myself clear," Haylin's father said. "Get rid of her."

Mr. Walker was utterly impossible to see into, closed as a

locked vault. Franny, however, was completely transparent at this moment, a woman in love who had just been fucked in the elevator and clearly didn't give a damn about anyone else's feelings, certainly not those of the bride-to-be, who had gone off to lock herself in the bathroom to weep, terrified she had already lost Hay before he was hers.

"Don't make an ass out of yourself," Walker said to his son. "She dumped you and she'll do it again. Do the right thing for once in your life."

Franny saw the expression set on Hay's face. When his father left them, she tugged on Hay's sleeve. "Don't listen to him. You never have before."

Haylin looked at Franny. "It's not about him, Franny. You know I don't care about my father's opinion. But all those years! You should have contacted me."

"I didn't want to ruin your life," Franny explained.

Hay laughed bitterly. "But now you do?"

Franny recoiled, stung. "Is that what I'm doing?"

Hay appraised her coolly and she could see how she'd hurt him. "I don't know, Franny. You tell me. Because I'm not sure I want my life ruined." He shook his head, his confusion evident. "I keep thinking about when I was drowning and you didn't come in after me. And when we were going to school together, and you didn't come with me."

"But you didn't drown! And you did fine without me at school! But you resent me for everything. I see I shouldn't have come."

Franny hastened into the elevator, but Hay threw his arm across the door, making certain it wouldn't close. "I couldn't go through losing you again," he said. "It killed me. It took me years to get over you."

"But you did get over me. *You* found someone else. *I* didn't."

"Tell me you won't walk away again and I'll call the whole thing off."

Franny took a step back, startled by his raw emotion.

"Tell me," he demanded. "And I'll do anything. I'll hurt her if I have to."

That was when Franny saw Emily. She had come to search for Hay and was watching them from the parlor. Franny lost her voice then, and felt the courage drain from her body. Who did she think she was to cause another woman such grief? Perhaps Emily was Haylin's fate and Franny would only be interfering in what was meant to be.

"You still can't make a promise to me," Haylin said, and in that moment he let the elevator go.

On the street Franny hailed a cab. She rode along past the gates into the park she and Haylin used to walk through. Love had to happen without any certainty, the ultimate leap of faith. But Haylin now stood beside Emily Flood while Franny was headed downtown, weeping as she looked out at the world she had once known.

Once a month Jet went to Massachusetts. She told no one in her family, but they knew. Sometimes Franny packed her a lunch and left it on the kitchen table. A cucumber sandwich, some cookies, a green apple. Vincent often left out cash for the bus. She was grateful, but she never discussed her plans with them. She simply went early on the last Sunday morning of the month. When she got to town, she took the local taxi to the cemetery, and she always brought daffodils no matter the season. She sometimes stopped at the local grocery that sold flowers. Everyone knew who she was but treated her politely all the same. In the spring she walked to the cemetery, and she picked her own flowers, the ones that grew in the fields that were the color of butter.

Isabelle did not consider it rude that Jet didn't stop in to see her, although once or twice she had spied her niece walking through town. One time in particular she'd happened to be going to the library when she noticed Jet standing in front of the Willards' house. Maybe it was a good sign or maybe it wasn't. Only time would tell. The Willard home was a white house with green shutters, more than two hundred years old, with a huge garden that had never regained its former glory once the Reverend had cast down salt on the day when April Owens blundered in, aiming to pick some of his pie-plate-size roses. Now the rosebushes were bare and the leaves curled up. The only things that grew here were daffodils, and Jet was surprised to see that there were hundreds of them.

There was an apple tree that Levi had told her about. He'd said he loved to climb the tree and pick crisp McIntosh apples, but now the bark of the tree was leathery and black, the boughs were twisted and bare. It hadn't borne fruit for years.

Jet was leaning on the white fence looking up at the second-floor window where Levi's room had been when the Reverend came out. He was putting out the trash, but he saw her and stopped. They looked at each other in the fading light.

"I'd like to see his room," Jet said.

The Reverend no longer attended to any services. He didn't attend to anything. He no longer watered or weeded his garden. The gutters on the house were sagging, and the roof needed work. There were two rocking chairs on the porch he never sat in. He didn't want neighbors passing by to greet him or wish him well or ask him how he was faring. He looked at the Owens girl with the dark hair and her serious pale face with the scar on her cheek and then he signaled to her. He didn't know what he was thinking or if he was thinking at all, but he watched her come into the yard and up the porch steps.

"I appreciate it," she said. "Thank you."

She followed the Reverend into the house and up the stairs. The carpeting was beige and the walls were white, but yellowing. There was the scent of mothballs and of coffee that had recently been brewed. No lights were turned on. The Reverend didn't like to spend the money on electricity bills, plus he could see just fine until it was pitch dark. After dark he went to bed. Or he sat by his window, looking into the yard as if he could see back through time into the past. His wife had died much too young, of cancer, and maybe that was when everything started to go wrong. He was strict with his son, and he feared bad luck, and then it seemed he had brought it upon himself, and upon everyone near him.

"Watch your step," he found himself saying, for the stairs were steep.

Once inside, the Reverend switched on a lamp. Jet had wanted to see Levi's room ever since they'd met. Whenever they sat in the park he would describe it in the greatest of detail. The blue bedspread, the trophies he'd won on the swim team, photographs of his mother and father on a picnic out by the lake. The wallpaper was blue and white stripes, the rug was tweed. Jet stood in the doorway now. If she closed her eyes she could see him sitting on the bed, grinning at her, a book of poems in hand. Her eyes were brimming and hot.

"Unable are the Loved to die, for Love is Immortality," Jet said, quoting Emily Dickinson.

When she opened her eyes the Reverend was standing beside her, crying. They stood together like that until the light changed, with bands of blue falling across the floor.

After a time, Jet followed him downstairs. He opened the screen door for her and they walked into the garden of daffodils. Everything else was black. Even the soil.

"I can drive you to the bus station," the Reverend said.

"That's okay, I like to walk."

He nodded. He liked to walk, too.

"You can come by next time," he said. When she looked at him, confused, he added, "I know you're here every month. I see you at the cemetery, but I don't want to disturb you. I know you want your time with him."

Jet stood on the sidewalk and watched him walk back up the steps to the porch. The lamp had been left on in Levi's room and it cast a yellow glow. Jet waved and then turned. She walked the long way to the bus station. She liked to walk through town, especially in the fading light. It brought her comfort to know that for more than three hundred years people in her family had been in this town, walking where she walked now. The next time she came she wouldn't wear this black dress, which was too warm for the season. And she would come earlier in the day so she would have more time, because for the first time in a long time, she felt she had all the time in the world.

On June 28, 1969, the weather was hot, eighty-seven degrees, un-usual for the time of year. New York City grew steamy, as if the heat rose from its core. On Christopher Street, between West Fourth and Waverly Place, the Stonewall, a restaurant that had originally been a stable, was burning from the inside out. The heat was trapped and it had to rise up. Organized crime ran it as a gay bar and everything about it was illegal. There was no liquor license and corrupt officials were handed enough cash to look the other way. Sometimes they did, but sometimes they chose not to de-spite the payoffs. There were raids and customers, including trans people, drag queens, and the young and the homeless, were beaten and humiliated and jailed, dragged onto the street, cuffed, blood-ied, and facing a legal system that saw them as without rights.

Late on this particular night, Vincent was walking with his dog when he came upon a crowd that was growing by the min-ute. He could have gone in another direction, but he came this way. Later he would wonder if he knew, if he needed to see for himself who he was and where he belonged. He usually paid no attention to anyone when he walked his dog at night, as he would have paid no mind to the crowd, which had been grow-ing in number ever since the brutal arrests, had the police not encircled the area.

Eight officers who had beaten customers were trapped in-side, and when tactical forces arrived as backup, a riot began. Garbage cans and bricks were being used by the crowd to de-fend themselves. Vincent stood there, frozen. When confronted with the enormity of what was happening, the pure revolution-ary action of standing up to be who you are, he was unable to move. Be yourself, his aunt had told him. Was this who he was, a man who feared to show himself? A rabbit? He could not have despised himself more at that instant.

"Why don't you do something?" someone shouted.

One of the homeless kids from Christopher Park was being beaten, doing his best to protect his face with his hands. Before he could think, Vincent pushed the officer off. He concentrated and a hail of stones fell, scattering several of the officers. When the kid limped away, the officer went for Vincent, tackling him. Vincent toppled, his face hitting the cement. Harry was barking like mad, and would have attacked whoever came after him next, but Vincent gathered his wits and rose to his feet, calling the dog off. They ran down West Fourth Street, off the pavement, cutting off traffic. Vincent was bleeding, a gash down the left side of his skull.

He let the dog into the yard at 44 Greenwich before going to the ER at St. Vincent's. For days afterward there were riots, and many of the wounded would be brought here. Vincent himself had a concussion and was in need of stitches, and there was the matter of his hand, which had bent backward during his fall. They sent an intern to take care of him.

"What have you done to yourself?" the tall rangy intern asked.

When Vincent gazed up he saw Haylin Walker, in his scrubs, a look of worry on his face.

"There's a riot out there, Dr. Walker. I didn't do this to myself."

Haylin then recognized him. "You!" He threw an arm around Vincent so heartily Vincent winced in pain.

"Are you sure you're a doctor?" Vincent asked.

Hay grinned. He still had the same easy smile he'd had at fifteen. "Pretty sure. I just got posted to a residency at Beth Israel."

He was good at stitchery, and, because there were many other patients waiting for him on this day, extraordinarily fast. "There. Your looks won't be ruined. What a mess today has been." He got to work on a cast. "You may have trouble with this hand for a while."

"I was lucky. It's mayhem out there."

Hay looked embarrassed, but he swallowed his pride to ask, "How's Franny?"

"Considering you let her go, do you care?"

Hay gave Vincent a look, then took a moment to sit beside him on the gurney.

"Does anything turn out the way we want it to?"

Vincent got up, leaving Haylin to the line of patients waiting for him. "You want to be smart?" Vincent said before he went to check out. "Don't waste time when there's someone you love."

When Vincent came home, Franny made him lie in bed with an ice pack on his skull.

"Wrong place, wrong time," Vincent explained, but the night had done something to him, and, in fact, he no longer felt as alone in this life. He was part of something bigger than himself. All the same, he wanted to protect William. "Do not call him," he told Franny. "He's out at Sag Harbor with his family. I don't want him to worry."

But William had the sight, and knew something was amiss. When he turned on the news the riots were on every channel. He came the next morning, driving his father's old Jeep, parking illegally, pounding at the door. Franny let him in and he paced in the parlor while she told him what had happened. He was already damning himself for not being a part of it.

He went upstairs and knocked at Vincent's door. When there was no reply he said, "I'm not taking no for an answer."

Vincent came to the door, his appearance shocking. William embraced him, then stepped back to take a better look. "We're getting out of the city," he said.

He found Vincent's suitcase and began packing.

"Why go?" Vincent said. "We can't escape from who we are."

"Of course not. Why would we want to do that?"

Vincent laughed, for he agreed. "We wouldn't."

"I'm glad you feel that way, Vincent. Because I certainly don't wish to be anyone other than who I am and I don't wish to deny it. I'm taking you to see someone who had to do that all his life."

"Who's that?" Vincent asked.

William opened the bedroom door. It was time for them to leave. "My father."

They went to the town of Sag Harbor, where William's family had a home dating back hundreds of years. The house had been a summer place, a ramshackle wood-shingled building with huge porches that overlooked the glassy sea and the shoreline of Shelter Island. But it had been insulated and a heating system had been put in. Now William's father lived there year-round. He was tall and Vincent saw that William resembled him in many ways, not just in his appearance, but also in his calm demeanor, which belied a passionate heart.

"William used to row out to the island in storms just to see if he could. He went in a hurricane once, despite my warning. He wasn't one to ever back down." William's father had been waiting for them at the far end of a great green lawn. He embraced William, and then embraced Vincent as well, extremely happy for their company. "My son has always been brave and

244

he reveals that to all who know him. I've always envied him this quality, for it escaped me completely."

They cut across the lawn, then walked down a lane past a small cemetery, where the Grants had always been buried, the first being Everett Rejoice Grant, who had died in 1695. Family mattered to the Grants. William had been an only child, but that had been made up for by scores of cousins and friends. William's mother had an apartment in New York, and stayed there year-round, but she came out to celebrate Thanksgiving with the family, despite having a separate life from her husband.

It was a clear, bright, beautiful day, the air tinged with salt, the climbing roses blooming. The graveyard was filled with sunlight.

Retired now, Alan Grant had been at the district attorney's office in Manhattan for nearly thirty years. All the while William was growing up, his father didn't come home until late, sometimes not until nine or ten, and then he would sit up even later, files spread out over the dining room table. He got lost in his work, and often forgot his family. Those days, however, were long gone. Today he had set out lunch for his guests on a porch that overlooked the sea. There were oysters and a salad and white wine. There were roses in a milky vase in the center of the table on a white lace cloth that had belonged to William's great-grandmother.

"I hear you were there at the riots," Mr. Grant said. "My darling son has always thought he could win over everything nature set before him, and I admire his attitude. We must fight against bigotry in all its forms, for it is prejudice that ruins a society."

"So says the DA," William said, clearly proud of his father.

"I'm proud of you, too," Mr. Grant said, toasting Vincent.

Vincent was abashed. "Me? I did nothing. I just stumbled into it and managed to get myself beat up."

"It's more than that. I'm proud you can be honest about who you are."

"Well, it's recent, believe me."

"I have every cause to believe you, especially because you are with my son. He knows truth when he sees it."

After lunch, Vincent and William walked down to the shoreline. The beach was rocky, covered with small mossy stones at low tide. Out in the water there was a blue heron that looked like Edgar, the stuffed bird in the shop. Herons mate for life, and Vincent thought this was a good sign, and an even better sign that Mr. Grant had seemed to like him.

"My father felt he had to hide the fact that he was homosexual. My mother knew, of course, and they had their arrangement, but at work and in the larger world, he couldn't have anyone know. It would have likely meant his job and would have left him open to blackmail, which he paid off once or twice. It was not a way to live, and it took a toll. On all of us, but especially on him. We loved him, but he despised himself, so it made for rocky going sometimes."

Vincent recounted the story his aunt had told about their cousin Maggie, who, having denied who she was, was turned into a rabbit. "That clearly didn't happen to your father."

"No. In spite of all of us, he managed to have quite a life of his own. He's no rabbit. He's a fox."

They both laughed.

"Well, so are you," Vincent said.

"He taught me what to be and what not to be and I'm grateful that I live in this time, now, with you. It's far from perfect but it's not what my father went through. He was the one that was usually out rowing, if you really want to know, not me, and sometimes

246

I feared he wouldn't come back. That he'd just keep going until he reached a place where he could be happy. Or happier. He took on the worst cases, murder, rape, because he wanted to change the world in his own way, but also because he needed to fight, and he couldn't fight for himself. That's one of the attributes that first attracted me to you. You're a fighter."

"Am I?" Vincent said.

"You'll see. When the time comes. You'll fight for the life you want."

After walking for a while, they stopped by a tide pool, and took off their shoes, and then, as if having the same thought at the same time, they undressed and raced into the water, whooping, for it was cold as ice. Vincent was alive, more alive than he'd ever imagined he'd be. He dove into the water and everything was green. His mind was clear and cold. His heart pounded in his chest. He was caught up in the water, but he knew he couldn't drown. All the same, William reached for him and steadied him, then pulled him out of the tide.

"You're mad," William said. "There's a current."

"It doesn't matter to us."

Vincent threw his arms around William. He dared to think that at last he was truly happy. He looked out to Shelter Island. He had the urge to swim for it, to try something impossible, for everything he'd done up to this time seemed selfish and small.

"You matter more than anything to me," William said.

Vincent shook his head. "You think too highly of me."

"I know exactly who you are," William responded. "Just as I always knew who my father was. And I loved him, not despite it, but because of it, the way that I love you because of who you are."

One still night, people happened upon a deer lying on the ground in Washington Square Park. No one knew where it had come from, although there were said to be deer in the Bronx and perhaps this one had come down along the riverside. It was an albino deer, said to bring bad luck. It was curled up beside a wooden bench, and the next morning all the children in the neighborhood came to see it. There it still was, sleeping in the park, and even children who didn't believe in fairy tales found themselves believing. They stood on the concrete paths, in awe of the woodland creature. It was so silent and it didn't seem the least bit afraid. The children left hay and grass, and a few brought other offerings: sugar, blankets, sweet herbs.

For many it was a time when miraculous things happened every day. This past summer, Neil Armstrong and Buzz Aldrin had been the first people to reach the moon, on *Apollo 11*, landing in the Sea of Tranquility. It seemed the distance between earth and the stars and planets was growing smaller, and perhaps the world, that floating blue orb, could be better than it had ever been. But there was no peace to come; instead there was unrest in cities that were brutal and brutally hot. In the park there were swarms of bees, so many that Franny took to wearing a scarf when she sat beneath the Hangman's Elm. She brought the deer a bowl of cool water, but it refused to drink. She could see in its eyes that it had given up.

Sometime in the night, someone shot the deer with a bow and arrow, as if hunting season had been declared in Manhattan. People were outraged and a sit-in began, with many of the protesters the same children who had tried their best to save the deer. The mayor took up the cause and a collection was raised so the deer could be buried on the grounds of the Cloisters.

For days after the murder of the deer, there was a trail of blood on the concrete path where the poor creature had last lain. Near that place the children of PS 41 planted a rosebush one murky afternoon. It bloomed overnight with masses of white flowers, though the blooms were out of season. It was a miracle, everyone said, and some were satisfied, but to anyone with the sight there was still a sense of doom in the park. Franny stopped going to Washington Square. Instead, she sat shivering in their own small garden and she waited for whatever was bound to happen when a white deer appears, when white roses bloom overnight, when bees follow you home to nest in your rooftop.

It didn't happen until October. A letter arrived at 44 Greenwich on a Sunday afternoon, a time when mail wasn't delivered. There was no stamp and no return address, but the cream-colored stationery and the slanted handwriting were instantly recognizable. The missive was addressed only to Franny.

"Aren't you the lucky one?" Vincent said drily. He had stopped by for coffee, as he often did in the morning when William left to teach his classes.

Franny looked at the envelope on the floor by the mail slot. She had no urge to retrieve it, in fact she had gone quite cold with dread. In the end, Jet was the one to get the letter. She looked at her sister and Franny nodded. "You open it."

Wren hopped on Jet's lap as she sat down to inspect the envelope. When the cat batted a paw at the letter there was the thrum of a bee.

"Better take it outside," Jet suggested to Franny. "It's addressed to you, after all."

Franny went out to the rickety back porch. The city smelled like possibility and corned beef hash. Franny used a dull knife to slit open the envelope, then watched as a bee rose into the cloudy air. The last time they'd seen bees they had portended a death.

The note inside was brief.

Come today.

Isabelle did not often make requests, and when she did it was best to comply. So Susanna Owens had believed and so her daughter did as well. Franny packed a suitcase and took the bus to Massachusetts within the hour. Jet had packed her a lunch, a tomato sandwich and a green apple and a thermos of Travel Well Tea, composed of orange peel, black tea, mint, and rosemary. Riding through the lush New England countryside, Franny thought of the first summer they'd come to visit, when Haylin wrote letters every day. She thought she could have what she wanted; she thought she could see the world from above, as if it were a distant blue ball whose sorrows had nothing to do with her. She had wanted to be a bird, but now she knew, as she looked out the window to see Lewis following, that even birds are chained to earth by their needs and desires.

There was a chill in the air and Franny wore her mother's ember spring coat and tall lace-up black boots, along with jeans and a shirt that had been Vincent's castoff. She had an awful feeling in the pit in her stomach. A one-line message was never good. It meant there was no recourse to something that had gone wrong. For what you can fix, there are a hundred remedies. For what cannot be cured, not even words will do.

To Franny it seemed that nothing had changed when she walked toward Magnolia Street, except that the Rustlers were no longer in residence. The house had been painted and two unfamiliar girls played in the front yard. Franny stopped and leaned over the fence, curious.

"What happened to the family before you?" she asked.

"They were stinkers," one of the girls said.

"We had to burn sage in all the rooms," the older of the two sisters confided. She was all of ten. "Bad karma. We got the sage from the mean old lady at the end of the street."

Isabelle.

"What made her mean?" Franny asked.

"She always wore black and a pair of old boots," the older sister said. The girls suddenly stopped their play and looked at Franny more carefully. Her black coat, her boots, her blood-red hair piled atop her head. "Oh," both sisters said thoughtfully.

The girls' mother came to the door with a skeptical expression. "Lunch," she called, clapping her hands. When the girls skittered into the house their mother walked onto the porch, hands on her hips, eyes fixed on Franny. "Is there something I can help you with?"

Franny detected a stain on the porch beneath the gray paint. Crimson. She felt her face grow flushed. She knew what it was and it didn't bode well. "What happened to Mrs. Rustler?"

"Are you a relative?"

Sometimes the truth was the best way to find out more of the truth. "I'm Franny Owens. I think you got some sage from my aunt."

The neighbor continued to be wary. "What if I did?"

"If you did, I'm glad she could help you." The woman relented and came a little closer. She no longer seemed quite as guarded, so Franny went on. "Mrs. Rustler was involved with my brother," she explained. "So I just wondered."

"Well, it's a good thing he wasn't around when it happened. Her husband? He was kind of a mild-mannered guy? He murdered her. I take it she had all kinds of improper flirtations. We got a great price on the house because of the crime, but I've had to go to your aunt half a dozen times to try to rid the place of her aura. It still smells of burning rubber in the basement."

"Try some lavender sachets. Put them in every room and bury one under this porch."

"Frankly, it's good you're here," the neighbor confided. "Your aunt hasn't had the porch light on for weeks. People in town are a bit worried about her, but we all know she values her privacy."

Franny thanked the neighbor and walked on. October was such a tricky month. Today, for instance, it was as chilly as wintertime, but the sun was bright. The weather report predicted that the following day would be in the sixties. Vines snaking around the old house were still green, but there were no leaves, only thorns. When Franny went through the gate she noted the garden hadn't been put to bed as it usually was at this time of year. The beds had not been raked, tender plants had not been taken into the greenhouse, where they would winter over in the faint sunshine. The new neighbor had been correct: the porch light, always turned on to let those in need of a remedy know they were welcome to call, burning for more than three hundred years, was turned off. Moths caught inside the glass dome were fluttering about helplessly.

Finding the door unlatched, Franny shoved it open. Colder inside than out. A sign of a passing over to come. Franny kept her coat on. Her throat tightened as she walked through the house, the echo of her heels clattering on the wooden floor. There were dishes in the sink, unwashed, and dust glazed the furniture. Isabelle was always meticulous to a fault. Now there were ashes in the fireplace. Herbal encyclopedias were scattered over her bed. There was one book of poems, a present from Jet one Yule. *The Complete Poems of Emily Dickinson.*

Franny came to see that the back door had been left open. A beetle squatted on the threshold. Deathwatch beetles are wood borers; they can be heard in the rafters calling for mates and there was a call from somewhere inside the ceiling. There was nothing Franny could do about the beetle hiding in the attic, but she stepped on this one and crushed it flat, then went on to the garden. The lilacs were bare but she swore she could smell their scent. *If there are lilacs,* her aunt had told her once as they'd worked in the garden, *there will be luck.* The spindly plant in the backyard of 44 Greenwich was one of the reasons she'd decided it was the right house for them.

She went on to the greenhouse, thinking of the night she learned to make black soap, and in doing so learned who she was. The door was ajar and she peered inside. There was Aunt Isabelle sitting in a wicker chair.

"You received my note," Isabelle said when Franny came to her, her voice a dry rasp. Her skin was sallow and she was clearly chilled to the bone, for she wore a sweater, a coat, and a shawl. Still she trembled. "I won't play games with you. It's pancreatic cancer. One can't escape every evil under the sun."

Franny sank onto the wicker ottoman and took her aunt's hands in her own. Her emotions swelled into panic. "Is there no cure?"

"Not yet." Isabelle was honest above all things, a trait Franny admired. It was an important rule. Nature could be shifted, but not controlled. "Not for me," Isabelle said. "But, darling, you can cure yourself. I wanted to make certain I spoke to you about this matter right away."

Franny smiled softly. It was so like her aunt to worry about her when she was the one who was dying. "I have no disease."

"You will," Isabelle said. "Unless you love someone."

Franny bent to rest her head on her aunt's knees. "You know I can't. It's not possible in our family."

"Maria Owens did what she did for a reason. She was young and she thought damning anyone who loved us would protect us. But what she had with that terrible man wasn't love. She didn't understand that when you truly love someone and they love you in return, you ruin your lives together. That is not a curse, it's what life is, my girl. We all come to ruin, we turn to dust, but whom we love is the thing that lasts."

"Maybe I'm afraid of love," Franny admitted. "It's too powerful."

"You?" Isabelle scoffed. "Who chose courage? You're stronger than you know. Which is why I'm leaving you what matters most. The book."

Franny raised her head, touched by her aunt's generosity. Her eyes were brimming with tears. "Can we change what's happening to you? You once said that just as anything whole can be broken, anything broken can be put back together again."

Isabelle shook her head. "Everything except for this. Death is its own circle."

"How long do you have?" she asked her aunt.

"Ten days."

Then and there they began the work that would take ten days to complete. They shielded the furniture from daylight and dust by laying down white sheets. They made soap out in the garden, the best batch that had ever been prepared. If used once a week it could take years off a person's appearance. They wrapped the portrait of Maria Owens in brown paper and string for storage, then put bay leaves and cloves in the closets to keep moths away. They telephoned Charlie Merrill, who could be trusted to keep their business private, and had him exterminate the attic and the rafters to rid the house of beetles. Before he left, they asked him to fashion a plain pine coffin and to please do so quickly. He stood there, blinking, choked up and not knowing quite what to say to Miss Owens.

"I can't do that," he said, distraught.

"Of course you can. And I'll appreciate it, just as I've appreciated all of your hard work over the years," Isabelle told him.

She handed him a check for ten thousand dollars, since she had been underpaying him for fifty years, and when he protested she simply wouldn't hear anything more.

"We have too much to do to argue," she said and off she and Franny went to the pharmacy, where they ordered hot fudge sundaes with marshmallow cream at the soda fountain.

"Much too fattening," Aunt Isabelle said. Her hand shook each time she lifted the spoon.

"But we don't care," Franny said, though she had noticed that Isabelle was only taking small bites and that her silver sundae cup was overflowing with melted ice cream.

They saw to all of their chores, readying the house and the garden, and on the eighth day, when Aunt Isabelle could barely walk, they had Charlie take them to the law firm in Boston that the Owens family had always used. There a will was taken from a file. It had been drawn up after Franny had come to spend the summer. Isabelle now confided that she had known right then. Franny was the next in line.

Once they'd been ushered into a private office, they sat in oxblood-red leather chairs facing the lawyer, Jonas Hardy, a young man with sad, moody eyes. His father and grandfather and great-grandfather had all worked for the Owenses. He shyly addressed Franny. "You are the trustee for your brother and sister when it comes to the house, in which you have equal shares. Everything else, however, goes directly to you. That includes all belongings: furniture, dishes, silver. There is a trust used to manage the house, so you never have to worry about taxes or upkeep. But you can never sell the house, you understand."

"Of course she understands," Isabelle said. "She's not a nincompoop."

Franny signed the necessary papers, then they had tea and sugar cookies.

"Your aunt gave me this tea when I first met her," Jonas Hardy said. "She sends a box here to the office every year." He lifted his cup. "Thank you, Miss Owens!"

Franny took a sip. *Courage.*

They all shook hands when the papers had been signed and the tea had been drained to the last drop, and then Franny and her aunt got into Charlie's waiting car, and they navigated the bumpy streets of Boston, which had been cow paths when Maria Owens first came to set up the initial trust for her daughter and her granddaughter and all the daughters to follow. Aunt Isabelle rested her head back and dozed. She woke once when they hit a pothole and was clearly disoriented. "Is this New York?"

"No. We're going home," Franny assured her.

When they arrived at Magnolia Street, Franny brought her aunt into the house and up to bed. She helped Isabelle undress and gently pulled her nightgown over her head. Her aunt was still shivering, so Franny found some wool socks and a knitted shawl. She brought in a basin of warm water and used a soft washcloth to clean her aunt's face and hands with black soap. In the morning she phoned Jet and Vincent and told them to come. They rented a car and arrived on the afternoon of the ninth day, having sped along the Mass Pike at ninety miles an hour, fearing that time was against them. They trooped into the house and, without bothering to remove their coats, came to sit at the foot of Isabelle's bed. They were all silent, too dazed for any emotion. All three had been half convinced Aunt Isabelle would live forever. What was happening seemed impossible. Things ended, and then they began again, only they would begin without Isabelle.

A sparrow darted inside the house and flew around the room. Franny fetched a stepladder from the linen closet, climbed up, and held out her hand. "Don't come back here on Midsummer's Eve," she told the bird. "There won't be anyone here to rescue you."

Because there was a wind from the north, and their aunt's condition was precarious, Franny took the sparrow down to the stairwell landing so she could pry open the green glass above the window seat. She watched as the bird lifted into the air. When she turned she was stunned. Her aunt was beside her.

"How did you get here? Let me help you back to bed," Franny said.

"I want to give you this." There on the velvet seat cushion was Maria Owens's sapphire. Franny had read about it in Maria's journal, the jewel her lover had given to her. "Wear it and your heart will come back to you. Do it now."

Because her aunt was so insistent, Franny slipped on the necklace, tucking it under her blouse. It was surprisingly warm.

Jet came to the top of the stairs and called to Franny. "Hurry. She's failing."

"No. She's right here." But when Franny looked there was no one beside her. She ran upstairs, where her aunt signaled for her to come near. Franny went to her bedside and knelt down beside her.

"Oh, dear aunt," Franny said. "I have so many more things I want to discuss with you. You can't go now."

"I don't make all the decisions, you know," Isabelle managed to say. "I just do the best I can to face what life brings. That's the secret, you know. That's the way you change your fate."

Vincent had edged closer to the door. His face was ashen. It was an awful sight to see such a strong woman become so weak, like a moth folding up on itself. "I don't know if I can stay," he murmured.

"You'll stay," Franny told him. "We owe her that and more."

"You don't owe me anything," Isabelle managed to say.

Franny patted her arm. "Don't exert yourself," she urged their aunt.

Isabelle had very little energy. She gestured for Franny to lean in as she spoke her last words. No one heard but Franny, for the message was a final gift, and one that brought Franny to tears.

When Isabelle sighed, the last of her breath rose to the ceiling, then followed the path of the sparrow, into the hallway, down the stairs, out the window. By then the house was dark. Somehow night had fallen. It was after midnight. The tenth day. Time had passed so quickly they hadn't even noticed.

The sisters washed their aunt with warm water and black soap, then dressed her in white. They went down to the garden, where the night was starry and clear. Later, Charlie came with his sons to carry their aunt down from her room in the coffin. She was taken in their van to the old cemetery where the children's parents had been buried. They knew she didn't want any fanfare, therefore no service was held. They sent a telegram to April in California, and to the Owenses in Maine, and to the ones in Boston, with the date and time of Isabelle Owens's death. Contributions in her name could be made to the town library. Charlie's two sons, who had been cured of drug addiction and thievery by Isabelle Owens, and who'd always been afraid to look her in the eye, wept as they lowered the coffin. Jet had phoned April when they'd learned Isabelle had taken ill, and April had sent a huge flower arrangement of white roses and ferns. Jet gave the blessing from the book of poems she had given her aunt.

In this short Life
That only lasts an hour
How much—how little—is
Within our power.

"She was a good woman," Charlie said.

Vincent insisted on refilling the grave himself. He stripped

off his black jacket and his boots and socks, then labored, digging, until he was sweating through his white shirt. He'd brought
along a bottle of whiskey, and they all toasted to the memory of
Isabelle Owens.

When Franny told her brother and sister they had inherited
the house, all three knew they needed to return to Manhattan.
As they were bound not to sell the property they would let it
stand empty. Franny hired Charlie to be the caretaker, to make
certain that no one vandalized the house in the absence of any
tenants, and ensure that vines or roots which might disturb
the plumbing or the foundation be cleared away. When they
returned to the house, Franny gave Charlie the chickens, and
said they might be reclaimed someday, but until then he was
entitled to all the eggs they would lay.

When the Merrills had gone, Jet came to stand beside her sister. They looked out at the garden, which had now turned to straw.
Isabelle had done all of the autumn planting, but she wouldn't
see anything bloom in the spring. "What did she say to you at the
end?" Jet asked. She'd been wondering ever since their aunt had
whispered something that had brought Franny to tears.

"She said you and I should share the *Grimoire*. She said the
sight would come back to you."

A blister arose on Franny's tongue as she spoke. Ever since
she and Jet had shared a room, they had shared all that they had,
but the one thing Franny wanted to keep for herself was her
aunt's last words.

Jet took her sister's hand. "You were her favorite."

It was true. Early that morning Franny had found a card Isabelle had left under her pillow. *If there be a cure, seek till you find
it. If there be none, never mind it.*

Today everything smelled earthy, the rich scent of mulch and decaying leaves and roots. It was an ending and a beginning, for the month itself was like a gate. October began as a golden hour and ended with Samhain, the day when the worlds of the living and the dead opened to each other. There was no choice but to walk through the gate of time. Franny had already packed up her suitcase and carried the *Grimoire* with her. The book, and all it contained, was now theirs.

While they waited for Vincent to shower and change, the sisters took a final inventory of the house. They found the keys to the front door in the silverware drawer, and Isabelle's bankbook in the vegetable bin. They packed up the remedies stowed in the cabinets into several boxes that would fit neatly in the trunk of the rented car.

The sisters sat in the shade of the arbor beside the shed. Wisteria grew here in spring and spread out like a canopy; grapes twisted along the structure in late summer. The town was sleepy, but without Aunt Isabelle's presence it was empty as far as Franny and Jet were concerned. They were tempted to uncover the black mirror in the greenhouse and take one last peek at the future, but they restrained themselves. Instead, they crammed the car with belongings, locked the front door, and cut down an armful of bare lilac branches to take with them before latching the gate. What the future would be was yet to be discovered. As for the past, they already knew it too well.

PART FIVE

Gravity

It came on the wind, the way wicked things must, for they are most often weighted down with spite and haven't the strength to lift themselves. On the first day of December 1969, the lottery was held. Men between the ages of eighteen and twenty-six would be drafted to fight in Victnam according to their birth dates. Lives were interrupted and fortunes were exchanged. A cold drizzle hung down and flurries of snow fell in swirls. There were no stones thrown or drownings, no pillories or burnings. Those chosen were computerized, their fates picked at random.

Life went on despite the lottery: traffic headed down Broadway, men and women showed up for work, children went to play. The world breathed and sighed and people fell in love and got married and fell out of love and never spoke to one another again. Still the numbers drawn had the weight of ruin and sorrow; they turned young men old in an instant. A breath in and a man was chosen to walk on a path he'd never expected to take. A breath out and he must make the decision of a lifetime. Some would leave the country, some went to jail, some were ready to take up arms and die for the country they loved despite the heartbreak of leaving families and friends. All were torn apart.

It was said that fate could not be altered, except by one thing, and that was war.

Because Vincent was born on the fourteenth of September, his was the first number drawn, the 258th day of the year. He was in a bar on the Lower East Side when it happened, a no-name place for lost men where the drinks were cheap and the company was rough. He hadn't wanted to be with William or his sisters on this day and see their shock and fear because he knew this would happen. He'd always known this was to be his lot, and he'd wanted to be alone when they called his number. He'd seen his fate when he was fourteen and had been foolish enough to gaze into the black mirror in the garden shed. His aunt had warned him not to look, but he'd wanted to know what his future held, and then, like anyone who can see what will be, he regretted his actions. Life is a mystery, and it should be so, for the sorrow that accompanies being human and the choices one will have to make are a burden, too heavy for most to know before their time comes.

He came home plastered, nearly unconscious, dragged to the front door by two somewhat less drunken men, who had decided to help when Vincent was booted onto the street. They were veterans and they pitied him the war of his time. Theirs had been terrible, but it had also been just and worth fighting. Franny gave them each a five-dollar bill, thanked them, and let Vincent sleep it off in the parlor. He looked cold and alone, his skin a faint blue color. The next step after being called up would be an order for a physical, and then, if he passed, induction by May of that same year.

Franny had little choice. After all this time, Haylin was still the only one to whom she could turn. She took a cab uptown, to Beth Israel, in a frantic state, urging the taxi driver to go faster, not caring as he skidded through changing stoplights.

"You're going to get us killed, lady!" the driver cried.

Feeling guilty that she'd placed him in peril, Franny tipped the driver twenty dollars when he got her to the hospital in no time flat. In admissions she got the runaround until a nurse found her pacing outside the ER searching for Dr. Walker. Franny was clearly so distressed that the nurse pulled her aside in the corridor.

"He's not here anymore, honey."

The nurse handed Franny a tissue, for she clearly thought that tears were to come. "He did what a lot of our young interns and residents are doing. He joined the navy as a doctor in order not to be drafted."

"What does his wife have to say about that?" Franny asked. Emily Flood. She could call up her image in an instant, so cheerful and friendly and so damned good-natured.

"The doctor's not married," the nurse informed her.

"Yes he is," Franny insisted.

"I filed his records from personnel. Trust me, there's no wife."

Franny called from a pay phone. He was not in, the housekeeper said, but she could take a message.

"Tell him it's urgent," Franny pleaded, leaving her phone number and address. "I have to see him. Do you understand what *urgent* means?"

"I do," the housekeeper responded. "It means you want what you want."

Which was true, but for good reason. Franny went home and

waited by the phone. When Jet came in with tea, Franny said simply, "We won't let him go."

"Of course not," Jet said.

At dusk there was a knock at the door. The sisters exchanged a look. They knew who it was.

"He'll help you," Jet said. "All you have to do is let him."

An icy drizzle was falling, but Haylin stood there without a hat or an umbrella. Franny threw open the door so swiftly she startled him, even though he was the one who had come to call. Harry had trotted after her and he now guarded the threshold protectively.

"May I come in?"

Hay was formal and he did not move to embrace her. It had been a long time, after all, and their last parting had been awful. When Franny nodded, he entered the vestibule and stomped the rain from his shoes, then took off his wet rain gear. Under his coat he was wearing a navy uniform. Stunned, Franny took a step backward. She knew he had joined up, yet the sheer reality that he was in the armed services threw her. The Hay she'd known would have fled to Canada, chained himself outside the Pentagon, perhaps even gone to jail. But this was a grown man before her, a doctor, and one she barely knew.

"Don't say how could you," he said when he saw her expression. "It's the better option. Better than being drafted at any rate. I go as a doctor, and maybe I get to do some good."

They went into the kitchen and Franny made her own recipe for Courage Tea, which they both needed.

"You didn't marry her," Franny said in as offhand a manner as she could manage. Color was rising in her face, but she forced herself to sound calm. "That Emily."

Hay shrugged it off. "That Emily didn't deserve marrying someone who didn't love her."

"Oh."

"Don't worry about her. She married someone else. Someone better."

"I doubt that."

"Do you want to discuss love and marriage? Is that why you phoned after all this time? Your message said it was urgent."

"I don't mind if I have to beg for your help if that's the way things are between us," she said. Then she added, "Do you want a slice of chocolate cake?" She had made it that very morning and the scent was intoxicating. They both felt mildly drunk just from the smell.

Hay laughed. "So it's the kind of help that needs a bribe. Just tell me, Franny."

"It's Vincent. He was the first number in the lottery."

"Shit."

"Of course he can't go."

"Thousands of men are doing exactly that, Franny."

"Not Vincent. It would break him."

"Is he so different from everyone else?"

"Yes," Franny said. She thought of the day the nurse had tried to kidnap him. How quiet he had been when he'd been found, how wide his eyes were. That was the first night she sat by his bedside, keeping watch.

"Because he's a homosexual? Plenty of homosexuals serve this country, they're braver than most."

Franny was taken aback.

"Of course I know," Hay said. "How could I not? You knew, so I knew, too. There was a time when I always knew what you thought. Or at least I believed I did."

"So you're a mind reader?"

"I'm a navy doctor with no power to help him."

"Well, that is not the reason he can't serve. Vincent cannot do harm to another. It's out of the question." It was the very first rule of magic. "And if he goes he won't come back." Anyone with sight could tell that her brother was a man whose fate was a brief life. "You can help him, and I know how. If there was any other way, I wouldn't ask."

"Will I wind up in jail if I do what you ask?"

"I don't think so."

"You don't *think* so? That's rich. This is the way it always is. Do you care about me at all or am I just some pawn?"

She cried then, hands over her eyes.

"Not that," he said, taking little comfort in how agitated she had become. She so rarely wept. "All right, fine. I'll dive in. I'll drown if that's what you want."

She went to sit in his lap. She didn't care if she was supposed to stay away.

"Franny," he groaned, as if in pain. "Let's not start this all over again."

"You're still angry because I didn't go after you into the pond. Because I wouldn't steal you away from your engagement party."

"It doesn't matter now," he said pointedly. "I'm likely going to wind up in jail doing whatever you want me to, so let's not talk about the damned pond."

"I want to explain! I physically can't go underwater. I can't be drowned. None of my family can, not unless they fill our boots with stones."

Hay laughed. "You're all witches?"

He likely didn't believe anything she'd told him, but still he kissed her and told her he didn't care if they were witches or warlocks or zombies or Republicans. He was a rational man, a doctor, ready to throw his life and career away for her, so what did it matter? They were entitled to do as they pleased, at least in bed. Eyes brimming, she now told him that what they did mattered greatly, for her family was afflicted and whomever they loved would be brought to ruin unless she could figure a way to break the curse.

"Is that why you were always running away?" Hay was moved to see her distress. "You should have told me, Franny. I have the answer. We'll trick the curse. We won't marry and we won't live together. We'll never speak of love. That's how we'll fight it. We'll just outwit the damned thing. We'll never say the word *love* aloud. We'll never think or breathe it. If we do that, nothing can get in the way." He shrugged then. "Well, almost nothing."

They went upstairs to her room. Haylin took his deployment orders from his inner coat pocket before he got undressed. He would be leaving for Germany in a few weeks. His specialty was surgery, and there, where the worst of the wounded would be airlifted from Vietnam, he would get his share of practice.

Once in bed Franny knew that, despite the curse, she could no longer fight what she felt even if she never spoke of it aloud. She thought of one morning at Aunt Isabelle's when she'd gone into the garden alone. The air was still and dark, the light just beginning to lift in the east. There was the rabbit in the grass. Franny went as close as she could to lay down a saucer of milk. *I will never be you*, she insisted. *I won't pretend to be something I'm not.* At last it was true. It felt grand to be herself, a woman who knew how to love someone. They would simply pretend, to everyone except one another. Franny whispered to Haylin all that she ever was and had been. She told him that she had always known what the future would be, and he said that if what she said was true, then she should have known a very long time ago that this was meant to be.

All that winter Vincent refused to tell William the date of his induction. He didn't want an emotional scene, so he began pulling back. He took to leaving Charles Street right after sex. He didn't speak much. He often looked out into the street as if memorizing the view, in case he should never see it again. He did not wish to fight in a war he considered to be unfair. He was not a warrior and he hadn't the skills to be a soldier.

"Are you angry with me?" William wanted to know.

"Of course not." But Vincent sounded angry even to himself. Angry to be in this situation where he felt he was a traitor with no courage at all.

He began to slowly move his belongings out of William's apartment. Each evening he went through the dresser where he kept his clothes and took a few shirts, a pair of jeans, some socks. He took a coffeepot, a hairbrush, his dog's water bowl.

"Do you think I don't know what you're doing?" William asked.

"I'm getting rid of things I don't need. There's nothing wrong with that."

"You're getting ready to leave. I can tell when a man is in denial. I grew up with one. I'm an expert. You won't even stay the night anymore. You're thinking of leaving me."

Vincent leaned to kiss William, who backed away.

"You don't trust me," Vincent said.

"You have that so wrong," William remarked. "It's you who doesn't trust me."

Vincent refused to discuss the situation any further. He would not allow William to be shattered by sorrow that belonged to him alone. Was this the curse, succeeding at last in breaking him? He went down to the Lower East Side, returning to the building where he'd once set up shop. He had *The Magus* with him, tucked inside his coat. It was as if he had two beating hearts, one his own, the other belonging to the book. All this time, the book had been his closest companion. He hadn't really needed anyone since the day he had found it, until now. Back in the abandoned apartment covered with graffiti, he brought from his shirt pocket the photograph William had taken of them when they were first together. Some love magic was brutal and quick and didn't give the other person a choice in the matter. It was dark and irrevocable, but in Vincent's opinion it was for the best if it would save his beloved from pain and grief. He tore William out of the picture. He had brought along the ingredients necessary to undo their attraction. His own blood, black paint, pins, a bird's broken wing, a thin strand of lead. He could fix it so that William would never even see him. It was emotional camouflage. Whom you had loved, you would no longer recognize. He would not know his voice, his touch, their history.

Without knowing why, William would throw out anything that might remind him of Vincent, letters he'd written, the tape of "I Walk at Night." He would open a book Vincent had given him and not know where it had come from. He would toss out the second pillow on the bed.

But when Vincent imagined William no longer knowing him he found he could not proceed. What would he feel when they walked past each other on Bleecker Street and William gazed at him as though he were a stranger? What was this world without love?

As Vincent passed a sewer he tossed the magical ingredients down through the grate into the watery depths below the city. Then he took out the book that had been with him since he was fourteen. He went to Washington Square and left *The Magus* on a bench for the next person in need to find. It was wrenching to do this. He had so treasured the book; it had spoken to the darkness inside him, it had been his true voice when he'd had none. But that time was over, and what magic there was, was inside him.

Know yourself, Aunt Isabelle had told him. They had stood in the garden when he had been so lost. He hadn't known how to reach the surface, all he knew was that he was drowning. Yet on the morning when his aunt tested him, he had chosen courage. So he walked on, to Charles Street, where William was waiting for him in his apartment, which overlooked the green plane trees and open sky right in the center of a city where anything was possible for those who were not afraid to try.

Before his appearance at Whitehall Street, Vincent called his sisters into the kitchen. "There's something I need to say in case anything happens to me."

"It won't," Jet assured him. "You'll be fine."

"But if something *does* happen," Vincent went on, "you should know about me and April."

Franny furrowed her brow. "Did you have an argument? I didn't even know you were in touch with her."

"No one can argue with April. She's always right." He paused. "We're in touch on and off. We have to be." When Franny gave him a look, he added, "Jet knows what I'm talking about."

"Does she really?" Franny said, annoyed at having been left out. "She no longer has the sight, so you must have confided in her."

"It was a long time ago," Jet was quick to say.

"I didn't confide in her," Vincent told Franny. "April did. It happened the summer we first went to Aunt Isabelle's. When I didn't know who I was or what I wanted. For a brief moment I thought I wanted April."

"Seriously?" Franny shook her head. "That's hard to picture."

"Well, picture that it ended up with Regina."

Franny was stunned. "Really?" She looked over at Jet.

"Really," Jet said.

"Well, I think that's wonderful," Franny concluded. "That's a gift. I thought you were going to tell us something terrible, but this is actually good news. I dislike children, but I liked her. I still have her drawing."

"Franny, I'm telling you about this now in case the worst

comes to pass. April and I decided that if we should both die early, we want Regina to be with you."

Franny wouldn't hear of it. "That's a mistake. I wouldn't be a good influence. Neither of us would be, really."

"Speak for yourself," Jet said primly.

"There's no way out of it. April and I agreed on this some time ago. You're Regina's godmothers. You'll be her guardians."

They sat at the table and he brought forth the legal papers he'd had the family lawyer, Jonas Hardy, draw up. He'd already sent the document to April for signing, and now the sisters signed as well.

"This is all very official," Franny said. "I happen to have something official as well, thanks to Haylin."

She handed Vincent a note that he then scanned.

"I have asthma?" he said.

Jet handed him the vial they had prepared for him. "You do now."

He explained to William that he had to go alone, but William wouldn't hear of it. "I thought we were ruining our lives together."

William hailed a taxi and they secretly held hands as they traveled downtown, and then on the corner of Whitehall Street, Vincent had the cabbie pull over. William was so honest and forthright, Vincent couldn't share with him the plan his sisters had come up with. It was somewhat dangerous, and he knew William would disapprove of him putting himself at risk, which made Vincent love him all the more.

"You're coming back," William said, leaning in close. "I have the sight, too. I know we'll be together."

Vincent walked the rest of the way to the induction center. He had brought along the official letter written on the stationery of the chief pulmonologist at St. Vincent's that stated that he had severe asthma and could not serve his country. The stationery was real, stolen from the chief's desk while he was at lunch, but the letter itself was forgery, written by a resident whose last radical act had been to chain himself to a rack in the cafeteria of his high school. Vincent was wired and jumpy; he could barely stay seated when brought into the spare office of the MD who would examine him. He was such a good liar, the best of the best, so why was it that his tongue felt thick and heavy in his mouth? Why, when the doctor walked into the room, did he fall silent?

Franny and Jet had decided to go to the induction center to wait outside for Vincent. They both were as nervous as birds. "Fuck Richard Nixon," Jet said.

"Agreed," Franny said.

"We're doing the right thing, aren't we?"

"Of course we are. He can't go. I've always seen his life would end too early. It's right there in the palm of his hand. We have to do everything we can to protect him."

They'd given Vincent wolfsbane, grown in their tiny greenhouse. He'd been advised to consume it with great caution, for the herb was dangerous, and could affect the heart and lungs with lethal action, interfering with his breathing. *Just a pinch,*

Franny had told him. *We don't want you to actually be dead*. Unfortunately, his emotional good-bye with William had caused him to forget the vial in the backseat of the taxi, something he didn't realize until he was already sitting in the doctor's office.

His lungs seemed fine when the MD had him breathe in and out. "Clear as a bell," he was told. "How long have you had the asthma?"

"At least five years," Vincent said. Having been in a rush he didn't bother to fully read the letter, which stated his asthma had begun at the age of ten.

"And what medications have you used?" the doctor asked.

"Various ones," Vincent said. "Mostly organic."

"But you don't know the names of any of them?"

"You know, my sister takes care of my health. She's the one who knows everything about my medications."

"But your sister isn't here, is she?" the doctor said.

Vincent waited in his underwear while the doctor went to confer. When he returned nearly half an hour later, a soldier in uniform accompanied him. The pulmonary specialist at St. Vincent's Hospital had been phoned. He'd never heard of a Vincent Owens and the files at the hospital had no information about such a patient. Did Mr. Owens wish to recant his story? Or perhaps he'd prefer prison? Actually, Vincent said, he'd prefer a psychiatrist.

"Are you saying you're mentally ill?" the doctor asked.

"That's for others to decide," Vincent responded, sick at heart but not seeing any other choice. He was desperate to get out of his service.

By now, hours had passed and Jet and Franny were freezing on the sidewalk. Men who had walked into Whitehall at the same time as Vincent had already left. They had no idea that their brother was being interviewed in the psychiatry department, where he explained that he was a homosexual, and that he couldn't serve because he was also a wizard and he would do no harm to anyone if they tried to send him overseas.

Franny finally went inside at six that evening. Her footfalls echoed, for the building had emptied. It was a place of fate and the scent in the hall was that of fear and sorrow and courage. Outside, the sky was dark blue, threaded through with clouds. There was a chill in every breath you took. Jet stayed out on the street shivering. On this day she wished she still had the sight. She had developed a fear of crowds and stayed away from public spaces.

At the front desk, Franny was told there was no information. Her brother was no longer in the building and they were closing for the night.

"That's not possible," she declared. "I've been right outside waiting for him all day. If he had left I would have seen him."

"Back entrance," she was told, "used for expedited departures."

The sisters and William were worried sick. It was as if Vincent had disappeared from the face of the earth. Franny went to the Jester to search for him, while William checked Washington Square and Jet stayed at home in case he should call.

"Maybe we should phone the police," Jet said when they had all failed to find him.

William phoned his father, then came back with his report. "No police," he said. "We just wait."

The following week, an official letter finally arrived. The three sat around the kitchen table that had been in the family's home, the one that had been tilted ever since Franny and Vincent first experimented with their powers. Jet was the one who finally opened the letter, and she read it aloud in a small voice that shook with emotion. Vincent had been examined and found to be psychotic and delusional. He had been admitted to Pilgrim State Hospital. There was no need to hear more. They needed a lawyer, and Franny called the only one she knew, Jonas Hardy in Boston, who had always handled the Owens family business. He would do the best he could, but once he acquired the hospital admission documents he conceded that getting Vincent released would be a problematic and lengthy process. Their brother had incriminated himself, signing a document that stated he was a homosexual and a wizard who had planned to defraud the U.S. government and avoid military service.

"First things first," William said. "They won't allow me to see him because I'm not family." He turned to Franny. "You go. They'll let you in."

"Me?" Franny said.

"You're straightforward and honest," William insisted. "And you won't burst into tears."

"You're right," Jet agreed. "It has to be Franny."

"When you come back, we'll sit down with my father and put together a plan," William said. "We'll get him out."

Franny took a cab to Long Island that same day. Before leaving she'd had to lock the dog in the bedroom and make sure the windows were shut, so Harry couldn't leap out and search for Vincent. He'd been distressed ever since Vincent's disappearance, pacing and whining and refusing to eat. "I'm going to find him," Franny told the dog. "You just stay."

It was a misty day, and the hospital was shrouded in fog. It was a dreadful looming place, built between two highways, made of brick, with the bleak look of an old factory. There was a great deal of fencing, and bars over the windows. The lights flickered and the hallways were painted a foreboding shade of green. Franny felt intimidated standing in the waiting room. She tasted metal, for this was a place that was dangerous, made of metal that diluted her power. There was no way anyone could make use of the sight here.

At last a social worker came to speak to her. She was a well-meaning woman, but there wasn't much she could do. Vincent was in the wing the army used and no visitors were allowed.

"Why would that be?" Franny asked. "I only want to see my brother. What harm is there in doing so?"

"Only army or medical personnel," the social worker said. She had a heart and patted Franny's shaking hands. "Trust me, it would be too upsetting for you to see him."

"What is that supposed to mean?"

It meant he was no longer in a straitjacket, no longer fighting or banging his head against the wired-shut window, but viewing the effect of the drugs could be disturbing. He had been too uncontrollable to be in the dormitory with the other patients and had been taken to a single room. He was disheveled and hardly alert, suffering from confusion, trembling whenever there was a loud noise. There would be a report at the end of the month.

"You mean weeks?"

"Unfortunately, yes. We're dealing with a bureaucracy here. Things take time. Sometimes months."

Franny walked out knowing that her brother would not last that long.

They drove out to Sag Harbor. It was early spring and the trees were budding, but the air was still cool. It was a clear, bright, beautiful day, the air tinged with salt, the climbing roses blooming. They were in William's car, and they all wore black. They barely spoke, especially when they drove on the Sagtikos Parkway, past Pilgrim State.

"It's dreadful," Jet did manage to say, and they all agreed.

Once in town, they stopped at the liquor store, thinking they would need the fortification. They needn't have worried. Alan Grant had wine opened on the table, and took a whiskey for himself.

"My advice will set you against the laws of our country." Mr. Grant's expression was somber. "And I'm also afraid that in saving Vincent, I may endanger you," he told his son. "You can be arrested if you aid a deserter." He gestured to the sisters. "All of you can."

"We'll take that chance," Franny said.

"Then my suggestion is that Vincent must run. He's already made it clear he won't serve. He needs a passport and a plane ticket."

"Pardon me?" Franny said. "He's in a hospital. He doesn't have a passport."

"Then find him one, and get him the hell out of that place," Mr. Grant told them.

"And then what?" Jet wanted to know.

Mr. Grant smiled and shook his head. "Then, my dear, prepare to never see him again."

When they left the sun was on the water and everything seemed to gleam as they walked across the wide lawn to the car. They were all saddened by this day, and by knowing what they must do. When they reached the car, they lingered, as if trying to avoid the inevitable return to real life.

"You cannot lose someone you love, even if he is no longer beside you," William said. "So we'll do as my father suggests. It's the only logical choice."

"Are you willing to?" Franny asked. "No matter the cost?"

Franny had her arm around William's waist. Jet walked close beside them. They were in this together, this perilous, wonderful business of loving Vincent.

"We've already decided we would ruin our lives together," William said. "So here we go."

Franny phoned Haylin that same night. When he heard what had happened he left work before his shift was over, something he never did. He was committed to his patients, but this was different. It was urgent, it was Franny, the only one who could give him a feeling of recklessness. He got to Greenwich Avenue in no time, and she was waiting for him. She was so worried and so pale that he lifted her into his arms. They went upstairs, pulled off their clothes, then got under the quilt together. Haylin was too tall for the bed and he always banged his head against the wall. He had such long limbs it seemed he might fall onto the floor at any moment.

Whenever Hay was there, the crow made himself comfortable on the bureau. Otherwise he spent his time in the kitchen, near the radiator. Lewis preferred to stay in the house. Long flights were past him, still he seemed full of cheer when Haylin visited, flapping around joyously before he settled down. Hay always brought Ritz crackers, which were the crow's favorites.

"I need your help again," Franny admitted.

"I suppose once you start breaking the law, it gets easier and easier to do," Hay said. "I could lose my medical license over the asthma incident. Now what?"

"Now we have to get Vincent out of Pilgrim State."

Hay had always thought Franny smelled like lily of the valley, which grew in wild clutches in the woodlands in Central Park each spring. He missed the past, but now that they were together again, he missed it less. Franny stroked his torso and his broad back, always amazed to find that he was now a man rather than the boy she'd first fallen in love with. But this wasn't love. They'd agreed to that. It was simply everything else.

"It's a secure facility," Haylin said. "Should we think about this?"

"There's nothing to think about," Franny said. "We have to get him out."

"It's *we*, is it? But isn't this when *I* go to jail?" he asked with a grin.

"It's when you rescue someone." Franny entwined her legs with his. She understood why ancient monsters were often made of two creatures, with two hearts and minds. There was strength in such a combination of opposites.

"Not you, I gather," he murmured. "Because I wouldn't mind

rescuing you." He held her beautiful red hair in one hand and told himself this wasn't love. He had to keep reminding himself of that. All the same, he knew he would step blindly forward to do whatever she asked. That had always been the case.

"Before you, I was the Maid of Thorns. I had no heart at all. You already rescued me," Franny said right before she asked him to risk everything, unaware that she had been asking him to do so ever since they'd first met, and that he had been willing to do whatever she wished him to, even during the time they'd been apart.

In the hospital, Vincent's thoughts were cloudy, fragile things. They'd shaved off his hair and had him wear a uniform that barely fit his tall frame. He was not allowed a belt or socks, lest he try to commit suicide with them by hanging. He had gone berserk in the dormitory and was then shot up with medication and plunged into a cold bath. Then they tied him up so they could carry him down the hall to this small room. There were mice, he could hear them. He could hear footsteps in the hall. Here were the things to stay away from: metal, ropes, water, fear. He felt himself weakening by the second.

His face was bruised from the altercation in the dormitory, and he had lost a good deal of weight. He was a wraith, a shadowy creature. He was thankful William couldn't see him, didn't know what he had become. They continued to feed him medication that caused him to be plodding; it was Thorazine, a wretched pill that made him descend into a woozy state of mind. The Vincent he had been previously had been banished to some distant part of the past, but not completely. He still knew how to play the game, and soon realized he could pretend to swallow the pills, even open his mouth to show they were gone, while keeping them tucked up along his gum. He would then spit them out when the nurse left him alone, then he'd hide them under the radiator. The first clear thought he had was a memory of an interview he had read with Jim Morrison, a singer and poet he admired for his rebellion.

Expose yourself to your deepest fear; after that, fear has no power, and the fear of freedom shrinks and vanishes. You are free.

Freedom was the instinct of every mortal being, even those who thought they had no hope. This was his deepest fear, to be trapped and jailed, like his ancestors. If he hadn't been surrounded by metal he could have willed his window to open and climbed out, then dropped to the ground. He then would have stopped traffic and hitchhiked to the city, slipping into a car with any stranger who would have deposited him on a city street, so that he might disappear into the crush of people at Forty-Second Street and call William from a pay phone. But he could not reach that part of himself. He had lost himself in this place, as had so many others before.

All he could do was keep his eyes closed and do his best to get through the day. *I've tried before, I've locked the door, I've done it wrong, I've done it right.* He did not eat or fight back. He shivered with cold even when the heat was turned up high, the old metal radiators pinging. He still had marks on his wrists from being bound when he'd thought he could fight his way out. At night he tried to get back the piece of his soul that had disappeared when they brought him here in irons.

He went over the spells he remembered from *The Magus*, doing his best to recall the magic that had once come to him so easily. He was convinced Aunt Isabelle's story of Maggie the rabbit was meant for him when he was hiding from himself, denying who he was. Now in the glinting half-light of the hospital room he practiced spells he had memorized. Although the newspaper on a cabinet fluttered and fell off the shelf, and a bowl and a plate rattled when he muttered curses, the aura of the place soon overtook him. It affected his brain and his soul alike. He couldn't even turn off the bright light that was kept on through the night. He was a rabbit in a cage. For most of the day he sat on a mattress on the floor. His feet were bare, long white feet that didn't look at all familiar, the feet of the dead.

To make himself aware that he was still alive, to save himself in some small way, he made himself think of the lake in Massachusetts, how cold and green it was, and of the garden where he'd played his first songs, and of April Owens standing in the grass in California, hands on her hips, telling him not to make promises he couldn't keep. He remembered Regina tagging after him, and the surprising swell of love he'd felt for her when she said she wanted to remember him. He transported himself to that moment, and he stayed there, in California. He no longer smelled the Lysol the janitors used to clean the floor, but rather there was the woodland scent of eucalyptus, so fragrant it made him dizzy.

He heard the door to his locked room open, but he was too far inside his head for it to matter. He had perfected the ability to hover somewhere outside of his own body, something he had learned from *The Magus*. He was in California and the grass was golden. Nothing else mattered. He could stay forever if he wished. *Would you like some flowers?* Regina was saying. All of the flowers were red, and in the center of each, a bee drowsed. Someone sat down on the chair. Likely a nurse with his medication. Best ignored. He stayed inside his mind, fading into the tall golden grass.

"Wake up, kid," a man's voice said. "You'd better pull yourself together."

Vincent gazed across the room, his eyes slits. He glimpsed a man in a naval uniform. It was Haylin.

"Medical personnel are allowed in," Haylin told him. "I have about twenty minutes, so you need to listen to everything I say." He then tossed something to Vincent, and without thinking Vincent reached up and caught it. It was a set of car keys. It woke him up.

"What are these?" Vincent's mouth felt like cotton when he spoke. His eyes hurt when he opened them wider. Light poured in and he rubbed at his eyes with his fists.

"They're yours. You're driving a Ford." Hay stood to drape his jacket over the pane of glass cut into the door. "We don't need the staff to know what we're doing." He took off his shoes and his shirt, then stopped and gestured when he took note of Vincent sitting there in shock, unmoving. "Can you hurry up? You leave for Germany tonight and trust me—you do not want to miss your flight. Your sisters and William will have my hide if something goes wrong."

Vincent smiled. He remembered how to do that.

"Let's go," Haylin urged. "Step one. Get the hell out. But just know this. You can't contact any of us. You have to make a clean break, otherwise we can be implicated and charged with abetting a federal offense."

In the parking lot the car was exactly where Hay said it would be. A rented Ford. He was to drive directly to Kennedy Airport, renamed in 1963 for their fallen president. He had Hay's ticket and passport and the two thousand dollars in cash Franny had sent along. She'd sold Maria's sapphire and was glad to have done so for Vincent's sake. Once safely in Germany, Vincent would be on his own, free to go where he pleased. Before leaving, though, he'd had to punch Hay.

"Right in the mouth," Hay had advised. "It's filled with blood vessels and will look much worse than it is."

Vincent then was instructed to tie Hay up—Hay had obligingly handed over his tie and his belt—and then to cover Hay with a blanket so no one would notice the switch until it was too late. And it was already too late. He was gone. A navy man and a doctor, with proof of it in his pocket. He looked official, with his buzzed hair, his head nearly bald. He drove with the windows down. He could feel his abilities coming back to him. He passed lights on the parkway and they clicked off. He turned on the radio without touching it. It was dusk, his lucky hour, the hour when he'd met William, when he'd gone onstage in Monterey, when he made his way to freedom, knowing he could never come back, understanding that this was the way one life ended and another began.

There was no reason for the authorities to doubt that Dr. Walker had been beaten and robbed. After the investigation he was given another ticket to Germany and a new passport. He and Franny knew they could not see each other in case one or the other was being watched. Still they dared to meet one last time, in Central Park, at night. It was easy enough to disappear into the lilac-colored shadows on paths they knew so well. The leaves on the trees looked blue, the bark violet. Franny had Vincent's dog with her. Harry walked slowly, for he had aged since Vincent's disappearance. All the same Franny kept him on a leash, for fear he'd take off and search for his master. She tied the dog to a bench when Haylin came up the path in the dark. They climbed the rocks above Turtle Pond and sat with their bodies so close they were touching. The water was green and luminous.

"Should we swim?" Haylin said.

It was a joke, but neither laughed. They wished they could go back to that moment when Franny didn't dive in and change what could never be changed. Franny rested her head on his chest. His heart seemed too loud. Lewis was in the tree above them. Looking down, he made a clacking sound.

"He's a funny pet," Haylin said. "He's so aloof, yet he follows you everywhere."

"I've told you before. He's not a pet. He's a familiar. And you're the one he's following. He's never really liked me. We're too much alike. Two crows in a pod."

"I see." Haylin threaded his fingers through her hair. "You're a beautiful bird."

He was still a drowning man every time he was with Franny, and now he had to give her up again. They would not be able to write or see each other, lest Hay's involvement with Vincent's disappearance be reexamined. He had done enough. Franny would not ruin him any more, although he very much wished that she would.

They did what they should have done years earlier; they took off their clothes and dove into the pond. Even in the shallows it was freezing, but once they went all the way in, they forgot the cold. The branches of the plane trees moved in the wind. There were snowbells, which bloomed for only ten days. Soon everything would be in leaf, a green bower as far as the eye could see. Tonight the city smelled of regret. Franny floated on her back, and Haylin came and took hold of her, pulling her to him. To want someone so much could be a terrible thing, or it could be the best hope a man could have.

"I can't be drowned, so don't even try," Franny teased. She could feel his sex against her and she moved so that he could enter her. She gasped because she felt the loss of him even now when he was inside her.

"Yes you can," he said, holding her closer. He would be going overseas and felt there was nothing to lose. To hell with the curse and the government and all the rest of the world. There were turtles below them and above them the firmament was starry. "Anyone can drown."

He walked at night, in a black coat acquired at a flea market. His hair was cropped, his complexion pale. He knew enough French by now to manage, but in truth, he rarely spoke. He had stayed only a short time in Frankfurt, where he'd practiced magic in a lonely room, then tried West Berlin for a month before heading for France, where he'd instantly felt more at home.

He lived in a small hotel in the Marais, a good place to hide out. In France, no one asked who you were or what you were doing there. They simply wrapped up the loaf of bread you bought, handed over the drink you ordered in a dive bar, and nodded when you bought cheese or meat. He was nervous when he saw Americans. He feared being caught for some ridiculous reason, a fan from Washington Square would recognize his face and bring attention to him in a public place. He'd forget to pay for an apple in a shop and be arrested and then found out.

What saddened him most was seeing people walking together in the hush that came to Paris only at certain dim hours of the day. He'd be wandering back to his hotel, having been out all night, eager to return to his room and sleep through till the late afternoon, but then he'd see lovers together and he'd feel a stab of loss cut through him. He couldn't help himself from missing William, but in response he'd turn his back to the scene that troubled him and keep walking, any idea of sleep shattered. If he thought too much about all he'd lost, he wouldn't be able to go on. Several times he'd come close to phoning William, but he couldn't take the risk of incriminating him.

Many times he'd thought of Regina, who was already nine. Likely he would never see her again, and that was most surely in her best interest. He couldn't ruin her with his love. The past seemed a distant thing, unreachable, as gone from him as ash. Once, in a bakery, he'd heard his own song, recorded at the Monterey Pop Festival. Someone other than William must have taped it and sent it out and now it had resurfaced. Vincent had turned and walked out. Soon the radio was muffled by street sounds and his frantic heart calmed down.

It was all so long ago, the golden hillsides in California, the dock where the sky was so blue. He was here, now, away from everyone he'd ever known in a place that also yielded beauty at every turn. He tried not to see that either; closing his eyes to the radiant light, and to the wood doves plummeting from the trees to the grass, and the lovers who didn't bother to hide their passion. This is why he usually walked at night, when the world was rife with blue-black shadows and pools of lamplight turned the streets yellow.

On evenings when Vincent felt the need to escape his room earlier than usual, he didn't bother to wait for nightfall. His hotel was musty, and there were times when he wanted freedom from his makeshift home. He went where no one knew him. It was dusk and he was having wine at a café in the Tuileries. The last of the daylight was sifting down in shades of orange. It was an illuminated world; one had to squint to see behind the paths. He knew William would have appreciated the beauty of the place; he would have enjoyed hearing the ringing of a bell tied around the neck of a goat there to eat grass, which was why Vincent himself could hardly tolerate any of it. Most of the young men in the city looked like Vincent: dark hair, bearded, dark coats and boots. He fit in well. He could be anonymous. He carried a newspaper, though he could not yet read French well enough to make much sense of the articles.

He was turning the pages when a woman sat across from him. She was older, extremely elegant, wearing sleek white-framed sunglasses despite the hour. She wore black, and took a cigarette and gold lighter from her leather purse.

"So here you are," she said.

Vincent looked up and shrugged. "Je suis désolé, madame. Vous avez fait une erreur. Nous ne nous connaissons pas."

"We don't know each other, it's true," the woman remarked. "But I am not mistaking you for anyone else. I knew your mother. To tell the truth, I knew her extremely well. I'm the same as you and your family, you see. From a very long line here in France. When your mother lived here in Paris, Susanna didn't deny who she was. That came later. We remained close, by long distance, and I know she would have wanted me to watch over you, which is what I've been doing."

"I see." Vincent put down his paper. So he was not anonymous after all. Because this was Paris and not New York, he did his best with the pleasantries of polite conversation when in truth he wished to merely storm off. "Perhaps I don't wish to be looked after."

"But you're one of us, so you see I have no choice."

Vincent shook his head. "I'm not anything."

The woman looked at him sadly. "We never change who we are from the beginning. You still have your inheritance from your bloodline. We may have experience and loss, but who we are at the core, that never changes. You are something special, the same as you've always been." She went on to introduce herself as Agnes Durant. "I have an apartment behind Place Vendôme. We often gather there. We've been here in Paris for so long we don't have to hide as Americans do. No one sees us if we don't wish them to. You think you're in hiding, but your presence is quite evident."

Vincent flicked down some money for the bill and stood, nodding courteously. "Then it's best for me to go."

"And keep running? That's the coward's way, isn't it? Please. Don't go."

Something in her tone moved Vincent. He sat back down

again. "Madame, I appreciate your offer of help. Really. I do. But there's no point."

"You have nothing worth living for?"

Vincent laughed. "Not so much. No, I don't."

"Because you can't go back to America? Because the government will never let you be?"

"Because I lost the man I loved."

"Oh." Agnes nodded. That she understood. "Many of us lose the man we love. And it's terrible. I know that for myself."

Vincent heaved a sigh and leaned forward, his expression bleak. He saw that this woman was the age his mother would have been and he felt a connection despite himself. "I have nothing left." He had always known his life would be over when he was still young.

Madame shook her head. "Vincent," she said with emotion. She clearly had the sight. "One life may be over, but another can begin."

Vincent gazed at the orange light. He could see every molecule of air, all of it infused with possibility. He picked up the scent of the sweet grass in the gardens, and heard the ringing of the goat's bell and felt the chill of the evening as it approached.

"You're in Paris," Madame said. "You might as well live."

So that he could live freely Madame Durant advised it would be best if he died. It must be public and final. He would no longer be a wanted man. His government would forget him, and so would everyone else. He could be himself, but with a new name and a new life, and what's more, he could then avoid the Owens curse.

He checked out of the hotel in the Marais. He had very little with him, but there was enough cash left from Franny's generous gift so that he could shop at a music store near the Sorbonne. There he spent the afternoon searching for an instrument that might replace his cherished Martin left behind in the States.

He found the guitar at the end of the day. A Selmer, the kind the brilliant gypsy musician Django Reinhardt had used. Reinhardt's third and fourth fingers were paralyzed and became webbed after he suffered burns in a fire, but he continued on with a style that was his alone. The guitar Vincent chose was made of laminated rosewood with a walnut neck and an ebony fingerboard. It had been made in the early fifties, and had been banged around, but once Vincent picked it up he didn't want to let it go. He hadn't played since his fingers had been broken, and so he was tentative at first, but he thought of what Django had gone through, and how he'd managed to become one of the greatest jazz guitarists of all time, therefore he couldn't feel sorry for himself.

He was not as skilled as he once was; all the same, strumming the guitar felt like sorcery. The tone was so singular, so nearly human in its trembling pitch, it was as though he'd found his soul in a dusty shop. He was in Paris and he felt alive. Perhaps Agnes had been right: you remained who you were. Vincent bargained, but not too much because he wanted it so. And then he saw a little record player in a corner, a clever little machine fit into a rose-colored leather traveling case. He bought it without bargaining, full price, and he took it with him, tucked under his arm.

He went to a stationery store, where he bought an airmail

letter. He then sat at a café, ordered a coffee, and composed a message to his sisters. He told Jet that one of the best days of his life was when they arrived at the hospital after the accident to find she was alive. He reminded Franny of the story she had told about the minstrel who lost his voice.

He wrote that when he thought of the past he envisioned the three of them lying on the kitchen floor, eavesdropping on their father's therapy sessions. There they were, children trapped in a house they couldn't wait to get away from, but which he now missed every day.

> *You both rescued me every time I needed you. I hope I'm worthy of such kindness.*
> *We were wrong about Maria's curse. It is simply the way of the world to lose everything you have ever loved. In this, we are like everyone else.*

When he went to post the letter, he also had the record player boxed up and sent to April's address in California. He jotted a note on a piece of thin, white paper. *To my dear Regina, to whom I made a promise that I kept.*

He did not need to write to William. Mrs. Durant had already taken care of that.

He tossed his backpack into a trash bin in the park where it could be discovered after he was gone. Everything he had, other than his guitar, was folded inside, including the key to 44 Greenwich Avenue. It was a portion of his life he would never get back. Friends of Madame Durant's were stationed in the Tuileries. They had hung posters on lampposts and a crowd was already gathering. There was an atmosphere of expectation in the streets. Vincent's music was known in France and his underground tape often played.

Vincent wore a black suit. He kept a photograph of William in his shirt pocket, the one taken in California when the world was open to them. They had been standing on the dock in San Francisco and had persuaded a stranger to snap them together, arms entwined, the sky behind them a vivid blue. Tonight he had sipped a tincture of dogwood Madame had given him, so that his voice would come back to him.

For the date of the concert he'd chosen Samhain, All Hallows' Eve, the night of death and transformation. The sky was black and filled with stars and the leaves on the chestnut trees curled up as a sudden flash of cold descended upon the city. He stood on an overpass near the Louvre facing the crowd. The lamps in the park blinked as though they were fireflies. This was the moment he had seen in the three-sided mirror when he was fourteen. When a hush fell he sang the songs he had written in New York, beginning and ending with "I Walk at Night." He had his fans, but most in the crowd had never heard of him. The last song was a river in which he would have happily drowned.

Isn't that what love makes you do? Go on trying, even when you're through, Go on even when you're made of ash, when there's nothing inside you but the past.

He felt the wolfsbane he had ingested earlier in the evening spreading through him. He was sinking into it as the herb slowed his heart and his breathing became shallow in his chest. He could see everything he'd never seen before as time slowed down. The glimmering of the world. Those he'd loved who'd loved him in return. The gifts he'd been given. The years he'd had. He was so beautiful in that moment. Those who watched him gasped and forgot where they were. An enchantment took over and people stood in silence. White moths appeared from the grass. They spun past, higher all the time, until they disappeared into the sky.

Vincent was grateful this was the way he was able to leave behind everything he had known before. He collapsed, and when he could not be revived, a doctor who was a friend of Madame Durant's signed the death certificate at 11:58. It was still All Hallows' Eve. The temperature had dropped. Raindrops fell and splattered on the sidewalks. A private ambulance was sent for. Reporters had been called so they might witness his death. The leaves were curling in the cold and no one seemed to have the ability to speak. All was still, except for the siren as the ambulance pulled away, and then, at a little after midnight, the sound of the falling rain turned hard as it became ice striking against the sidewalks and the brown leaves of the chestnut trees.

Madame Durant was the one who made the funeral arrangements, acting swiftly so no questions would be asked. She had placed a very old disappearing spell over Vincent as he'd lain prone. *L'homme invisible.* From that moment on no one would ever figure out the private details of his life. All the same, the newspapers were filled with reports of his strange death. There were insinuations, with some convinced he had taken his own life and others vowing there had been foul play. A small vigil had begun outside the hotel where he had stayed in the Marais, with flowers deposited in a fragrant muddy pile and white candles lit so that wax flowed into the gutter. The radio stations played "I Walk at Night" and people who didn't know Vincent's name found themselves singing the lyrics as they walked home from work.

The burial was at Père-Lachaise, the cemetery opened by Napoleon in 1804. Jet and Franny's plane was hours late, delayed by a storm in New York. William had traveled with them, wearing a black suit, carrying only a leather backpack. He spoke very little, and seemed so distant the sisters wondered if because he had the sight he had known this was to be his fate all along, to be traveling to France for a funeral.

They took a taxi to the main entrance of the cemetery on Boulevard de Ménilmontant, with William telling the driver that if he ignored stoplights they would pay him double his fare.

"We must be there," William said.

"We will," Jet assured him.

Franny simply stared out the window. She had barely spoken since the news had come. She was meant to protect him, and she had failed. Her plans had gone awry, and now he was lost to them. Once at the cemetery, they had soon become disoriented among the angels and monuments until a young man sent by Agnes Durant to search for the missing Americans guided them to the freshly turned grave.

"It can be very confusing here," the young man said, as he led them down the gravel paths.

"Yes," the sisters agreed. They had never been more confused in their lives. Why did their thoughts become blurry when
they tried to think of their brother?

"This place is very old, and there are so many dead people," explained their guide, who dressed much as Vincent might
have, in a dark coat, with black Levi's from America and suede
boots.

For Vincent to have had a heart attack at such a young age
was unthinkable, but such was the doctor's report. The sisters
could not conceive of a world in which he was gone. They had
decided to wear white dresses that Jet had found in the resale
shop next to the Chelsea Hotel. They refused to wear black
on this day. It was only now that Franny realized what Jet had
chosen.

"These are wedding dresses!" she whispered, annoyed.

"You said white. These were all they had on the rack," Jet
said apologetically.

Though it was November and chilly, they slipped off their
shoes out of respect. The other guests were friends of Agnes's
and, as it turned out, of their mother's. The brevity of the service
was fitting. Vincent did not like an excess of emotion, unless it
was real love, and then nothing was too much. Agnes hugged
the sisters, then kissed William twice. "It's a pleasure to meet
you," she said to him warmly. "I've heard so much about you
and now here you are."

The mourners went to a restaurant nearby for a light dinner.
The place was small, lit by candles even in the daylight hours,
decorated with trompe l'oeil wallpaper and velvet couches to sit
on while they dined.

"Susanna and I came here often when we were young,"

Agnes Durant said. "And we often went to the cafés in the Tuileries, where I first met Vincent. Susanna and I looked so alike people thought we were sisters."

"Well, we look nothing alike and we *are* sisters," Jet said, taking Franny's hand in hers. She felt as though they had somehow lost Vincent to this stranger who gazed at them with curious dark eyes.

"I only meant, I feel that I'm family to you," Madame Durant said, trying to soothe Jet's ruffled feathers.

"Thank you," Franny said. "Please understand we have lost an actual member of our family."

"Of course. I would never intrude. I have your best interests at heart."

Franny found that difficult to believe but she was distracted by the presentation of their supper, which included hors d'oeuvres of oysters and cheeses. The restaurant owner had a little dachshund that lounged on one of the velvet couches.

It was only then Franny realized that William wasn't among them. She imagined he was still at the cemetery, unwilling to leave his beloved. How horrid they had forgotten him in his hour of need.

"I'll be right back," Franny told Jet as she dashed out, hoping she would find her way back to the burial site. The hour was late and night was falling. She felt panic rising in the back of her throat as she darted along the streets in the evening light, finally finding the pedestrian gate of the cemetery at Porte du Respos and hurrying inside.

There was ice on the paths and her breath came out in cold puffs and the white dress was much too sheer and flimsy for the chill of the day. Gravediggers were flinging clods of earth over the open grave. Franny stopped. Her heart felt too heavy for her chest.

There was the shadow of a tall man.

"William!" she called, but if it was he, he did not respond.

Franny held one hand over her eyes as the sun went down, and the orange light made it difficult to see. The leaves on the trees were rustling and swirls of earth rose up from the ground.

"Is it you?" Franny cried.

She couldn't tell if she saw one man's shadow or two. And then she knew. She felt her brother near, just as she had when they played hide-and-seek in the basement and their mother could never find them. She followed the path, but the orange light was blinding, and she bumped into a woman bringing flowers to a grave and had to apologize. She didn't realize that she was crying until she spoke to the other mourner. Her apology was accepted with a shrug, and then she was alone. She stopped and watched as the light grew darker and the shadows longer, and then, when it was clear she would not find her way, she returned the way she'd come.

She went back to the restaurant, arriving as Haylin was getting out of a taxi. He'd flown from Frankfurt, where he'd been stationed, and now he embraced Franny on the sidewalk. He kissed her and could not stop. It was Paris so no one looked at them twice.

"I should have been here sooner," he said.

"You're here now." Franny seemed more in shock than grief-stricken.

She barely spoke that evening. As the dinner was ending, with aperitifs and small cakes, Franny went to Agnes and asked if she could call on her the next day. "I want to thank you and perhaps get to know you better, as my mother did. I was rude before, and I apologize."

"I'm so sorry," Agnes demurred. "I'm closing up my apartment. I really won't have time. I'm going out to my country house."

"So that's it? Vincent is gone and we don't speak about it?"

Agnes shrugged. "How can we understand life? It's impossible. To the world, Vincent is dead and buried. Let's leave it that way, my dear."

"And we don't speak of William either? I'm not even sure where he is. What do I do when his father calls me and asks where he is?"

"William is where he wants to be. How many among us can lay claim to that?"

Franny rushed back to the hotel and Jet's room.

"William lied to us," she told her sister. "He let us go through that charade of a funeral. All the while, that Madame Durant had placed a disappearing spell on Vincent so we wouldn't know the truth. He's alive, Jetty."

"If William lied, he did it for Vincent. You knew we were going to lose him. I suppose this was the best way."

"To make us think he had died?" Even for a few hours it had been horrible.

"He has died. For us. And we must keep it that way if we want him to be safe."

At the hotel, Jet was happy to leave Franny and Haylin to each other. She preferred to be alone to grieve. The loss of her brother affected her deeply. She went to her room and when she took off the hat she'd been wearing all day, she found that her hair had gone white all at once. It had happened at the funeral. Her best feature, her long black hair, gone. She gazed into a mirror above the bureau and spied the woman she had seen in their aunt's black mirror. She wondered what Levi would have thought if he was with her. Perhaps he would have lain down beside her and told her she was still beautiful, even if it wasn't true. He would have read to her from a book of poems, then perhaps planned where they would go for a drink, someplace somber, but warm, where they could sit close together. But now, without him, she had stepped into her future, and, like it or not, this was who she'd turned out to be. He was a boy, and she was now a woman who had lost nearly everyone she'd ever loved. She thought of what she'd told April once. This was what happened when you were alive. She called the desk and asked for some coffee, since she already knew she wouldn't be able to sleep. Paris was too noisy, the room was too cold, the injury of losing Vincent too fresh. She did not mind being alone. She sat beside the window and wrote a postcard to Rafael. She always wrote him postcards, even when they were both in New York City, and then when they got together they would read the postcards in bed. She wished he were here with her now. Just as a friend, of course. The friend she wanted to be with more than any other.

It had begun to rain, a thin green drizzle that made the sidewalks shine.

Paris is sad, she wrote, *but beautiful enough to make you not care about sadness.*

Franny fell asleep beside Haylin, exhausted. When she woke he was sitting on the edge of the bed watching the rain falling. They were supposed to stay away from each other, but their pact didn't need to apply yesterday, nor today. The sky outside was thick with rain clouds. Paris was so gray in November. Wood doves were gathering on the small balcony. Franny held out her hands to them and they pecked at the glass. She wished they never had to leave this room, but they did. Haylin had told her he was being transferred to the field. He would be leaving in less than eight hours for Vietnam. They spent those eight hours in bed, telling each other they didn't love each other; they did so for luck and to do their best to ensure they would one day see each other again.

The sisters packed up and called a taxi. They went to the Tuileries and walked down the gravel paths. The leaves were turning brown. They had their suitcases with them, so they stopped at the first café they came to in the park. They ordered white wine, but they didn't drink much. They were thinking about their mother when she was young, and the rules she'd made up to protect them. They had their own rules now. Franny cast a circle in the gravel beside their table. Then she took one of Lewis's feathers that she had in her pocket. She let the feather fall. Outside the circle, and their brother was gone. But it landed inside, right in the center. Jet let out a sob. Franny reached for her hand. It was good news. He was somewhere close by, but when the feather blew away they knew the other side of the truth. He was lost to them now.

When the sisters returned to New York, Franny took to spending the night in Vincent's room. From here she could hear the echo of children in the school yard in the mornings. She let the crow remain inside. He was aging and he liked to perch on the desk near the heater, where he dozed in fits and starts. The dog followed Franny around, but she was a poor substitute for Vincent, and he began sleeping at the front door, waiting for his master to reappear.

Both sisters slept uneasily upon their return, disturbed by sounds of the city, the rumble of buses, the shrill sirens, the ever-present traffic on Seventh Avenue. When Franny opened the window she found that New York City had only one scent now and it never changed. It was the sharp tang of regret. She longed for something darker and greener, for a silence that might allow her to find some peace.

One night she dreamed that Isabelle was sitting on the window seat of the old house in Massachusetts.

You know the answer, Isabelle said. *Fate is what you make it.*

When Franny awoke, she realized she was homesick. She was at the kitchen table when Jet came downstairs. To Franny, Jet seemed even more beautiful with her white hair, for her beauty was rooted inside of her now.

"I'm ready to go," Franny told her sister. In fact, she had already packed up her room.

Jet looked at her surprised. "Go where?"

"The place we feel most at home."

"All right. We'll shut down the store."

"I'll call the attorney. He can manage selling this place. It was temporary for us. Now the rightful tenant can have it."

Jet understood her sister's wish to leave New York. 44 Greenwich Avenue was already becoming the past as they sat there. It was disappearing in front of their eyes. It had been a home for the three of them, but they were three no longer. She thought of Vincent playing "I Walk at Night" for the first time, of April visiting with Regina and eating chocolate cake in the kitchen, of the plumber who did work for them in exchange for a love spell, and of the night when Vincent came home and told them he was in love. As for Franny, what she remembered most was standing outside on the sidewalk, looking up at the windows, knowing that lilacs grew here and that she would buy this house and that for a while they would live here and try to be happy, and, in a way, they were.

During the course of two years Franny collected 120 letters from Haylin, all wrapped in string, kept in the bureau in the dining room. The house on Greenwich Avenue had been sold and divided into offices. A literary agent had taken the rooms on the third floor, and her desk was now in the space where Vincent's room had been. She was a lovely woman with a beautiful smile who filled up her bookshelves along the wall where his bed had been. For a while the shop was a mystery bookstore and occasionally the owners found red thread and wishbones in unexpected places. The ramshackle greenhouse Vincent had built was pulled down and carted away, but some of the seeds scattered through the neighborhood so that foxgloves and sunflowers grew in the alleys for several seasons. They took the tilted kitchen table that had been in their family house on Eighty-Ninth Street, and they took Edgar, the stuffed heron, whom they kept in the parlor of Aunt Isabelle's house and decorated every Yule with silver trimmings and gold tinsel.

The sisters settled into the Owens house on Magnolia Street. It felt like home in no time. Franny took Aunt Isabelle's room, where Lewis, now so aged his feathers had begun to turn white, nested on the bureau. Jet was happy to have the guest room where April Owens had stayed when they refused to share a room with her. The attic, where they'd spent their first summer, was a place for young girls, not for grown women who needed more comfortable beds, so they used it for storage. Harry still slept by the door, waiting for his master, while Wren kept to the garden, where she chased off rabbits and mice.

They had an entire winter in which to restore everything that had been ignored for so long. Charlie came to clear out the gutters, cut back the vines on the porch, and deliver a cord of wood for the fireplace. He said it was grand to see people in the house again.

"I miss your aunt," he told the sisters. "She was one of a kind for certain."

On days when the sky was spitting out snow, Jet took possession of the window seat to read from one of her beloved novels. Magic came back to her slowly, like a long-forgotten dream that hovered nearby.

Now that she lived in town, she visited the cemetery every Sunday. She walked no matter the weather. Some children called her the Daffodil Lady, because she always carried a bunch of the blooms. Sometimes the Reverend gave her a ride home, especially if it was raining hard. He was there every Sunday as well. In nice weather he brought two lawn chairs, and when the sky was overcast he brought a large black umbrella.

They didn't talk very much, although the Reverend noticed that Jet still wore the moonstone ring Levi had given her, and Jet saw that the Reverend kept one of Levi's swimming medals pinned to his jacket. When they talked, they talked about the weather, as people in Massachusetts often do.

"Cold," he would say.

And she would agree with a word or two, and then one day she brought mittens she had knitted for him out of soft gray wool. The next time he brought the scarf she had made for Levi, which made her cry. She ducked her head so that the Reverend wouldn't see, although he could tell all the same. He carried a handkerchief, and gave it to her, and gently said, "This comes in handy."

In the spring he handed her a new business card he'd had printed. He had gone back to work and was now a justice of the peace. He had already married six couples. He told her that one couple had phoned him in the middle of the night, desperate to marry, so he had performed the service in his living room dressed in his pajamas.

One day he said, "Maybe you should move on with your life."

Jet was grateful for his kind thought. Years had passed. She still met Rafael in the city several times a year. For a while he saw another woman, and thinking he wanted a family, he was married briefly. But in the end he divorced. His wife didn't know him the way Jet did. They could talk with each other in a way they couldn't with anyone else, and so they began to see each other again.

Rafael was the principal of a school in Queens and several times a year they went to the Oak Bar at the Plaza Hotel for old times' sake. They often spent the night together in his apartment. Once he had suggested marriage, but Jet told him she thought it was a bad idea. It would get in the way of things. The truth was she still worried about the curse; even though she hoped such things could be broken, she didn't want to chance its ill effects. She thought it best if Rafael was only a dear friend. He agreed to this, even though he was in love with her. He didn't tell her so, but she knew, just as he knew what her intentions had been that night at the Plaza Hotel. They didn't need the sight to know how one another felt.

"I'm fine," she told the Reverend on the day he told her to get on with her life.

And she was. She did not discuss her grief with anyone, but she could share it with the Reverend. But then one Sunday, Jet failed to appear. The Reverend scanned the field, waiting for her to arrive, but she didn't. It felt strange without her there, not right somehow, so he drove over to Magnolia Street and parked outside the house. He sat there in his idling car, until Franny came outside. The Reverend rolled down his window. He'd never spoken to Franny, he'd only see her walking through town in her black coat, her red hair piled on top of her head. People were afraid of her. They said she was not one to cross. Up close, she was taller than he had expected, and prettier.

"She has pneumonia," Franny said. "I wouldn't let her go to the cemetery."

It was a damp, drizzly day and the Reverend more than understood. He nodded. "Tell her I'll see her next week."

"Tell her yourself," Franny said.

They looked at each other, then the Reverend got out of his car and followed Franny into the house. He noticed that the wisteria was blooming, always the first in town to do so. This was the house that had been built with money his ancestor had given to a woman he had loved, then had called a witch. He wondered how often that had happened both then and now. He carried the burden of his family with him and was weighed down by the wrong they'd done in the world.

The Reverend had arthritis so Franny slowed her usually quick gait. Jet was in the parlor, a blanket around her, drinking tea, reading *Sense and Sensibility*, which she could happily reread time and again. When she saw the Reverend she was so startled she dropped her book, then quickly bent to retrieve it. She felt fluttery having him in the house, as if something momentous was happening even though everything was so very quiet.

"Sorry to hear you're not well," the Reverend said.

"I'll be better by next week," Jet said.

"I expect you will be," the Reverend said. "The weather will be better then, too. So they say."

"Yes, I've heard that, too. No rain."

"Good," the Reverend said. He looked around. "The woodwork is nice."

"Yes. It is. It doesn't need much care. But I use a little olive oil on the dustcloth every once in a while."

"Olive oil," he murmured. "I never would have thought of that."

"It's natural. No chemicals," Jet said.

"I'll try that sometime," the Reverend said, even though he hadn't dusted the woodwork in his house for years.

The next week was sunny and dry, and on Sunday Jet went

back to the cemetery. She wore boots and a sweater and woolen slacks. She still had a cough, but she'd had a cup of licorice tea before she left the house that would quiet it. She didn't want Levi's father to worry. When he did there was a line across his forehead, the same line that Levi had across his forehead when he was concerned. The Reverend looked relieved when he saw Jet walking across the grass and he waved. Jet thought perhaps she was fine, considering everything that had happened, and that by coming here each week, she had made her own fate. She was a woman a person could depend on, in fair weather and foul.

The sky was very blue and the Reverend said this was because in Massachusetts if you waited a few minutes the weather was sure to change, and she agreed and said that in her experience that had always been true.

On the harshest days of the year Franny could be seen stalking through town on her way to Leech Lake without use of a hat or gloves. She had discovered that the woods circling the lake fell into the pattern of migration of scarlet tanagers. On the grayest days, the nearby bushes were bright red, as if each branch had a heart, and each heart could fly away in an instant. All Franny had to do was hold out her hands, and they came to her. She laughed and fed them seed. She knew they would be far away in no time, to warmer climates near the Mexican border. She herself no longer had the urge to fly away. She was happy to be where she was.

That first winter Franny walked to the library on the day the board convened. There was muffled shock when she arrived. The president of the board shook Franny's hand and offered her a cup of tea, which she declined. The members of the board didn't know whether to be flattered or terrified when Franny then stood to announce her intention to serve on the board, and all raised their hands to vote yea to include her.

When Franny's first request was permission to have the rare book room dedicated to Maria Owens, assuring them that in return she would make a donation to the library, the members of the board were relieved. As that room had been Maria's jail cell, it was only right that she be remembered here. Pages from Maria's journal were framed and hung on the wall. Teenage girls, especially those who considered themselves outcasts and were interested in the town's history of witchcraft, often came to study the pages. They didn't understand why a brave, independent woman had been so brutally treated. Many of them began to wonder why they themselves often feigned opinions rather than speak their minds, no matter how clever they were, for fear they'd be thought of as difficult. Some of these girls came to stand at the fence so they could gaze into the garden. At dusk, everything looked blue, even the leaves on the lilacs.

When spring came around, and the lilacs bloomed, Franny began to leave blank journals on the bureau in Maria's room in the library, and every week they were taken home by girls who questioned their worth in the modern world. Walking past Leech Lake, Franny often spied one or two perched on a rock, writing furiously in their journals, clearly convinced that words could save them.

Summer came and with it the sparrow. This time, however,

the bird that could bring a year's worth of bad luck was met by Lewis, who had perched on the dining room mantel. The poor hapless sparrow swiftly flew out the window.

"Good work," Franny said to the crow.

Despite her flattery, he eyed her with suspicion. They were wary allies who both happened to adore the same person.

"Even if you don't like me, come have a cookie," Franny said, for she knew the crow liked anise biscuits and she'd just made some. She had been thinking of various ways for them to earn money. The house had its own trust to support its upkeep, but without the shop, the sisters had no regular employment. Franny had made the rash donation to the library and there was no shop to help them pay the bills. She thought of baking for profit, but it was so time-consuming. Her biscuits were chewy and probably wouldn't sell, and the ingredients of the tipsy cake were so costly—the bars of chocolate, the extrafine, aged rum— they'd never bring in a cent.

Franny put in an application at the dress shop, but when the owner saw her name, she quickly said the job was filled, a blister already forming on her tongue as she spoke. So much the better, really, as Franny had no interest in clothes and wore the same black dress and red boots, which were mud-caked and in need of new heels. Her rejections continued at the pharmacy and the grocery store. The baker looked positively terrified when she walked in the door. His customers didn't favor anise, he said, and as for rum in a cake, well that would never do. The shopkeepers did their best to be pleasant enough, though they all had a frantic look in their eyes when she came into their shops, the bells over their doors refusing to ring. She had that effect. She stopped things with her chilly manner.

"It's really not a job for you," the bookshop owner had said when she went to ask for a job. "Perhaps your sister?"

Of course people would prefer Jet. She was kinder and much more well mannered, and Franny *did* look savage with her wild red hair and her threadbare black coat. She had lost weight and was gawky, as she'd been when she was a girl. Even when she dabbed powder on her freckled skin she looked sulky and unkempt. And those boots, well, they gave her away. Red as heartbreak. An Owens woman, through and through.

In the summertime, Franny missed Vincent more than ever. She went to Leech Lake, where she stood on the grassy bank to strip off her clothes, then she waded in to float in the cold, green water. No leeches came near. There were only dragonflies skimming over the surface of the lake.

You know who we are, Vincent had said to her that first summer, and she had, but she hadn't wanted to admit it. She didn't want to be condemned because of her family history or be pigeonholed as an Owens. She longed to be free, a bird in the sky over Central Park, unconnected to the fragile world. None of that seemed to matter anymore. In the shallows of the lake, she closed her eyes and floated through the cattails. The water turned jewel-blue once she reached the depths, which were said to be bottomless. There were rumors of ancient fish living in the deepest parts of the lake, creatures that hadn't been seen for a hundred years, but all Franny saw were frogs in the shallows, and occasionally an eel slipping through the reeds.

One day she noticed some girls watching her. She swam to shore, where she ducked behind some thornbushes and swiftly dressed.

"You're a good floater," one of the girls said to her.

"Thanks," Franny said, wringing out her hair. The water that fell onto the ground was red. The other girls all took off, but one stayed behind. The one who had spoken.

"Is that blood?" the girl now asked.

"Not at all. It's hair dye." It was neither, it was simply the way her hair reacted to water, but Franny wasn't about to explain that to a ten-year-old. She'd never cared for children. She hadn't much liked herself when she was one.

The other girls had scattered to climb up the rocks.

"That's dangerous," Franny called. No one paid attention to her, except for the one girl who was still staring at her. "Not that it's any of my business," Franny said brusquely.

"Is it true that you can't be drowned?" the girl asked.

"Anyone *can* be drowned. Given the right circumstances." The girl was plain but had a bright spark of intelligence in her eyes. "Why do you ask?"

"I thought you were a witch."

"Really?" By now Franny was slipping on her boots. She wore them in every season. Even in summer. They were so much better than shoes for gardening. "Who told you that?"

"Everyone says so."

"Well, *everyone* doesn't know *everything*," Franny responded. She sounded crotchety, even to herself. The girl was carrying a backpack. A blue journal peeking out caught Franny's attention. It was one of the notebooks she'd left in the library. "Are you writing?" she asked.

"Trying to," the girl said.

"Don't try, *do*." She realized she sounded exactly like Aunt Isabelle when she was irritated. She hadn't meant to be a wet blanket and had no wish to discourage this clever little girl, so she changed her tone. "But trying *is* a start. What is your story?"

"My life."

"Ah."

"If you write it all down, it doesn't hurt as much."

"Yes, I can imagine," Franny said.

The girl scampered onto the rocks to join her friends. She waved and Franny waved back.

As she walked home Franny thought that the girl at the lake had been perfectly right. It helped to write things down. It ordered your thoughts and if you were lucky revealed feelings you didn't know you had. That same afternoon Franny wrote a long letter to Haylin. She had never told anyone what her aunt had whispered with her last breath. But now she wrote it down, and when she did she realized it was what she believed, despite the curse.

Love more, her aunt had said. *Not less.*

Jet remembered how much she had enjoyed puttering in the garden when she began working there again. Everything flourished under her touch. She planted spring onions and mint and cabbages and rue and basil and Spanish garlic. She put in lemon thyme, lemon balm, lemon verbena, foxgloves, and zinnias, making sure to plant rosemary and lavender by the back door, where it had grown when Isabelle was there. The Reverend gave her some of his bulbs so she could grow clutches of daffodils and bring her own flowers to the cemetery on her visits. Some were white with orange centers, some were golden, some were butter yellow. When they bloomed she cried because she knew another year had gone by and it was all happening so fast.

The more dangerous plants were ordered from the Owens farm in Rockport, Maine, and these Jet grew in the greenhouse, still locked with an old iron key. No reason to take a chance that teenagers who could easily mistake wolfsbane for marijuana might manage to get inside and binge on poison. There, behind glass, she kept belladonna; hemlock; nightshade, which could induce visions and was said to be in the ointment that allowed witches to fly; henbane, known as black nightshade, used by men to attract women and by women to bring rain; mandrake, an herb said to scream when plucked from the ground by its roots; thorn apple, used for healing and for breaking hexes, but only in tiny amounts, otherwise death might result.

One day she saw the old rabbit, Maggie, near the greenhouse, hiding from the cat. Franny had come out and they stood there together. It was definitely Maggie, with her black whiskers and sad eyes.

"Let's set her free," Jet said.

Franny went over and grabbed the rabbit before it could hop away. "Now what?" she asked.

Jet went to open the gate, and Franny followed.

"She'll just wind up in someone else's yard," Franny said.

"Yes, but it will be her choice."

Franny put the rabbit down on the sidewalk. For a minute it huddled there, staring at them.

"You're free," Franny said, waving her hands. "Go on!"

Maggie took off down the street, running so fast they never saw her again.

"Good riddance," Franny said.

"Good luck," Jet called after the creature.

The cat always followed Jet about, but one day Wren disappeared and when she returned home another black cat, soon called Sparrow, followed. After that there was another named Goose, and then yet another enormous long-haired cat, whom they called Crow, since he seemed far more interested in Lewis than he did in the other cats, even though the bird did little more than spend his days drowsing in a sunny spot on the porch. As it turned out, Wren was bringing home cats from an animal shelter on the other side of town, climbing in through a broken window, then leading them to Magnolia Street.

"You're becoming a cat lady," Franny observed.

"They chase away the rabbits," Jet responded.

"Yes," Franny said with a grin. "But they never catch them. I'll bet old Harry could. If he wanted to. Which he clearly does not."

The dog was usually up on the porch with Lewis. Two old creatures who never were pets, and who now needed their food to be mixed with water, which was easier on the digestion. She wondered if the old dog dreamed of Vincent, as she did. She liked to imagine her brother in a village in France, strolling through the dusk with William, past fields and woods. Occasionally his song came on the radio. Jet always turned it off. Vincent's voice was too painful a reminder for her. But Franny would take the radio into the garden. She loved to listen to Vincent and was glad that people remembered him. Sometimes cards would arrive in the mail, postmarked from Paris. She kept these and tied blue ribbon around the stack she had collected. Only their address was written out, but the message was clear. *I'm still here.*

The light on the porch was broken. Charlie Merrill had tried his best to fix it, but to no avail. "Circuits are shot," he said. "It will cost a fortune to rewire. I recommend leaving it be."

Franny, nervous as ever about money, was quick to agree. So what if their doorway was dark? They certainly didn't expect visitors. It was fall, their favorite time of the year, and the evenings grew dark at an earlier hour. Jet had visited New York, as she did once a month, keeping her destination to herself, meeting Rafael at the Oak Bar. He was by far her oldest and best friend.

"You look different," he had told her the last time she saw him. "Happy."

Indeed, Jet had the feeling something was about to happen. And then one day when she was collecting the last of the rosemary that grew beside the door, thinking about Aunt Isabelle's clients who often arrived at this hour, the porch light switched on.

Jet stood up, holding the rosemary. It was wilted brown, but as she watched, it became green in her hands. Her gray eyes rimmed with tears. What she had lost had returned. When two girls passed by the fence she knew what they were thinking, although she was too well mannered to ever tell.

She had the sight once more.

It was Samhain, the last day in October, when doors between worlds are open and impossible things are accomplished.

She began to work from Isabelle's *Grimoire*, starting with the easy recipes: chamomile for blessing, hyssop and holly to dispel negative energy, and after a few weeks she progressed to one of the most complex spells, the dove's heart love charm. She went to the butcher's for the heart, and afterward there was all sorts of chatter on Main Street. People peered out their windows as she walked home with a bloody paper bag. She was to prick the heart she had carefully prepared for a client who was to say, *My lover's heart will feel this pin and his devotion I will win. There'll be no way for him to rest nor sleep, until he comes to me to speak. Only when he loves me best will he find peace and with peace rest.*

That night the porch light was on.

No trick-or-treaters ever came to the Owens house on Halloween. They were warned away by their parents and by tradition. But there were other people who were desperate to walk through the gate. The first woman came at dusk, knocking tentatively at the door.

"It's probably someone trying to sell us something," Franny said. "Ignore it."

All the same, Jet opened the door. There was the woman who had bought Mrs. Rustler's house, the one Franny had run into years back when Isabelle had fallen ill.

"What on earth are you doing here?" Franny wanted to know.

"Your light was on." The woman was unsure as to whether she should cross the threshold or back away. "I know what that means."

Franny tossed her sister a dark look. Still Jet motioned to

their neighbor, who after a glance around, proceeded to enter the kitchen.

"I suppose she wants something," Franny groused.

"Everyone wants something," Jet responded. "Even you."

"It's about my husband," the woman said.

"Oh, God, not this again." Franny groaned.

"What about him?" Jet had already put the kettle up for tea.

Their neighbor began to cry. Her husband was unfaithful, and it was tearing their family apart. It was then Franny realized that the girl she had met at the lake with the blue notebook was this woman's daughter. Franny now wondered if that was why the girl had asked if she was a witch, if she'd been in search of a spell to set things right in her family. Perhaps she'd been the one to suggest her mother come to them.

"I may be able to help you," Jet said.

"Really?" Franny said to Jet. "Are we going to do this?"

"Go to the refrigerator," Jet told her sister. "It's on the second shelf."

For once Franny did as she was told. When she spied the dove's heart on a blue willowware plate she laughed out loud. Here it was, their future and their fate. She had often found such unsavory items in the pantry or in the fridge where their aunt had stored away the more questionable ingredients. It might also be a way for them to survive their dismal financial state.

Franny turned to her sister, who was pouring cups of chamomile tea, good for the nerves. "Remember," she told her sister. "There's a charge for these things."

"I'll pay anything," their neighbor told them.

Franny brightened then. Perhaps this wasn't a completely worthless endeavor.

Jet went to the cabinet. There was the jar of engagement rings they'd forgotten all about. "Do you have one of these?"

The neighbor slipped off her diamond ring and handed it over.

"All right," Jet said. "Let's begin."

When Haylin was wounded he was posted in a makeshift hospital in the delta, where the air was so hot it turned liquid. He had been there so long he no longer counted days. He no longer counted patients. One man after another was injured, some so dreadfully he would go outside and throw up into the dense greenery after he cared for them. When he himself was injured, he felt nothing at first. Only a rush of cold air, as if the wind had cut through him, and then the heat of his blood. He was immediately airlifted to the hospital in Frankfurt where he had previously worked, and, after surgery and intensive rehab, he was transferred to the American Hospital in Paris, on the Boulevard Victor Hugo. His father had insisted he be sent to the best private hospital in Europe, and the navy had relented. It no longer mattered; Hay was done with his service. He had read all of Franny's letters, three times over, but he didn't wish to upset her by informing her of the magnitude of his medical situation. Instead he called the last person anyone would have expected him to contact. His father. Later Franny would always say, "So if you had died your father would have been the one to contact me?" And he would always answer, "I wasn't ready to die."

Months had passed and she hadn't heard from him. She was dizzy with worry, writing on a daily basis to the navy. She called and got no information. She phoned the Walker residence and was told there was no one there who wished to speak to her. Well, that was nothing new.

At last, Haylin wrote.

This is one thing I didn't wish to share with you. The human body is so fragile, but more and more I think the soul has real possibilities.

She flew to Paris immediately and took a room at a small hotel near the hospital. She didn't even take note of the name of the place. She left her suitcase and quickly showered and changed. She'd packed real clothes, not the raggedy stuff she usually wore. A Dior suit that had belonged to her mother. A pair of black heels. A purse her parents had given her one Christmas, purchased at Saks, which she had never before used. She didn't intend to spend much time at her hotel, perhaps not even to sleep. It was merely a place to leave her suitcase.

At the hospital, the nurses were very kind, too kind. She had been alarmed, and now her worry intensified. People spoke in hushed voices, and although Franny had excelled at the French language at school, everyone talked too fast for her to follow. They spoke to her in English then, slowly, as if she were a child. She was told she must see the doctor before she could see Haylin and was brought to a well-appointed office. She was offered a coffee, and then a drink, both of which she rejected.

"There's really no need for this," she said, pacing the room. Then the doctor arrived and she saw his expression and she understood the news wasn't good. She sat down and kept quiet.

The unit where Haylin had been posted could not be called a hospital; it was a surgical tent. It was hidden by greenery, but on windy days it was possible to see their location and there was a wind when it happened. During times of war, no one is immune, the doctor told her, not even those who are there to heal the wounded. When the medical tent was bombed, Dr. Walker had thrown himself across the patient he was working on. He did so without thinking, because it was in his nature, because he had always thought of others before himself. And so it had come to pass that he was the injured party.

"He's lost a leg," the doctor told her.

Franny made him repeat himself so she could be sure she hadn't imagined what he'd said. And there were burns, he informed her, now not as severe.

She stood then and thanked the doctor for his time and asked if he could excuse her for a moment. She went into the hall, where she turned to the wall and sobbed. She felt a rushing in her ears, as if she had lost her hearing, as if the doctor had never said anything to her, as if none of it had happened. A nurse pulled her into a washroom so she could dash water on her face and compose herself. When she had, Franny reached into her purse for a comb and tidied her unruly hair, which the nurse pinned up so that it chicly framed her face. It was barely possible to see that she had broken down.

"Much better," the nurse said. "Let's not upset Dr. Walker. He doesn't like anyone to fuss. When you visit, you'll be calm."

Franny nodded and was taken upstairs. Hay had a private room overlooking the leafy street. His father had spared no expense and made sure there was always a private nurse on duty. Her name was Pauline and she was quite beautiful. When Franny shook the nurse's hand she was terribly jealous that this stranger had been here to watch over Hay and care for him so intimately while she, herself, had been clueless, worrying about the library and the garden and all manner of frivolous things.

Hay was usually in constant motion, always at work in some way, so it was a shock to see him trapped in bed. Franny was reminded of the time she went to Cambridge to visit him at Mass General and Emily Flood came in, beautiful and young and windblown, there to ruin Franny's plan to win him back. She had had the same lump in her throat then, the same tumble into fear. She could not lose him now. It was unthinkable, for how could anything happen to Haylin, who was so confident and sure of himself and of the world?

"There you are," he said, his face breaking into a grin when he saw her. He reached for her and she went to take his hand. She leaned to kiss him, then drew back and said, "Is this okay?"

He pulled her to him and growled, "This is the most okay thing that's happened in eighteen months."

When the nurse found them in bed, Franny was made to wait in the hall while Haylin was bathed. She was jealous yet again. But he was still Haylin, and still hers, no matter what had happened. All the same, he refused to talk about the bombing to her or anyone else. He had seen too much as a doctor to ask for pity or even compassion. He would be in France for some time, to be fitted with a prosthetic leg and learn how to deal with his medical reality and care for himself.

"Good thing I'm a doctor," he said.

He had no need to tell her what had happened. She had the sight. She saw everything in his eyes, the grief and horror he had seen. She saw that he was still worried over patients he had known, men he'd worked on, but never saw again, whose fates he would never know. Franny had been so worried about Vincent serving in Vietnam, but had always imagined Haylin would be safe, especially if she stayed away from him.

He saw her regret and said, "This is not the curse. This is fucking war, Franny. This is what happens to people."

She stayed late that first day, until at last the staff asked her to leave and return in the morning. She had not eaten and went to a café where she cried as she ate, but it was Paris, and no one seemed to notice. She wished that Vincent were with her; he was the one who had always best understood her. She was not as tough as she seemed. She wished she could speak with her brother. As she had no idea where he was, she went to the place where she had last had a glimpse of him and William. She took a taxi to the cemetery, but found it was closed for the evening.

"You can climb over the far wall," the taxi driver told her. "Everyone does. There's a stepladder to help you. Run if you see the guard."

And so she entered the cemetery after hours. Inside it wasn't as dark as she expected. There was a moon, and lamplight. She took note of some shadowy figures. Not grave robbers, but fans, there to pay homage at Jim Morrison's grave. They had left flowers and candles. She asked the group if they knew the way to Vincent Owens's grave. One of the girls, an American who wore a torn T-shirt, said, "Who?" and the young man with her said, "You know the guy. 'I Walk at Night.'"

He then turned to Franny with a map he allowed her to use. After she found Vincent's grave listed she made her way to it, past Marcel Proust's grave site; past the site of Adolphe Thiers, the prime minister under King Louis-Philippe whose nineteenth-century ghost was rumored to tug on visitors' clothing if they came close; past the lipstick-kiss-covered grave of Oscar Wilde.

There at last was Vincent's headstone. Agnes Durant had

ordered it, since Franny and Jet had been too distressed to do so at the time. It was very stark and beautiful. A white stone with his name and the dates of his birth and death. Franny leaned down and kissed the stone. She stayed until it was pitch dark. Perhaps she thought if she waited long enough he would manage to find her. But the place was deserted, and at last she went back to where the taxi was waiting. Vincent had always known his life would end young, but she was thankful that somewhere a new one had begun. She asked to return to the hospital. She would sleep in a chair in the lounge until visiting hours began.

She had become jealous of Paris. Haylin had fallen in love with the hospital. Every day that he was stronger he seemed more at home. He had begun to meet with the doctors not just about his own case but also to discuss the histories of other patients. He'd been an excellent surgeon and would be again. Rather than stand during an operation, he could sit in a chair that rose up so there would not be pressure on his good leg.

On days when Hay was busy, Franny walked through the city. She liked to go to the café in the Tuileries, a place Madame Durant had told her Vincent had frequented, and to the Ile de la Cité, where she sat on a wall near the cathedral so she might watch the river, and to the garden of the Rodin Museum, where the budding roses were impossibly large. One day she found herself in the Place Vendôme. She had been following a crow, aimless, with no particular destination in mind, until the bird had led her here.

She went into the Ritz and asked if she might use the telephone. Allowed to do so, she called Madame Durant, who lived around the corner, on the Boulevard de la Madeleine. She was invited to tea. Just a short visit, that was all that could be managed, for Madame was preoccupied with plans to leave the city for her country house. The housekeeper was waiting at the door, poised to show her in. It was a very beautiful tall house, covered with vines. The shutters were painted black, but the light was so glorious who would ever want to try to shut it out?

"Well, here you are," Madame Durant said, kissing Franny lightly. "What a surprise."

But the truth was, she knew Franny would arrive someday. It was difficult to keep the truth from someone with the sight. Every once in a while Franny thought she could see Vincent in a field of yellow flowers. Now, she and Madame Durant sat by the window at a marble table. The light fell through the room in bright bands, illuminating some things, and leaving other items in the dark. The furniture was upholstered in apricot silk and the walls were fabric, gold brocade. The woodwork was all painted a pale blue that might have been white, but wasn't. Franny thought her mother would have loved the room.

"We were roommates during her time here. We had a small apartment that we adored. But Susanna thought everything was beautiful," Agnes said. "When she was in love."

"Yes, the man she ruined."

"She didn't ruin him, dear. He drowned. They were on a sailboat and she, being one of us, couldn't save him because she could not dive underwater. She tried. She was hospitalized after because of the cold. But it did no good."

Franny was stunned by the idea that she and her mother were so alike. She remembered waking from a deep sleep as a child to find her mother sitting in a chair by her bed, watching over her.

"She was crushed, but she went on with her life in New York. When she gave birth to you she wrote me a long letter about how perfect you were."

"You must be mistaken," Franny said. "I was her problem child."

"Oh, no. With your red hair and your curiosity you were perfect to her. She said she knew you would grow up to be a beauty and to be difficult. Which I see has come to be true."

"Difficult, yes," Franny said, embarrassed not to have known anything about her mother's true feelings.

"Well, we can't really know our parents, can we?" Agnes said, reading her thoughts. "Even for those with the sight, parents are unfathomable creatures."

After the maid came in with tea in bone china cups, Franny took note of a photograph of Vincent on the mantel. He was wearing a white shirt, sitting under a striped umbrella, the blue sky behind him.

"When was that taken?" she asked.

"When he first arrived in Paris. We met in the park."

"He was here in autumn. That looks like the height of summer."

Madame changed the subject to more current issues. They spoke a little of Haylin and his interest in the hospital. Then Madame glanced at her watch. Her car had arrived. It was time to go. Madame Durant walked Franny to the door.

"Can I not see him? Or know where he is?" Franny asked.

"It's best to let go," she told Franny. "That way he stays safe. In truth it is easier to let your old life disappear in order to start anew. And there's the matter of the curse. Now it can't find him either. He has a new name and a new life. Therefore love is possible."

They were at the door when something overtook Franny and she simply couldn't leave. Without a word to her hostess, she turned and took the staircase to the second floor. The carpet was plush, cream-colored. The walls were a lacquered red. Off the hallway was a bedroom, and then a sitting room, and then a plush bath tiled with marble. The last door in the hallway was closed. Franny hastily pushed it open, her heart thudding. The room, however, was empty.

"Please, Franny, I have to leave," Madame Durant called from the front hall.

And then Franny saw it. A guitar, propped up against the bookcase.

Madame came up the stairs after Franny. They met in the hallway. She wasn't young, and chasing after Franny was an effort. "My car is here."

"To take you to the country?"

"Yes."

The yellow flowers. When Franny concentrated she could see two men walking in the pale sunlight. "Is that where he is? And William?"

Madame shrugged. "What do you want me to say? He is not here. You've looked for yourself. He'll never go back, Franny. You must know that."

"That is his guitar, isn't it?" Franny asked.

Madame looked at Franny and Franny could see it was true.

"Do they stay here when in Paris?" she asked.

"Occasionally. Paris wouldn't have suited Vincent in the long run. There are fields of sunflowers out in the country. It's beautiful and peaceful. And, you must understand, Franny, he's safe."

"Considering who he is?" Franny said.

"Considering what the world is like."

Franny took a taxi to her hotel and sat looking out the window of her room, watching the darkness fall. She felt Vincent's presence in the world, in the beauty of the evening and in the sunflowers Madame Durant had had sent over in a glass vase. That was the message, that bouquet, the most Madame would tell her.

Franny telephoned Mr. Grant at his home in Sag Harbor. It was early in the morning, but he was glad to hear from her.

"They live in the countryside," she said.

"That would be William to live someplace that reminded him of home. Do you still get the postcards?" he asked.

"Yes," Franny said.

"They're happy," Mr. Grant said. "So we must be happy for them, dear girl."

They made plans for Franny to visit Sag Harbor. She would bring Jet and they would sit on the porch and have lunch and look out at the sea and the island William used to row toward even in high seas. She had been in Paris six weeks. Soon it would turn cold and the paths where Franny liked to walk would be covered with ice. In the countryside the sunflowers would be cut down and their stalks would turn brown. Birds in the hedges would rise, twittering, to fly over the meadows in the last of the daylight.

"Yes," she agreed. "Let's be happy."

Now when Franny came to see Haylin he was no longer in his bed or at physical therapy, but in consultations. The nurses shrugged. A doctor was a doctor, they said. A man's situation might change, but the man himself never did. Such was Haylin's character. He was more interested in the well-being of others than he was in himself.

One day she took him to the Tuileries on an outing from the hospital. He struggled with his walking at first, and called himself a damned peg leg, but by the time they reached a café, he had caught a second wind and his stride was fine. His French was impeccable, hers merely good, so Franny let him order for her. They had white wine and salads with goat cheese and everything was cold and delicious. He spoke about a surgery that had been very successful earlier that day. A sergeant who had taken a bullet to the spine. It was a delicate operation, one Hay excelled at, so the patient had been sent from Germany so that Hay might supervise. He was taking measures to get his French medical license so he would be able do the surgeries himself. He was excited to be helping servicemen who had lost limbs, as he had. He thought he would use some of his father's money to bring these patients here to France to be treated. He lit up when he spoke of his work, and Franny recalled the way he would speak about science when they were young, the way a lover might speak of his beloved.

He poured more wine. It was a perfect afternoon, one Franny

would think about often. He would be in the hospital another six months.

"Just promise me you won't fall in love with anyone else when I go," Franny said. "That's all I'm asking. You can take them home, do whatever you want, sleep with whomever you want, just don't fall in love."

"I never would."

"What about Emily Flood?"

"Emily who?"

They laughed and finished their drinks. "What about the nurse?"

Haylin gave her a look.

"Aha." Franny made a face. "She's your type."

"You're my type," Haylin said. He took her hand and brought it to his mouth so he might kiss her. "You're leaving, aren't you? Why? Because you think it's safer for me if we're apart? After everything that's happened to me do you think I give a damn about being safe? I'm coming back to wherever you are."

He refused to listen to any arguments against his plan. They walked back to the Rue de Rivoli, where they found a taxi. It was still difficult for Haylin to shift his leg into a car. "I'll get better at this," he vowed. Once inside the taxi, Haylin drew her to him so that she was on his lap. The driver didn't pay the slightest bit of attention, no matter how heated their kisses became. "We'll outwit the curse," he told her. "Wait and see."

Franny liked to sit in the yard wearing her black coat and her old red boots no matter the weather. These days she kept to a schedule. Every morning, she wrote a long letter to Haylin. She ate the same diet, noodles and apple tart for dessert, or beans and toast and soup. Simple, practical things. She loved the garden: the bats flickering over the pine trees as they devoured insects, the frogs that came to sing in the spring. On most evenings, women arrived, in search of remedies. But tonight was different. She spied a girl standing inside the gate.

Nearly everyone in town was too afraid to walk into the yard. Even the ones who came to the back porch to knock on the door felt they were taking a risk. They remembered the boys who had been struck by lightning and the stories their grandparents told about the women who could turn a hair into a snake and call birds to them and change the weather if they had a mind to. People still crossed the street when they saw the sisters coming, and at the library no one dared to defy Franny when she made suggestions. The grocery boy who made deliveries wouldn't set foot in the kitchen even when offered a ten-dollar tip. But here was a girl, utterly unafraid, staring at Franny.

She thought it was her neighbor's child at first, the one who was writing her life story in a blue notebook, but as the girl came closer Franny recognized her. It appeared to be Regina Owens. Franny still had the drawing of the black dog and the cat. It hung in the kitchen in its original frame. The girl resembled Vincent, with her long black hair and her confidence. She had bloomed and was a true beauty, but then she would be, considering who her parents were.

"You're in California," Franny said. "You can't be here."

The girl gazed at her and Franny was reminded of the time when she saw Isabelle on the window seat, or the essence of Isabelle at any rate, when their aunt was actually up in her bed.

It was a spirit that had come before her, a wisp composed of thought rather than deed.

"My mother will be bitten by a spider. I'll run away with the man I'll marry. You should have told me to stay away from love. Not that I would have listened."

"Well, why don't you listen now?" Franny asked.

"Because I'm not here, silly. Remember one day you must do as you promised. And then you'll get a big surprise."

"Really? What's that?"

The image of Regina had already begun to fade into transparency. It was possible to see right through her to the leaves of the lilacs.

"Wait," Franny called.

Regina shook her head and smiled and then there were only the lilacs in the garden, no girl at all.

That night Franny phoned April in California.

"I wondered if you were ever going to call me," April said. "I read about Vincent in the newspaper, and then Jet called me to tell me he was still alive."

"Did she?"

April laughed. "He was always *too* alive. Anyway, I knew. He sent Regina a record player of all things. And she always gets a box of her favorite cookies from Paris on her birthday. No note. But it's him."

"Were you bitten by a spider?" Franny asked.

"Are you mad? I don't even work with spiders anymore."

"And how is Regina?" Franny wanted to know.

"She's fine. What's all this about?"

"I had a vision, I suppose. Regina was beautiful. She looked like him."

"She does," April said sadly. For all this time she had never been in love with anyone else. "It could have been different."

"No," Franny said. "We were who we were. No more, no less."

"He told me we could depend on you."

"Of course." Talking to April now, Franny wondered why they hadn't been friends all along. Perhaps they were too much alike. Headstrong, willing to do anything for Vincent, refusing to accept certain aspects of their upbringing and their fate. She looked out the window and saw a fleck of white in the garden. A single rose bloomed.

Dusk was falling. Vincent always said it was the best time of the day. Half in one world, half in another.

"Always," Franny said.

Haylin came back the following year. He rented a small house near the town green, saying the curse would never be able to figure out where he was, since he slept there on some nights and at Magnolia Street on others. Whenever he came for dinner, he would ask for a salad, since their garden was so marvelous, and of course Franny always obliged. They went out together at dusk. It always smelled the same here, the green scent of weeds, and lilacs, and rosemary. They had several rows of lettuce, the best in the commonwealth. Butterhead, red leaf, Boston, looseleaf, curly oak leaf, Red Riding Hood, escarole. They were both reminded of the evenings when they would meet in the park, when they were sixteen. In all that time Franny had never loved anyone else. He'd kept his promise and she'd kept hers. They pretended that they meant nothing to each other to keep the curse at bay, but everybody knew the doctor had come here for her.

Hay's favorite season was August. He and Franny always swam in Leech Lake, and he never drowned and Franny never had to rescue him. They didn't wear bathing suits, though he had that leg he had to unhook before hopping in, which could make for precarious going over the flat rocks. All the same, they swam on a daily basis even though half the town knew and was scandalized. People avoided the place and privately called it Lovers Lake and rumors grew up around it. A dip in the water could bring the man or woman who'd broken your heart back to you, and some women took to wearing vials of lake water around their necks on a string to ward off evil and bring luck to their families.

For several years Hay commuted to Boston, where he was on the orthopedic surgery team at Mass General, the hospital where he was treated when he was a student. He continued to be on staff and often consulted, but he decided to open a practice, setting up the first floor of his house as an office and hiring a nurse and an assistant, local women Jet had suggested, as they were clients of hers and in need of jobs. Haylin was the only doctor in town, which was a blessing to everyone. When a child was sick he always made himself available to make a house call. He impressed everyone with his pet crow, and he let well-behaved children feed it a cracker or give it a pat on its gleaming head.

"Shall I tell you a story about a rabbit?" the doctor would say, and the children would always say yes because they all knew the story by heart. It was the one about a rabbit who had once been a witch. They knew that a witch must never deny who she is, and that no matter what happens it's always best to be true to oneself. Hay also gave out lollipops, which the children liked, especially when they had scratchy throats, and black bars of soap for their mothers, which were very much appreciated.

Folks often saw Dr. Walker leaving the house on Magnolia Street early in the morning, whistling, followed by that old dog of theirs, which had taken a liking to him. Frankly, people wondered what a wonderful man like Haylin Walker was doing associating with the Owens sisters, he was so kindhearted after all. He knew everyone's name, and all of their ailments, and when walking with Franny to the library for board meetings he reminded his patients to stop eating salt and take their medications. At night he came up to Franny's room. After she undressed he sometimes brushed her hair. He said there had never been a more beautiful color on earth, or a more beautiful woman, even though she knew that if that had ever been true, it wasn't anymore, except to him. She always wanted him in her bed, even though he was so tall and took up so much room. Even after all this time, when he kissed her everything left her mind except for the moment in time they were in, and the heat went through her, slowly, and she fell for him all over again, as if it were the first time.

Hay was still a whirlwind, working all hours, though Franny did her best to slow him down. With every step they took time was passing, spring was ending, summer was gone, ice was covering the windowpanes. Vincent's old dog passed away, the vines grew taller, Haylin's young patients grew up and began to bring their own children to him. Before they knew it, twenty years had gone by. They didn't know how time had moved so quickly, but these were, by far, the best twenty years of their lives. For all that time they had managed to avoid the curse, meeting at midnight, then sneaking into each other's beds, saying their good-byes at dawn.

"The curse will never find us," Hay always said.

"Is that possible?" Franny would then ask.

"Isn't that what we've done? We're here together, darling."

"You two are like teenagers," Jet teased them when she came upon them kissing in the parlor or the kitchen.

"But aren't we still?" Hay said with a grin.

"Oh, yes," Franny said. "And you're still refusing to eat a tomato sandwich."

"And you're still difficult."

There was that grin, so how could she be annoyed? Still, she protested. "I was never difficult."

"No," Hay said, linking his arms around her, pulling her near. "Never once."

As most doctors do, Haylin diagnosed himself. He had cancer and he knew enough to know it was too late. He conferred with an old friend at Mass General, a specialist in oncology and hematology, but he already knew what the advice would be. Live now.

He told Franny at the lake, where she wept in his arms. Still, he insisted there was always some good to come out of every circumstance. Now the curse could not touch him. They'd held it off with trickery. He was dying and nothing more could bring him to ruin. They could finally be husband and wife. It was too late for many things, but it was not too late for that. Jet had been right. Whenever they looked at each other they saw the people they had first fallen in love with. She was a gawky, beautiful freckled girl with long red hair who liked tomato sandwiches for lunch and had shivered when he first kissed her. He was a tall boy who cared more about other people than about himself, one who had almost died of appendicitis at Harvard and who had refused to stop loving her, no matter what fate decreed.

That same afternoon when he told her he was dying, he went out and bought her an engagement ring, an emerald, which some people say is much preferable to a diamond, for it causes love to last. In certain lights it was the gray-green of her eyes, and in full sun it reminded her of the garden, a deep, lush green.

Haylin went to Jet for her permission to ask Reverend Willard if he would officiate at the service. Jet telephoned the Reverend, who said he would be honored to do so. Haylin then went over to his house and the men drank glasses of whiskey. The Reverend said he liked to get to know the people he would be marrying; it was more personal that way.

"We've been together since we were kids, sometimes more so and sometimes less so," Haylin told him.

The Reverend congratulated Dr. Walker and said he was a lucky man. Franny was waiting for him at home. He walked so slowly now, it broke her heart to see it, but she waved and rushed out to meet him. She worried that the Reverend had changed his mind, and that Hay would be disappointed, but instead the men had wound up having several drinks.

"I told him it was the end of the curse," Haylin assured Franny. "At least for us. If we're choosing anything, let's choose love."

On the day the doctor married Frances Owens the whole

town came out to stand on the sidewalk and watch through the window of town hall, moved by the power of love. Some of the children had never even seen a member of the Owens family, for they weren't allowed to walk down Magnolia Street, and they wondered now why their parents had always been nervous about the tall lady with red hair. The Reverend wore his old black coat and his thin black tie. He had aged greatly, and was now quite stooped. His arthritis made it difficult for him to drive, so on Sundays, Jet often picked him up in the station wagon she and Franny had bought and she would drive the Reverend to the cemetery. They usually brought plastic lawn chairs so they might stay awhile, especially in fair weather. When the daffodils were blooming they brought armfuls along. They remembered Levi better than anyone, and because of this they often didn't need to speak. Jet still wore the moonstone. She had never once taken it off, not even to bathe.

As the wedding service was about to begin, the Reverend nodded to Jet, who was the maid of honor, dressed in a pale green shift. She nodded back, and in that quiet way they shared the grief the feud between their families had caused as well as the joy of the day.

Unable are the Loved to die, for Love is Immortality, the Reverend quoted when he ended the service, a blessing not only for the husband and wife but for Jet as well, who understood his meaning in his choice of Emily Dickinson. Levi would always be with them.

When the happy couple walked out of town hall there were wild cheers. Franny hadn't even known there were so many people in their town. She hunched down, unused to all the attention. The doctor's patients threw rice and the children's chorus from the elementary school sang "All You Need Is Love." Franny carried a bunch of long-stemmed red roses. Hay was slowed down a bit by the problems with his leg and by the pain he was suffering, but he grinned and waved as if he had won a race, his arm around his bride, who was crying too much, right there in public, to notice much of anything other than how crowded the street was on this day. Even people who had always disliked the Owenses, and blamed them for every misfortune in town, had to agree that Frances Owens made a beautiful bride, even at her age, even though she dressed in black.

Dr. Walker moved into the old house, for he had no fear of curses, just of the pains and suffering of real life, and anyone could tell he was happy. People would see him watering the garden. He weeded between the rows of lettuce while singing to himself. He had to close down his office, but he'd talked a young doctor from Boston into taking over his practice, which was fortunate for him and even more fortunate for the town. These days Haylin wanted to spend as much time as he could with Franny, who liked to tease him about his new gardening mania. He'd put out a wooden box just inside the fence, filled it with lettuce, and urged their neighbors to take as much as they'd like.

"The best lettuce in the commonwealth, if we can keep the rabbits away," he told people passing by.

"They're never going to walk through the gate," Franny insisted.

And then the oddest thing happened, they did. His patients and her neighbors all came past the gate, and although some appeared to be nervous, they gratefully took the lettuce, heads of all varieties, each so good that people who made salads of the stuff dreamed of rabbits and of their own childhood gardens.

Charlie Merrill was now deceased, so Franny had asked his sons to bring over a bench so Hay could sit and rest out on the porch, which he had begun to do. He had slowed down, but not completely. He let Jet water the garden now and Franny weed, but all that summer he set out lettuce for his friends and patients.

"Aren't I lucky," he said one evening when he and Franny were sitting on the bench holding hands, watching the dusk sift down. Hay remembered walking through Central Park, lying on the grass looking at stars, swimming in the cold pond just before he went away. He remembered Franny with her red hair pinned up haphazardly lying on the floor with him in the cook's room at her parents' house, naked and beautiful.

He tried not to take painkillers because he didn't want to spend any of his time with Franny in a haze. "I might have drowned long ago, and then we wouldn't have had all of this."

Franny had no idea how it was possible to love him more, but she did. She thought perhaps that was the curse, to love someone so much when you knew he would leave you. But Hay was right.

"*We* are lucky," she said.

"It was all because of third grade. When you walked into the classroom in a black coat, looking pissed off."

Franny laughed. "I was not pissed off." She looked at him. "Was I?"

"You most certainly were. Until I sat next to you."

Haylin grinned, which undid her, as always. She leaned her head against his chest and wondered how on earth she could ever let him go.

"Was it fate?" she asked.

"Do we care?" he answered.

The truth was, they had managed to get what they wanted. It just wasn't lasting long enough, not that it ever could. When he passed, the doctor was sitting on the porch on an autumn night. The lilacs were blooming out of season. There were so many stars in the sky it was impossible to count them all. They had turned off the light on the back porch, the better to see the swirling show above them.

Oh, how beautiful was the last thing he said.

There was no warning when it happened, and no pain, he just was there one moment and then he was gone. Franny sat outside with him all night. She was so cold in the morning that Jet brought her a pair of gloves. Charlie's sons took him to the funeral parlor in their new truck, with Franny insisting she go. She sat in the bed of the pickup with the doctor, who had been covered by a woolen blanket. She did not notice what roads they took or that the sky was piercingly blue. They made sure he was dressed in a black suit, with no shoes on, for that was the way people were buried in their family, in a plain pine coffin. Franny sat in the funeral parlor all night. Near midnight Jet came with a thermos of tea and a blanket for her sister and they sat together, not speaking, but holding hands, as they had when they were girls sitting on the roof that first summer they visited Aunt Isabelle's house, wondering where life would lead them.

The Walkers did not argue or protest Haylin's final resting place in the Owens cemetery. They were all buried in Bedford, New York, but they understood his place was not with them. His family came up to Massachusetts in three long, black cars. The Reverend performed the service. It was brief, and allowed time for patients and friends to stand up and say their piece or give a blessing. The youngest speaker was nine. Dr. Walker had cared for him when he had appendicitis, and the speaker, who had been bought his first suit for the occasion, wanted to say that he had decided to become a doctor because of Dr. Walker.

Mr. Walker was old by then, and he had lost his only son. His wife had been gone for some time. Even though he was rich and had a new wife, even though Haylin had spent a lifetime quarreling with him, Mr. Walker was bereft. Franny made sure Haylin's father sat next to her, with Jet on his other side.

"It was always you," he said to Franny. "That sort of thing doesn't happen very often. It was never going to be Emily Flood. Even I knew that."

Love of my life, Franny thought.

The day Haylin was buried was beautiful and clear. The crow was in the tree, old Lewis, who was going blind, his eyes filmy and white. Seeing him broke Franny's heart. The bird cried, even though crows are said not to have tear ducts. Afterward Franny called Lewis to her and she carried him home, where she wrapped him in a blanket, for he coughed and fretted. He died the following day and one of the Merrill boys buried him behind the shed. He had never belonged to Franny, and had always preferred Haylin, and she'd never once blamed him for that.

Franny stayed out on the porch for seven nights. The vines began to grow over the bench where Haylin liked to sit. They grew and grew until passersby could no longer see Franny Owens in mourning. The bin where Dr. Walker had offered lettuce to passersby was empty. Children asked for him when the new doctor in town made a house call. They wanted the story about the rabbit and the kind, tall man who had lollipops in his pockets.

People in town pitied Frances Owens her grief, and many felt bereaved themselves by the loss of such a good man. They brought casseroles and salads, pies and cakes, all of which Jet accepted gratefully. But Franny did not try a bite and she left it to her sister to send thank-you cards. People in town had lost a doctor and a friend, she had lost her life. She looked at the trees and they grew taller, and the vines covered the fence and the gate, and people stayed away, the way they used to, before Haylin Walker came to town.

For seven days Franny Owens did not brush her hair or wash her face or have a meal. The birds in the thickets came to nest in the vines, but she couldn't even hear them sing and they wouldn't come to her when she held out her hands. She had lost some of who she was when she lost her beloved. Though Jet had draped sheets over the furniture and drawn all of the curtains, Franny couldn't bear to go inside and leave the place where she had last been with her husband. The man Haylin had been lingered in the dark. All she wanted was to hold his hand. To see the way he smiled at her. She saw bits and pieces of him out of the corner of her eye, or maybe it was the fireflies. He was a man of integrity, a man of honor, the boy who had chained himself up in the school cafeteria for the rights of others, the doctor who kept lollipops and bars of soap in his pockets, who had helped five hundred men learn how to walk, who had known how to make her shiver with a kiss when she was a seventeen-year-old girl. She had loved one person in her lifetime, and for that she would always be grateful.

On the eighth night she came inside and got into bed beside Jet. She was shivering and still wearing her coat. Haylin was gone and there was nothing she could do about it.

"How will I ever love anyone again?" she said to her sister.

That was when the telephone rang.

PART SIX

Remedy

*T*hirty years after Vincent's disappearance, his granddaughters, aged three and four, lived with their mother and father in a house in California, in a town called Forestville, where the trees were so old and tall it was impossible to see the sky. Regina Owens had grown up to be a beautiful woman with long, black hair and gray eyes the color of mist. She had a lovely singing voice and was so graceful the birds came to watch when she hung the laundry on the line. She knew how to have fun. She didn't believe in drudgery or boredom and had a trick so that the broom swept all by itself when she cleaned the house. Her daughters, Sally and Gillian, were thirteen months apart, as different as chalk from cheese, but best friends all the same, a good thing, for there were no other children for miles.

Their world was mossy and green with rain that splattered down for days on end. The girls' father, Daniel, was a fisherman and a guide on the Russian River; their mother was a painter whose subject matter was trees, not surprising given their location. The girls liked to climb the trees surrounding their house, and often had tea parties with their stuffed animals aloft, using the branches as the table and chairs. When they concentrated they could make the wind come out of nowhere and shake the branches and then they would laugh and hold on for dear life. Sally would open her hands and birds would come to her as if they'd been called and Gillian could dangle on the farthest branch and let the wind blow right through her and not be scared at all.

The girls' grandmother April, who had been their favorite person in all the world, had recently and unexpectedly died of a lethal bite from a brown wandering spider that had been hiding in a bunch of bananas brought from a market. They had not eaten fruit since. They had not laughed or climbed trees. They had been in mourning, and their mother especially had been so sad she took to her bed. It was not at all like Regina to be mournful, but sometimes she could be heard crying while she hung the laundry on the line, and now the birds scattered. She spent her birthday under the covers, even though the box from Ladurée Royale that always came to her from Paris on that day had arrived and the girls knew there would be delicious macarons inside, a treat to be savored. First a pale orange cookie that was apricot, then a green pistachio, then chocolate, of course, then the best of all, pink ones that tasted like roses. Regina brightened up then, as she did when anything came from Paris. Sometimes there was a postcard with a single heart as the message. Once there was a beautiful box of pastels.

They had the macarons and a fragrant tea that always made them feel especially brave. "Always choose courage," Regina told her girls. She wasn't worried about Gillian, who loved to walk on a tightrope set up between the trees, but cautious Sally was another story. "Don't live a little," Regina would whisper to her older daughter when she tucked her in at night. "Live a lot."

Regina had fallen in love with the girls' father when they

were students at Berkeley. They'd dropped out to live on the land and for the first year they'd lived in a shack, sleeping together in one sleeping bag, mad for each other. They were still so in love they hadn't spent a night apart. Sorrow was not in either of their natures. At last their father told their mother that it was high time they had a little vacation. He surprised her with plans for a second honeymoon.

Regina my beautiful queen, he said, *let's celebrate our lives*.

He kissed her on the mouth and made her laugh and after that she seemed more like her old self, the one who knew how to have fun and who always took her daughters outside to dance in the rain. They packed their suitcases, promising to bring home presents and chocolate bars. The girls stood at the window waving, and they watched their parents dance on the lawn before they waved back and headed off for their trip.

But something had gone wrong. That much was evident. The girls were woken in the middle of the night by their babysitter, a teenager who had become so hysterical the sisters couldn't make out a word she said. They clutched each other and tried to make sense of the babysitter's ramblings. She mentioned a phone call from the sheriff, and then she talked about fire and water, which they knew never mixed. She called them poor pathetic creatures and wondered what would happen to them now. As the babysitter considered their future, her despair set her into fits of uncontrollable weeping.

It was pouring, buckets of cold, stinging rain. No one could dance in this sort of weather. The trees were shuddering without the sisters willing them to do so. Leaves fell like a black blanket. Birds that always gathered at Sally's window disappeared. The girls waited for their babysitter to catch her breath and stop crying. They had never been up in the middle of the night and they knew bad luck when it came to them. It tapped on the door, quietly at first, then it pounded, insisting on being let in.

Gillian, fair and usually fearless, clutched her stuffed bear and stood in a corner, terror creeping up her spine. Sally, dark and serious, sat on the bed and held the babysitter's hand to calm her. This was the moment Sally had been dreading, when the life they had enjoyed was turned upside down. Her grandmother had confided that it happened to everyone sooner or later. Sally had always thought it would be later, but as it turned out it was now.

Their parents had taken a canoe down the Russian River, loaded down with their father's fishing equipment and their mother's paints and canvases and the pastels that had been sent from Paris. When the rains commenced, suddenly and without warning, the canoe overturned. Daniel nearly went under in the rushing tide, but he managed to hang on to the hull of the boat. Their mother, so buoyant she could not be drowned, floated alongside him, saying encouraging words so he wouldn't give up. When they at last made it to shore, they were grateful for their luck. There was a small motel, and they checked in to wait out the storm, but they must have dozed off and they didn't hear the storm worsen. When lightning struck the building they were tangled together in bed, deeply asleep, not recognizing that there were curses in this world, and they were still there, their arms around each other, when the fire began, with smoke filtering through the walls of their room.

The babysitter informed the girls that the sheriff's office would soon be sending someone over. Since there was no family, the sisters would be taken into protective custody. "They'll find you someplace to live. It might not be together, but you won't be alone."

"But where will Mommy and Daddy be?" Gillian asked. Her voice trembled and her eyes brimmed with tears. "When are they coming home?" Gillian said.

Sally had very dark gray eyes and a somber expression. "Don't you get it?" she said to her sister. "They're not."

"That's impossible," Gillian said. "We have to have parents."

Sally turned to the babysitter. She was the take-charge sister, and in this moment it was clear that she had better begin to do so. "Can you make a phone call?"

The babysitter covered her puffy eyes with a damp cloth and said, "Maybe later. I'm too upset right now."

Sally stood up, took hold of Gillian's hand, and led her into the parlor.

"No one is splitting us up." She went to the telephone and opened her mother's datebook. She quickly began to page through it. Fortunately, she knew how to read. She remembered an enormous bouquet of wildflowers from Massachusetts had been sent to their grandmother's funeral. The card had been signed *With love from Bridget and Frances Owens*. That meant they were family.

"What are you looking for?" Gillian wanted to know.

The girls were in their pajamas and their feet were bare. They both had a shivery feeling.

"Granny said that if anything ever happened I should call our family."

"We have a family?"

Sally brought the phone to the babysitter, still reclining on the couch, and had her dial.

"Go pack," Sally whispered to Gillian as she took hold of the phone. "Get our best dresses. The ones Granny bought us."

"What about everything in our room?"

Sally shook her head. They would be traveling light from now on. "You can take Arthur and Pip." Gillian's stuffed bear and her toy mouse. "I'll take Maxine." Sally's stuffed black dog.

Sally waited for someone to answer. The person who picked up turned out to be a mean old lady.

"Do you know what time it is?" said the annoyed voice on the line.

"I can't tell time," Sally admitted.

"Who is this?"

"Sally Owens. Who is this?"

"Frances Owens," the old woman said, sounding surprised.

"You sent the flowers. My grandmother said to call our family if anything happened."

There was a pause. "And did it?"

A police cruiser was pulling into the driveway. The headlights were so bright Sally shielded her eyes. When the lights were turned off Sally blinked. She would have to tell the people at the funeral parlor that her parents should be dressed in black, with no shoes. That was the way their grandmother had been buried. She and Gillian would wear their best dresses and, out of respect, be shoeless as well.

"Oh, thank God," Sally heard the babysitter say when the officers knocked on the door.

Sally held the phone receiver tightly. "We're coming to live with you," she said to the mean old lady. At least she and Gillian would be together. Gilly had returned, dragging along their party dresses. Hers was violet and Sally's was pink trimmed with lace. "Good," Sally said. "Those are the right ones."

"What are you saying?" the woman on the phone asked in an upset tone. "What happened?"

The officers approached the girls solemnly. They'd taken off their hats and one policeman got down on one knee so he could talk to the sisters at eye level. "I think you need to hang up the phone, little girl," he said.

"Oh, no," Sally answered. She handed the receiver to him. "This is our aunt. She'll make all the arrangements for us to go and live with her."

The plane ride was their first and it was horrible. There was a storm over the middle of the country, with lightning streaking the sky, which terrified both girls.

"Lightning never strikes twice," Sally said firmly, to reassure both herself and her sister. All the same Gillian vomited twice into a paper bag that Sally then handed to the flight attendant. They were in their flimsy party dresses and they both had small leather suitcases under their feet. Sally had taken along practical things, toothbrushes and toothpaste, photographs of their parents, a comb, pajamas and slippers. Gillian had stuffed in all of her other party dresses, so many that her suitcase barely shut.

"Don't you girls have anything warm to wear?" the flight attendant asked when they were finally landing. "It's Boston, after all. There could be snow."

Neither girl had ever seen snow. For a moment they were excited as they peered out the window and spied huge white flakes.

"Oh, Arthur," Gillian said to her stuffed animal. "I think you're going to like it here."

Sally sat back in her seat, worried. It was dark in Boston and the snow was swirling and their parents weren't coming back and the old lady she'd spoken to *had* been mean.

The flight attendant walked them off the plane and through the terminal. It was already cold and they weren't yet outside. Ice coated the windowpanes. People spoke loudly, in rough voices. Someone said it was wicked nasty out tonight. The sisters held hands. They didn't like the sound of that.

"I actually don't think Arthur's going to like it here," Gillian muttered in a dark voice.

"Of course he will. Where do you think bears come from?" Sally said primly. She herself was shivering. "They like cold climates."

"There are bears in California," Gillian protested. "Daddy said he saw one."

"I think that's your family," the flight attendant said, pointing.

The sisters turned quickly to look. There were two women in black coats, one very tall, and the other shorter, with snow-white hair. They both had red balloons tied to their wrists so the girls would see them. The shorter one carried a black cane with a carved raven's head. She waved and called out their names. Sally and Gillian stopped, frozen in place. This most assuredly could not be their family.

"I don't like them," Gillian said.

"You don't even know them," Sally said reasonably.

"I don't want to." Gillian's voice sounded the way it always did before she began to cry. "They're old."

"Granny was old."

"No she wasn't. She was beautiful. That's why her name was April."

"Let's go, girls," the flight attendant urged.

They had reached the arrivals gate. What was done was done. What was to begin was on the other side of the gate. They could run, but to where? The police were in California, and they'd be split in two and given to people who wouldn't care if Gillian was afraid of the dark and Sally liked to eat the same thing for breakfast every day, oatmeal topped by a spoonful of honey.

The girls looked at each other, then approached their aunts.

"There you are!" the one who said she was Aunt Jet cried cheerfully. "Aren't you opposites! I think I'll call you Night and Day. You're late, but a late start means an ending that will be right on time."

The aunts smelled like lavender and sulfur. They wore boots and gloves and knitted scarves, and they'd brought along scratchy black wool coats for the sisters. When the girls put them on, it felt as if spiders were crawling up their arms and backs and the girls didn't like the idea of spiders at all.

"What did I tell you?" the tall one, Franny, said to the nice one. "People in California dress like fools."

"No we don't," Sally said, insulted.

This tall aunt was clearly the mean one. She appraised Sally coolly. "You're not a troublemaker, are you?" she asked.

"She's not at all!" Gillian said protectively.

"Then I suppose you are," Aunt Frances said to the younger girl.

361

"What if I am?" Gillian said, her hands on her hips.

"Then you'll bring trouble upon yourself, which I'd hate to see."

Gillian's eyes widened. She was seconds away from tears.

"Well, you're probably blind and couldn't see it anyway!" Sally said in an effort to defend her sister.

"I am not blind or deaf and if you have any sense you'll listen to what I say," Franny advised. "I will always have your best interests at heart."

"We'd better go," Jet said, having had enough of the squabbling. "There's snow."

Flakes were falling as they walked through the parking lot to a battered Ford station wagon. Aunt Frances took the car key and burst the balloon that was tied to her wrist. The pop made Gilly put her hands over her ears.

"Really, Franny," Jet said. "Must you?"

"Well, it wouldn't have fit into the car." Franny popped Jet's balloon as well, then feeling some remorse because their nieces looked so nervous, she stuck her hands in her pockets and brought out red licorice and gumballs for the girls to suck on during the long drive from the airport. "I suppose this is what children like," she said. "I always preferred lemon slices."

The flight had been a red-eye and dawn was breaking as they turned onto Main Street. The snow had accumulated and it was slow going. There were crows perched on the rooftops of many of the houses and almost no stores on Main Street. A pharmacy, a bakery, a grocery store. As they drove past, the streetlights flared, then went out.

All at once they had reached their destination. In the backseat of the station wagon, the girls were still holding hands. When they got out their shoes became soaked with snow.

"Of course," Franny said. "No boots. People in California probably don't believe in them."

They walked up the path to the Owens house. Sparrows were nesting in the twisted wisteria. When Sally held out her hand one flitted over to sit in the center of her palm. "Hello," she said, comforted by the warmth of the bird and its bright eyes.

"How unusual," Jet said, tossing a knowing look at Franny. Another Owens to whom birds flocked of their own accord.

"It always happens," Gillian said proudly. "She doesn't even have to whistle."

"Really?" Franny said. "Then she's clearly a very talented girl."

There were so many vines the girls could barely see the door. The garden had been put to bed for the winter, with some of the shrubs wrapped in burlap, which made them look like monsters. The wisteria twisted around the pillars of the porch, like a goblin's fingers. The house itself was tall and tilty, with green glass in the windows and a fence that circled the property like a snake. Gillian was not a fan of snakes, or vines, or trees that looked like monsters, but Aunt Jet offered her hand and said, "I have something special for you for breakfast."

"Is it macarons? That was our mother's favorite. She always got a box sent from Paris on her birthday."

Jet and Franny exchanged a look.

"Did she?" Jet said. "Well this time it's chocolate cake. The best you'll ever have. And we have Dr Pepper if you're thirsty."

They went up to the porch as if they'd known each other for years.

That left Sally and Aunt Frances standing on the path.

"Do you live here all alone?" Sally asked.

"Of course not. Your aunt Jet is here."

"You don't have a husband?"

"I did. Once."

Sally stared at her aunt. "I'm sorry," she said.

Franny stared back, a bit shaken at having been asked about Haylin. Hay would have been so much better with children. If they'd ever had their own, she'd be a grandmother by now. She would be different then, softer, not so quick to frighten small children.

"I'm sorry about what happened to your parents," Franny managed to say. "I knew your mother when she was a little girl. I still have one of the pictures she drew when she visited me. I have it right in the front parlor."

Sally looked up at Aunt Frances, waiting to see what she would say next.

"I was a friend of your grandmother's, you know. And your grandfather. I miss him every day," Franny said before thinking better of it.

"We didn't have a grandfather," Sally said despite her inner vow not to give out any information.

"You did, but he went away to live happily ever after in France." Franny gave the girl a closer look. "You resemble him. You're lucky in that."

"If all that was true he'd have had a name."

Sally was stubborn and not afraid to talk back. Her chin was raised, as if she were ready to have Franny say something terrible. All at once, Franny felt something she'd never felt before. She felt another person's loss.

"He has a name," Franny said. She sounded different when she spoke. Sadder. Not mean at all. "Vincent."

"I like that name," Sally said.

"Why wouldn't you?" Franny said. "It's a wonderful name."

"If he's living happily ever after you shouldn't sound so sad," Sally told her aunt.

"You're absolutely right."

"Is he the one who sends the cookies?" Sally asked. "The ones made of roses from Paris?"

Franny looked into Sally's clear gray eyes. It was an honest, innocent question. She felt a surge of relief but also a swell of sorrow for all of the years that had been lost. "Yes. I'm sure he is."

"Will he ever come back?"

Franny shook her head. "Unlikely."

Sally thought it over and took her aunt's hand.

"What's this about?" Franny said, surprised.

"Vincent. What will happen when he sends the macarons to California? He'll worry about us."

"When they're sent back to Paris he'll know you live here, with us, and he won't worry."

Standing on the porch where the light was always turned on, Sally felt her aunt's loss as well. Franny lowered her gaze so that the girl wouldn't see tears in her eyes. She thought children were better behaved if they had a little fear and respect. But rules were never the point. It was finding out who you were. In the kitchen there was a chocolate tipsy cake for breakfast. The girls might as well learn early on, this was not a house like any other. No one would care how late they stayed up at night, or how many books they read on rainy afternoons, or if they jumped into Leech Lake from the highest cliff. All the same, there were some things they needed to learn. Do not drink milk after a thunderstorm, for it will certainly be sour. Always leave out seed for the birds when the first snow falls. Wash your hair with rosemary. Drink lavender tea when you cannot sleep. Know that the only remedy for love is to love more.

ACKNOWLEDGMENTS

My deepest gratitude to my editor, Marysue Rucci. Thank you to Jonathan Karp and to Carolyn Reidy.

Many thanks to Zack Knoll, Dana Trocker, Anne Pearce, Elizabeth Breeden, Wendy Sheanin, Mia Crowley-Hald, Susan Brown, Carly Loman, Lauren Peters-Collaer, and Jackie Seow.

A huge thank-you to Amanda Urban and Ron Bernstein for their faith in this book.

Many thanks to Kate Painter and to Pamela Painter for insights into fiction and fact.

Gratitude to Madison Wolters for assistance in all things.

Thank you to Alexander Bloom for historical expertise.

Thank you to Sue Standing.

Gratitude to my early readers Gary Johnson, Kyle Van Leer, and Deborah Thompson.

Love to everyone who has ever passed through the doors of 44 Greenwich Avenue, especially to Elaine Markson, who made dreams come true.

ABOUT THE AUTHOR

Alice Hoffman is the author of more than thirty works of fiction, including *Practical Magic*, the Oprah's Book Club selection *Here on Earth*, *The Red Garden*, *The Dovekeepers*, *The Museum of Extraordinary Things*, *The Marriage of Opposites*, and *Faithful*. She lives near Boston.

SCRIBNER